THE SCHOOLMISTRESS WITH THE GOLDEN EYES

*'The isles of Greece,
the isles of Greece!
Where burning Sappho
loved and sung.'*

BY THE SAME AUTHOR

"The Mermaid Madonna"

The Schoolmistress with the Golden Eyes

Stratis Myrivilis

Stratis Myrivilis, born in 1892 on the Isle of Mytilene in the Aegean Sea, is today the most highly respected and foremost literary figure in Greece, and occupies an assured place in the world of letters.

Myrivilis studied philosophy and law at the University of Athens. From 1912 to 1922 he was a volunteer in the service of his country, participating in the Greco-Turkish and Greco-Bulgarian wars and in World War I. Twice wounded, Myrivilis received many medals and citations. During World War II he was active in the Greek underground.

By profession Stratis Myrivilis is an author and journalist. He has written numerous successful novels *(The Life in Tomb, The Schoolmistress with the Golden Eyes, The Mermaid Madonna, The Argonautes, Vassilis Arvanitis, The Goblins, Pan),* short stories *(Stories, Red Stories, The Green Book, The Blue Book, The Red Book, The Vermilion Book),* essays *(Man and Art, Lonliness and Art, Woman and Art, The High Peak, Byzantine Music, Thought and Heart, The Law of the Heart)* and poems *(The Song of the Earth, The Small Flames)* and has published newspapers and literary journals. His works have been translated into many foreign languages, and as author and scholar he has won the plaudits of critics throughout Europe.

Originally published in Greek under the title

Η ΔΑΣΚΑΛΑ
ΜΕ ΤΑ ΧΡΥΣΑ ΜΑΤΙΑ

Stratis Myrivilis

THE SCHOOLMISTRESS WITH THE GOLDEN EYES

Translated by Philip Sherrard

EFSTATHIADIS GROUP

EFSTATHIADIS GROUP S.A.
14, Valtetsiou Str.
106 80 Athens
Tel: (01) 5254650, 6450113
Fax: (01) 5254657
GREECE

ISBN 960 226 088 2

Greek edition © 1954 Stratis Myrivilis, Athens
English translation © 1964 Hutchinson & Co. (Publishers) Ltd.

First published in Great Britain
by Hutchinson & Co. (Publishers) Ltd., 1964

© **Efstathiadis Group A.E. 1998**

Printed and bound in Greece

1

SO MANY YEARS. So many years he'd longed for it, dreamt of it—this final hour of his homecoming. In the trenches. In hospitals. On journeys. It would be summer-time on the island, nature and man revived. The pots would be full of carnations, the path covered with daisies and flowering capers, even if it were the middle of winter. All in festive mood: the sea, the dancing mountains, the sky. Romantically beautiful. How many times had he dreamt of this happiness, a happiness which he alone could measure in the scales of his nostalgia. To be but a small shell buried in the sands of the Lesbian shore, no more than a humble shell, unknown to everyone, dwelling in insignificance, out of the sight of God. But to return there, to be there, on the shore of the island, in the sun of the island, wet with its sea, coated with the salt foam of the island.

And now how different everything was.

The ship stopped outside the harbour, and when he got down into the small boat that was to take him ashore his eyes were clouded with tears. And yet it was summer-time on the island, and the sea was blue, and the boat was gay: a small blue felucca, rapid in the water, it leapt with small joyful cries at each stroke of the oar as it made towards the beloved land. And there was the Venetian castle, the little pine-wood, the public garden with its poplars, the kindly provincial quay. All in its place. But this wasn't it, this wasn't the homecoming. It was as if he'd emerged from a shipwreck . . . . And he was alone, quite alone with the boatman in the blue boat. A ship had sunk, big as a continent. Gone totally. An engulfing abyss had opened, had swallowed a whole world—thousands dead—and had closed. Then the blue singing sea had passed over it, calm, full of silver butterflies and amorous dallyings. All milk and honey. Wasn't there now something dishonourable in that feast? Dishonourable and lacking respect.

A bitter silence awaited him at the house. The creepers hung dustily from the walls of the courtyard, the windows were tightly barred. He heard the bell ring as though in a huge echoing void. His sister threw her arms round his neck, sobbing. She was in black, and couldn't speak through the knot of her tears, and there was no mother there to welcome him. He understood, and a new sorrow cut like a knife into his heart.

'Mother?'

'It's two months now .... I didn't write .... You'd enough with the war ....'

He kissed Adriani's tears, tasting their bitterness on his lips as though they were a symbolic drink to his arrival. He received the blow squarely, with a tired composure. A poison, a new wound, began to drip, drop by drop, within him. The vision of his beloved mother passed before his mind's eye, as though in the forecourt of an empty church. Calm, slow-moving, graceful: so she passed, tall and slender, very white in the black weeds of her widowhood, which she still wore six years after his father's death; so, as always, soundless, in her soft unechoing slippers. No marks of death were on her face, but it was as it is with those whose last moments we haven't witnessed, whose features we haven't seen loosened and deformed by death.

'Our house is ruined, Lilo .... We're two orphans now, complete orphans ....'

He buried her girlish face in his arms for protection. He caressed her golden curls as though she were a child.

'You have me, Adriani .... Don't cry like this.'

'Lilo .... Ah, Lilo ....'

She still called him by the caressive nickname of his childhood. It was strange to him. It had in it something like the down of a young bird, the down of the warm nest of the house. He had retained it during his school years, he had taken it with him through the Polytechnic at Athens. Then he took it to the war. There, like everything else, it had been killed. He had become Leon. Leon Drivas, son of Nicholas, acting lieutenant of the infantry, machine-gun section.

Now hearing his sister murmur it after so many years was strange to him, its music reviving in him the memory of many half-forgotten songs. It was like those deep laments that come half heard out of the past, voices passing over the sea, sweet, quivering, and then lost. And again .... and again: 'Lilo', the soft call of his mother. 'Lilo,' his sister's shout. And further back: 'Lilo', the deep bass of his father as his unforgettable blue eyes mocked at him—those eyes exhausted by the stomach sickness he had suffered so long but their smile still full of love. Then there were voices, many voices, parties and festivals, carnivals and Easters and New Years, the summers full of swallows and the winter rains singing from the gutters and playing the piano on the large sheet of corrugated iron over the outside door. The great deputations of the storks whose companies passed over the castle 'in formation' and whose journeying voices came down into the alleys. Voices full of human sadness saying 'good-bye' and leaving because winter was coming on. And the children, masses of them, herding into the streets, and seeing them off with the urgent appeal that they take their laziness with them:

Take away my laziness,
And bring me back quick spirits . . . .

Then the memories from Megalohori, where they spent the summer holidays. The strong smell of the vintage, the tread of the feet in the winepresse, the hot scent of boiling pitch, the ebb and flow of the sea. So much and so much. As if a cloud of birds swarmed round his head. The confused echo filled him like a gentle wave . . . . And all—scents and sounds—preserved (so many years: how was it possible?) in that childhood nickname.

'Lilo . . .'

Seeing him so sunk in thought, his sister raised herself up, clasped his cheeks between her two hands and turned his face towards her. He smiled imperceptibly, smiled at that whole litany of the past, and sighed deeply. Then he seized her hands and raised them up, smiling then as his father used to smile.

'Listen,' he said. 'Leave Lilo where he is. He's been dead for years. We're grown up now. Look at us. Me as tall as the ceiling and you a girl ripe for marriage. Call me Leon, as in the regiment . . . .'

Without paying much attention to what he said, she continued to gaze at him insistently. Then, half surprised, half in rebuke:

'You haven't cried yet because of Mother. She died with your name on her lips and you haven't cried . . . .'

He didn't answer, only looked at her sadly, knowing it was natural she didn't understand him. Also perhaps because ever since childhood he'd found excuses difficult.

But in himself he said to her, quietly:

'You can't understand, little sister, and it can't be explained. Even I don't understand it fully. But I don't think I have tears any more . . . There's a great emptiness here inside, and it's got to be filled before I can weep again.'

If only indeed he could surrender himself to that voluptuous release. He would cry, almost joyfully, drunk with the sweetness of his sorrow. So he would wash his soul clean of so much poison; would weep for so many things, for so many dead, for such horror and such humiliation: that deep degradation of man that he'd seen and experienced at first hand. He'd weep till he'd drenched the gravestone the war had left in his breast, till he'd softened it, crumbled it like wet bread. His siter, the others—there was no way they could understand, and they wouldn't understand. For wasn't there a whole crowd of those who'd known the war who still 'didn't understand'?

Arranging his cupboard, he found on the shelf a pair of his mother's fine woollen gloves. They were black and elegant. They'd have lain

9

there from the time she'd come back from church one Sunday, and they still kept the shape of the white hands she'd had before she died. One of them was mended with great care round the fastening. He held them like small living animals on his knees, spreading out their black empty fingers, stroking them. He recalled his mother, tall, wax-like in her black silk, buttoning them at the door as she left for the service. He inserted his fingers and stroked his cheeks with them, and again that still sadness filled him, and again he saw the image of his mother, shining in her vibrant black silk, the joy of Sunday upon her white forehead and in her silver curls and no sign of death's terror showing.

He put the gloves down again, trying to compare those hands with those other thousands of dead hands—'hands of the war': those he'd seen twisted and blackening like wood in the trenches, grasping the rocky outcrop in their final spasm, or in the dried-up river-bed, their broken nails clutching in despair at the torn and dissolving garment of life. Of the whole body they were the last to surrender, vanquished in the struggle. He'd seen them fighting feverishly even when the light of life had left the shattered eyes . . . . Suddenly he felt stabbed by a sharp sorrow for all those hands left in Anatolia—hands, a whole forest of them, beckoning from far away, supplicating, contorting themselves into ugly symbolic shapes. They sprouted from the rocks and the brambles, stretched towards heaven their black fists, skinned by the vultures. The sky rained upon them, covered them with mud, the north wind knifed them, at night the jackals shredded them and dragged them to their lairs, crying together like children.

Those hands had no relationship to these soft clean gloves of his mother, with her gentle hands, bending as though still alive, scented with lavender and kindness, knowing how to caress even from beyond the tomb.

He remembered two other small female hands, poor hands, scarcely more than fifteen years of age. It was at Pergamos. He had gone into a ruined house and found a young girl, a child, dead on a satin coverlet with red and blue stripes. Her eyes were blue, enormous, wide-open, her breasts no bigger than two apples. They had stripped her naked, had tied her feet, her legs apart, to two railings near the staircase; and when the whole herd of male beasts had passed over her, they had nailed her down, there on the floor, with a long ancient bayonet. The iron had pierced the childish body, passed through the coverlet, and had stuck in the floorboards. Such force had not been needed. And the hands, of that child clutched onto a thick cushion and wouldn't open when they went to free her from the vile position in which she'd been abandoned. She'd been dead many hours, but the terror still hadn't left her.

If only he could free himself from all those terrible, hateful hands of the war whose blue nails had seized upon his soul, so that he dragged them behind him, with him, even here into this house of peace. . . .

He knew that the war had written in horrible characters a large part of his life, and he wanted obstinately and passionately to seal that book with seven seals. He wanted the war to be like a bit of surplus flesh on him, that he could cut off and throw away like rotten meat, so he could begin a new life, open a new book, with large innocent pages, white as angels, stainless, without the marks of human blood, without splashes of mud, of dirty sweat, of greasy secretions. If only he could take a sponge swollen with fresh water and wash his memory clean of all that filth, calm his soul, exorcize the visions of slaughter, the nightmares of terror that visited him in sleep. If only he could let his mind rest, lull it to sleep like a small child. . . . so that when he woke the red parenthesis didn't exist any longer.

. . . . . .

With what passion he took up his bone-dry brushes. He set to work furiously. He wanted to paint children with joyful eyes. Hundreds of children, a whole new generation of men unstained by crime, laughing with innocence in the face of life. Or a boat, light as a rose petal, forgotten in the calm blue sea, beneath the blue sky, sailing no one knew where. Or the peaceful olive-groves of the island, their ashen and silver leaves wet in the light, their trunks twisted, gnarled like the hands of a peasant, with the sun dropping its golden stains like oil on the earth. He struggled, struggled—a joyless effort to deceive himself.

As soon as he put pencil to paper a host of pale wide-eyed forms crowded forward, seeking expression: a sorrowful tormented army of condemned souls clamouring in the purgatory of his soul, seeking with savage and commanding cries their form as though through it they would regain their peace. There were faces yellow as the oilskins of fishermen, shrunken lips, eyes with motionless staring pupils or pure white and without pupil. There were chins hanging loose, mouths gaping at the sky, their tongues black as a dead dried-up snail.

Anatolia. The destruction of a conquering army! The defeat of the ten thousand. Then the return. . . .

The sea was blue, full of light and ripples, festive and joyful, its naked breasts stroked by the trembling fingers of the sun. Adroit prostitute, it laughed with playful laughter, while over its amorous waters sailed a terrible company of black ships, ships smutty and filthy, loaded to the hatches with women and half-naked children. Herded together, they reached out their arms, stretched their frail voices towards the Anatolian shore which slowly vanished, vanished over the stern.

The ships groaned and spat smoke, and the night came and covered them, and the land they had left behind them was red from the glow of an enormous fire that wrapped it in flames and blood, red as the cloak of Christ. There had been left the fathers and the young men and the finest girls of a whole people; there they trod the road of martyrdom, a road untrodden by gods or men. Their innocence found no justice either in heaven or on earth.

He closed his eyes and he saw them walking, an endless procession moaning and weeping. Their feet left on the burning earth red imprints. They were in long columns four abreast, beaten bodies and accursed souls, tied like beasts one to another. Shoeless, trouserless, dishevelled, their beards full of spittle, camel bells tied to the neck, pitiless butt for the Asian mob, their eyes darted right and left like a trapped beast's, their backs bent nakedly, raw from the whip and the bayonet.

When such memories mastered him he felt a pain, a shame, disgust with himself, eat into him. So strong was this feeling that he nearly cried out as though mad.

It did not take Adriani long to see the state he was in, to measure, with her love's sensitivity, the depth of the crisis through which he was passing. She forgot her sorrow and her grief and stood by him like a mother. And she did this with such thoughtfulness and tact that not for one moment did Leon feel that irritation which the tiring love of relatives often produces in the sick.

In spite of his self-absorption he realized the effort she was making, and many times he was overcome by an impulsive tenderness for this child who was able to carry out her heroic task with such delicacy.

In this unhappy atmosphere he struggled to find himself again. His artistic consciousness, which throughout the war years he'd felt ripening in him like a rich harvest, compelled him to the realization of his great ambitions. He wanted to transform into pure art those visions which had been his secret consolation in the trenches and under canvas. The time for which he'd longed was now upon him, and his heart beat as though he was preparing himself for an assault beneath the metal hail of bullets. He measured his powers, trembled lest he'd been deceived about them. He decided he'd work for an exhibition which would be the great decisive step towards fame. He wanted to resolve into colour flowers and flames, to catch dreams as though they were butterflies. He wanted something violent and burning, challenging public and critics alike: an assault that would end with victory. That would be his salvation.

One day he received a letter. He'd have to go for a few days to Mega-lohori, in the country, now that the vintage was near, to see what state the lands which he'd hired out to his godfather were in. It was his god-father who'd written to him, a Mr Spanos, second cousin of his father and common godfather of both Leon and Adriani.

He'd been working and harvesting the lands for years now, sending half the income regularly to the orphans. And there was the tower, too, the beloved country house of their childhood—that too would have decayed and would need repair. His godfather wrote of that also. Leon must go himself and see it, and they must decide together how much they'd need to spend on it.

His godfather's letter roused his longing for the countryside and the sea. It was a nostalgia that had tortured him in the mountains of Serbian Macedonia and in the treeless deserts of Anatolia. He longed to plunge again like a lithe animal among the shady trees of the village, to strip himself on its beaches, to crush the leaves of walnut trees, to chew the bitter-sweet vineleaf and to feel on his body the sun and the sea.

The sea!

2

ONE day the maid knocked on the door of his room. There was a note for him, brought by a soldier who stood outside waiting for the signed receipt. It was a form from the Garrison Commander. They wanted his discharge papers and a list of his 'postings' for their records. The military débâcle in Anatolia, the desertion of whole units, the loss by many regiments of their archives, had played havoc with the records. The Services were in a complete muddle.

He called to Adriani to ask her to search among his things for his military papers. They were in a big satchel which hung on a narrow strap. The discharge papers, folded under the transparent cover of the portfolio, showed the last organized unit to which he'd belonged before the catastrophe: the advanced guard of Seyndi-Gazi.

A slight shiver passed over his heart, and it seemed as if the point of the small compass on the portfolio trembled in response on it axis. He unbuttoned the large swollen leather pocket, took out a military cross, two medals, his discharge papers, a booklet of purchases of public goods from the military stores of Eski-Sechir, and a small black wallet with a silver monogram in the corner.

Leaving everything else, he seized that small wallet, gazing at it fixedly. He'd forgotten about it, and now he had it in his hands it reminded him of a sacred task he'd undertaken and which the hurricane of the catastrophe and the longing to get home had driven from his mind.

Slowly he opened it, his heart beating rapidly.

Inside was a photograph of a woman, a wedding ring, a sharp fragment of shrapnel as big as an oyster, and a small wrist-watch, the strap eaten by sweat.

They were the belongings which his fellow soldier Vranas, Stratis Vranas, had given him before he died. They'd been in hospital together at Eski-Sechir, in the 2nd Diakomides Hospital, when they'd brought him there with his thigh shot through. The sight now of those small objects shook him. He got up, locked the door of the room, to be alone, and sat wearily down in the armchair, still without taking his eyes from those sad memorials of his dead companion lying before him on the desk. Of all the events of the last year of the war it was the one which they recalled that had made the most powerful impression on him.

Imperceptibly he found himself again in the long narrow ward of the 2nd Hospital, the ward of the Saviour. It was a bare room, desperately like all the other rooms of military hospitals. It smelt of iodine, had its walls coloured a dismal pink, and contained two iron beds of the folding type. On the wall opposite the door hung an icon, taken from some ruined church: Christ the Saviour. The face was long and austere, the eyes fierce, their whites shining from the darkness of the icon as if from some hidden depths. One could just make out also the chin with its forked beard, and a hand raised in formal blessing, the fingers forming the symbolic letters I.S.X. unbelievably long and thin.

It was to this room that they'd brought them the same day. He was in one bed, Vranas in the other. Both had thigh-wounds. Only his was minor, a pistol bullet having passed through the flesh without causing any infection, or damaging any part essential to movement or circulation. But Vranas's was far more serious, a bad wound, as large as the palm of a hand, crushing the muscles and the nerves and breaking the thigh-bone.

At first the treatment had gone well. The only fear the doctors had was that the wounded man might have one leg shorter than the other, something anyhow which could be got over with a special shoe made with a sole an inch or so higher than normal. He might have nothing worse than a slight limp. It would depend on how well the bone mended. Yet from the time when their beds were placed next to each other Leon felt something, a secret communication, which only later became clear to him. He felt as though Fate was linking them together beneath the fierce eyes of the Byzantine Christ who raised his hand in blessing over them as though he raised it to strike whatever head came beneath it.

Until now Vranas had been simply an old acquaintance who came from the same island. Together they had passed through the Officer's Training Corps at Salonika, though there they'd hardly exchanged more than a few words together: good morning, good evening, and sometimes not even that. He'd been also in a different platoon, and each platoon had its own quarters. Now that they'd been brought so close together they felt a powerful friendship bind them together inseparably—one of those friendships forged only in war: the friendship of two men in the face of death.

Leon felt a kind of protective tenderness for his companion from the moment he saw how much more seriously injured he was. He followed his treatment with ceaseless attention, especially after he knew his own wound to be healed safely and perfectly. It was a duty that was like a propitiation for his normal self-indulgent egotism.

Vranas, in his turn, felt a sense of gratitude nourishing his friendship, and if he had not been such an unemotional type who regarded every form of demonstration as humiliating he would have shown to Leon, from the first days, the tenderness of a loved and sensitive child. But he was by nature so hostile to every confession of feeling that he was never able, while he was well, to express to Leon the extent of his love and gratitude.

Leon was soon moving about on crutches. And the first day that he was allowed to get up he celebrated his 'restoration', as he called it, in every way he could. His most successful turn was a somersault performed between his two crutches, when he looked like a locust leaping up on its long legs. As he did it, Vranas could not help a smile appearing on his thin lips—a slight melancholy smile.

'You're marvellous,' he murmured.

'But you should see old Wooden-leg,' said Leon. 'He really is marvellous. Did you ever see him?'

'No,' said Vranas, knitting his brows.

'When we're released we'll go to the carnival in Athens and I'll show him to you. He walks on two stilts high as the ceiling and wears trousers three yards long. He goes like this up and down the pavements, dignified and unsmiling in his tail-coat. Suddenly he'll stop in front of a window, lean negligently on the balcony, and say to the girls: "Would you give me a light please?" They strike a match for him, he lights his cigarette up there on the first floor, and then he doffs his top-hat and thanks them.'

He did all he could to cheer his friend up; he gave him books he'd ordered in the Greek bookshop in Broussa, he drew caricatures for him, told him stories from his Polytechnic days, tried with endless conversation to distract him.

Vranas was a stocky youth, dark, with black eyebrows thick above his sharp, slightly curved nose. His eyes too were dark, unbelievably dark, like two beads of jet. He was a primary-school teacher who'd got into the officers' corps through a special law of the revolutionary government, which had wanted to create out of the educated element in the army a new body of officers with antiroyalist feelings. He was himself a fanatical idealist about his country's destiny. He felt a childish delight when the Anatolian army every now and then came across relics of ancient glory: a bas-relief, a peristyle, an inscription half eaten by time, one of those exciting mosaics scattered among the Turkish villages and which signified that Alexander the Great had passed that way. How all those things stirred him. They were the marble spray from the wave of that Greek civilization which had once risen, broken, and spread joyously over this land, leaving behind it white theatres and temples and works of beauty and art. They seemed to him to be signs of welcome which from the depths of the past came to him from familiar, from beloved lips. He spoke of them with a fanaticism that was like a fever.

'We're in our own home, Leon,' he said. And he bit his lips, trying to move his numbed limbs into a more comfortable position. 'They're no myths, these things. They're unbreakable marble. They're true titles. We walk over Greek roads, camp on the sites of our forefathers. What we do is no more than a change of guard. Each keeps watch in turn. Alexander, then the Byzantine borderers, now us . . . . Put your hand on the earth and you'll feel how the ashes from their camp-fires are still warm. Our tents are pitched with their tent-poles, Leon!'

In spite of his pain he was genuinely proud of his wound, and one day, while Leon was doing his acrobatics on the crutches, he told him, with an altogether child-like maliciousness:

'Yours wasn't a wound, my friend. It was simply a fifteen-day home leave. If it wasn't for the gold stripe on the sleeve no one'd believe you'd been wounded . . . .'

Leon laughed warmly, joked, and told him funny stories. Mostly Vranas listened without interest, sunk in thought. The fact that he couldn't move made him irritable, especially now that Drivas was up and about on his crutches.

'If only I could change my position,' he said. 'Turn on my side, lie on my front—just shift a bit. It's as if my whole backbone was aching . . . .'

'Patience till the bone's mended and they've taken the splints off. It's the being motionless that'll bring you afterwards into—perpetual motion,' Leon told him. 'Think of the fakirs of India: they stay without moving for years in the most fantastic positions. That's how they develop the ease of movement which they need to slip into paradise after their death.'

'After their death . . . ' repeated the wounded man, like an echo.

Suddenly the hospital was shaken by savage howls, terrifying the patients. Eyes staring, everyone listened, while all other sound in the wards and corridors of the first floor came to a stop. Only that harsh cry was heard, seeming to contain all the sorrow and all the pain of the hospital.

'Go, lad, go and see what's happening in there!' Vranas ordered the orderly on duty.

In a few minutes the soldier was back. He smiled stupidly, obediently.

'It's nothing, sir,' he said with that serenity which all doctors and orderlies of the operating theatre develop. 'They were just cutting off a sergeant's leg, here at the knee, and he woke up from the anaesthetic while they were still operating.'

Leon felt the wounded man's eyes fixed on his, as if measuring their fear, or as if seeking for unconfessed information. A shaft of uncertainty passed rapidly through their black depths and vanished. He tried to conceal his anxiety by turning it into a joke. Imitating the voice of the orderly: 'You see, it's nothing,' he said to Vranas, who smiled.

He was straining his ears to listen. The beast-like howl of the sergeant was beginning to die down, like that of an angered animal being slowly overcome and falling exhausted. Finally there were only long moans, sobs, hardly audible from behind the closed doors. He would have been given a fresh dose of anaesthetic and was again sleeping.

Vranas fixed his glance intently on the orderly as he came and went in the room of the two officers. Leon saw that he wanted to say something but was hesitating. Finally, as the orderly was arranging his bed, he twisted his moustache with his finger and said with an air of unconcern:

'And why were they cutting off this leg?'

The orderly paused in his work, looking questioningly at the wounded man.

'Whose leg? You mean the sergeant's?'

'Yes, the sergeant's of course,' said Vranas, irritated.

'But . . . because of the gangrene. But he's not the first—every day they're cutting off arms and legs. That's all they're doing. The mortuary, in the basement, is full of 'em. The Director's ordered the quarter-master to have extra wide coffins sent up, so with every dead body they can put some of these other relics in.'

Leon noted with what horror Vranas listened to the soldier's slow, quiet, hopeless words. It was that day too that he saw for the first time a slight tremble appear in the corner of his mouth, on the left side. Later the wounded man, in a voice which, weak and hesitant, hid his anger badly, asked:

· 'And how . . . how is it they let them get gangrened?'

The orderly shrugged his shoulders as he wiped the washbasin, and answered indifferently:

'They don't let 'em. But most of those that come in to us now haven't had their wounds dressed for days, or they're without bandages . . . . Take for instance the other night, midnight, when a whole group arrived, four days ago. Till they could be settled in the serious ones stayed on the stretchers, the others were left on the ground, there in the big corridor of the main wing, where there's the hanging lamp. I happened to see them: those that could were themselves taking the worms out of their wounds by the light—white thick worms. They threw them on to the floor, and they wriggled, like this'—and he curled and uncurled his forefinger.

A troubled silence filled the room, broken only by the orderly's damp cloth, as again, desperately slowly, he began wiping the basin, first to the left, then to the right. The two officers watched that monotonous movement, their eyes going first left, then right, as if it were a significant sequel to his revelation. Then the soldier wrung the cloth out into the bucket, slowly and decisively. Afterwards he hung it over his arm so that he could carry other things in his hands, and he went out, treading as quietly as he could in his boots.

Suddenly the two officers felt that they didn't any longer know what to do.

Seeing his cigarette case on his pillow, Leon took out a cigarette, put it in his friend's mouth, lit it, lit one for himself, and blew a great cloud of smoke out of his chest towards the ceiling, breathing in again with relief. He spoke conclusively:

'We're among the lucky ones, both of us, though we don't say it....'

Vranas was silent, staring at the end of his cigarette where the blue thread of smoke rose straight and trembling into the tepid air.

He often did this when there was some thought troubling him which he hadn't clarified yet, or which he didn't want to speak about. It was at those times that Drivas realized that his friend was a true peasant, full of reservations and suspicious of every demonstration of feeling. Sometimes this irritated him, as though it were a form of insult, and he tried then to repress the over-impulsive mood which now and then came over him.

He had recounted to him, in that somewhat exaggerated way that artists have, a thousand and one incidents from his own life: humorous flirtations, a host of youthful stupidities, his dreams, his visions. He did all this to amuse him, to show him his trust and his devotion. And his friend listened as though it were something that was due to him, locked in himself, sad and thoughtful. His eyes were so dark that you couldn't see anything in them except a flame burning in their depths, burning slyly and then vanishing.

'Can't you tell me anything, anything?' Leon broke out one day. 'Can't you tell me about your childhood, your follies, about your affairs with women?'

Vranas saw that he was angry. He slowly clasped Leon's long white hand between his own, yellow and hairy—gazing for a while at the contrast between them, only now so noticeable. Then he said tightly, the tips of his ears reddening:

'Believe me, Leon, I haven't anything to tell you. I've never had a childhood, never had adventures. I haven't played about with women, ever . . . . '

'Please, I was joking. Joking,' said Leon, overcome with emotion. 'I like telling you things. You've no need to tell me anything. And you'll always have my friendship. You'll see. Always.'

Vranas looked at him, and clasped his hand nervously. He moistened his dry lips to speak, but couldn't say anything.

It was then that Leon saw two large tear-drops form on the flaming black of his eyes and disappear again without spilling. As if they'd been burnt.

3

THE days passed and Vrana's wound still didn't get any better. A silent melancholy more and more took hold of him, although Leon did all he could to relieve him of his gloom: read him selected pages from his favourite books, sung him comic songs, drew fantastic caricatures, of, for instance, the surgeon in charge of the hospital, a short dark man, of few words, conventional—extremely conventional—more a soldier than a doctor, though a good man at heart: he drew him in the act of performing operations with his sword, raising its huge blade in his two hands to bring it down on the cucumber-like legs of the soldiers laid out on the ground in front of him; or of His Excellency, the assistant chemist of the hospital, an excellent type from Smyrna. A volunteer, he was a well-built man of about forty, with red cheeks and a fat belly which made him lean backwards when he walked in an effort to hold it up with dignity. He had two tiny eyes which disappeared altogether when he laughed. And he was almost always laughing, with loud guffaws. He was one of the world's happy spirits. He played the guitar and sung songs, in all European languages, with a perfect pronunciation. He had organized at Eski-Sechir the 'company of laughter-lovers', the members of which had to laugh as much as possible and at the smallest thing. When the company was 'in session' the sound of their laughter shook the roof. There was a scandal and a reprimand: His Excellency must be more serious, as became his rank. He was known throughout the camp as 'His Excellency', a name which he chose for himself and by which he was known even to the ordinary soldiers. Kind, fond of amusement, women, and food, he always wore highly polished riding-boots, like a general, their bright spurs ringing behind him. He used to be teased about this:

'But you've never ridden a horse. What d'you want spurs for in a hospital, man?'

'Each to his choice,' His Excellency would answer. 'Am I entitled to wear them according to the regulations? I am. A man should enjoy everything he's entitled to.'

He sketched him marching between two rows of beds, their blankets and sheets dragged behind him on two enormous spurs, big as the wheels of a railway engine with their terrifying pistons, while the soldiers goggled at him with their eyes starting out of their sockets like eggs.

Vranas smiled at these caricatures, and his eyes filled with gratitude.

One day Leon brought important news from the pharmacy. His Excellency had told him that today or tomorrow a group of Athenian nurses would arrive from Broussa. They would be divided, he said, among the hospitals, one girl to each.

He brought his crutch down like a sceptre in front of Vranas and shouted dramatically:

'Do you understand? An Athenian girl in Eski-Sechir. That's news for you now. The title of a novel: *The Girl from Athens in Eski!* What is an Athenian girl in Eski?'

'Well, what is she, after all?' said Vranas.

'What is she? She's a feminine voice among the groans and the whinnies of an animal-farm. The note of a violin in a coppersmith's. A dove in a jackal's lair. A tender star in the darkness. A skirt among— among so many trousers! What is she? Take a walk through the hospital and see what she is? The barber had no work but he's got work now: they're all trembling in case she comes before they've got shaved! Mirrors here, combs there, brushes. An alert. You'd think they were getting ready to greet the spring. And don't speak of His Excellency: his eyes are gone for good now, he's laughing like a full moon, and his spurs are ringing as if it were the resurrection. Ah, it's a miracle!'

'And you?'

'Me? I'm already love-sick to the marrow. She's only got to make a sign, and I'll be down on my knees offering her a heart—my own heart —on the point of a cane. A flaming heart. Help yourself, my lady, but take care not to be burnt. But you? What are you?' He turned to Vranas, who smiled obligingly. 'Tartuffe or simply a teacher?'

Then Vranas stopped laughing, and answered gravely, looking at the ring on his finger:

'I . . . It's different,' he said. 'I . . . I am married.'

This he said with such a serious air that it at once put a stop to any wish for further talk.

The same thing had happened on the one other occasion when he'd spoken about his marriage. Leon was careful not to touch on the subject, avoiding respectfully any discussion which the sick man might take for thoughtless curiosity. He felt him to be untouchable on this point. On the other hand, whenever he saw him in one of his difficult moods he sought to distract him by telling him of various episodes in his own life, tragi-comic incidents for instance during his period of training at the Officers' Training Corps. All these he spoke of in a light-hearted manner, and he was indeed often successful in amusing the sick man. Vranas had belonged to another platoon. (The platoons were divided according to the height of the cadets, and Vranas, a short person, had been in the third platoon. Leon had been in the first platoon, which contained all the tall cadets.)

It happened that most teachers were on the short side. So that nearly the whole third platoon was made up of bent, underfed school-teachers, most of whom were older men, pedantic, complaining, with small old-fashioned spectacles the cord of which hung down at the ear. they wore their blue army berets as if they were nightcaps. They read much, never sang, never made merry on Sundays, the one day on which the cadets were allowed out into the town.

Leon's lot used to call them the 'uncles', and the name stuck. One day even the Commander of the Corps yelled out exasperated: 'For God's sake raise your heads for once, you "uncles" down there.' When Leon and his friends returned in the small hours from their Sunday nights-out, more or less dead beat, they used to see light shining through the cracks of the third platoon's hut. The 'uncles', their candles lit, were still studying. On the theoretical side no one could touch them. Leon's group, for instance, never read at all, but made up for it by their lithe immaculate appearance, proud bearing, powerfully enunciated words of command echoing with military violence from the wooden walls of the barracks, accurate shooting (impossible with glasses tied with a cord), and expert throwing of the grenade, it being essential to be tall if you wanted to throw them any distance. It was a tight-knit group, enthusiastic and tumultuous, a kind of 'Three Musketeers' of the Corps, although in this case they were four.

Douras was the first, an ugly journalist: you never knew when he spoke whether he was being serious or joking. He used to compose satirical songs which were at once taken up by the Corps, then by the whole camp, and finally by all the cabarets in Salonika. Beneath his sarcasm he hid, fairly successfully, a tender and sensitive soul. His great desire was to complete his two collections, one of local pipes and the other of every kind of hand-grenade. Among his pipes were some as large as spade handles, made from cherry and jasmin. Leon looted his kit-bag one day and erected a tent for seven people with them, hammering them in for pegs. His other collection, that of the hand-grenades, he could add to only with great difficulty, much begging and beseeching, and in any case he'd discovered it was quite impossible to take it with him. It weighed several stone. When the training came to an end and the cadets had to go back to their regiments he tried to find some dealer in Salonika to give it to, praising its importance and the trouble he'd taken. But it was utterly impossible for him to find anyone: no one would accept such a dangerous gift. In the end he handed it over to the quartermaster's store and forgot about it.

Then there was Minas, a volunteer from Cappadocia. 'Minas the Cappadocian'. he was called by his friends. He was the Hercules of the group, a huge powerful man, with a delicate girlish face, clear blue virginal eyes, and blond curly hair. Douras called him 'the Cherubim in trousers'. Minas was the only member of the group who was neither an amateur nor professional artist. But he was endlessly good and uncorrupt. He didn't allow any bad talk to go on in his presence and he blushed to the whites of his eyes when stared at greedily by a woman. His dream was to organize in Greece a workshop for Anatolian carpets: the secret of making them had been handed down from generation to generation in his family.

Then there was Doukas—or the Duke, as the others called him. He was an intellectual from Aivali, tall as a chimney, with the large, slanting, sympathetic eyes of a faun and a long, El Greco-like face. He was a mixture of mysticism, eroticism, and modesty. Drivas made a caricature of him as a monk with goat's hooves. He called it 'The Satyr in holy orders'. When a woman didn't look at him he stared at her hungrily and his nostrils quivered. As soon as she turned round and saw him he gazed down terrified at the toes of his boots. He was the acknowledged aesthete of the group, a critic of all the arts, and he wrote excellent essays in his notebook for trench warfare. One day he summoned all the members of his group to the café where they used to gather and read out to them a study in praise of simplicity in art. He had given it the title 'The Simple', and had made that rather unusual theme the repeated leitmotiv of the piece. The simple and the simple.

'What do you think of it? ' he asked when he'd finished, a bit anxious because of the suspicious silence of his companions.

They looked at one another, embarrassed, and at once, to their intense relief, realized from the look in one another's eyes that none of them had understood a thing. So they kept silent, till Minas said, with indescribable simplicity and sincere admiration:

'It's the first time I've ever heard such a complicated "simple".'

There was a roar of laughter, in which finally Doukas himself joined. They laughed for a long time, weeping and holding their sides, such innocence had Minas's short criticism.

The group was always together. They had a common bank, held by Minas, for generally he was the only one who put anything in it. They had common secrets, common adventures, and common Sunday 'nights-out with cabaret'. What held them together was their good spirits, their humour, and their artistic bent.

Drivas recounted thousands of stories about that unforgettable group of friends to the sick man, which he liked hearing because they reminded him, now in amusing terms, of the harsh life of the Training Corps.

4

ONE morning the doctor on duty, changing Vranas's dressing, paused in his work thoughtfully. Smiling awkwardly, he sent for the Director. When he arrived he too looked at the large open wound, said something privately to the duty doctor, and then told Vranas that they would have to scrape the thigh-bone.

Vranas gazed anxiously at the Director and asked him what this new operation involved. The latter smiled with his narrow lips and took hold of his hand, as if to reassure him.

'Oh, it's nothing. We're simply got to remove a skin that's forming over the shattered bone and that's stopping it joining together.' If he wished they could perform this small clean-up without even putting him to sleep—simply giving a local anaesthetic.

Vranas, as if offended, spoke firmly:

'It's not the pain, Doctor. It's that I'd like to save the leg . . . . '

The wheeled stretcher was brought to the bedside and he was carried off to the operating theatre. As he went through the door his eyes sought those of Leon.

'Good luck.' And Leon waved his hand encouragingly.

When the door shut the room seemed very empty. Leon felt a sharp prick of sorrow when he turned and saw his friend's bed still hollowed by his body. He leant standing against the window and felt terribly alone, straining his ear to catch even a cry of pain from the operating theatre: that at least would be a sign of life.

Time passed.

Nothing . . . .

He'd already smoked his third cigarette.

When they brought him back Vranas was a pale green in colour and was biting his lower lip with stubborn restraint. He didn't speak, only the blanket rose and fell jerkily on his chest. Drivas didn't dare say anything to him. Finally the sick man fell asleep. He slept as if dead-beat, but the upright groove between the black eyelashes of his damp forehead didn't disappear.

Leon sought out the doctor. He told him that it was not certain that one of his friend's legs would be shorter than the other. They had removed a piece of bone and had cleaned the surrounding flesh.

The next day Vranas begged his friend to try to find out from the doctor what his real state was.

'I've found out without waiting for you to ask me to,' said Drivas. 'They had to clean the bone so that the broken thigh could mend better.'

'If it were a question of mending...' murmured Vranas sceptically.

To get him out of his depression, Drivas read him part of Papadiamandis's story *The Royal Oak*. He enjoyed hearing it, light flashing in his eyes like swords in the darkness.

'It's the joy of vigour and strength,' he said with excitement in his voice. 'A song of health. Like a hymn, a paean. The royal oak. It sinks its roots deeply into the earth and embraces the sky in its arms. But...'

He tried to smile, gazing sideways at Drivas, and broke off.

'But what?' asked Leon, glad at the effect his reading had had.

'You mustn't laugh at what I think,' the sick man said awkwardly. 'You see, I was thinking that, in spite of all that, trees live a fantastic tragedy. I... I'm a schoolmaster, and it's never come into my mind to write poetry. But now when you read that piece to me and I listened to it without moving, swaddled like a baby, something suddenly occurred to me: there's a bitter tragedy that faces all trees. All those royal oaks, all the plane trees and the poplars—well, all those creations of God that rise up with strength and vitality are condemned all their life to stay in one place, immovable. Imagine it. Many of them live for centuries. And for all those centuries, thousands of nights and days, they stand on the same spot. . . . And think: even if the wood catches fire and all the animals rush out of it to escape . . . . It's terrible. The smallest insect, a worm--is there anything more exposed than a worm?—is better off compared with the majestic royal oak. . . . That's what I wanted to say. That, or something like it. Is there anything in life more delightful than movement? No, there's nothing. Clouds, waves, ships, birds . . . '

'Well?'

'What well?' said the other excitedly. 'Look at me. What am I now? Worse off than a child at the breast. If I'm not helped I'll dirty my own bed . . . . What am I? A woman could come and beat me and I could do nothing except cry . . . . Some filthy sod of a man could spit in my face, in my mouth . . . as though I were a spittoon. . . . '

His eyes clouded, and, ashamed of himself, he tried to smile. And the corner of his mouth again started to tremble, to tremble . . . .

The next day was His Excellency's 'great event': the Athenian 'sisters' arrived in Eski-Sechir, and the 2nd Hospital received one of them. Disappointment was general. All those men—doctors, orderlies, sick, and wounded—had been waiting now for days and with such anticipation for the woman who would sweeten their lives, filling with her femininity the savage atmosphere of the hospital. And now that she had come they were almost furious with her because the poor creature happened not to be beautiful. There were one thousand five hundred patients in the hospital, ten doctors, two administrators, and eighty orderlies—in all one thousand five hundred and ninety two men. All of these, waiting for the 'sister', had built out of their dreams her ideal image; and now all were angry because she didn't correspond to a single one of those one thousand five hundred and ninety-two images. She was a woman of some forty years old, breastless, without curves, the same before as behind, with a dry expressionless face, a slight moustache—the one thing not lacking in the hospital—and some reddish marks on the throat from an old glandular operation which she tried to hide with a tall starched collar that reached up to her ears. Her only bit of çoquetry was some miserable curls, made with paper curlers, which protruded like worms from beneath her blue cap.

Leon, with his sense of humour, was able to make Vranas almost cry with laughter. He told him that all the patients had asked for their discharge so as not to have to see the sister. She, on the other hand, was a true nurse—patient, skilful, courteous, and devoted to her work. It amused Drivas to sketch caricatures of her.

'How superficially you speak of women,' said Vranas solemnly. 'You've never been in love, that's clear.'

Leon was thoughtful for a moment.

'Never,' he then said emphatically. 'Till now I've always gone to a woman as a thirsty man goes to a spring. I don't understand how anyone can turn a glass of water into a tragedy. Especially since the good God, placing springs at every step, makes it so readily, so plentifully, available to his creatures. Sometimes even, when there haven't been any springs, I've splashed about in the mud—like the pig that rolls over and smears himself with it. Can you imagine it?'

'I don't want to.'

'Well, then, listen. A month before I was wounded the 3rd Army Corps had sent us at Seyndi-Gazi a whole lorry-load of women of that kind. A lorry-load, that's the exact word: it was the big lorry belonging to the Admin. Section which used to carry slaughtered cattle. I'll tell you how it happened. 3rd Corps' chief Admin. officer was a colonel from the Peloponnese who used to take his wife with him everwhere. I don't know what he was by profession, but he knew as much about soldiering as my boots. One day an army amateur theatrical group gave a performance. The Admin. officer was present. There were turns from old Athenian reviews, with ambiguous jokes. In one of the turns the compère spoke about some young girl: "She came from the village to Athens. She'd nothing in the world, not a penny. What could I do? Leave her in the street? It'd have been a crime. So I took her in, protected her. I gave her an opening by which she could earn her daily bread." Laughter from the soldiers. The Admin officer was livid with rage. He yelled at the actors, had them parade in front of him. "What's all this? Do you want to corrupt my men?.... They're all clean village lads, and you come and put filthy ideas into their hands!" A few days later a crime was discovered, a brutal murder. We found a soldier lying in a cornfield a little way out of Seyndi-Gazi, killed. His head had been pounded to mincemeat with a stone. Investigations were made and a number of cheerful things came to light. The dead man had been the mistress of a whole company of "clean village lads". He'd been killed by some lover he'd turned down. Sensation in the audience, eh? Then something else was discovered. In the theatrical troupe of a division in the same Corps there was a soldier who played female roles with enormous success. With his blonde wig, his make-up, and his movements he was the idol of every man in the division. One day the prompter of the troupe was taken away bound because he'd shot the "leading lady" with his pistol. At the trial it was revealed that a whole group of officers had come down from behind the curtain, had seized the "star" dressed and made up like a woman, as she had been on the stage, and had caroused with her till dawn.

'So it was that the Admin officer of the 3rd Corps of the Army began to come down to earth. And one morning we heard that he was going to provide the army at Seyndi-Gazi with women. How the men got wind of it I don't know. Nor how they even knew the time they were due to arrive. I imagine it was something like the instinct of those insects who fly for miles, straight as a die, to find their females.

'It was one afternoon, a scorching afternoon, that far away in the yellow landscape appeared the lorry that was bringing them—a huge green lorry, making the ground shake as it passed. It was uncovered, and they were standing up in it, holding on to the sides or on to the metal supports which normally held the cover, and jerking about like a load of goods. Ugly, angry, dizzied from the sun shining straight down on them, painted like masqueraders. A cloud of white dust rose up around them and stuck to their faces along with the other make-up. Oh, what a welcome! Where had so many soldiers come from? It was as if they'd sprang out of the earth like moles. All branches of the service, all kinds of uniform, all ages. They'd been waiting for them for hours in the Phrygian heat, hungry, filthy, hairy, and full of lice. They howled like a single enormous mouth when the lorry came into sight. In one swift movement they were all round it, in front of it, behind it, lost in that cloud of fume-filled dust, plunging into it intoxicated, running to keep up with the lorry: a herd of dogs mad with hunger behind a cart loaded with slaughtered beasts, howling, whining, swearing, spitting vulgar words, gesturing at the women, making disgusting signs, shouting "air" as they used to when they went into attack with the company, while the sweat poured from them like muddy tears. There were seasoned soldiers, fathers with children and beardless raw recruits. It was a strange sight, wild as a nightmare. It was then that I understood what the carrying off of women could mean in ancient times, a death-struggle between two races for the possession of females. I saw the soldier-driver, once he'd got among the mob, seized by the same delirium. Suddenly he started blowing his horn and shouting, his face twisted as though in pain, his eyes red, starting from their sockets.

'They put them in a house, posted a guard over them—they'd have been lynched if they'd been left unprotected—and had them registered and looked at by the doctor. Well, would you believe it? I went with all those women. It's the sensuality of a plunge into the mud. Have you ever felt it? You go barefoot into the mire and sink up to the knees, splashing and sploshing, and you like it. You destroy your innocence deliberately and spitefully. . . .'

'No,' said Vranas strongly. 'A woman is something better. . . . Only we're not always able to accept her as she is. . . .

Leon stopped, was quiet for a time, and then spoke with lowered voice:

'That's not at all unlikely. In fact I often think it is like that. I told you about Douras: here's another story about him, the other side of the coin that I've just shown you. You remember that small open-air café near the barracks—the one with the little pomegranate tree? You remember the barracks? There wasn't an army camp more dry and treeless. Well, Douras, whenever he wanted us to go to that café, used to say: "Let's go to the wood." The wood, you see, was that little pomegranate tree—the only tree in the whole district. And I shall never forget it. It's as though it grows and flowers with all its flowers in some corner of my soul. One whole spring, the spring we passed at that camp—the whole of it came and went for me only in that tree. At about the end of March, before it had any leaves, it began to break into blossom. It was a miracle. Suddenly it was full of buds, thousands of red-tipped buds, like pieces of burning charcoal. Then those tight knots began to burst like fireworks. Every bud became a small rose-coloured explosion, one after the other, a few more each night: we used to count the new ones we found every morning. Once Douras said: "I'd like to spend the night with it, to hear how they burst in the darkness!" When they'd all opened the pomegranate began to put forth tender green leaves.

'But Douras didn't go there, "to the wood", only for the pomegranate tree. There was a girl there also, opposite the "wood", on the other side of the road. She was a Slav-speaking girl, lithe and pale. Pale as transparent porcelain. She had delicate bloodless lips, small unripe breasts, and extraordinary blonde hair. Quite extraordinary. When she wound the golden plaits round on the top of her head it was as if she wore a royal crown. She was slim and proud, and we didn't know her name. She was living with her aunt— or it may have been her grandmother; we weren't certain—whom we used to call Maiko. She was an oldish woman with grey hair, most sympathetic, very clean, and always smiling. She had a little shop in her house where she sold things that were of absolutely no use to soldiers: coloured darning wool, small metal boxes for marriage crowns with two pigeons of yellow tin kissing each other with their beaks—even spices, multi-coloured moulds—angels with blue gowns —and wooden combs for looms and red vases hanging in rows on the low ceiling.

'The girl was always embroidering, sitting at the window. The window was green and she was blonde. I remember her still in that position, like an icon in its frame. Opposite this window we used to set our chairs, sit down on them, and drink our coffees, watching her. As in the song: "All day in the coffee-house I sit drinking coffee. . . " She had hyacinth eyes, which she scarcely ever raised from her embroidery, and her hands were small, transparent.

' "What shall we call her?" the 'Three Musketeers' asked one another one day.'

'Then Douras, the journalist, said in a quiet warm voice:

"We'll call her Contessa. Simply 'Contessa'. I think she's worth it."

' "She is worth it," we all repeated, drinking our coffee to the health of the Contessa.'

At this point Vranas suddenly frowned. He raised his head.

'Contessa?' he said, smiling.

'But I assure you it fitted her absolutely, that name. She was like some chatelaine risen from an ancient miniature.'

'I didn't mean that,' said the sick man, blushing slightly. 'But they gave my wife the same nickname at Megalohori. . . .'

'At Megalohori? You don't mean it,' said Drivas joyfully. 'You taught in my village. And you haven't told me all this time!'

He quickly told him how he had the two properties of his father there, and the tower where he passed his finest childhood summers.

'Of course! Now I remember,' said Vranas. 'The villagers still speak of your family with affection. So it's you they call "the people from Kastri". They used to tell a lot of stories about your father—everyone there loved him it seems. Well'—and he hurriedly changed the conversation—'what were you saying? I believe we left the Contessa embroidering at the window.'

'Yes. And to cut a long story short, one day, at two o'clock in the afternoon, to be precise, the journalist Douras finally fell in love with the Contessa. He assured himself of the hour at which this event had taken place. From then on he used to gaze at her intently, smiling at her, trying to catch her attention. And at the same time he developed an affection for Maiko. In order to have contact with her he began to buy whatever he could. At first it was vaseline. He found a tin of it in her shop and from then on he had an absolute mania for cleaning his rifle. One way or another he succeeded in making all of us polish our rifles and bayonets till they were like mirrors. Everything about them was dripping with vaseline—sights, bolts, magazines. Then when he'd exhausted that line he began buying paper angels and blue beads, those that villagers wear for charms. And he would even have bought the wooden combs for looms if Minas hadn't politely pointed out to him that the group's resources weren't quite sufficient for that kind of purchase. The Contessa was not slow in responding to his love. Her cheeks flamed every time she saw him, and she bent even lower over her embroidery. Then she began adorning herself for him, and we learnt from Maiko that she was desperately trying to learn Greek. It was very moving. The rest of us, who till now had regarded the girl as our common love, much like the little pomegranate tree, saw that the romance was developing. So every so often we'd find some excuse to retire from "the wood", to let Douras exchange smiles and flowers with the Contessa in peace."

'And then?'

'Then . . . . Nothing. The affair got as far as a kiss, the first and the last. Douras, the sarcastic Douras, told us this, and his lip trembled. When the period of training was over we got ready to return for exercises to our regiments. Douras was terribly upset. On the night before we left he broke away from us to go and take leave by himself of Maiko and the Contessa. It was dark, and he sat for some time in their little house. When he came back to the platoon he brought with him a woollen scarf, two pairs of knitted socks, all done by the Contessa. There were even six blue handkerchiefs. In the corner of each of these there was a small rose-coloured flower embroidered in silk, which was meant to be the pomegranate flower. Douras had asked her to embroider that instead of an initial. Duras agreed—it was the most fitting emblem for the Contessa, he said—and a duke should know where crests are concerned. Then some time passed. We'd been posted as lieutenants, and had been given our platoons, when one day a note was handed to me from Douras. He'd sent it with a liaison officer. I remember what he wrote almost word for word: *"Leon, my old friend. Do you remember the Contessa? I thought of her a lot, and I'd no news of her since we left the training camp. So much I thought of her that last week I managed to get them to send me from the regiment to Salonika, to buy some materials we needed. I did this only for the Contessa—you know how I like my platoon, I wouldn't have done it for any other reason. From the station I went as fast as I could to Maiko. I found her aged, shrivelled. How could she have changed so much for the worse in four months? A bag of bones, that's all. 'Where's the Contessa?' I asked, and my heart trembled. I was carrying a small parcel for her—five silk handkerchiefs, a copper bracelet. Maiko looked at me without speaking, bent double, her hands clasped at her waist. 'Where is the Contessa?' I asked her again, frightened to hear the answer. Then she unclasped her hands, raised her finger and pointed to the sky. My dear friend, the Contessa died two weeks after we left with galloping consumption. Maiko told me she was smiling as she died and holding to her cheek the photograph I'd given her—that one we'd had taken together by the street-photographer, standing by our pomegranate tree."* Yes, that's how the letter finished. And the story of the Contessa. . . .'

There was a short silence; then, his voice broken, Vranas asked:

'And Douras. . . . Does Douras still love her now she is dead?'

'Douras was killed a few days later in the attack on Skra,' said Leon simply. 'Minas was killed as well. . . . .'

5

THREE or four days later the doctor again brought the Director with him on one of his visits. A civilian doctor was with them, a fine man, who wore a superb gabardine with a belt and a blue cross on the arm. He was one of the leading surgeons of Constantinople, now serving with the 'Blue Cross'. They examined the wounded man, and then the Director and he spoke together in German. Vranas interrupted rudely:

'Would you please tell me clearly what is wrong with my leg. I think it is humiliating to a Greek officer that you should speak in front of him in a foreign language.'

The civilian doctor at once apologized. It was, he said, a professional habit. Then the Director, not at all angry, explained to him that from what was happening it was evident that the scraping which they had done wasn't enough for the bones to join together. It would be necessary to carry another operation . . . .

Again there was that slight trembling in the corner of Vranas's mouth.

'Don't be alarmed,' said the Director, as if he as well as Leon had noticed that scarcely visible movement. 'Don't be alarmed, it's not serious.'

And he rubbed his finger on the buckle of his belt.

'I'm not alarmed, Doctor.' Vranas spoke dryly and crisply, with something like spite and hostility in his voice.

The civilian doctor turned to him:

'Only . . . I would ask you to allow me to use chloroform, Lieutenant, so that we can operate successfully.'

'Do as you wish,' said Vranas tightly, looking at them challengingly.

So the sick man was again carried off to the operating theatre. Again they brought the wheeled stretcher up to the bed and placed him on it. Drivas noticed with surprise how light and thin his body had become: the two orderlies lifted him like a child. As he left the room Leon clasped his hand. The wounded man held it for a moment, and stared at him silently. It seemed to Leon as if in that fiery glance lay a desperate appeal, stubbornly hidden by the sick man's angry pride.

They took him away, the door of the room closed, and Leon heard the wheels of the stretcher squeaking.

'They need oiling,' he heard himself say.

This time the operation lasted a long time. Drivas imagined that he heard from behind the closed door of the operating theatre a low subdued groan, which stopped and then started again monotonous and long, drawn-out. He remembered the sergeant who'd woken up during the operation, and he shuddered, feeling a wild desire to smash through the lock of the door with his crutches and to rescue his friend who was lying there like a beast beneath the butcher's knife.

'Stupidities!' he thought at once. 'There they are doing all they can to save his leg and I'm getting in a temper and behaving like an idiot....

At last he heard the door of the operating theatre open, and he quickly opened the door of their room. He saw the orderlies with their white overalls pushing the stretcher gently towards him. In the operating theatre he glimpsed through the open door the Director, an assistant doctor, and the civilian surgeon talking urgently together. They also had on their white overalls. The sister was there as well. He saw one of the orderlies emptying a white basin full of red liquid, bloodstained gauzes, and cotton wool.

Vranas was still dead asleep, yellow as death, as if they'd taken all the blood out of him and then brought him back. Leon watched anxiously as the stretcher came slowly nearer, slow as a boat bearing a dead body. He noticed how extraordinarily black the thick eyebrows and the unshaved beard of the sick man seemed against the yellow skin. And when the orderlies drew aside the sheet in order to lift him up and lay him on his bed Leon froze with sudden terror, and a sharp cry escaped him as he looked.

The 'thing' they were putting on the bed next to him wasn't Vranas any more. It was a miserable relic of Vranas, hacked up and quartered. It was a senseless defective body, ending in a single leg, which they lifted like a piece of junk. It ended in a single leg which, dark and hairy, protruded from a pair of brand-new pyjamas. The other leg had been cut off high up, right up by the hip, where big safety-pins held in place a thick pile of bandages.

At this moment the Director came out of the operating theatre and entered the room. He gave some instructions to the orderlies, and then, seeing the shock that Drivas had had, touched him lightly on the shoulder.

'What have you done to him? ... What have you done?' he said, sobs suddenly shaking him.

'It had to be done,' said the Director, nodding his well-groomed head thoughtfully. 'It had to be done. You see, gangrene had set in ....'

'But shouldn't you have told him? Shouldn't you have asked his permission? To do it without him knowing—just like that—without him knowing . . . . That's a terrible thing. . . . '

'Don't be upset,' said the assistant doctor to him. 'He's a stubborn type, he wouldn't have let us do it. In which case, death would have been certain. He's a family-man, don't forget. He can still be of use in the house and even do his job with an artificial leg.'

'But it's a terrible thing.'

'It is a terrible thing. Do all you can to keep him going. Don't tell him anything till he's gathered a little strength and his nervous system's calmed down—it's thoroughly disturbed at the moment. He's very fond of you. In fact it was you he called for even when he was under the anaesthetic. The orderlies have strict instructions about what to do. But I'm relying mainly upon you. Protect him from the great shock he'll have as much as you can. You understand?'

Leon nodded his head affirmatively, not able to speak. He took his crutch and went out of the room, not wanting to be found tearful and unprepared when the sick man woke up from his sleep.

At the same moment an orderly came out of the operating theatre carrying a large white bucket. From the mouth of the bucket a leg was sticking out, a bare, blackish-yellow, hairy leg, the heel upwards. The reddish cloth covering the bucket allowed it to protrude as far as the calf. As the orderly passed, Leon stopped him:

'Where . . . where are you taking it?' he asked, shivering all over.

His eyes were glued to the leg. Only in a frenzied nightmare could he dream of a leg in a bucket, the heel upwards. Two of its toes were crossed over each other, and there was a yellow corn on the little toe, which had been slightly deformed by the boot and was squashed up against the others. As if from some great distance he heard the orderly answering him, a slight tone of surprise in his voice:

'To the mortuary. Where else?'

He tried to understand.

'Ah yes, of course. To the mortuary. But . . . . are you going to bury it?'

The orderly put the heavy bucket down.

'Yes. Of course. At the first funeral. And I believe this bit's going to be lucky.'

'How's it going to be lucky?'

'A transport officer's died in the St. Barbara Ward: he'd got pneumonia, and just lasted out till midnight. They'll be putting this bit in his coffin. Another leg's been waiting since yesterday. That'll have been nibbled at by now . . . . '

'Nibbled at?'

'Yes. It's the mortuary rats that do it. They've got used to eating human flesh, you see. Last week they ate the nose and heel of a machine-gunner that'd gone with enteritis.'

He saw that Drivas had nothing else to ask, so he picked up his bucket and went off carefully down the stairs.

Leon watched the leg as it was carried in such an unusual position down the steps till it was out of sight. Then he felt a strange anguish, something which came from the inability of his mind to grasp how his friend could be sleeping there nearby, in the Ward of the Saviour, at exactly the same time as one of his limbs, half of him almost, that whole leg from the thigh downwards, went off independently down the stairs bound on its own journey—and went, too, in a way that was altogether unnatural, with the heel upwards. But—and this was even more perplexing—it still bore all the marks of life: the corn of the little toe, the toes crossed over each other, even, if one bent down to look, the lines of the stockings. And all these were testimonials of life. Yet in spite of that, off it went down the stairs, marching away like another person, and Vranas, the other half of Vranas, was sleeping unsuspectingly in the ward of the Saviour.

When sometime later—how much later?— they told him that Vranas was beginning to come round, he raised his head, lit a cigarette to give his face a more or less normal expression, tried out a smile, and entered the room with as joyful an appearance as he could manage. He stopped at the door, pretending to be pleasantly surprised.

'Bravo! . . . You're already awake again?'

The sick man lay for some time without answering, only his eyes showing that he was awake. His hands still lay in exactly the same position that the orderlies had placed them in on the sheet, without his having the strength to move them. . . . Then he spoke tiredly, very tiredly, and his voice was feeble and colourless as a whisper:

'Yes . . . . It's nothing . . . . Only the chloroform . . . . The moment you go off . . . . It's an indescribable struggle . . . Afterwards there's a terrible taste . . . . Everywhere . . . . In the mouth . . . . In the stomach . . . . In the head . . . . A nausea everywhere . . . . I want to be sick all the time . . And the tiredness . . . . What a tiredness. . . .'

All night long he slept deeply, in what was more like a stupor than a sleep. He seemed to have some pleasant dream, for Leon heard him talking in a quiet cheerful voice:

'Come on, stop joking, let's have a look . . . .'

Drivas, his mind on the sick man, didn't get to sleep for a long time. When he awoke it was already daylight and the sun was spilling gaily into the room. Vranas had been awake for some time, and had drunk the milk they'd given him hungrily. He was still extremely exhausted and had not even the strength to turn his head. But he was in a good mood, and filled with a strange talkativeness. He spoke hurriedly, almost nervously, with a voice which seemed to have got smaller.

'Do you know, I'm much better,' he said to Leon when he saw him sitting on a stool at his bedside. 'That operation's given me new breath, brother! And I didn't feel anything, you know. Only that chloroform. They told me to count, one, two three . . . . But I'm much better this time.'

'Of course you are. . . . '

'I bet it's that civilian doctor I owe it to. I've got a suspicion, you know, that our own chaps aren't much good. A bit amateurish . . . . '

'He seemed to me to know what he was about . . . . '

'There you are, you see. In any case, that's how it is. It's all a matter of confidence. It's that which sets up the healing current between the doctor and the patient. Now . . . of course it's true that the uniform makes our doctors a bit unsympathetic. To be a colonel, with pips, with disciplinary rights, with swords and spurs, and then to be called "Doctor". A doctor's something else. He can't be an old battle-axe...'

The murmur of a priest chanting came from the road beneath the window: a slow chant, that slowly passed, one they'd heard often.

Drivas shivered. He knew what was passing in the road below.

'Listen!' said the wounded man, interrupting his haphazard talk. 'Listen! Another funeral . . . . What a lot of them. . . . Like flies.'

'Yes, it's nothing . . . . What were you saying to me just now?'

'What do you mean, it's nothing?' said the patient excitedly. 'You sit there and talk as if it were a dog they're going to bury. It's bound to be one of us again. Go and have a look, would you.'

'I know who it is. It's one of the transport officers,' said Leon in a strained voice as he rose as if to look out of the window.

Over the rough cobblestones the funeral hearse passed creakingly, covered with a large sheet. In front, the priest, a wooden cross in the hand, murmured the prayers through his nose, chatting meanwhile with a soldier at his side. Leon knew very well why the coffin was extra large.

The sick man was silent, his eyebrows contracted, until the sound of the funeral had vanished. Then he said clearly and slowly:

'You see? While one sleeps like an animal snoring away so that one can wake up hale and hearty in the morning someone else down below is fighting for his life. Existence! . . . You know what, Leon?'

'What?'

'It's strange . . . . As soon as I heard the priest I was as sad as a woman for whoever it was they were burying. That's why I got nervous at what you said just now, though you didn't mean anything. Forgive me. You know, I'd have liked to have been at the funeral of that poor transport officer.'

Drivas said nothing.

The sick man suddenly turned angrily to the orderly who was standing motionless in a corner of the room.

'You, you fool' he said to him, 'what are you standing there for like a bloody statue? Haven't you finished your work? Get outside and day-dream out there.'

I'm sorry,' said Leon. 'I forgot to tell you. He's been given to us exclusively, you see. Last night he even slept in here. And he'll go on staying here with us for anything we want. It's an order of the Director.'

The news didn't seem to please him.

'What the hell do we need all this looking after for?' he said. 'That explains why I thought I heard snoring all last night in my sleep. And I said to myself: "Leon doesn't snore." But I don't want that to happen again. You sleep outside, d'you hear, orderly?'

The soldier stood to attention and looked questioningly at Drivas. Drivas nodded to him.

'The lieutenant's quite right: you can sleep outside, there in the corridor, near the door. It's summer, so you won't be cold. And if we need you we can call you. You might as well go now. I'll arrange things with the Director.'

The orderly started to go.

'Just a moment.' Vranas called after him. 'Get my boots for me, would you, from the storeroom. Clean them and then bring them here.'

The orderly stopped short and looked at Drivas.

'Go and get them,' the latter said to him. 'He's given you the order.'

When he'd gone the sick man started again.

'I simply can't lie here all nights swallowing the breath of one person after another.... It's like drinking dirty water.'

After a while the orderly came back with Vranas's boots. They were indeed a splendid pair of polished boots, shining like the sun. The sick man smiled contentedly.

'That's the way. Lift them up, so I can see'em well. Aren't they fine, Leon?'

'Absolutely marvellous.'

'I had them made in Broussa. Broussa, you know, makes much better boots than Athens and Salonika.'

'It's been a military centre for centuries, you see.'

'And, you know, I haven't worn them yet. It seems they're lucky.'

'Lucky?'

'Yes, of course. The first time I'll wear them will be when I go on leave. Ha, ha! I'll go back to my wife like an officer out of some opera. She'll be expecting to see some ragged old warrior, covered with hair and beard and stinking of gunpowder. And she'll find instead a clean dandified shirker.... Won't that be a joke?'

'Yes, very funny.'

'What about it. Leon? Shall I try the right one out for a second? I'm longing to put them on, you know. Yesterday I dreamt I was wearing them....'

Leon paled at the thought that he was going to uncover himself.

'Are you mad?' he asked.

'I'm joking, brother. How's it possible when the mending of this famous thigh depends upon being absolutely still? In any case, it'd break the plaster.... You can't imagine, Leon, what an unpleasant thing that plaster is. It's as if my whole leg were encased in a marble tomb. There's a tightness from the ankle right up to the hip. Only that wife of the chief mason, that they built into the bridge at Arta, could tell you what it's like.'

'And those lovers of married women the jealous barons used to wall up in their cellars.... Imagine. What a time!'

'I can understand them,' the sick man said seriously. 'When one's really in love one can do anything.'

'To wall someone up because he's seduced a woman? In cold blood, bit by bit, with lime and stone?'

'That as well.... But that shouldn't prevent one from shaving a little. Look at me, I'm getting like a priest. The truth is I haven't been able to bear the thought of a razor. I'd decided I'd shave the day I got up. But today.... Ah, today I'm in the mood. The mood! If it wasn't for that plaster I'd kick the bedclothes off and I'd dance... a Pyrrhic dance!'

It was not long before the barber came, attentive and fully aware of the situation. Vranas flooded him with his chatter as well. When he'd finished he sprinkled him with scent and put a mirror in front of him.

'Like a bridegroom,' said Vranas with relief.

Then he touched his ear with the tips of his fingers, looked again into the mirror, and said quietly, so quietly that it might have been simply the sound of a thought:

'How thin I've got....'

It was not long before his cheerfulness vanished, though he went on talking until the evening. Then, when he had made sure that the orderly was sleeping outside the room, he too went to sleep, and didn't wake until it was dawn.

The next day he suddenly remembered that his toenails hadn't been cut since the day he came into hospital. He ordered the orderly to cut them.

Again Drivas intervened.

'First of all,' he said, 'it's impossible to cut your nails because they're in plaster.'

Vranas seemed sceptical.

'Do you mean to tell me' he said, 'that even the lower part of the leg's in plaster? What for?'

'Because every movement you make with your toes or your heel moves the whole muscular system up to the thigh.'

'You're quite right,' said the sick man, after testing it out on his sound leg. 'But it's curious how I can move it. Mostly it's the nails on my wounded foot that bother me . . . . It must be that they've grown and press against the plaster. It's a most irritating feeling, you know.'

'That's what it must be. So you've got to be patient till they break the plaster.'

But Vranas went on till he was almost angry, insisting that the nails of his sound foot should be cut and there was no alternative but to do what he wanted. But he still complained of the unpleasant feeling he had 'because the nails of the other foot are pressing against the plaster.'

When it got dark he begged Leon to leave on the electric light which lit the room with as little strength as a candle.

'I'm not tired tonight and I want the light,' he said. 'But if it bothers you and you can't sleep it doesn't matter.'

'Ba, I'm not tired either tonight,' said Drivas. 'Let's talk a little, if you want to.'

'I'd like to. Read me something, if it's not a bore.'

'I'll read you something you'll like.'

He read him stories from Papadiamandis for quite a time. Vranas didn't say a word. His eyes were half closed and Leon thought he'd dozed off.

'Shall I stop now so you can sleep? The reading's tired you . . . . '

The sick man raised an eyelid and asked doubtfully:

'The reading?'

'Don't tell me you've been sleeping all the time I've been struggling away with Papadiamandis . . . . '

'Papa . . . Papadiamandis . . . . Papadiamandis,' said the sick man, as if he were trying to remember.

'Yes, Papadiamandis of course. Do you mean to say you didn't recognize him from his language, his style?' Drivas asked in astonishment.

The sick man answered him in an entirely unexpected way, saying, hesitatingly, his eyes still half closed:

'Of course I recognized him. How could I not recognize him? As soon as he came in I knew who he was. "How are you?" he asked me. "As well as I can be," I told him. "I'm really much better. I'm just waiting for my thigh to mend." "The thigh?" he asked. "Yes, the thigh," I told him. "The thigh." Then . . . '

Drivas, alarmed, let the book fall. He got out of his bed and went over to him, leaning over him and taking him by the hand, which was slightly feverish. The sick man looked up at him, his eyes shifting in a curious way, as though he were trying to see some object in front of him that was continually changing its place. Perhaps, Drivas thought, it's because of the light that's falling straight into his eyes.

'You've got a temperature, Strati,' he said.

He sat down beside him on the stool, still holding his feverish hand.

The sick man twisted his face into a grimace in his effort to answer:

'A temperature? . . . Rubbish . . . . I'm very well . . . I'm even sleepy . . . Good night, my friend. . . . '

Drivas was a little less anxious. He'll have been talking in a half-sleep, he thought. He turned out the light, lit the night-light, and went to bed. He'd just gone to sleep when he heard himself being called. The sick man was quietly repeating his name: 'Leon! . . . Leon!' He realized then that all the time he'd been asleep his mind had been awake, listening and attentive. He got up at once, put the light on, and went over to the other bed.

The sick man's face was full of fear and suffering. His nostrils were twitching nervously, as if he'd just escaped from some great danger. He was breathing heavily and rapidly through his nose.

'Is there anything you want?' Drivas asked.

'Nothing. . . .No, wait a moment . . . . Yes, a little water, if you would . . . .'

He filled the glass, raised the sick man's pillow slightly with his left hand, and gave him the water.

He hardly took a sip—probably he'd only asked for it as an excuse —and indicated that he didn't want any more. Leon laid his head back carefully and put the glass down on the bedside cupboard, covering it with a saucer. The sick man followed all these movements with intense curiosity, as if he were struggling to understand something. When Leon again sat down beside him he began looking first at one arm, then at the other, from the fingers up to the shoulder. Then he looked at him in the eyes, his forehead, at his nose, his mouth, his chin, his chest. Then he glanced sideways at his own left shoulder, and then at his right.

'Why are you looking like that?' asked Leon, his heart tightening.

Vranas again looked searchingly and suspiciously into his eyes without speaking. After a bit he murmured:

'Nothing.'

But he continued looking at him, as secretly as he could, until finally, not able to restrain himself any longer, he asked firmly and energetically:

'Look, Leon ... I want to ask you something. You won't misunderstand me, though? You promise?'

'Ask me whatever you like, my friend,' he answered, deeply moved.

'Tell me: who put on the electric light just now?'

'I did .... You saw me .... The orderly's sleeping outside the door...'

'I know .... But .... It was you? You yourself? Are you certain?'

'But of course I'm certain.'

'Strange,' said the sick man, thoughtfully, 'With which hand?'

'With this one.'

'With the one with which you gave me the water?'

'Yes. The right hand.'

'And which hand did you raise my head with?'

'With this one.'

The sick man seemed astonished. He pursed his lips and frowned with perplexity and terror. Then he said hesitatingly:

'And ... the other hand?'

'What other hand? Who do you think I am—Shiva?'

Vranas again looked at him suspiciously and said, trying to make his voice sound normal and untroubled:

'Nothing... I'm teasing you. Didn't you realize? ... I must be tired ....'

Drivas smoothed his forehead, wet with a cool sweat.

'You've a temperature,' he said to him. 'Stop talking now.... Try to go to sleep .... Close your eyes ....'

'Why should I close my eyes?' he asked quickly and anxiously.

Drivas saw his eyes watching his movements, fixing for a second on the hand he held to his forehead. Then he carefully reached out his finger and touched Leon three times on the shoulder as he bent over him. He saw Leon was looking at him, and he tried to smile.

'That's what it is,' he said after a moment, as if he had realized something. 'I must have a temperature. That's the reason. Leave the light on, if you don't mind .... And ... the door ...'

'The door?'

'Is it open?'

'Yes.'

'Please lock it. There's no reason why we should sleep with the door open, is there?'

43

'None at all.'

Drivas slept fitfully and as soon as it was light got up to go and tell the Director of what was happening. Vranas was still asleep, terribly pale, his hands in the dawn light lying thin and green-looking on the white blanket as they emerged from the sleeves of his blue pyjamas.

Leon switched off the light, drew the curtains, and went quietly out into the corridor. There he stopped, leaning on his crutches, in front of an open window looking out on the big courtyard. A cheerful noise came up from below and poured in through the window with the pure dawn air. It was the orderlies passing in a queue past the porridge-pot from which they were taking their morning meal. They were wearing the light-striped service pyjamas and were complaining good-naturedly at the wateriness of the milk.

A moment later the big iron gates of the courtyard clanged open, and with a great shouting and turmoil the cart of the Administration, loaded with slaughtered animals and vegetables, burst in like a war-chariot. Skinned lambs, their bellies open and their feet cut off, hung from its sides. Opposite, in front of the stables, a trooper with his one arm off stood idly slapping his gaiters with his whip. His empty sleeve was unstitched up to the shoulder, where it was fastened with a large safety-pin that shone like silver. He was dressed with extreme smartness. His buttons flashed, his epaulettes were new, green as fresh spring grass. He was a tall, thin-waisted youth. It seemed that his cure was over and he was waiting to go back to his home. Drivas noticed the silver stripes on his sound arm: there would have been as many as six of them. Then the clown in him made him say to himself: 'A soldier loses an arm on the sleeve of which he has, according to regulations, to wear the silver stripes awarded for being wounded. He loses his arm and so he loses the sleeve as well. Where now is he to sew the testimonials of his gallantry?' The trooper, his lithe body swaggering in the early light, went out of the big gate into the road. He walked with a curious vanity, as if the loss of his arm had given him some superiority over others. It was exactly like the pitcher in the Lesbian poem, the pitcher with the broken lip which when it was taken to the spring said compassionately to the other unbroken pitchers:

Ah, my poor pitchers,
All with your sound lips!

The doctor on duty examined the slaughtered animals, checked their weight on the scales, and took over the day's supply. It was the same doctor who'd first noticed Vranas's gangrene.

Drivas descended slowly into the courtyard and called him over. He gave him all the details of his friend's behaviour during the night. The doctor promised to report them at once to the Director, so they could come and visit the patient before they began their rounds. And indeed it was not long before the three of them—the Director, the duty doctor, and the civilian surgeon from Constantinople—came into the room.

Vranas by now was awake, and lay there motionless and thoughtful. He had no appetite and it was only after great difficulties that Drivas managed to persuade him to drink a few drops of milk. When the doctors came in he looked at them one by one with that searching regard which Drivas had noticed during the night. He gazed intently at their overalls, their hands.

The Director touched his forehead.

'Well, my friend, how are things going?'

'Well . . . very well. There's nothing wrong with me now,' the sick man answered, looking all the time at his fingers, as though he were counting them.

'Excellent. Excellent. May we have a look at the wound for a second?'

Vranas frowned, his eyes filling with fear.

'But there's nothing wrong with my wound now, Doctor. There's no need for you to see it. It's getting on fine, I tell you. Just leave it to get better for a while, so I can get up and get out of here. . . . '

'Ah, there's no need for you to be in such a hurry, Lieutenant,' said the surgeon in a quiet reassuring voice. 'One has to change the dressing from time to time, to help the wound to heal itself more quickly. It's its day today. . . .'

The sick man bit his lips, hesitated a moment, and then, turning his frightened eyes from one doctor to another in turn, asked, defeated now:

'You won't do anything bad with me, eh?'

'You know that we try to do everything for your good,' said the Director as gently as he could, making a sign to the duty doctor to remove the bandages.

In case of accident the bedcover was bundled up on Vranas's chest, so he wouldn't be able to see easily. As the bandages were removed, he moaned, clenching his teeth, while two orderlies stood by with gauzes and cotton wool in a shining nickel tin, tweezers, and bandages. The inspection was soon over. Again the Director said something in German to the civilian doctor, who looked at him and answered quickly:

'No, of course it's nothing. It's coming along splendidly.'

'There you are, it's over,' the Director turned to Vranas. 'There's nothing the matter with it, you see.'

They told him to try to eat, to eat whatever he liked, to ask for whatever he wanted, and they prescribed a medicine and some injections.

'When'll I be able to walk with it?' asked the wounded man.

'With what?' said the Director absent-mindedly.

'With my leg.' He spoke imploringly.

The Director flushed slightly and gave a cough.

'Well. . . . You must lie absolutely still for twenty days or so. Just as you are.'

'It's the nails, you understand.'

'The nails?'

'Yes. They're growing inside the plaster and they're a terrible irritation. An ugly spasm shoots from the toes right up the leg. . . .'

The doctors exchanged glances. Then the surgeon spoke, smiling:

'When we break the plaster in fifteen day's time. . . .'

'Fifteen days' time,' repeated Vranas, trying to grasp quite how long that would be. Then, his voice timid, he asked: 'Tell me, please: shall I be able to wear my boots in fifteen days' time?'

6

FROM that morning the uninterrupted relentless struggle began. Drivas could recall its progress day by day, hour by hour; could retell all its details. And when now, after so long, he saw those poor mementos of the dead man spread out on the table in front of the black wallet with the silver monogram, the photograph of his wife, the gold wedding-ring, the bit of shell, and that cheap leather strap with the silent wrist-watch—when he saw them lying there he still had to shudder.

The civilian doctor told him of the patient's condition on that same day. He was condemned to death—had, in fact, only a few days more to live. The gangrene had introduced a kind of toxin into the organism, a fine but terrible poison was spilling from the wound and spreading through his whole body, infecting his nervous system and the centres of his brain. It was the irritation of these latter which produced various illusions in all his senses. From now on the sick man lived in an imaginary world, pleasant or terrifying according to the scenes that his mind played before him. He spoke with people that he alone could see, hear, and touch. He responded to sounds which echoed only within himself, cohabited with extraordinary beings who came and went in the long narrow room of the hospital, sang, paraded, moaned, howled, or grimaced between the two beds of the wounded officers.

What made this martyrdom more tragic and Drivas's position more difficult was that frequently at first, and more rarely later, the sick man had moments when his mind preserved a strange critical control over these visions. It was as if some corner of his mind still remained unaffected and it was there that his reason had withdrawn, and it was from there that it tried to illuminate with the small light which it still retained the chaotic and monstrous confusion of irreconcilable impressions with which his afflicted nerves filled his head.

The sick man realized that in all this confusion there was something terrible and unusual, something not normal; and his mind sought to reconcile the new hallucinary world with those logical criteria which up till now had been valid. He made concessions, ever larger, so as not to have to admit his degradation, he struggled to escape with pretences and cunning reservations. It was then that his anguish reached a climax. He begged Leon for help, never losing sight of him even sometimes at moments of delirium. At first he didn't dare tell him exactly what he saw and heard around him, but tried to give a semblance of truth to things by speaking indirectly of them. In this way he sought some confirmation or at least indication of their reality, which he still doubted. It was the final attempt of his reason not to hand the reins over to the monstrosities breeding uncontrollably like worms in his infected mind.

Leon, who'd suspected the presence of this unconfessed drama from the first night, began consciously to take up his improbable part in the sick man's fantastic world. He did everything he could to give his friend some slight evidence, or at least the shreds of some evidence, that his mind was in order and that his senses were working normally. It was an endless duel of craft and suspicion on both sides, with the sick man every so often setting traps for him, or on rare occasions becoming altogether quiet.

There were times when the orderly began to imagine that Leon too was mad, so that he had to explain to him exactly what he was trying to do. It was at this moment that Vranas glanced sharply at the door.

'Listen! But listen!'

'I am listening,' said Leon, trying to guess what it was.

'If you're listening why don't you get up and open the door? They'll break it down in a moment and you sit there doing nothing.'

So Leon got up and opened the door. The face of the sick man lit up in delighted surprise.

'Oho! Look who's arrived . . . . Come in, come in! Thank you, and how are you? . . . What? You heard we were lying here wounded and you've come all this way to see us? . . . . Bravo. That's what I call friendship. . . . And, you know just last night we were speaking of you, weren't we, Leon?'

'Yes, indeed we were.'

' "Yes, indeed we were", and you don't do anything to make them welcome. And you know them better than me . . . . Excuse us, my friends, we're short of chairs. . . . It's a hospital, you see. But, Leon, you could at least offer your bed for Minas and Doukas to sit on. Doukas used to manage very well on the divan. . . . '

'Of course, of course! Please sit down,' said Leon, offering his bed to the invisible visitors.

Meanwhile the sick man had begun talking with Minas:

'Leon was quite right. . . . You're an absolute colossus, God bless you. Gulliver among the dwarfs, you are among us. . . . Let's hope you don't go through Leon's bed. . . . But wait a moment, Leon.'

'What is it?'

'Didn't you tell me that Minas and Douras had been killed at Skra?'

'I told you such a thing? No, it's quite true . . . there was a rumour of it once. One of those war-time rumours, you know. Anyhow, here are both of them, large as life.'

'It seems to me ... But come now, Douras, don't go on like that. I've heard all about your Contessa. That's what the rotten world's like. Cheer up if you can. In fact, you know, nearly all those girls with very blonde hair, blue eyes, and skin transparent as porcelain are tubercular. . . . Come, don't cry. Men don't cry. They suffer only. . . . And I'll tell you a curious fact. You know, Douras, I've got my own Contessa. But she's neither pale nor blonde. She's. . . Ah!'

'What is it?' asked Leon anxiously.

'What do you mean, "What is it?"?' said the sick man, suddenly frightened. 'Sometimes, my friend, you are so indifferent that I can't explain it. How did our friends leave without me knowing about it? What time was it they left, so that I didn't see them? It's as if the earth'd opened and swallowed them!'

'Nonsense, I saw them,' said Leon, trying to calm him down. ' "We'll go now," Minas said to me quietly while you were talking with Douras. "We'll go now, so he doesn't get tired with talking so much." '

'And what's it matter if I do talk? Is there anything wrong with my chest? It's my thigh that's wounded, and I certainly don't speak with my thigh, so why should I get tired? . . . Well, would you believe it? I simply didn't notice when they got up and left the room. I didn't see anything, and I didn't hear anything.'

'Naturally, since you can't turn your head round. And, anyhow, when you talk you're so involved in what you're saying that you don't notice anything.'

'That's what it must have been. . . . That's obviously what it must have been . . . . That's what it was, certainly. . . .'

He was quiet for a while, then began to look angrily and anxiously first at the walls of the room, then towards Drivas. Drivas bent over his book, waiting to find out what was happening. At last Vranas called out to him:

'Leon!'

'What is it again?'

'But why don't you look up for a moment and see what's happening round you for a bit? Are you blind to everything? Don't you hear at least? Ts,ts,ts! Where on earth did they get the idea of coming to decorate the room again? Hey, are you all mad? . . . Listen to that! He says the Director's given them orders. . . . Cement! . . . First, he says, they're going to build in the door, then the windows . . . . What absolute rubbish! So the microbes can't come in, he says, and infect my leg. . . . What an absurdity! You bloody fools, you've got the order all wrong! How's it possible? What about the air? And the light? How long will the oxygen in the room last? Look! There's hardly enough left for us to breathe already! Ah!... Leon!"

'Strati!'

'For God's sake get up and drive the idiots away! Get up and stamp your feet if you can.... What cheek! And they go on hammering, making the mind ache.... They don't give a damn for us.... Get up and go for them with your crutch!... Do you mean you're afraid? Give me your pistol, then, and I'll settle them from where I am.... Forgive me, men, don't you see... Leon.'

And Leon got up and began waving his arms and shouting and prodding with his crutch.

Gradually the sick man calmed down, his breathing became more regular, his heart beat more gently. But still, in the spell of his terror, he shot sidelong glances towards the door and tried to turn his head towards the windows. Leon wiped his sweating forehead with a handkerchief soaked in eau-de-Cologne, and he closed his eyes, or pretended to close them, for suddenly he opened them again suspiciously and asked, fear in his voice:

'So they've gone, Leon, those bastards?'

'Yes, we got rid of them finally.'

'All of them? All? Have a look behind the curtain.'

'Nothing.'

'And the other curtain?'

'Nothing there either. I got rid of the lot of them. They'd made a mistake, he said, it was the storeroom they should have been building....'

'We must report them. I'm certain it was deliberate.... Listen!'

'What it it?'

'Have a look, if you would, under the bed. One never knows what's going on.'

And all the time his condition grew steadily worse. He stopped eating altogether, and thinned rapidly, his skin clinging to his bones. All he asked for was water. Simply to drink, to drink that was all he wanted. The poison spread, the resistance grew less, and the doctors were now quite outspoken with Drivas:

'Not a scrap of hope. He'll die today, tomorrow, the next day.... It's a matter of how long his heart holds out. How long can it?'

The sick man continued to live his double life, only his struggle became greater, the deliriums more frequent, and the light of his reason ever less: the intervals of clarity were shorter, came more rarely. His colour became that ugly yellow of people about to die, his features bit by bit sunk away: his nose became pointed and seemed to be longer, and in the middle, where it curved, a small bone stuck out beneath the skin like a small stone beneath greaseproof paper. His life was now concentrated in his voice and in his eyes which circled, circled

50

endlessly, tirelessly, hither and thither, full of fear and suspicion, so that you grew exhausted watching them. Their pupils were able to move into the most improbable corners of their sockets. He threatened, supplicated, joked. He tried with his altered voice to repeat some song which only he could hear, and at night he would chant weirdly and wildly. There were times when Drivas shuddered with secret terror. 'There are many things in heaven and earth.' Perhaps those about to die hear and see, their senses stretched to breaking point, some world which our senses cannot grasp? And Drivas would be seized by a strange panic, and didn't dare turn his eyes to look at the icon of the Saviour in case His fierce eyes with their white motionless balls were turned towards him.

Finally the sick man wasn't able to sleep any more, and lay wrestling all night with his self-created world.

One morning he said to Drivas:

'You slept like a log last night, Leon. Like a log you slept, and you didn't see the trick I played on you. You know that I went off for the whole night? Hehe!'

'You went off?'

'Yes,' he said triumphantly. 'I went off and not one of you saw me. I got up carefully, put my boots on, and away I went. I left Eski-Sechir and made for Ankara. I walked and I walked till I was exhausted. . . . My leg got numb, and where the wound is it began to ache and I couldn't go any further. And then, just at that moment, there right in front of me by a stroke of good luck was a Turkish soldier. An infantry captain on a white horse. He saluted me, I saluted him. "Stop a moment, " he said to me. "What do you want here?" He spoke to me in the plural even: "What do you want over on this side, officer?" I was surprised at his manner. I thought: "That's done it. I've wandered into the Turkish outposts. Now they'll take me prisoner. And the Turks'll beat me," I said, "as they did at Pergamos; they'll nail my cap to my forehead, driving the nail straight through the badge." And I shivered, shivered. But my leg ached terribly. "Brother," I said to him, "aman, captain, I'm wounded badly. It's the fatal thigh," I told him. "But I couldn't bear it and I escaped from the hospital, and I made for the front lines. If only my legs weren't numb," I said, "and I could see the fellows of my platoon again!" I wanted to see them. The Turk smiled, put his weight on the stirrup, and swung himself down from the horse, down from his white horse. "You're very tired," he said to me. Did you ever hear anything like it, my friend? "You," he said. "You're very tired, brother. Come, get on my horse and go your way. I've got my legs." And he slapped his healthy thighs with the palms of his hands. Do you hear friend? He even helped me to get up into the saddle, and he put the reins into my hands. "Aha," he said "you've got a splendid pair of boots." "Yes," I said, proud that he should have noticed them. "I had them made in Broussa. They make fine boots in Broussa," I told him. The Turk said: "Of course, of course! It's been a military centre for centuries, you see. But you don't know," he said. "You don't know the news." "The news?" "Yes," he told me. "Peace has been signed." "How do you mean, peace has been signed? You mean the war's over?" "The war's over. The two armies laid down their arms, and all together, officers and men, declared: 'We're not fighting any more. Let every man go back to his home and let us part like good friends. We're both of us fine peoples, and we've proved it.' " And now they're staying outside Ankara and there's no fighting. "If you want to," he said to me, "you can go there as well. The entrance's free. And there's a lot of fruit in Ankara—the kind you're longing for." "Ah, yes," I told him, "I am longing for it. For oranges above all. Large oranges, and you make a hole in them, and suck them like breasts, hanging from the orange trees. And grapes. A plate of cool grapes!" "Well, get going, then," he said to me, smiling and waving his hand. And I spurred the horse and before I knew where I was I was there, outside Ankara. The people! Like millions of ants. There's a broad road, about a mile across. On the one side are our men, on the other are the Turks. They'd piled their weapons up, thrown down their haversacks. For hours I passed between the two armies and they didn't come to an end. Such a gathering! They all smiled at me and pointed at me. He's going to Ankara, they said, to get fruit. "Good luck to you," they called, pointing with admiration at my boots. I got to Ankara. A town full of fruit, Leon: melons here, figs there, pomegranates, oranges, grapes. Ah, the grapes! You go through the little alleys and you see them hanging above your head from the vines, bunches large as babies. I glutted myself, picked and picked.... But just imagine it, all the roads covered with vines and you simply reach out and pick. I took some away with me. You can have them if you like—I left them downstairs, in the stable, where I tied the captain's horse up. We'll have to give it back, won't we? But I'm too tired now. I can't even move my fingers. Such tiredness.... But it was quite something, all that, wasn't it?'

'Don't talk so much,' Leon said to him, trying to calm his excitement. 'You make yourself more tired....'

'No, I don't. When I talk I don't get tired. Don't you bother, I know what I'm doing. And then ... when I talk I'm less frightened.'

'Less frightened?'

'Yes. There are some strange things going on now in here, and neither the Director nor anyone else knows anything about them. We ought to report them to the Garrison Command. There are some people who've got their knife into me. They don't have any pity for me. When you were out just now four of them came in and they treated me brutally. I was alone and there were four of them. What could I do? And they were tall and strong as porters and I was lying here on my back, my leg in plaster. And, again what really troubled me was that the four of them hadn't a single face. They were all quite normal, but they hadn't a single face. You can't imagine how terrible that is. I thought at once that they'd come to do something bad. Otherwise they would have had their faces, like everyone else. It was so they wouldn't be recognized, you see. And they came in without making any noise. But I was aware of them, mind you, from the first moment. They stood in a row there, by your bed. I was trembling, and I began to sweat a bit, but I pretended that I hadn't noticed them, and I didn't even turn to look at them, so that they could say that I made the first movement. They came up close to me then, stood on each side of my pillow, two to the right, two to the left. They shook me by the shoulders. "Come on," they said to me, "what are you pretending you don't see us for? Get up and dance the Pyrrhic for us." I tried to make a joke of it. "The Pyrrhic?" I said, as if I found it very amusing. And then they set to work, the dogs. "Don't you see that my left leg is broken," I told them, "and that I've got to lie absolutely still if the bone's to join?" They didn't take the slightest notice. They forced me to get up and to leap, to leap and leap on my one leg. On my left leg. What a pain. . . . I wept. Luckily the orderly came in and they made off.'

'I shan't leave you alone again,' said Drivas.

After a while the sick man called out to him again:

'Leon!'

'Here I am.'

'Come nearer to me. . . . Nearer. I want you to tell me the truth.'

'I give you my word.'

'Good. Well, then, tell me seriously: how does my leg look to you?'

'How should it look?'

'Listen. You promised. So tell me seriously. Has it got much longer, or do I just imagine it? It's something I only noticed today. Don't deny it—I can feel it. It's longer than the good leg. I can feel it protruding quite a bit beyond the end of the bed. Look! Do you see? I'm moving my big toe in the plaster and I can feel it beyond the end of the bed. Is that how it is, or . . . ? '

'Or?'

His eyes filled with tears, and, his voice still lower, his lip trembling, he said:

'Leon . . . Listen to me. . . . There are times when I think . . . '

'Come on, be quiet now; you're behaving like a child.'

'Tell me, has it got longer?'

'Well, yes. Compared with the other, it has got a bit longer. But it isn't important. The doctors say it's a natural consequence. . . .'

'Natural? It's the first time I've heard of it. In what way?'

'I don't know—the doctor gave me some explanation about it, but don't ask me to remember exactly what he said. You know what doctors are: to everything they know, and, even more, to everything they don't know, they stick a name, half Greek, half Latin, and there they leave it. All I can understand where your leg's concerned is that where the break took place there's been a kind of expansion. An expansion of the bone and of the muscles round it. Something of that kind. It'll pass with time, the doctor said, once the leg starts working.'

The sick man seemed to be comforted. He breathed deeply.

'If that's what it is,' he said, 'then it's all right. And of course it must be like that. Otherwise there's no explanation. I was frightened, you know, very frightened. . . . I kept on thinking of that man on stilts in the carnival. And I thought and I said to myself: "It can't be otherwise. Either there's something wrong with my leg, or with . . . my mind." And I'll tell you something else. Yes. I made up my mind after the second operation. If I should have a limp I wouldn't go back, you know, to my wife. . . . My pistol would see me out of it. . . .'

Two or three hours went by quietly. Vranas slept or was half unconscious. His eyes were half shut, but they weren't making that endless movement which they made when he was going through one of his attacks. And his breathing was more regular. But, none the less, just before dawn he let out such a cry that Leon leapt up in alarm. It was long since he'd heard the sick man shout so loudly or so joyfully.

'Ba! Ba! Leon! Get up! Leon!'

He himself was struggling to rise but wasn't able to. His face was contorted in a most strange manner, his features becoming like those of an ancient mask and his forehead filling with beads of sweat as large as dewdrops. It was as if some uncontrollable force was working within him.

'What is it?' said Leon, now thoroughly frightened.

'But open it! Open it!'

He jabbered, shouted breathlessly, his eyes staring towards the door, and his fingers, stretched out in the same direction, trembled violently.

'Quickly, quickly, can't you hear how she calls?'

Leon got up, opened the door, closed it again. The sick man's eyes filled with tears, unspeakable emotion twisted his features. He moved his head this way and that on the pillow, and his eyes were both weeping and laughing.

'You! Are you here, Sappho! Holy Mary, how is this? And Father as well! But what came over you? What came over you? Come, no crying please . . . . You know how I don't like that in front of other people . . . . Leon!'

'What is it, Strati?'

'Forgive me, my friend . . . . but I didn't expect this, you know. This is something quite out of the blue. May I introduce you. . . . This is my wife, the Contessa I told you of. And my father. . . . Please, Father, do stop; you ought to be proud of me. . . . And this is Leon. Leon Drivas, one of my colleagues. He's lame like me. Thank him, both of you. He's the best of men and my best friend. . . . . But more, much more than a friend. . . . Much more than a brother even. . . . No one knows, only I know. . . . Yes, here inside there's something. . . . Here . . . . That's for Leon. . . . But, Sappho, my child, what madness, what madness is this? And how did you allow it, Father? For a woman to leave home and to come into this terrible world. . . . Here in the depths of Anatolia. . . . Among so many soldiers ready to devour each other like wolves at the sight of a woman. Among so many Turks. . . . So many men who've all grown savage and don't respect anything. . . . Ah, it's not a good thing you've done. . . . You've poisoned me with this mad joy. . . . O Holy Mary. . . . My Holy Mary. . . . You shouldn't have allowed it, Father. . . She always does what she wants to do. . . But she's only a child. . . . You should have stopped her. . . . What? You brought clothes and presents for the army? . . . . What'd been collected in the village. . . . But couldn't the village have arranged for some men to have brought them? . . . . Did they have to send an old father and the wife of a wounded man? . . . . There it is again. . . . Our honour! But how did they hear about it? I didn't write to you. . . . I didn't write to anyone that I'd been wounded . . . . The newspapers! They are bound to have stuck their filthy noses into the military hospital. . . . Come, don't go on like that, Sappho. . . . I was only joking. . . . Tell me, Sappho. You've come so many miles, did nothing happen to you on the way? Did no one bother you? No one? Didn't you hear any nasty remarks as you went by? Good, good. Forgive me. I was always like that and it's too late for me to change now. Come, be quiet. . . . Listen, Sappho, tell me. . . . The child? Ah, no. However careful they'll be, you shouldn't have left it alone. . . . What? He's all right? No, impossible. No, truly! He's beginning to talk? To talk? . . . . He asks for his father . . . . His father . . . . His father. . . . '

And the tears began to pour down his fleshless face uncontrollably, running down beneath the lobes of his ears and wetting his pillow. He wept quietly resistlessly, and the black brush-stroke of his eyebrows shrunk like a thick leech wounded and convulsing. On his throat, next to the Adam's apple, a fine vein was pulsing, pulsing rapidly.

The whole scene was too much for Drivas. He sat down beside him, wiped away his tears and his sweat, and wept himself. The sick man went on talking with his wife. He spoke hurriedly, breathlessly, as though he'd been running, and his words were smothered by his sobs.

'Holy Virgin. . . . Holy Virgin. . . . Thank you, that you came. I've been thinking of you so much, so much. . . . Ever since I went away. . . . You'll never be able to understand. . . . One person is never able to understand anything about another. That's how it is. . . . You were so good. And you're still so good, even now. And I . . . . know. Do you think I don't know how much I made you go through? . . . There are times when. . . Yes, I'll tell you now, since it's turned out like this. . . . Otherwise I would never be able to tell you. . . . I wanted to throw my-self at your feet, to kiss your hands. . . . But it was your pride that restrained me. . . . And my own pride. . . . That's what it is that poisons everything. . . . Our pride. . . . I always said that to the end we'd not be able to find the way into the heart. . . . How shall we go back, being so misguided? . . . In the dark. . . . Searching. . . searching. . . . But you, you see, secretly, in your heart, you are good . . . good. . . . Ah, how very good. . . . Now it is that I understand. And those clothes, the collec-tion. Excuses. . . . I understand you. . . . Excuses to conceal your pride. . . . For me. . . . They were for me. . . . Yes, you see, I too, in the same way, secretly, I loved you. . . . Secretly I was so good with you. . . . So bad with myself. . . . I think that's why I volunteered in this way. . . . To bring an end to things. . . . But you'll see. You'll see when I come back. Ah! I'm not the same person any more now. . . . I've thought so much about our life these years I've been away. . . . I've written love-letters to you and torn them up. . . . I wondered how I could have been so unjust with you. . . . But how much I love you, Sappho! Ah, no I never stopped loving you, loving you madly. . . . I could kill someone for you, Sappho. Thank you . . . . That, of course, is not said. . . . It isn't . . . it isn't said. . . . '

He started speaking more rapidly, but now there was no voice, only the lips moving. His face was motionless, with the nostrils stretched taut and only the lips moving endlessly, rapidly, trying now and then to a form a smile which turned into a small ugly grimace. And when that stopped there was only, in the corner of the mouth, a slight trembling a tiny nerve flickering, flickering tiredly. . . . Tsipi-tsipi-tsipi-tsipi. . . .

When the crisis was over he shut his eyelids tightly and then, after a while, fluttered them slowly, sceptically, finally opening them wide and looking at Drivas.

'You know, Leon, this morning I had unexpected adventures, ... My wife came to see me. . . . Do you believe it?'

'Ba, I hope you received her well. . . . '

'Imagine, didn't they tell you?'

'I heard something about it.... She brought clothes for the soldiers. ... Gifts from the island....'

'Yes! Or, rather, that was a way she found of being able to come. She shouldn't have done it, of course, and I was very upset.... But she's here now. So, tell me, what's to be done? I've been puzzling my mind for hours about how to look after her. Where'll she stay while she's here? She can't of course, spend the night outside.... There are so many filthy people around.... And I don't want to ask the doctors to take care of her. There's a whole crowd of officers over there.... I don't like that at all ... That's why I wanted to ask you .... I don't know whether you'd be willing to do this for me....'

'I'll do anything you like....'

'It's a lot that I'm going to ask of you, but I've thought and I've thought and I can't find any other solution.... Would you be willing to give her your bed while she's here? Do you think you'd be able to fix yourself up in another room till she's left? I'd be terribly indebted to you .... though how I can be more indebted than I am, I don't know ....'

'Don't bother at all—I'd thought of it before you. It's all arranged already. My bed's at your disposal.... It's such a simple thing that it's not worth the fuss you're making over it.'

'Thank you. You're invaluable.... It's only you who could be so good in such a simple way.... Eh, Leon, I think sometimes what a world it is. Just consider. We were months together in that training camp, but we were strangers to each other.... We were something more than strangers.... I ought to tell you about it, seeing that the subject's come up. It's been on my conscience, you see, since the day I've been with you here. Well, then: at that training camp I didn't like you at all. I didn't like any of your group and in particular I didn't like you.... All those easy successes you had in the gradings, the airs you all took on during exercises.... The way the officers favoured you.... All that. One day you happened to pass by my platoon. I was reading there with the rest of our lot, teachers. You stood over us, your hands in your pockets, and you said: "Good morning, lads." I turned and looked at you as you stood towering over me and then I turned back to my book again without returning you the "good morning". I did it on purpose. I wanted to provoke you. But you didn't notice it, and that was more humiliating for me. You'll say, what's all this about? Nothing. But there you are, it came back to me and I've been worrying about it since the day we've been together here.... And now I've told you about it it's as if some weight's been lifted from me... And I ask you, how many people are there who meet one another in this way?

They pass by close to each other, jostle each other with their elbows out of carelessness. "Pardon me! . . . . Nothing!" And in spite of that they may be destined together. . . . You, for instance. . . . No one has done so much for me in my whole life. And I didn't return your "good morning" to you that day. . . . '

He began to weep again. And his defeated pride wept with him.

Leon took his hands, bony and warm, within his own.

'Come, don't worry. That's how life is. And all those things aren't our responsibility. The only thing we can do now is to say "thank you" to the war that has introduced us to each other and that has brought us so close together. It seems that man is a marvellous creature, wrapped up in the prickly hide of a hedgehog. Coincidence, or some powerful event like a war, now and then breaks through the armament, and the heart responds and understands. . . . '

'Yes . . . . That's how it is. . . . I could die for you today, Leon. . . . '

Some time passed, and the sick man continued speaking of various things with an extremely clear mind. At one moment his forehead suddenly puckered, as if he were trying to remember something.

'There's one other thing I'd like to ask you, Leon.'

'Ask whatever you like.'

'Bring my service chest out from beneath the bed. You got it? Good. . . . Now take the key, the one that's hanging on a chain on the bedside table—the one that's with my whistle. That's it. Open the chest and give me the black leather wallet that's in my summer jacket. It's in the top pocket. . . . That's the one. Open it. . . . It's got in it the bit of shrapnel that hit me, my wife's photograph, and a small wrist-

'Correct. They're all here.'

'The watch has stopped at twenty minutes past four-the morning it was. That was the time the shell burst, and it stopped. The time I was wounded. I want the hands to stay like that. . . . I don't want them to be moved, ever . . . . A memento for my son. . . . Did I tell you that I had a son? Now come over here. . . . Take the wedding-ring from my finger. . . . Good. . . . Put it with the other things in the wallet and close the lot up. . . . There are moments when I'm afraid one of the orderlies'll pinch them. . . . Not that they're worth anything to anyone else, but . . . You see, they're the only heirlooms I've got. . . . You must look after them, and you'll give them to my wife. . . . I, no, don't say anything—there are times when I don't know what's happening. My mind goes dark and I can't remember. . . . It's odd, but . . . . Well, will you give them to her?'

'But . . . . it won't be long before you have leave and'll be able to take them yourself.'

'Yes . . Of course. . . . But you're sure to be out in a few days. Don't listen to the doctors, Leon. I've still got many meals to eat in this hospital. . . . How did the old priest put it? . . . . "I sir, as things have fallen out, will spend here this year's Christmas and next year's Easter." You know what's happening? . . . . But in any case you'll give them to her?".

'I'll give them to her.'

'You'll promise me, Leon.'

'I promise you.'

'As an officer and a gentleman?'

'As an officer and a gentleman.'

'Good . . . . Now I'm at peace. At peace. . . . Thank you, brother.'

Those were the last coherent words that he spoke, and after a while he again began his inconsequential ramblings.

Now it was the beginning of the death struggle. Broken phrases, distorted words, shreds of conversations could sometimes be distinguished through the nightmare of agony. 'My rifle! . . . . My rifle! . . . .' In his delirium he saw men circling round in a truck that was like a fire-engine and squirting gas through the hoses in order to poison the wounded. He sought for his mask, begged for help with his eyes that suddenly came to life again, darted nervously this way and that way, supplicated and appealed. His breathing became short, rapid, tortured. Towards the evening he died.

It was the hour at which the sun was setting beneath the low yellow hills of Eski, sending a shaft of violet rays through the western window and filling with colour the sick man's water-jug. His rapid breathing stopped with a long heavy sigh that raised his hairy chest and then let it fall restfully for ever, as though it were a pair of bellows emptying of its own accord. Only then did his lips cease their terrible play, the vein on his neck stop beating, his eyebrows thicken and remain motionless, like a bracket closing a long parenthesis.

A few days later, before Drivas had had time to receive his leave, the collapse of the Greek army took place. The catastrophe. The slaughter of the innocents. The martyrdom. The shame of chaotic flight. Days and nights full of savagery. But it was his time in the hospital that remained most firmly fixed in Driva's mind. Its bitter charm dominated his memory, all its terrifying details printed clearly, its poison still fresh.

He was surprised to find how many words, how many movements, had been so carefully stored up in his mind; how his imagination could call forth vividly, one by one, a whole host of gestures and feelings that had taken place during those strange days. He thought: 'What a treasure life stores up in a man whose senses and spirit are awake. Then suddenly he was ashamed of this egotistical thought. He gathered together the dead man's belongings as they lay before him, sadly looking again at each one in turn. He recalled the oath of his friendship, the solemnity of the moment when he'd made his promise about these few poor objects. He put them back again into the small wallet, took out a large envelope, closed them up in it, and wrote on the outside with a blue pencil: *Mementos of Stratis Vranas.*

7

ONE Sunday in June brother and sister loaded their things on to the bus and set off for Megalohori. It was a journey of some three hours among olive-groves, pine trees, and figs. It was still early and the cicadas were already shrilling furiously, a sign that it was going to be very hot. Drivas loved the heat: it added to his enjoyment of the countryside and the sea. They were both very moved when they reached their Tower—an old country house, dignified in its simplicity and similar to many others standing here and there on the Lesbian coast, dating from the time when the Aegean islands lived under the perpetual threat of raids by the Corsairs. They were like small fortresses, with huge doors at ground level, sheeted with metal and with stone doorposts and monolithic lintels, sheathed in lead held in place with enormous nails and bound with iron. The ground floor, with its two grilled openings for light, was used as a storeroom. In the olden days it was there that the surrounding peasants used to gather with their provisions and their animals, barricading themselves in when the watchers above sighted the Corsairs out at sea or suddenly heard them on wild nights disembarking, armed to the hilt, at the nearby Cape of the Rocks. Those were the terrible incursions that destroyed the peaceful seashore villages; and it was because of them that the lower parts of these towers were built of stone and lime, great thick and castle-like walls, without windows and without wooden beams that might be set fire to and cut through with the axe. The rooms were high above, and had ceilings and shelves decorated with carved wood. The fine balconies were strutted out into the air on the outer side of the stone walls of the tower, giving the impression of a dovecote to the building. They swept out a couple of the rooms and then Leon immediately went to see his godfather to arrange about the further odd bits of work necessary to set the place in order.

They both felt a gentle melancholy on entering their ancestral house after so many years. It held for them such a store of childhood memories, took them back to vanished, love-filled years. It was a venerable building, well worn but well preserved. It welcomed them warmly and protectively, like a forefather clothed in the dress of a past age. It opened its door to embrace its children and at once began to tell them of a thousand and one incidents of their untroubled life which they thought they had forgotten for ever.

Adriani suddenly recalled the fears she had when she was very small because of one of her father's umbrellas. It seems it must have been an exceptional umbrella, black, enormous, tall as a giant. So at least it had stayed in her memory, wide as the dome of a church. While it had been hanging on a wooden peg in the wall, just to to the right as you went in, she hadn't really understood what a monster it was. It hung there closed up, its wings folded, full of cunning. But one summer it had been opened in front of her for dusting and she'd been terrified out of her wits. Only then she realized what a prodigious thing it was. Without giving her any warning it had suddenly gone 'zdroom' in front of her and had opened over her its monstrous black wings. It was as if a bat had detached itself from the wall and leapt at her. She bawled, began to tremble from head to foot, and to cry out. She thought it would drag her into its black maw, close her up within its cold membrane, and would begin to scratch her, to scratch at her eyes with those metal claws that protruded from the end of its wings.

What didn't they do to try to free her from that terror! What stories didn't they invent to reconcile her with that umbrella! All was in vain. She pretended to listen, pretended to accept them, pretended even to laugh when they opened and closed the umbrella in front of her. But she alone knew how her heart beat every time they did it. She pretended to be brave when the grown-ups were with her, certain that they would defend her should there be any need. But once the two of them—she and the umbrella—were there by themselves, then nothing could control her fear. While it was still daylight she used to pass by it hurriedly, her back to the wall, as far away as was possible from the peg on which it was hanging. But at night it was absolutely impossible for her to pass the spot. She knew that that black demon was watching out for her, lying still in the darkness, waiting for her to be alone in order to seize her.

'Yes, this is where it hung!' she said, touching with her finger the old peg which had seemed so high to her when she was small. And, true enough, that curved wooden peg was still there, just to the right as you went in. But the terrifying umbrella of their father's had gone. And their poor father had gone also. They saw him again stooping his tall shoulders as he went out of the low doorway.

Leon took his sister to the northern room and the wooden stair creaked loudly as they ascended to the upper floor. It had always creaked like that—it and godfather's shoes. Grast! Grast! He showed her the walnut jambs of a window.

Remember?'

She remembered. . . . There was the full record of their heights as they had grown up. It was on those pieces of wood that Leon had measured and marked his own and his sister's height each summer, when they'd been taken for the holidays to stay here by the sea. He had stood his sister upright against the left-hand post and then had drawn a pencil mark and with his penknife had made the inscription: *Nannie, August, Nineteen hundred and so-and-so.* Then he had stretched himself out as much as he could and had given the pencil to Adriani to make the mark of his height. And when she couldn't reach high enough he'd said loftily: 'You can't do it like that, child; get up on the sill.' On the right-hand post of the window there were only two marks, with a single date. It was with emotion that they looked at them: they showed the heights of their mother and father. Leo had one day insisted on scoring their heights as well. They had laughed, looked, and had stood there—just as though it had been yesterday or the day before. First one had stood there and then the other, and in turn they had lifted Leon up so that he could draw the lines on the wood. Afterwards their father had cut them with the knife and had written the dates.

Adriani's eyes filled with tears. Leon pretended not to see, called to her gaily, with that childhood name which he used to use:

'Nannie! Stand up against here.'

She stood in her old place, laughing through her tear-filled eyes. She again assumed that sly look she used to have as she rose as unobtrusively as she could on her toes, so as to gain half an inch or so. And Leon, again as he used to do, pressed his hand down on the top of her head. When he had marked her height she said, as then she used to say:

'Your turn, Leon!'

Leon stood himself to attention, towering above her, and said with that same old protective superiority in his voice:

'You can't reach like that, child. I suggest you get. . . . a table to climb up on.'

The two new marks, so much higher than the previous ones, were again carefully notched on the wood, and Leon carved out the new date beside them. And the girl again stared absentmindedly at the splinters of wood as they fell to the floor, as she used to stare then. He saw her, and put his hand on her head.

'These marks mark the beginning of our new life' he said. 'May this starting point be a fortunate one for both of us.'

'Amen,' she said, quietly.

On the day of their arrival Leon learnt from their godfather, who'd come to the bus station to meet them and to give them a hand with their things, that Vranas's wife had been appointed as a teacher to the primary school of the village immediately after it was known that her husband had died. Vranas's father had himself died from sorrow over his son's death a short while after him. Mr. Spanos also said that the Director of the school and all the other members of the staff were extremely impressed by the energy and determination of the new mistress. Leon was glad to hear of this, and felt respect for the unknown woman who'd given herself so courageously to the task of mending her life so soon after losing her sole support. Another woman in her position might well have gone down hopelessly under the blow, unable to lift a hand to help herself and making a profession of acting the rôle of war widow, living in the meantime on the small pension she would get, and on the charity of whatever philanthropic organizations could be persuaded to take an interest in her home and her fatherless child.

Leon often thought of making her the sad visit which would mark the fulfilment of the task to which he was so solemnly committed. But he always hesitated and put it off, and on two occasions he cut off down a side road as soon as he got close to her house. It was a tiled house that stood high up overlooking the sea, with an outside door, painted green, that was almost square, and with creepers spilling over the wall surrounding the courtyard. He had put the black wallet in his pocket and had said to himself: 'This time there's no going back; this time I'll knock.' But as soon as he had come up face to face with the iron knocker on the green door his courage had failed him and he'd passed on.

One day he found himself confronting the teacher without in the least expecting it. He had gone up to visit the Genoese castle that stood on the hill above Megalohori, as incongruous and forbidding as a medieval helmet on the head of a peasant. There, turning in one of the labyrinthine alleys that climbed the slope, he suddenly heard childish voices, many voices, coming out of some large wide-open windows. His heart beat, and he asked an old woman who was sitting on her threshold spinning:

'Please, could you tell me what this is?'

The woman stood up and answered, ready to engage him in conversation:

'You'll be a stranger, my son. This is our primary school, you must know.'

'Do you know if Mrs. Vranas teaches here?'

The old woman nodded her head from right to left several times.

'Mrs. Sappho, you'll mean, my son, wife of the teacher Stratis, God bless him, who was killed as an officer in the war? Is it her you speak of?'

'Yes, I mean her.'

'Here she is, my son—where else could she be, poor thing? That's her class there, opposite. The door's on the other side. Ah, my child, what a fate for that unfortunate young man. . . . '

He thanked her, interrupting the maudlin recital on which she was embarked, and turned decisively. He entered the iron gateway, crossed the large courtyard of the school, and found himself in front of the door of the main schoolroom. From within he could hear the subdued murmur of the children's voices and over them the voice of a woman. He braced himself for a second and then knocked on the door. At once the noise of the children died down and the woman's voice called out clearly:

'Come in!'

He turned the door-handle, and entered, hat in hand. The children —there must have been some fifty of them—stood up at attention in front of their desks and saluted him in military fashion, their fingers held together correctly against their foreheads. They obviously enjoyed doing this; it was a game they'd practised on other occasions and liked repeating. Some glanced at him slyly, their eyes laughing, and others, who took the game very seriously, stood rigidly upright, their lips pursed and their wide-open eyes fixed straight ahead.

Startled somewhat by this strange reception, he bowed and came forward into the room, barely able to refrain from returning the salute and ordering the class to stand at ease, so strongly had the habit become part of him from long years of military service.

'Sit down!' he said to them, seeing that they continued to stand rigidly there in the same position and had obviously been taught to wait for that command.

The children sat down noisily, extremely pleased with themselves. Then there was a complete silence, and as the teacher came down from her desk to meet him he felt all their eyes fixed upon him in curiosity.

He gave her his hand.

'Please excuse me,' he said to her. 'I'm Acting Lieutenant Leon Drivas, and Stratis Vranas was my close friend and fellow officer. I've come—'

'Won't you please sit down,' she interrupted, pointing to a chair that stood close to the front desks.

It was an old chair, full of holes, and where the rush had been worn away it had been repaired with the string used for fishingnets. He sat down immediately, perturbed, as soon as she asked him to, and saw her standing up in front of him holding in her left hand a closed reading-book, the marker between its pages. And he smelt the scent of jasmin.

'You were his friend?'

Her voice was clear, musical, and firm. He tried to make his own sound less nervous.

'Yes. And he'd entrusted me with a sad commission. And . . . . now that I've been released and have come here with my family—we have, you know, a house and some land here—'

'I know,' she again interrupted. '"The tower of Drivas". . . . Down by the sea. . . . The "children of the fort".'

She smiled, laying the book down slowly on her desk. There was a short silence and she looked at him.

'Exactly,' he went on. 'The "children of the fort" returning after so many years. Only half of us aren't there any more. . . . . I am alone with my sister. . . . .'

'I had heard,' she said, nodding her head. 'Your mother died quite recently. Everyone here was very devoted to your parents; they used to wait for them to come each year.'

'Yes. . . . It's most kind of you to say so. . . . But now I wanted to speak about something else. We arrived three days ago, and since then I've been thinking about seeing you. But what with one thing and another—the repair of the house, builders—I haven't managed it. Also I have to confess I was a little hesitant about bringing you any fresh sorrow. . . . '

'Fresh sorrow?'

Her eyes opened anxiously, and he felt beneath the strong light with which they looked at him a sense of pain. He spoke quickly:

'Yes. There are a few personal things which he gave me to bring you. . . . He gave them to me during his last hours, and I promised. . . . So . . . '

He put his hand into the pocket of his jacket.

'What things?' She spoke loudly.

'A wallet with some. . . '

He felt a fool, an absolute fool. The dead man's wallet wasn't in his pocket. He realized it immediately, as soon as he put his hand in to find it. It was the wrong jacket. And in spite of that he continued to search blindly, seeing her waiting with such evident impatience, as if somehow by doing this he would be able to change the situation or his jacket. On the desk he caught sight of a small bowl of jasmin.

'I'm terribly sorry. . . . I've changed my jacket,' he finally began to explain, covered with shame. 'You see. . . . I came in here entirely un-expectedly. I was going up to the castle and I heard the children's voices. ... Till yesterday I'd got it with me. ... I'd intended to bring it to your house. ... Please excuse me.'

'It doesn't matter,' she said politely. 'In any case that would be better. Come to my house this afternoon. I'll be there from four o'clock onwards. I'll wait for you. ... Only do you think you'll be able to find it easily?'

'Certainly. I know it. A tiled house with a green door and creepers, isn't it?'

'That's it exactly. ... Thank you and I'll wait for you.'

He got up with relief from the terrible chair, while she again shook his hand and led him to the door. And with a flurry of sound the children repeated the military salute.

Out in the road, Drivas felt a cool breeze on his ears and realized that they must be bright red, burning, as if someone had pulled them violently. He no longer had any desire to visit the castle. He wanted to go back, to shut himself up somewhere, and to try to put his thoughts in order. And he was about to turn round, to make his way down to the seashore, when he glanced up at the windows of the school and again saw the teacher there, looking down at him while she announced something to the class. So he checked himself, and with large strides set off up the cobbled alleyway which led straight up to the castle.

He passed without a glance some of his old secret hiding-places which called out to him with the voice of far-off memories, and sat exhausted in a shady corner on the half-ruined walls. He let his gaze wander swallow-like over the wide view that spread out beneath him, over the village and over the sea where the sun played, blue and silver. He saw the houses at the foot of the hill climbing up towards the castle, tired in the intense heat, defeated by their efforts. But his mind was on that unexpected, that ridiculous, encounter, and he felt an anger for the whole incident, and above all for himself, slowly mount within him: for the old woman with the spindle, for the children and their army salute, that tragic puppet-show, that stupid militarism which they tried to instil into the young. And she among them—she who at least ought to have tasted more than others the horror and disgust of war. Then the chair with its knotted strings; why had he sat there like an ass for so long while the mistress stood facing him—not even facing him, but over him, so that he'd had to raise his head whenever he spoke to her, like a hen drinking water? Then that idiotic pretence of his, that searching in his pockets. 'You see, it's because I've changed my jacket.' As if the woman was waiting for him to tell her how he'd changed his jacket or anything else. ... And in addition—that spontaneous inclination which he'd only just managed to control to return the children's military salute and to order them to stand at ease. He still hadn't forgotten the fool he'd made of himself in somewhat similar circumstances the first day he put on his civilian clothes again. He'd gone to the post office to ask if there were any letters for him and as he'd turned away from the counter he'd seen the Garrison Commander standing behind him; whereupon, with the same spontaneity, he'd made a proper turn, had clapped his heels to attention, and had raised his hand towards his head when the fingers, correctly held together, had knocked up against the brim of his hat. Reddening with embarrassment, he'd pretended he was simply setting his hat straight and had fled as fast as he could. But he had had time to see the colonel give a smile, take hold of the peak of his military cap, and doff it to him, civilian-wise; and until he was out of the main hall of the post office he'd felt the colonel's mocking eyes bore into the back of his neck.

'How is it that there are times when I can be such an idiot?' he thought, saying the words out loud as he uprooted a tuft of camomile from a crack in the castle wall.

For there was no doubt of it: he'd been an idiot, blundering from one absurdity to another. What need had there been, for instance, to tell her about the builders repairing the house? And the reference to the 'fresh sorrow': why a fresh sorrow? And when he'd seen the teacher again through the window, why that movement he'd made to go down towards the shore which had ended by him turning and almost running like someone in a panic up the hill towards the castle? That movement too had been made against his will, and he'd made it simply because he'd happened to mention to her that he'd been on his way to the castle when he'd unexpectedly come across her school. And she'd have noticed that he'd turned to go downwards and would have thought that he'd been lying. Her glance down at him had said as much: 'You're making a mistake, my lad. You'd set off for the castle. Continue on your way up, then, and stop playing.' And he like a puppet had obeyed her order, as if he'd been caught in some guilty act. . . . How many humiliations. . . .

He automatically lit himself a cigarette, throwing it away as it began to burn his fingers.

And was his confusion and nervousness, he now began to wonder, due to other causes? Was it perhaps a reaction to the affront given to his inflated egotism? He discovered, for instance, with surprise that without noticing it he'd built up in his mind the whole scene of his meeting with the wife of the dead man—a scene prepared down to its smallest details and which was to have been played in her house. He discovered that even before he'd come to the village, even perhaps while he'd still been at the front, he'd formulated all the phrases with which he would accompany the handing over of the wallet. Even the gestures he'd make had been thought of and rehearsed—solemn studied gestures that were in keeping with such an emotional presentation. And the expression of the face, serious, full of sincere feeling. (How does one successfully make a face 'full of sincere feeling'?) And a slight tremor in the heart. 'Allow me to introduce myself, madam. I am so-and-so. Acting lieutenant of the infantry. Close friend of Vranas. I was with him during his final hours. . . . He died in my arms. . . . It was I who closed his eyes. . . . He said to me: "Promise to give these to my wife." And I promised.' Those were the words, and others like them; all ready, with the i's dotted and the t's crossed. And she would have listened to him, choked with sobs. She was to have been a village girl, huddled in her badly made provincial dress, in deep mourning and grief: a small woman, slightly ugly, with a large mouth. She'd have held in her lap the precious mementos of her dead husband and would have watered them with tears, struggling to hold back her sorrow in front of a stranger. . . . 'Please forgive me, madam, or ma'am' (if she were entirely a peasant woman) 'for opening your wound again. . . . I will leave you to indulge your grief alone. Your tears are a sacred obligation to the dead man. He loved you intensely. . . . Your image was with him even in the depths of Anatolia.'

He went through it all, discovering now for the first time that it was all there and realizing with disgust how he was unable to escape from that slavering philological beast which he always carried around in himself even in the most sacred moments of his life. He would sit and imagine all his emotions and would enjoy them 'artistically' with self-centred insensibility. . . . And now he'd caught this philological beast waiting for months for this meeting, licking its dry lips sadistically in anticipation of the feeling which the distress of the dead man's wife would give him.

A sudden thought made him shudder: suppose through all that tragic comedy which he'd played in the hospital he'd simply been the same fraud shamefully delighting in it? Suppose he'd simply been collecting as 'experiences' even the shocks he'd received from the Dantesque hallucinations of his delirious friend? He felt a stinging anger and shame at this suspicion, for in a certain sense it was not altogether without foundation.

He got up from the stones and fled. He went down as slowly as he could towards the house, taking a short cut through the fields. And he thought how it would be better to send the dead man's wallet to the teacher through somebody else—through his sister, for example. Yes, that would be the most correct thing to do.

It was midday when he got down to the Tower and as she saw him coming Adriani waved her white hand at him from one of the high-up windows.

'Lunch ready,' she called gaily. 'Shall I put it on the table? We've got those fresh beans you like so much.'

He ate without appetite and grumbled unnecessarily at the two workers on the verandah who were finishing off some odd bits of plastering. They looked at him in surprise, and muttered some joke between themselves. He noticed this and became more irritated. Finally he took himself off to his room, locked himself in, stripped, and lay down on the bed with a book. He felt the coolness of the fresh sheet on his naked body thankfully. After three pages he realized that he was reading mechanically and that he had to go over what he'd already read again. His mind was elsewhere.

He heard the cicadas drumming in chorus outside the window, stirred by the noonday heat, the monotonous march of summer. With their massed commotion the salt smell of the sea came into the room, so that he felt its freshness in his nostrils like a breath coming from the green bowels of the sea. There was no doubt: that was the best thing for him to do, to send his sister with the wallet. In this way this unpleasant incident, which was beginning to irritate him seriously, would be brought to an end.

He tried to recall the schoolmistress's features, to recompose them out of whatever he remembered from that brief meeting and from the portrait in the small photograph. He soon realized that there was no connection between his two sources, and that in addition he was quite unable to put together any definite image. He discovered that all that remained with him was the impression of a slender, well-knit figure, and a powerful but imprecise sense of two large deep-shaded eyes. Also there had been a rather pronounced mouth with lips strongly delineated and painted very red. There was something unpleasant in that for a schoolmistress and in a school. Especially as she was a widow. They ought to have spoken to her about it. . . . He broke the train of his moralizing, waking the joker in him just in time. But that torch-like stature! The truth of the matter was that he could never have imagined Vrana's wife to have been like this. Among all his endless affronts this had been the most striking: that in the place of the peasant girl he'd found a lady, a coquette, a girl smart and impressive, who'd made his ears burn as red as poppies. But perhaps he retained that impression of her because he'd seen her while he was sitting down on that low chair, forced to raise his chin every time he spoke to her. It was certainly true that he didn't know whether her eyes were black or brown—not, of course, that any of that was of any importance. Nor was it his task to sit making comments on a woman deeply smitten by misfortune, and with whom he'd been brought into contact only because of a sacred obligation and of a promise given to a dead man. And in any case it was all decided now: Adriani would finish off for him what still had to be done.

He smoked cigarette after cigarette, lighting the one from the stub of the other. He suddenly saw the book lying open beside him like a tactless gossip insisting on carrying on a conversation although he'd no inclination to listen. He shut it up, phlap! revengefully. Then he got angry, or pretended to get angry, in order to appease his conscience: he'd caught himself in the act of getting up to see the alarm-clock relentlessly ticking off the minutes on the table opposite. It was the third time he'd got up to look at it. That was it: he was waiting for four o'clock in the afternoon. And now it was nearly four. 'I've hardly time to get dressed,' he thought. He leapt up, shaved, washed in cool water from the well.

Leaving the Tower he again felt into the inside pocket of his jacket, to make sure that this time he had Vranas's wallet with him.

'Since the thing's got to be done, let it be done, so I shan't be bothered with it any more,' he said to himself.

And he set off for the schoolmistress's house.

8

HE KNOCKED on the iron knocker and after a while the door was opened to him by a woman of some fifty years in age, tall and with her head wrapped up in a black scarf.

'Mrs. Vranas?' he asked.

The woman nodded and gestured with her hands for him to enter. He was impressed by this unsmiling silent figure with her burning, almost savage, eyes.

They passed into a narrow paved courtyard in which the paving-stone was held in place with unmixed lime. All round were rows of earthenware pots filled with village flowers and herbs and all cleanly whitewashed. On either side of the door two green poplars shook their cool leaves like gay lackeys, and a jasmin, snowed under with flowers, climbed against the wall, reminding him how he'd smelt its scent in the schoolroom. At the far end of the court was a large cherry tree. The whole atmosphere was one of cleanliness and care, such as should have brought delight to the heart. But in spite of this he felt through the cool silence as though some sense of secret sadness were enfolding him.

'It must be this black-dressed woman,' he thought to himself. 'This depressing feeling of silence comes from her gestures. She must be dumb, without a doubt.'

The woman led him into a wide drawing-room furnished in a picturesque village style. The schoolmistress was sitting at the far end on an enormous sofa which filled the whole wall on the side towards the sea.

'Welcome to our poor house!' she said, putting a piece of embroidery she was holding into a wicker basket and getting up to greet him. She made a sign for him to sit down on the same sofa. There were two windows looking out over the sea and across to the Anatolian mainland. She herself sat down opposite him in a large armchair, asking the woman at the same time to bring them coffees and sweets. As she turned her head in profile he noticed her dark eyelashes, thick and curving.

She seemed calm and untroubled, and again he wondered how she would receive the message and the sad package which the dead man had given him. She looked at him openly, frankly, with quiet expectation in her clear eyes.

He anxiously took out the wallet, got up, and went over to where she was sitting.

'This is it,' he said, moved suddenly in a way he'd not expected. He began to give her, one by one, the dead man's mementos.

'Here is your photograph.'

Without wishing to, he once again noticed how little it was like her. She took it silently. Then he gave her the wedding-ring, then the piece of shrapnel, which she touched with obvious repulsion, and finally the wrist-watch.

'It has stopped,' he said, listening attentively to the sound of his deep voice. 'It has stopped at the moment the shell burst, and since then has always shown what time that was. Vranas said that he wanted it always to stay like that. So that his child should see it when he grew up. . . . '

He felt something quiver inside him. He gave her the wallet and went back to his place on the sofa.

The woman looked at the watch for moment, then raised her eyes up to him. Putting the things back slowly into the wallet as she spoke, she said: 'Yes. . . . It's a cheap watch. It hardly cost anything. . . . But thank you very much for all you've done. . . . For the trouble of keeping these things, of bringing them to me. . . . It is very kind of you. But the chest which was given to me by the Service of Inheritances has been looted. . . . '

Her voice was cold: with insult or simply out of insensitivity?

He felt as though he'd been slapped across the face, and suddenly realized how absurd was his own place and the place of the dead man in that room. Hidden anger and disgust took the place of the sympathy he'd had.

'He none the less loved you very much,' he said finally, with a bitter austerity. 'He used to rave about you. . . . In his delirium he always saw you close to him.'

As he spoke he was thinking that that 'none the less' was a bit unnecessary. It wasn't his business to cast judgement on things that were nothing to do with him. And the teacher had certainly noticed the changed tone in his voice, for she blushed and the great arch of her eyebrows moved slightly. She lowered her eyes to the black wallet. She spoke slowly, with a voice that was coldly explanatory:

'He loved me . . . . That is true. . . . And I did everything I could to make his life happy. . . . He was an unfortunate man. . . . '

She hesitated a moment, then raised her eyes and said emphatically:

'There are many unfortunate men.'

The woman with her head wrapped in the cloth of mourning came into the room again with the tray of coffee and sweetmeats. The teacher got up, put the black wallet into a drawer, closed the drawer, and took the tray from the woman's hands, setting it down on a low table and offering him one of the cups of coffee. Her movements were definite and graceful, her hands pale and well cared for. Drivas still had not recovered from his anger. He was full of protestations that he had no right to utter, doubts that he was unable to resolve.

'May I recommend the cherry to you,' she said with evident pride. 'I made it myself from the cherry tree in the court. . . . It's turned out excellently.'

She looked at him, waiting with a strange simplicity (or irony?) for him to give his opinion of her sweetmeat.

At that moment there was a series of wild shrieks from the far end of the courtyard. Discordant and tragically harsh, it was impossible to say, whether they came from a human throat or from that of some animal being tormented.

Drivas turned in alarm. The girl, clearly disturbed, nodded 'Go' to the tall woman, who had looked directly at her the moment the voice was heard. She withdrew, quiet and black, without making a sound. The shrieks slowly subsided and finally stopped, as used to happen with the wounded in the hospital. There was an awkward silence, when suddenly Drivas asked:

'Doesn't that woman speak?'

The schoolmistress welcomed the question with relief and related to him her story. No, she didn't speak. She was from Asia Minor. Her tongue had been cut out by the Turks. They'd found a Greek flag in her house. They'd tied her to the flagpole, laid the flag on the ground, and then had set upon her two daughters. When they'd finished they'd slaughtered them with the meat-knife from the kitchen. They'd laid their throats down on the meat-board and had cut their heads off. The woman had writhed in her bonds, had entreated and cursed Mohammed. Then they'd opened her mouth, drawn her tongue out with a pair of pliers, and cut it off. When she'd first come to the island she'd been half crazy with grief. Sappho had taken her into her house and since then they had lived together. She looked after the house while she was away at school; she took care of the child. . . .

He turned sharply.

'The child?'

He'd wanted to say: 'Where is Vranas's child?'

He again saw that reddish flush pass quickly over her face, and she tensed, as though she regretted having let that word escape her. She lowered her eyes to her hands and spoke crisply:

'The child. . . . But, you know, the child is ill. . . . Let us not talk of that now. . . .'

And she began to question him about his house, about his sister, about his life in the village, here at Megalohori. Wasn't it a place where one could die of boredom? He protested strongly: not at all, he

74

enjoyed it enormously. From the moment that he plunged his feet into the sand, that he sunk down among the foliage of the vines, he began to relive a genuine, an expansive, life.

'Don't let us confuse things,' said the schoolmistress, smiling almost mockingly. 'For you your life here is a brief interlude, a change of key. But for us who live here and stay here the year round that refreshing change takes place only with an escape into the city. That's how it is. . . . Each of us sees things from his own point of view.'

That's how it was. Drivas admitted that she was entirely right, and wondered whether in that simple thought was not contained a whole philosophy of life. But in spite of this he still felt a stubborn resentment within him, due to the failure of this meeting to correspond to the original imaginary picture that he'd made of it. How many disappointments there'd been. He wanted to speak to her of his dead friend but didn't know how to bring the conversation round to him.. Finally he saw beneath the looking-glass a photograph as big as a postcard set in a cheap black frame. Under it and in the same frame a medal was hanging. He got up and went over to it. It was Vranas, photographed in his brand-new uniform—it would have been the first time he'd worn it after having been made an officer. On his sleeve could be seen the row of active-service stripes, and it was obvious that he'd been posed so that these marks of warlike gallantry should be displayed to the best advantage. He was also wearing his sword, which he carried in the way that provincial schoolmasters carry their sticks. Beneath was the military cross, which had been sent by the Regiment to his widow on his death. There was a note of pride in her voice as she told him this. She also showed him an official document from the Division, typed and sealed, in which it was written that she ought to be proud of his glorious death.

He turned and looked at her, and saw indeed that she was proud of it, or at least was appearing to be proud of it. He felt his lack of sympathy for this woman grow more intense. She in her turn was troubled by the glance of his eyes upon her and, facing now the open window, raised her arm with a wide sweeping gesture towards the sea.

'Look,' she said. 'Always at this time a breeze arises. Every afternoon it's the same, almost down to the minute. You see that blue line furrowing the sea near the Anatolian coast? Soon the whole sea'll be like that. It means that the currents are running over there.'

She was leaning slightly towards the window, and he could not but admire the firm slender line of her body, strong and yet graceful, reminding him of the lithe splendour of the wild cat. Her hair was as thick as Athene's shield, deep chestnut and glinting like bronze, and the head itself was tilted slightly, almost challengingly, backwards as it rose from the arched neck. He remembered Vranas's words, that the villagers had nicknamed her 'the Contessa'.

He realized now that that abundance of life which flowed from the source of her being increased his antipathy for her. Before his eyes rose vividly the image of a tormented body which he'd seen dissolve like wax. And the final glimmer of life in that body had been a cry of love for this woman that stood before him. Now disintegration would have obliterated Vranas's crippled body more terribly, while her life flowered like an open rose, pulsing splendidly beneath her magnificent firm skin. She ate, had excellent digestion and had sweet-smelling jasmin in a bowl on her desk. She indicated the sea with a sweeping gesture perhaps to show off the fullness of her arm, and she spoke of the breeze that turned the sea blue, using the phrases of sailors or fishermen with the tang of the waves in them: 'It means that the currents are running over there'. For Vranas the currents weren't running over there any longer. For him there was now neither the sea, furrowed by the afternoon wind, nor this woman rippling with vitality, health, and beauty. But Vranas had adored her, and once she had been his. . . . Once? Why once? She had been, she was, and she would be always the dead man's wife. The power of his love had been such that it had been able to summon her image from here into the depths of Asia Minor so that she would be near him. Would not that same power be able to do the opposite now, bring Vranas's image close to her? It would have given him a pleasant feeling of revenge to have told her of his thought, simply to see her grow pale with fear. . . . In addition to this, he wanted very much to ask her about Vrana's child, but he did not dare: he felt that that was something which it would be difficult for her to speak of, and he thought of the diseases about which it would be terrible to remind a mother. He thought suddenly that the child must be crippled, or blind, or mad.

She spoke to him in measured tones about her own affairs, about things which fundamentally didn't interest her. He answered shortly and formally, while the bad impression he had of her grew ever stronger.

'I would like very much to know your sister,' she said to him. 'I've heard them say she's an absolute angel.'

'It's quite true,' he answered simply. 'Come to the Tower and you will meet her. She's been so busy setting the house straight that she hasn't had time yet to go out. Then there's the fact that she's in mourning which stops her from going about a great deal. In a day or two I hope to have got rid of the builders. So come, if it's not a bore for you.'

'I'll come, quite definitely,' she said. 'This year, because of the requisitioning of the school building for the army and for the refugees, we've had to prolong the term slightly. But once the schools are closed

I'll be able to see her quite a lot—if she would like it, that is.'

'What superfluous and pointless formalities,' Drivas thought to himself, as they went on speaking about one thing and another. 'Both of us are playing a disgusting farce.'

Reaching the outside door he again heard the ugly screams. They came from a yellow outhouse, a kind of annexe to the main house built at the far end of the courtyard. He suddenly thought that it must be in there that Vranas's child, mad, was kept shut up, with the tall, tongueless refugee as its keeper. The whole house was a place of horror. A feeling of extreme revulsion swept over him.

He made straight for the seashore, taking deep breaths of the clean air. The sun rested on the sea like a great shield fired a glowing red, so that you expected at any moment to hear the waters hissing and crackling round the flaming bronze. Gold and yellow reflections played over the sea's surface, and the mountains of Anatolia had taken on a delicate strawberry shade, soft as a child's skin.

Among the seaside cafés that jostled round the harbour he saw one that seemed whiter and more clean than the rest, with a fine platform supported on wooden piles jutting out over the sea. He sat down and ordered himself an ouzo.

9

IT WAS not long before the platform on which Drivas was sitting filled with people and the noise of conversation, and he became the centre of a large gathering which circled him round in such a way that there was no chance of escape. The godfather, Mr. Spanos, was there, being addressed by everyone with his official title: 'Mr. Mayor'; and there were the Director of the school with two other masters, the Customs officer, and a Mr. Daphnis, the rich man of the village, owner of an olive oil and a soap factory, as well as of the village's electricity plant. The godfather spoke of Leon's father, and this pleased him. But the great bore of the party was the Customs officer, Mr. Philippas, a slightly deaf middle-aged man, dressed up like a bridegroom, always freshly shaved, scented, and ready to talk endlessly about himself. Once he'd managed to get hold of a listener he would relate to him for hours a whole host of trivial details about his life, every so often asking his victim: 'Are you listening?' He was—naturally—from Athens, as generally speaking were all the officials sent from mainland Greece to fill provincial posts in places which only recently had become part of the mother country. 'Ah, yes, I'm an Athenian.' His little eyes were wrinkled up like currants, presenting to the inhabitants of Megalohori the latest Athenian fashion. He was a well-preserved bachelor, with the happy conviction that every woman in Megalohori was either slightly or wildly in love with him.

He was a type that amused Leon, who began now to bait him sadistically.

'Well, Mr. Philippas?'

And Mr. Philippas leant foward enthusiastically and began talking in that confidential tone of voice which the deaf often assume:

'Yes, as I was saying, Mr. Drivas. Our climate here is extremely pleasant, but it does no harm to be a little careful. I—do you hear?—I have this light overcoat for the summer and I always throw it across my shoulders when I get up in the morning and also at evening when it begins to get cool. Also I pay particular attention to my diet. Healthy and nourishing foods only. A little fresh butter in the morning, toast with tea. There's fine honey to be found in some of the mountain villages here. And the fish—are you listening?—which are straight from the water and very cheap: they're seldom missing from my table. The phosphorus, eh? I avoid meat as much as I can. . . . Of course, I'm not a vegetarian, but. . . . one should follow the new dietetics.'

'I understand. . . . That's why you're so well and flourishing.'

'How did you say?'

'Flourishing,' repeated Leon in a loud voice.

'All right, no need to shout like that, please. Flourishing. Of course. It's a matter of keeping oneself fit.'

'Yes. . . . And I've heard that quite a number of the women of the place have noticed it.'

Mr Philippas smiled contentedly, biting his finger as he glanced round.

'Ssss, we'll be overheard. . . . So you've hardly arrived here and you've heard that already. . . . That's the provinces for you! But don't believe it, Mr Drivas. It's all exaggeration. . . exaggeration. To be sure. there are one or two presentable girls here not entirely lacking in taste, but that doesn't mean. . . doesn't mean. . . '

Mr Daphnis asked Leon what his profession was. He assumed a sympathetic interest.

'What? A painter? And what income do you think you'll get from your work? . . . Of course, artistic work. . . . In other places they know the value of a good painting. But in Greece. . . hm, in Greece . . . I myself have naturally a great esteem for artists.'

The godfather got up to go, saying that one of these days he'd come and pay them a family visit now that the tower had been put in order: godmother was very anxious to see her 'children of the castle' whom she'd missed so much all these years since they'd been away. Shortly afterwards Leon himself got up and set off in the direction of the house. One of the schoolmasters got up with him—the younger of the two, called Mr. Xynellis, Mr. Patrocles Xynellis. He was a most unattractive type of person. He wore cinnamon-coloured clothes—the same colour as his hair—and they hung from him as if from a coat-hanger. His eyes were secretive, with a perpetual look of astonishment in them, and were armed with thick glasses because of their shortsightedness. And they could swell to an alarming degree, seeming to emerge like snails from their sockets in order to come closer to the object they wished to scan. He appeared to be particularly pleased that he'd been introduced to Leon. He tried to catch his glance through his thick lenses whenever he could, he leant over closely to him whenever he spoke, hung from his lips when he was relating some incident, and burst out into loud laughter at his slightest joke. He wanted to demonstrate in whatever way he could that he was the intellectual of the village, isolated and misunderstood. . . .

'If you like I'll come part of the way with you to the Tower,'he said to Drivas. 'I'd like very much to take a stroll along your beach on this lovely evening.'

'It would be a pleasure for me.'

They said good night to the others and set off.

'Your Customs officer is a delightful type,' said Leon in order to say something.

'Yes. He's an exceptional man. He has the idea that all the girls in the village worship him. It's his great weakness.'

'Ah, well, we all have our own.'

'Of course. And then Mr. Philippas is quite harmless,' said the schoolmaster hesitatingly.

'Harmless?'

'Yes. . . . They say, anyhow, that he doesn't marry because he's frightened to. He's got no confidence in his capacities. But he likes to pretend he's a bit of an old devil. . . . It's a consolation for him.'

'How curious!'

'It seems that people of his type are like that.'

'Possibly. The truth is that everyone tries to find sexual release in his own way.'

'That's exactly how it is. Mr. Philippas finds it in the rumours which he manages to put into circulation, or which others put about in order to please him. But I'm certain that in the end he himself really believes them and all his happiness lies in that illusionary world of his own making. For instance, he's recently convinced himself that our schoolmistress has got her eye on him. Someone put the idea into his head and now he's absolutely certain that it's the truth. He's frightfully pleased about his new victim. . . . '

'What victim? Mrs. Vranas?' he asked, with an interest which didn't escape Xynellis's notice.

'Yes. Do you know her?'

'Hardly at all. I met her today. I had to give her some things belonging to her husband.'

'A wallet with some mementos?'

Drivas stopped, and the schoolmaster stopped as well, so that for a few moments only the sound of the small waves was to be heard.

'How do you know anything about the wallet?' he asked in surprise. 'Did Mrs. Vranas tell you about it?'

The master laughed.

'But the whole village knows about it, my friend! No one talks of anything else.'

Leon's astonishment grew.

'But how?' he asked.

'Heaven's above! From the children of the form which Mrs. Vranas teaches.'

Of course! It was so obvious and it hadn't occurred to him. He felt perturbed.

'And why is "the whole village" interested in this incident, which, after all, is a purely private affair?' he asked the teacher, obviously irritated.

The teacher realized that he too was included in this 'whole village'; and as he replied he waved his arms about as if making a personal defence:

'But it's only natural, my friend!' (His continual repetition of 'my friend' only added to Drivas's irritation.) 'It's absolutely natural. It's trivialities like this that are the great events of the village. What do you expect people to talk of here? Of the new piece that's been put on at the theatre, of the latest novel or the latest film? Back home the children said how you'd visited the school, they told everyone of the wallet which you'd left in your other jacket, and of how Mrs. Vranas had asked you to come to her house. And the same afternoon, drinking their coffee, the villagers discussed the whole subject. I'm quite sure even that several pairs of eyes were watching out for your visit from behind the closed shutters. Ha-ha, you don't know what goes on here behind the closed shutters. . . . '

Leon felt a wave of anger sweep over him.

'It's simply disgusting,' he said.

Xynellis made a bow, and his thin figure, all corners, elbows, and knees, was like a large penknife that half folded up and then opened out again. His unpleasant voice was quiet when he spoke:

'It's quite possible you're right to condemn it in this way. And truly, yes, it is disgusting. But that doesn't prevent it from being entirely natural. We have to judge everything in terms of its environment and relationships. At least, that's how it seems to me.'

'All right. But in that case allow me to ask you, Mr. Schoolmaster Xynellis, how you judge such vulgarity in terms of your environment and of your relationships?'

The teacher uttered his small cold laugh.

'Oh, my friend! I of course deplore all that village scandal about the private affairs of this, that, and the other person. Besides, Mrs. Vranas is a much-loved colleague and that alone would prevent me from gossiping about her in the way her enemies do.'

'In what way do her enemies gossip about her, if I may ask?'

'Oh, stupidities! They say that Vranas's death, which of course, was a matter of honour for the village, hardly affected her at all, and that on the contrary it came as a relief to her—'

'I can imagine,' Drivas interrupted, speaking with bitterness, 'I can imagine the sorrow that Megalohori would exprerience if tomorrow the newspapers announced the news that Vranas had not died after all. That he was, for example, living in captivity and carrying railway lines on his back. They'd lose the one dead officer they have among Greece's glorious fallen heroes. What a disappointment that'd be for them, eh?'

'Of course,' laughed Xynellis. 'What a fine dilemma to face the villagers with! How ridiculous we human beings are....'

'And what else do they say about Mrs. Vranas?'

'That she hates her idiot child.'

'What, as a matter of fact, is wrong with her child?' asked Drivas seized by an uncontrollable curiosity.

'Ah, she didn't say anything to you about it? It's a kind of monstrosity, though no one in the village has seen it yet. It's a crippled, deformed child, and she has a refugee looking after it, a half-crazy woman whom they say she chose because she's had her tongue cut out and so can't say a word about anything. She feeds it and cleans it....'

'But what's wrong with it?' repeated Drivas.

The schoolmaster put his hands in his trouser pockets and stopped walking, glad to be able to hold forth.

'I told you. It's a child that's been mad from the time of its birth. They say it has a disproportionately large head, with a swollen brow and squint eyes. It's now three years old and still can't stand on its feet or say a single word. Its limbs are under developed and flabby, and it's got a king of insatiable greed that makes it howl like a beast. They've got it isolated in the house, in a sort of annexe. It shrieks until they take food to it. It eats endlessly and dirties itself endlessly. And if they don't get the food to it in time it eats its own excrement. It is, it seems, something quite horrible.'

Leon recalled the long, drawn-out cry he'd heard, and the sign which the schoolmistress had made to the dumb woman: it had been full of dismay and sorrow.

'If things are like that,' he said thoughtfully, 'then she must be a most unhappy woman.'

'Hm,' interjected the master doubtfully. 'I rather think that people are not unhappy as we imagine them to be but as they are capable of being.'

'You think, that is, that Mrs. Vranas is not aware of her misfortune?'

'That's what they say at least,' answered the master. 'I know nothing about it. But they say she'd let the child die of hunger if it wasn't for the fact that if she did she'd lose with it the small pension it gets as a war orphan.... They also say that she makes the dumb woman beat it with a switch of wild olive, so that it's frightened and doesn't yell.

'I imagine that is just plain infamy,' said Leon firmly. 'If she's as vile a woman as that she'd have no reason to work for a living. In fact she gave me the impression of being an extremely proud person. . . . '

'That's my impression also,' said Xynellis, repeating the movement of the half-closing penknife. 'Then she is as well a colleague of whom I'm very fond, something which naturally forbids me to say anything against her.'

'Yes, of course, that's something we'd completely forgotten!'

Drivas said an abrupt good night, pretending that he didn't see in the twilight the hand which the schoolmaster held out to him.

The Tower stood some hundred and fifty yards beyond the last house of the village, on the way down to the shore. Its solitary trunk rose up out of a splendid vineyard surrounded by various kinds of fruit trees. This property, together with the olive-grove, was the best-tended property in the district: it had been the great passion of Leon's father, and now Mr. Spanos worked it and looked after it in the same spirit and like a true farmer. The vineyard carried its reddish shoots down to the edge of the beach—a fine sandy beach which stretched along the whole lower side of the property. One came out of the Tower straight on to the sand through a wooden door large enough to allow a large cart to pass through it at vintage time. The door was known in the village as the 'Portara', and the whole shore was called by the same name.

Leon walked by himself through the blue evening close to where the sea licked the sand like a cat. He liked walking there, spoiling with his footmarks the smooth surface of the washed beach. His head was dizzy with all the incoherent impressions and revelations which he'd received during the day. He was glad to be alone, to withdraw for a while into himself, to find some order in the confusion.

He recalled with a strange melancholy the picture that he'd imagined: of an afflicted village girl, immersed in her sorrow as only village people know how to immerse themselves. And at her side grew the child of their love, the child of the dead man, a flower growing above his grave. And now the whole of that romantic picture had been torn to shreds, had been destroyed as if he'd been given a heavy blow on the head. Now, dizzied and miserable, he felt himself struggling among the fragments of broken scenery. Had it indeed been still this scene, this ideal picture that he'd imagined, that he'd been defending a short while ago with such comic intensity? Was he an egoist, or a knight? The Fool or Don Quixote?

In a few words he told Adriani of his visit to the widow of his dead friend and of how he'd handed over the mementos. He also told her that the schoolmistress was very anxious to meet her, and that for this purpose she was one of these days going to come down to the Tower.

'It must have been a sad moment when you gave her her husband's things,' said the girl sympathetically.

He smiled sarcastically.

'Not so sad,' he told her. 'Altogether I'm beginning to believe that our social judgements are made in an entirely subjective manner. In most cases all we do is to project our own feelings into other people's situations. In this way we make the most ridiculous fools of ourselves. . . . Perhaps that's the result also of our romantic upbringing.'

All night his thoughts circled round the impressions of the day, and when finally towards morning he fell asleep the same impressions mingled with his half-waking dreams. He saw an unnatural child, its head as large as a barrel of beer, crawling about on all fours, the extremities of which were soft as dough, lean and long, and all four of which depended directly from the beast-like head. The knees were thick as knots in a mooring-rope, and the whole monstrosity walked across the floor in the same way as an enormous spider. It came towards his bed, and as it got near it Leon saw its broad face looking like that of some supernatural mask. It was the face of an aged child, the skin stretched taut across the cheeks and the forehead wrinkled with a thousand wrinkles like the creases in crushed silk. Its eyes too were enormous, tumefied like those of Xynellis and circling round in their sockets as if in shells. Watching their movement, he saw that one of the eyes had a watch in the place of its pupil—a flat wrist-watch with numbers. Somewhere he'd seen this watch, but where he couldn't remember. Its hands circled, circled unrestrainedly, endlessly, so that the eyes tired in trying to keep up with them. But he knew that now at any moment they would stop, that it couldn't be otherwise, they would have to stop. And he waited with agony till suddenly, hop!, they stopped. It was at exactly twenty minutes past four. 'Twenty minutes past four!' he thought, with a relief that was almost voluptuous. Of course, that was it: it was Vranas's watch! And he grew calm, and listened only, and there was the wave talking in whispers on the sand, but it wasn't any longer the wave that was murmuring in this way, it was Vranas, Vranas talking in his delirium on the hospital bed. It was Vranas's mouth that rambled on senselessly, that smiled and trembled in the corner, while the rest of the face was absolutely motionless.

It was very late when he got up. He ate a few grapes and called out to his sister to go down for a bathe together. They changed in the house, and, towels over their shoulders, they passed through the vineyard and out of the big door, the Portara, on to the beach. It was almost midday and the sun was plunging silver swords into the passive sea. Their straw sandals made deep indentations in the cool shining sand. Then the small waves reached out their wet tongues, licked silently at the footmarks and obliterated them.

Brother and sister threw off their towels and plunged with cries of joy into the sea. The water smacked their strong limbs as they ran through the shallows till they came to where it was deep enough to dive in. Adriani swam cautiously, not daring to go far out: as soon as she saw the sea getting dark beneath her she became frightened. And Leon, for whom the sea was one of the great joys of life, left her far behind as he struck out into the open, drunk with the sense of the boundless waters whose blue crystal mass the sun only slightly penetrated. He played with the sea as with a woman. He caressed her, he provoked her, he tormented her. He rolled over on her surface as though on an enormous animal, swathed in indestructible bonds of youth. He pushed her with his powerful shoulders, so that she ran over his back, rose up before his throat, murmured behind his ears. He made her foam between his legs, he sucked her in by mouthfuls and spat her out again, he beat her with his hands. And while he played this game he shouted like a child mad with delight, discovering again the feeling of his own childhood. He tasted his life now like a strong wine, tangy and full of body. And he enjoyed it to the limit of his capacity, lived it with all his senses, awake now and insatiable, stretched out voraciously. Because it was now that he found recompense for all the years he'd dragged out under the heavy shadow of death.

When he'd taken his full pleasure of the sea, submissive beneath him now like a throughbred mare, he voluntarily abandoned himself to her mercy. He turned over on his back, smilingly closed his eyes, let his hands float idly, and drifted like a piece of seaweed wherever she wished to take him. The sun then drew its burning fingers over his face and chest and the sea gently rocked him up and down on her wide bosom as though she were breathing beneath him. The indolent movement of the lukewarm water gave him the sensation of a woman's thighs stirring rhythmically at the touch of her lover's hand. Beneath his closed eyelids the sun exploded in orange and green fireworks that flowered in circles, made wavelike patterns, changed one vivid colour for another as the eye played with them. And the water kissed him, tickled his nostrils with salt splashes, reached with its cool fingers into his ears and slipped between his toes.

Then he felt himself to be endlessly happy, annihilated with happiness, voluptuously at one with nature, the great mother of all. He felt his body changed into blue water, pure and undefiled, pierced through and through by the sun. He had no weight any longer, no limbs. He had no thought—thought that is the sleepless worm in the ripe fruit. And in the place of thought there was this festive indigo, peaceful, full of a quiet joy and a lazy kindness. He wasn't anything material now—was simply an idea floating lightly, happily, the dry leaf of a plane tree on the surface of the Aegean. And when he made for the shore, swimming sluggishly on his back, the sea, the flatterer, had made a fine parting down the centre of his head.

Adriani was already lying in the sun, spread eagled on her towel. He lay down beside her laughing.

She raised the end of the towel which she had pulled down over her nose and asked him what was the matter with him.

'With me?' he answered. 'Nothing. I'm laughing. With thankfulness. With health. Health, you know, is a wonderful thing. So wonderful that it doesn't even let us know when it is with us. It's only when it leaves us that it gives notice of its existence . . . retrospectively. Isn't that curious?'

'Very curious.'

'I used to think about that when I got wounded. The moment the bullet went through my thigh I at once discovered one of my legs. Till the day I was brought to bed I'd never once thought: "I'm well. My arms, my legs—they're wings. I don't feel the weight of my body. I move about in the air as though I were air. This is to be healthy!" Have you ever thought like that? Have you ever been consciously healthy?'

'No.'

'You see. But from that time on . . . ah, how burning now is my sense of life! That's the only good thing that war leaves with those who get out of it alive and unmutilated.. It teaches them the value of life. . . . And to think that there are those who've been killed and who all the time they lived were never aware that they were well, were well!'

He threw a handful of sand into the sea and heard the grains pattering down with a cool sound.

Adriani looked at him thoughtfully. After a while she said:

'I rather think that that powerful sense of life has taken possession of you. . . . It corrupts you.'

He laughed.

'Oh, yes, certainly it corrupts me.'

'It's true. It makes you egotistical. You forget those who no longer live, for whom all those gifts of life have now dried up. And many of them have lost them out of love.'

Leon didn't reply for a while. Then he said, his voice thick now, suddenly without a trace of its former joy:

'I don't forget them. I don't forget them for a second. . . . Even though. . . . even though I don't imagine it makes the slightest difference to them. . . . '

'Probably not,' said Adriani quietly. 'But it makes a difference to us. It makes us less concerned with ourselves.'

Leon didn't argue. His sister was simply repeating his own ideas. His cheek was flat against the warm sand and through his half-closed eyelids he saw the whole rose-coloured beach giving off its transparent vapours. They mounted trembling and made the air quiver before his eyes like liquid crystal. He heard one of his veins, somewhere near the ear, knock against the sand on which it was pressed. He heard it beating firmly and regularly, with the sound and the rhythm of a powerful engine, as if it were working down in the hold of a voyaging ship: doup-doup, doup-doup. . . . He closed his eyes and once again he saw Vrana's yellow face: the thick eyelashes knotted over the waxen forehead, as if painted there with a broad brush dipped into black printer's ink; the thick neck, the sharp nose, the mouth with the discoloured lips, closed stubbornly; the shining half-closed eyes, frozen in terror at what they saw. Vranas wouldn't see again the sea whipped with the silver lashes of the sun. He wouldn't see the sky, the stars in the water, the grapes, women . . . Woman!

Sappho's image passed like a warm flash before him. How fine was her honey-coloured skin, her heavy eyelids that fell over and shadowed her eyes like two velvet curtains. Her breasts rose firmly and in her eyes there was a colour . . . a colour. . . . What colour?

He leapt up, shaking the sand from his arms and legs.

'She is, you know, an absolute bitch,' he said out loud.

'Who?' asked his sister in astonishment.

'She is! Who, indeed. Mrs. Vranas. Imagine, she's hung on the wall the iron cross that they sent her which had been awarded to her husband. She's got it in a frame and she's proud of it. . . . And she's got the official citation from the Division: "You should be proud of your heroic husband's death. He fell in the manner of a Greek officer"!'

And he swore to himself he would never set foot within that accursed house again.

10

THE next day the godfather made a family call on the brother and sister. He found Leon at the Portara, at work in front of his easel. The young son of their woman help was also there—he prided himself on being the one who carried Leon's painting equipment on his artistic excursions. Spanos's family at once swamped him with its warm greetings. Madam Evtychia ran up to him with tiny little bouncing steps, as if she were a red india rubber ball, closed her red umbrella and kissed him on both cheeks, standing up on the tips of her toes in order to reach him. She was a short stoutish little woman, with delicate rosy skin like a new-born babe, and her small blue eyes were full of sympathy: they would tremble with tears at the slightest thing and Mr. Spanos was continually having to remind her of the doctor's warning: 'Your heart, Evtychia!'

For Madam Evtychia suffered from her heart. She discovered this by chance while she was still young, when she went to Athens shortly after her marriage to see the Olympic Games. This was a memorable journey, and marked one of the great occasions in her life: from then on she used to count the years with reference to the Olympics, like the ancient Greeks. Anyhow, she took this opportunity of going to have herself examined by a distinguished doctor, a professor in the university: it wasn't every day of one's life that one went to Athens. At first he didn't find anything wrong with her. But she insisted. She told him how she got tired going up steps, how she got out of breath easily. Then the doctor made her do some marching on the spot—one-two, one-two—and afterwards he measured her heart-beats. That was it. He got up cheerfully: 'Weakness in the right ventricle of the heart—a slight contraction. Don't get worked up, don't get tired.' Thus the journey wasn't wasted. Their return home from the capital was a veritable triumph. They had seen the king, they had seen the evzones, they had seen Louis beat the Franks in the racing, and they had come back to the island with a 'weakness in the right ventricle of the heart', which was and continued to be of the utmost importance. No one else in Megalohori could boast of such a thing, or of anything which had even a remote resemblance to 'a slight contraction'. For her it meant that she had to be careful not to get over-excited. Otherwise she would forget about it. Fortunately the poor woman was only too easily stirred. As for instance now: she stroked Leon, she kissed him, she shook his hand, she clasped it within her small soft palms.

'Our castle-child, our Lilo! Ftou, ftou, ftou, how you've grown, may God protect you. To think that I used to let you ride on the girls' shoulders when they were treading the grapes! Ah, my son, if only they could see you now. . . . '

She remembered his parents and again the tears ran, so that she had to wipe her kindly eyes with a small handkerchief, that also red.

'That's enough, Evtychia. We must introduce him to our daughters. He'll have forgotten them completely, it's so many years that he hasn't seen them.

Leon shook hands with Loulou and Aspasia, who were both a few years younger than him. How did they appear to him? Well, they'd changed, changed a great deal. That's how it is: girls change from one day to the next. 'The lad will be as he is born, the girl as she is moulded' —that was what was said.

The girls laughed at his remarks. They too wouldn't have recognized him if they hadn't been told who he was. How tall he'd grown!

'He's got his father's height,' said Mr. Spanos.

Loulou was the eldest of the two girls. She had large chestnut eyes and beautiful hands. But she also had an enormous bosom. As she walked on the soft sand she leaned slightly forward and it seemed as if it was the weight of her breasts that pulled her down. Aspasia was the prettier—she was in fact extremely pretty, with dimples in her cheeks and small gleaming white teeth. Unfortunately, to show the latter off, she would frequently smile when there wasn't any reason for it, which made her appear to be slightly stupid.

Leon gave a sign to the small boy to gather up his equipment, and at the same time he took from the easel the large canvas that he was painting so that he could put it into a thick folder which held the pieces on which he was still at work.

'Please!' said Mr. Spanos, raising his eyebrows and also raising his hands to the level of his eyebrows. 'We don't in the least want to interrupt you at your work. We'll go on ahead and find Adriani, and when you've finished you can join us.'

'There's no question about it,' said Leon, laughing. 'The landscape won't disappear.'

Loulou asked to see what he was painting.

'It's a sketch,' he said. 'A child in front of the sea. There. It's really more a study of the powerful light. . . . '

It showed the sun-drenched child of the maid with his chocolate arms and legs standing in front of the blue playful sea. . . .

Madam Evtychia glanced first at the model, then at the picture, comparing them, and on her round face showed all the desire she had to find some resemblance between the two. She went on doing this with touching insistence for some time.

Aspasia bent over the canvas and discovered that the boy hadn't got any eyes. She laughed, showing all her white teeth and making her cheeks dimple. Loulou more tactfully concluded that Leon had not yet finished the painting and that it was because of this that he hadn't yet painted them.

Leon was used to this sort of criticism from the villagers and women who gathered round him while he was painting in the open air, and he laughed good-naturedly as he heard it, trying at the same time to explain things as much as he could. What he was chiefly trying to explore in this painting was the combination of the powerful light of the sun with the reflection from the sand and the sea. It was this brilliant light that consumed all those details which he'd omitted and which weren't of importance for his subject.

The godfather murmured: 'Of course, of course,' which Madam Evtychia repeated after him, at the same time making a small move-ment as though she were saying: 'Yes, it must be like that, since that is how Leon says it is.' Loulou raised her breasts forbearingly and said nothing. Only Aspasia laughed again, as much as to say that though the others might be taken in, she wasn't, about it being a mere detail whether the eyes were painted or not and about the sun and its reflection consuming the child's eyes.

At last they all set off for the house, with Aspasia plucking a grape here and there as they made their way through the vineyard.

There were more expressions of delight when they met Adriani. The girls found her very beautiful, and they stroked her blonde hair and exclaimed at the silkiness of her skin: she had no business to let it get brown in the sun.

'The world's changed,' said Madam Evtychia. In her time they used to tie charms on the arm, and the girls had to veil themselves up like women of the harem, so that the sun shouldn't touch their skin. And now. . . . Even so it was a crime to let a milk-white skin such as that of Adriani get burnt by the sun.

Loulou had a small complaint to make to Leon. Since he'd wanted to be the first to make a visit to some house in Megalohori, that house should have been theirs and not the schoolteacher's.

'She's quite right,' added Evtychia, nodding her head scoldingly. 'Yes, my child.'

Leon, a little put out, tried to explain to them that that wasn't a visit, it was a sacred duty he'd undertaken and which he had to discharge.

Unavoidably the conversation again veered round to Sappho.

Evtychia thought she was a most unhappy girl who since the time she'd become a widow lived almost entirely by herself. She had the school, her home, her solitary walks, nothing else. Exactly like a nun. And she was honourable beyond words. Evtychia appealed to her husband for confirmation.

Mr Spanos nodded in agreement. Loulou, completely without envy, admitted she was the most beautiful girl in Megalohori and in all the surrounding villages: that was quite clear from the first moment that one saw her. And it was not only that she was beautiful, she also had great sweetness. She had what they call charm.

Aspasia laughed and laughed again and said that Sappho was nothing but a vain romantic. She'd got it into her head that she was beautiful and now she played at being a cloistered virgin in order to get married an hour or two sooner. Everyone knew what a conceited creature she was. 'The Contessa'! The Contessa indeed: was that the kind of idea for a widow to have of herself?

The Mayor rebuked his daughter gently, saying that those were remarks put about by evil tongues and that no one had the right to decide what another person should do or should not do. It was sufficient if he or she didn't do you any harm and wasn't absolutely worthless. That was the proper way to look at the matter.

'I agree with you,' said Leon. 'Where I'm concerned, she's simply the wife of a dead friend who used to worship her. I would be only too delighted if I could be of any assistance to her in any way. I would even ask you, godfather, as Mayor, to protect her and to keep an eye on her like a father.'

'I do as far as I can, and I shall continue to do so,' said Mr. Spanos emphatically. 'It's our duty to, in any case. War widows and orphans are under the protection of the whole nation, and as Mayor I represent a small fraction of the nation. Isn't that so?'

Madam Evtychia, who had a boundless admiration for her husband's official status, nodded her fat double chin in agreement several times, pleased with the successful way he'd expressed things. How did he know how to speak in this way, how did he know! And her small eyes began to cloud again.

Aspasia, however, wasn't to be quieted so easily. She smiled and bit a piece of chocolate.

'At least she could take fewer romantic walks and could stay at home a little more looking after her child instead of leaving it for someone else to look after.'

Leon recalled those wild cries, and the woman with the unsmiling face, and the conversation he'd had with Xynellis.

'One can't tell,' he said, 'what's going on in someone else's heart.'

'Quite right!' agreed the godmother, who found hearing about crippled children too much for her.

Aspasia, beginning to anger now because no one took her side, said spitefully:

'They even say now that the Customs officer is after her.'

'So?' It was the first time any of them had heard it. No doubt it was simply Aspasia's invention. Loulou looked at her in frank surprise—she was in general extremely interested in who was going to get married or who was to be engaged. She herself had now reached the marrying age and such matters had begun to occupy her, in spite of the fact that with her ample dowry she had nothing to worry about.

'Are you sure?' she asked, knowing what a tease her sister was.

'It's what I've been told,' said Aspasia. 'Mr. Philippas they say has now himself taken a liking for solitary walks. And one night at the club it seems that he made some pointed remark about Sappho....'

'I've never heard of any such thing,' laughed Mr. Spanos. 'Unless, of course, your ladyship knows better than us what is said and what isn't said at the club....'

'What a blessing if there were some truth in it,' said Madam Evtychia, speaking with genuine sincerity. 'She'd have someone to support her then, the poor thing.'

'But the Contessa'd never accept a person like that, you can bet your boots,' said Aspasia mockingly.

Leon was beginning to get irritated by this tiring and trivial gossip and would gladly have left the company if he could. He felt an irrepressible need to defend the schoolmistress, as he always felt when he considered that someone was being dealt with unjustly.

'Aspasia,' he said gently to the girl, 'you are so pretty, and so fortunate to be among your own people.... And I know you're good as well. But now you're trying to make us believe that you're really not nice at all. Why are you doing that?'

'Not being nice?' said Aspasia, blushing.

'Yes, I'm sure that inside yourself you respect a woman who has to work for a living, who is entirely alone in the world, and who on top of all this has the misfortune to have a child who is deformed.'

Adriani was now thoroughly confused. She recalled her brother's epigrammatic judgement of the schoolmistress which he'd made after the bathe, and now ...

'You at least know her in person,' said Aspasia. 'You've met her, isn't that so? Well, then, tell us how she appeared to you. I'm most curious.'

She looked at him challengingly with her mischievous eyes, and her eyelids fluttered mockingly.

'How she appeared to me,' he said thoughtfully, as though he were posing himself the question. He glanced round and saw that all of them, Adriani included, were waiting for his answer with evident interest. 'How she appeared to me . . . I saw her so briefly . . . and I was so disturbed by the wretched mission which I had gone there to fulfil . . . I don't think I really know. She seemed to me to be a very respectable girl.'

'And beautiful?' asked Aspasia, a note of annoyance in her voice. 'They say she's the most beautiful of the lot.'

He laughed, relieved that he'd found a way out.

'So the truth of the matter is that I haven't yet formed an opinion of her. First because I haven't had either the time or the inclination to look at her as a woman, and second because . . . apart from those here present, I haven't yet seen what other beautiful girls there are in the district!'

As he was speaking he glanced also at Loulou, so that she should be included in his compliment. It was then that he noticed that the girl was looking at him silently with her kind tender eyes—the eyes of a dog that is looking for a master to whom it can dedicate itself. He smiled hurriedly and looked away again.

When they got up to go the brother and sister went with them to the end of the beach. And Leon, seeing Loulou's figure as she swayed on her high heels trying to keep her balance on the soft sand, could not help thinking of her enormous breasts which she would have to carry with her, whether she wanted to or not, all her life, and wherever she went. . . .

11

IT WAS a Sunday morning and all the bells of all the churches in Megalohori were tolling slowly, mournfully. The local Union of the Reserves had decided to hold a large memorial service for all those from Megalohori who'd been killed in the war, to be conducted by the Bishop with all the clergy in the neighbourhood in attendance. Megalohori alone had lost eighty-two of her sons. Round the cenotaph which had been set up in the middle of the church eighty-two candles were burning, and within their circle was a huge wreath of the Refugee Union in memory of the women and children who'd been killed and for the prisoners who were still in captivity. On top of the cenotaph was a military helmet crowned with laurel.

Leon, a member of the Central Executive Committee, had an official invitation to the service, and the Union had reserved him a seat of honour near the cenotaph. Next to him were the presiding members of the local organization, and the standard-bearer with the silk banner, white with black border and with the initials U.R.M. (Union of the Reserves of Megalohori) embroidered in blue in the centre.

Crowds gathered for the service. The big church was completely filled, the people milling like ants both in the church and the surrounding garden, and out in the road. In the church were the reservists, the mothers and widows of those killed, children dressed in black and black-scarfed refugees.

Leon saw Sappho in one of the neighbouring pews, near the Mayor and alongside the other teachers. She also saw him and spontaneously they greeted each other with a scarcely visible nod. The service was conducted in deep silence, broken only by the sobs of some of the women. The long mournful hymns mingled their bitter poetry with the clouds of incense that spread over the bent heads of the congregation, a heavy scented mist which intoxicated like a heady drug. When the service was over the 'roll-call of the dead' was carried out. The president called out the names of the dead reservists one by one, and the secretary replied, naming the battle in which each had fallen or been lost.

It was very hot, and the atmosphere in the church became suffocating from the smoke of the candles, human breath, and the incense. Now and then, as some name was read out, a shrill uncontrollable cry of lament rose from where the voice had come, and an immense murmur of sympathy filled the church and echoed in the hollow domes above. It was like a calm sea that is suddenly ruffled, stirred, and then becomes quiet. Two or three of the elder women who'd fainted or who'd broken down under the emotional strain were carried out.

As the roll-call was coming to an end, the teacher Xynellis, who'd been sitting near the right-hand chanter, came out of his pew and started to move towards the pulpit. By the time that the Bishop was rounding the service off with a few formal and unimportant words, Xynellis was standing next to Drivas. He shook his hand significantly and whispered to him:

'You know, I've been appointed by the Union to make a speech.'

Leon signified his congratulations with his eyes: whereupon the teacher came closer and, signing to Leon to bend down, said:

'You see that plate over there with the gold rim, with the candle with the blue ribbon. That's for Vranas.'

Leon turned his head. He saw the plate with its little offering of barley neatly covered over with icing-sugar like a cone of snow. In the centre burnt a white candle which instead of the usual mourning ribbon had one with the national colours. On the white surface of the icing-sugar were outlined in small black raisins and gilded kernels of almond the words: 'Once each of us dies'. The letters ran the whole way round the large dish.

Leon again felt a wave of anger against the woman sweep over him. Was this a case of plain insensibility or of pedantic puritanism in extremely bad taste? The gilded almonds stood out like an officer's pips among the poor plates of the simple soldiers, the inscription was blunt mockery, and the candle with its ribbon a piece of cheap patriotism. He recalled Vranas's medal hanging on the wall with the framed official notification of his death. He involuntarily turned to where she was sitting, but he wasn't able to see her: Mr. Spanos, bending forward in order to catch what the Bishop was saying, completely hid her face from view. He could see only her long hand with its slender fingers standing out whitely against her black dress. An extreme curiosity suddenly seized him. He would have liked, had it been possible, to be standing near her, so that he could have watched her eyes without her being aware of it, looking down into them as though into a well to see what shadow crossed them the moment the name of her husband and the battle in which he was wounded were called out.

In the meantime Xynellis had begun making his speech, standing on the first step up to the pulpit. He had a sheaf of notes and as he read from them his hand trembled. He himself had gone terribly pale so that the red spots on his chin stood out clearly. Twice he stopped and with his handkerchief wiped the thick lenses of his glasses, clouded over from his breath and his sweat.

Xynellis thanked the reservists for the honour they had done him in asking him to salute their dead colleagues on their behalf. At this moment their white souls were fluttering above the trembling flames of the candles, flames which had been lit in inextinguishable love for the dead companions of battle, victory, and misfortune. He himself Xynellis considered it the greatest honour he could have, his most sacred distinction, that he too bore the title of a reservist. (Drivas knew that he'd acquired it in the base-regiment, where he served as a clerk till he'd been released.) And he continued in the same strain, ending up by saying that in the name of the living and of the dead fighters he wished to make a plea and to express a wish. The plea was for the Fatherland not to let the widows and orphans of those who'd been killed go begging in the streets, or those who'd been lucky enough to get back home. And the wish: that sometime, sooner or later, we'd be able to give the dead the revenge they desire. . . .

At first Drivas had not been paying much attention to the speaker— he'd been amused only to see how nervous the schoolmaster had been when he started. But bit by bit as he began to listen he was filled with disgust and anger. And no sooner had Xynellis, sweating and yellow, stepped down from his stand than Leon uncontrollably pushed himself forward and without asking leave of anyone himself mounted the steps up to the pulpit. A murmur of sympathetic surprise greeted his appearance. Then there was a total silence, broken only by the sound of his own voice, resonant, almost angry.

First he asked his comrades of Megalohori, the Bishop, and the Refugee Union, to forgive him for pushing forward like this to speak without their permission. But he felt that his 'comrade' who'd just spoken hadn't perhaps been altogether able to express what he wanted to on this moving occasion. He further felt that in this church of the God of Truth and Love only words of Truth and Love had any rightful place, expecially now when what was said was said in front of the eighty-two small flames which indicated the presence among them of the eighty-two dead men. But to get at Truth and Love we have to search behind the mere words. What for instance is this 'Fatherland' which is requested not to allow the orphans of the dead and homes of the living reservists to die of hunger? It is all the others who've had the good fortune not to suffer from the war. It is, above all, those who govern the country. It is not petition, then, that we make to them, as the previous speaker had put it. It is a demand. It is a question of justice, which must be resolved with positive laws and not with beggar-like entreaties and romantic philanthropy. Second, it is not true, not in the least true, that the dead desire to be revenged with further human slaughter, fresh murders, more dishonoured women, new bestialities. No, the dead are now with God. They are without passions, without fanaticism. With their flesh they have put off also all their brutishness. The dead do not drink blood. Even less do they drink the blood of their comrades. No new war can pay back the debt they're owed. All it can do is to create new debts to pay. If the dead were able at this moment to speak their pale lips would move only to utter the great words of Christ: 'Love one another. . . . Peace be unto you . . . . .' They would say: 'You are many. Make love your law and be ruled by that. As soon as you wish it, it will come about.'

He spoke impressively, his conviction showing in his eyes, his gestures sweeping, his hair falling across his forehead with the strength of his movements. He'd become as white as one of the candles, but his voice was deep and warm.

No sooner had he finished and was pushing his way out through the crowd than he regretted what he'd done, that he'd not been able to control his impulse. Many hands reached out to shake his own, and many of the eyes he encountered were filled with tears.

Close to the exit of the church he almost knocked into the schoolmistress. He felt her look at him, and had an impression of her large eyes full of shadows and questions. Outside he thought: 'It'd be amusing if she believed that I was wanting to teach her a lesson.'

Adriani reached home after him. She clasped his hands, still strongly moved.

'It was good what you did,' she said. 'Thank you.'

'I lost my temper,' he answered. 'I couldn't bear listening to such rubbish. But the truth of the matter is that soldiers do get a pretty raw deal. Do you know, Adriani, what soldiers are? You have to have been in a war before you can find out. That's where I learnt what they are. Soldiers, my girl, form a very special race, the flower of the human race, which all the other races of the earth do their utmost to destroy. They deceive them until the time comes when they can kill them, and when they've killed them then they slander them. It's a shameless business. . . . '

'But if,' Adriani asked quietly, 'but if what they do and say is done and said in good faith. . . ?'

'No,' he said emphatically. 'At bottom it is an egotism—the imbecilic egotism of shirkers which makes them go as far as trying to cut figures in the name of the dead. They assume theatrical poses standing on corpses whose wounds still stink. . . . Didn't you see Vranas's widow?'

He told her of the military cross, of the inscription on the offering in the church, of the gilded almonds, of the candle with the national colours. . . .

Adriani looked at him in surprise.

'But you took her side so strongly the other day when godfather's family was here,' she said.

He was going to answer that that was beside the point, that what he was defending then was the wife of his dead friend. But he only gazed at her and said nothing.

That evening Drivas found a large company gathered at the seashore café. As soon as he was seen approaching there appeared to be a change in the conversation, and he felt the air still full of some discussion of which he'd been the object. Women were also present. There was the Mayor and his daughters, the factory owner Mr. Daphnis with his wife, the Customs officer and all the schoolteachers except Sappho. The new doctor of Megalohori was also there, a well-dressed, regular-featured type, handsome as an opera tenor with his dark eyebrows and red cheeks. He'd just come from Paris, the island newspapers reported, with a very rich collection of ties that were already beginning to be talked about in the village. The Customs officer was absolutely furious with this new representative of fashion: it was no longer a question now of Athenian chic and such nonsense but of the real stuff from Paris. He took the wind straight out of Mr. Phillippas's sails whenever this latter dared open his mouth to defend the taste of Athens. He would say quietly full of self-satisfaction and of indisputable certainty:

'Athens? A French province, certainly. But pretty backward on the whole. . . .'

Drivas greeted the assembled company, his mocking disposition well to the fore.

The Mayor introduced him to the newcomers. Xynellis got up as soon as he saw him, placing a chair for him next to his own, full of attention.

'You put me in a very difficult position this morning,' he said with a smile, as though he were in fact saying: 'Please excuse me for making you put me in a difficult position.' 'But you spoke excellently, my friend, you spoke excellently! It was a triumph! And it made, you know, a great impression. Congratulations! I don't bear you any malice. . . .'

'Yes . . . yes,' said Aspasia with enthusiasm. 'It was so beautiful and unexpected!'

'And . . . just a wee bit daring, wasn't it?' the doctor smiled protectively, raising his regular eyebrows as though making an important reservation.

Leon looked smilingly round the circle, his glance finally resting on Xynellis.

'Forgive me,' he said, 'if I spoke about things that you don't altogether believe in. I've no doubt there are others' (he glanced at the doctor) 'who also don't agree with what I said. I assure you that I regretted not to have been able to prevent myself from speaking. But I felt there was both a need and a duty. . . .'

'I entirely agree with you,' said Aspasia, and as she smiled all her teeth sparkled whitely beneath the electric light over the terrace.

The doctor noted her smile. With an elegant movement he tapped the end of his cigarette on his nail and began to explain. He spoke in an affectedly long-winded manner, emphasizing even the most trivial points.

'There is no doubt that the Fatherland has obligations towards those who fight for it, and generally speaking towards every victim of war. But I think we have to make a distinction. The duties of the community towards the reservists and the refugees are one thing, the "demands" of the reservists and the refugees are another. To recognize the latter means social insubordination. It is to open the door to anarchy. . . .'

'It smells of Bolshevism.' Mr. Daphnis concluded the sentence, while his wife's curved nose described a regular arch as her head moved up and down in agreement.

'I didn't wish to use the word,' smiled the doctor.

Loulou didn't speak, but she kept glancing first at the doctor, then at Leon, and then from Leon back to the doctor again, like a child trying to make up its mind in which of the two fists its mother holds out before it to choose from is hidden the sweet which it wants.

Leon was becoming increasingly irritated by this so polite and so serious rebuke he was receiving. As for Aspasia, she seemed to be highly amused by the whole scene.

'We've no need to fear the demands of the victims of the war,' said Drivas, 'since they're just demands. Only the guilty fear what it just —those guilty of the war, whoever they are: people in the army, politicians, those in the rear. Fortunately among us no one is in this category, so there's no need for any reservation.'

'Certainly!' said Mr. Daphnis, blushing slightly. 'Here we've all done our duty, both while the war was on and afterwards. The list of those who've given in the collections has been published in the papers. The thing's as clear as daylight. And the Municipality has done its duty as well. Isn't that so? Food for the refugees, a welcome and assistance for the discharged reservists, memorial services. . . . The public council's even voted four hundred pounds for the erection of a war memorial. . . . It's going to be carved in Athens out of Pentelic marble.'

'There you are, you see?' said Leon. 'What I said——'

Xynellis broke into the conversation:

'What I most have to congratulate you on, Mr. Drivas, is the artistic aspect of your speech. You spoke, I believe, without any preparation, and yet you spoke superbly.'

'Oh I don't think so,' said Leon. 'You flatter me with your exaggerations. I'd been meditating on the thing for years. Five years, to be precise. From 1917 to 1922.'

'All right, make a joke of it if you like,' smiled the master. 'But that won't prevent me from saying and from repeating that your speech was a marvellous lyrical poem. As a person, you know, who has a certain interest in the arts, I can't conceal my enthusiasm. It was a true piece of war literature. . . . '

Drivas patted him on the back.

'You're excessively kind,' he said. 'Unless, of course, you don't demand very much from literature.'

The doctor interrupted with quiet insistence:

'May I take this opportunity,' he said, 'of recommending the newspaper *Hellenism* to you. There indeed you'll be able to find a genuine piece of war literature. It's a page written by some ex-officer of the artillery. It's truly wonderful reading. In this defeatist period through which we're passing it's like a bath of rebirth. The man who writes it didn't leave either his patriotism or his courage behind him in Anatolia.'

'It's quite true,' said Drivas. 'From the way he writes he seems to be a hero. He was present at all the battles and fought like a Titan. So were all the soldiers and they fought like Titans too. When his battery was shelled they stood to attention and saluted in proper style. After that . . . we were defeated. He was taken prisoner and the Turks submitted him to every kind of humiliation. But he sacrificed his honour and didn't commit suicide. Luckily for history, that is, for now he can write his page in the paper. Otherwise we'd have lost our bath of rebirth, and the State a few hundred pounds.'

'The State?'

'Yes. Didn't you know? The man's making some retribution to the public funds because of a small irregularity in the handing over of some military stores in which he happened to be involved. . . . Yes, that truly, my dear Mr. Xynellis, is a fine piece of war literature. . . . '

'You're marvellous,' said the schoolmaster, as though with enthusiasm. 'You're in splendid form this evening.'

'I thought I was listening to his father,' said the Mayor warmly. 'He also used to get angry like that whenever it was a question of injustice.'

The doctor felt for the knot in his tie, made sure it was in place, and said to Leon in his most smooth professional manner:

'You know what has happened in your case, Mr. Drivas? It is something only too natural. You have the psychology of those who have returned from some terrifying disaster.'

He smiled artificially, full of politeness.

'Yes,' said Drivas, 'that is one more very just observation. And it is certainly also natural that I would far rather that I was in the situation and had the psychology of those who have not returned from some terrifying disaster.'

At this moment two little girls approached towards the company. They were two barefoot refugee girls, who stood in the shaded part of the café's extension in order not to be seen by the owner. They were encouraging each other with signs to go up to the table. At last the smaller of the two made the decision, came close, and indicated with her eyes and chin the various left-overs and uneaten bits of food.

'Shall I take them?'

Mrs. Daphnis said promptly: 'Of course, of course,' and got up from her chair to give her whatever there was. Then the elder of the two girls took courage and also came near. They began to eat hastily and greedily, and the smallest buried her face into the skin of a water-melon, tearing at it with her teeth so that the juice ran down her chin. Her tiny pitch-black eyes darted right and left like those of a hungry animal.

Mr. Philippas showed with a grimace his disapproval of this proof of bad upbringing. The factory owner took from his pocket a couple of drachmas and gave them one apiece, telling them to go home because good children don't go about like this at such an hour. Loulou didn't find any small change in her bag and had to give them a larger coin. The doctor was about to put his hand into the inside pocket of his jacket when he caught Leon's smiling glance following his movement. He stopped, displeased, and managed to divert his fingers to the lapel of the coat, where they pretended to set his buttonhole straight. Aspasia in her turn was carefully watching that glance of Leon's.

When the little beggars had left there was a short troubled silence, broken finally by the Customs officer.

'But did you see what delightful little faces they had?' he said. 'So full of intelligence and expression. And that sparkle in the eye! What a devilish race it is, the Greek race.'

'They'll be handsome young girls in a few years' time,' Leon called over to him.

Mr Philippas pursed his lips with anticipatory admiration, as though he were someone who knew about such things.

'Handsome! . . That elder one is full of promise.'

'What a pity that in the meantime we will have got old,' said Drivas feeling disgust and boredom overcoming him like a kind of sickness.

'You're wicked this evening,' said Xynellis, tapping him playfully on the knees.

The gathering began to break up. The first to rise were the Mayor and his daughters, and all immediately followed suit. Taking her leave, Aspasia said to Leon that one of these evenings he must certainly come with Adriani to their house. They were all expecting them. Did he promise?

Only Leon and Xynellis were left on the empty platform. They drew their chairs over to the balustrade at the end over the sea and lit cigarettes. The moon was new and the sky was glittering with the starlight. Leon asked the café owner to turn off the electric light. It at once seemed as if the sea had come closer. The blue night and its woven skies enfolded them gently. Beneath the planks of the platform the small waves knocked and plucked, and the stars danced in the dark waters, now visible, now disappearing again.

'How beautiful it is!' sighed Drivas.

The schoolmaster threw his cigarette into the sea and it sizzled as it went out.

'At first,' he said, 'I didn't realize you were joking. You spoke so seriously.'

'Can't you drop the subject?' said Leon dully.

'No,' insisted the schoolmaster. 'Excuse me for saying it, but I greatly admire you. I have a great respect for the spirit. . . . '

'And for literature,' Leon leaning down over the water, completed the sentence for him.

'You persist in taunting me, but it doesn't matter. I greatly enjoyed this evening. You put them all in their place magnificently. That doctor's the most pitiful of the bunch. You humbled him in front of the Mayor's daughters—he'll never forgive you for it, you mark my words. Aspasia, in any case, clearly showed her preference for you. . . . '

'Are you by any chance in love with her?' asked Drivas, for want of something to say.

'I?' The cold laugh of the schoolmaster grated harshly against the ebb and flow of the water. 'I? Of course not. Where on earth did you get that idea from?'

'Simply an idea....It seemed to me you were looking at her strangely. In any case, there's nothing wrong with it. She's a well-shaped attractive girl. Any man might be taken up with her.'

'Yes, now you speak of it,' Xynellis muttered. 'Those small dimples, the breast....'

'There you are, you see' Well?'

'I'll tell you, my friend. If it were really a question of my marrying some nice well set-up woman there's no doubt that I'd cock my hat at Mistress Aspasia. Supposing, that is to say, that a wretched schoolmaster had any chances in this direction. But...'

'But?'

'Yes. But she's not a woman who'd really get hold of me. She's not, let us say, a Sappho.'

Drivas raised his head. He saw the master's thick lenses glinting in the reflected light of the water.

'Are you very fond of Sappho?' he said slowly and with indifference.

'Everyone's fond of her!' Xynellis's voice was warm and gentle. 'Her, yes. She's a woman. She's *the woman*. She stands out from the others, don't you agree?'

'It's a matter of taste.'

'No, you can't put it like that. And you don't believe it, either. Sappho is the woman that all the men of Megalohori dream of. All, do you hear? Married and single, young and old...'

'I believe you. You can see how they gossip about her.'

'You're right. For she doesn't give a damn for anyone.'

'She is, so to speak, a kind of Penelope without a loom whose Odysseus is never going to come. And all you men of Megalohori represent the suitors!

'No. She's simply of a rebellious and proud breed. You don't know her. She's "the Contessa". You can't imagine. There has to be someone who can bridle her, subdue her...It would be something extraordinary.'

There was silence. A silence full of the schoolmistress's presence.

'You...Why don't you try?' asked Leon suddenly.

The teacher swallowed and spoke humbly.

'I,' he said, 'I haven't the gifts that are needed. I'm neither handsome nor courageous. I'm an intellectual who's got no capacity for such ventures....'

'But you love her, none the less?'

'That... Well, not exactly, unless you want to say that everyone here loves her. But I admire her. I'd do anything for her, if she wished it. Don't you think she's worth it?'

'It depends. . . . Does she know you love her?'

'How can she know? She's a sphinx. . . .'

He took a deep breath, hesitated a moment, then continued:

'I once wrote four songs for her . . . .'

'Aha!'

'You're right to mock. . . .'

'Not at all. I'd be only too pleased if you'd read them to me sometime.'

'It would be an honour both for me and them,' the schoolmaster said warmly. 'Besides, I've published them in an Athenian periodical which I know she takes.'

'Hasn't she noticed them, then?'

'I doubt it. . . . Even though there were things in them that gave an indication. . . . But I'm certain she's not noticed them. Because one evening, in the winter, when the Mayor was giving a family party and we were playing various games, I repeated one of the verses to her and she asked me with surprise: "So you also write poetry, Mr. Xynellis?" That was her phrase. . . .'

Leon sat up, stretching his arms.

'Time for us to leave also,' he said, getting up. 'You'll let me hear your poems sometime, won't you?'

He gave the schoolmaster his hand and said good night, so that he wouldn't keep him company. Xynellis also said good night, deeply moved.

Leon went slowly towards the house, hearing the sound that his steps made on the pure sand. The whole beach was flooded with the sweet sad song of the sea, the sea's evensong. Off shore a boat was moving, its mast-light now hidden by the gunwale, now showing red, its reflection making a snake-like crimson track on the water. The fisherman's silhouette stood out black in the pinkish mist of light. Leon stopped for a moment, repeating to himself the lines of Palamas:

> *At night he shines, at night he goes*
> *Beyond the harbour's quay.*
> *At night his burning lantern glows*
> *Like blood upon the sea.*

He stopped and saluted the sight, and then continued on his way. He was thinking of the various members of the company he'd recently left, turning them over in his mind like the pages of a book that were either interesting or stupid. He saw through the night the thick glasses of the schoolmaster who because of his great desire for a woman had spoken badly of her; and he repeated to himself: 'Each of us finds his erotic release in his own way.' He recalled Xynellis's warm subdued talk of the passion that smouldered in the whole male population of the village—a passion that was unconfessed, cunning, and cruel, and which wound itself in a thousand suffocating ways round Sappho. 'The Contessa'.

All, married and single, wanted her. She was young, she was beautiful, she was a widow. She was alone. She was Penelope without Odysseus. Without a loom either. And so everyone spread his desire over her. They all wanted her, they'd all swarmed round her with their hot breath, the whole herd, a pack of hounds with hungry eyes and hanging tongues. She troubled their dreams, a thorn in the flesh. And all played dumb, each watching the other, but no one daring to look his own longing in the eyes, to give it its true name. Only that ridiculous Xynellis. All the rest of them concealed their lust carefully, converting it into gossip, into social criticism, even into patriotism, so that they could parade it openly. And she, the Contessa, passed through this herd of he-goats untouched, smelling of jasmin, swaying like the bough of an apple tree in flower. How did her ancient compatriot and namesake put it? 'To a delicate sapling most would I compare you.' Thus would the ancient Sappho have spoken to her had she met her walking on the seashore.

And this was Vranas's wife. And he, poor devil, had been longing to come back to her one day, to come back to her unexpectedly in his shining boots, just as though he were an officer from the opera. He'd taken those famous boots with him finally. One of them had been empty. The leg that should have been with it had already gone. Vranas had been very anxious to keep his leg company into the graveyard! But he'd taken one or two superfluous arms with him to make up the weight.

That night in bed he couldn't help smiling at the thought which kept on recurring to him: that of the valley of Josaphat, when the trumpet of the Second Coming would have sounded the terrible reveille, and from all the tombs the dead would rush forth in crowds for the great roll-call. God's day of judgement. And then all the dead from the 2nd Military Hospital should rise up astonished from the graveyard at Eski. Vranas would be holding his empty boot not knowing what to put in it. He would see his third arm and he would say, as he'd once said in his delirium: 'There you are, you see, I'm right. There are three arms.' And the other fellow with pneumonia would find along with his own limbs, Vranas's leg, and he would try to remember—after so many thousands of years of death—how many legs in fact he had while he was living.

At last he fell asleep, lulled by the distant whispering of the sea. Such a sound the light steps of those shadows rising would make in the biblical valley, millions together, coming from far away. And now it was no longer the waves, it was simply the hollow tramp of the dead on the soft sand outside the Portara: an endless, weightless sound, as though innumerable naked feet were walking over dry leaves of the plane tree.

12

IT WAS at about this time that the schools closed for the summer holidays, and the Mayor, as was his custom every year, gave a dinner party for the whole teaching staff of the village. Drivas and his sister were also invited, and so were the doctor and a certain Sismanoglou with his partner Mr. Scaliotis and his wife. This Sismanoglou was a merchant from Smyrna who together with Scaliotis had bought up all the material on an Austrian ship which had struck a rock and gone down just off shore. They'd come from the main town and had all set themselves up in the little hotel by the harbour, where they were going to stay till they'd raised the vessel and stripped it of anything of value. A diver was also expected to arrive shortly. They had come with an introduction to the Mayor, and they had indeed tried to persuade him to join their company, the Smyrna merchant giving him a very attractive picture of the profits that might be expected. Mr. Spanos had, however, refused the offer, not being a person who liked to indulge in such speculative ventures. But this occasion of the dinner party gave him an opportunity to invite them to his house. In addition, a cousin of the Mayor was also present—a person everyone knew by his Christian name, Mr. Yanni. He was an elderly wrinkled little man, all skin and bone, who did what he could to make himself smart in Mr. Spanos's cast-off clothes. At heart he was a useless idler, and the Mayor gave him odd jobs such as the house-hold shopping—keeping him as a kind of general handyman—in order that the tips and the food he gave him shouldn't give him the womanish voice, and whenever he was spoken to he would open his colourless eyes ecstatically and say in a whining tone: 'Very odd.' Even if you spoke to him of the most natural thing in the world he would still find it 'very odd'. Mr. Yanni was, in addition, a virgin, something which everyone knew, although in spite of this he used to make eyes at all the girls who took his fancy. He was also to some extent literate and read with passion every kind of encyclopaedic journal he could lay his hands on. He had in this way succeeded in convincing himself that he was a man of great knowledge, an unrecognized sage. He'd got hold of various theories which he used to expound furiously whenever he could find anyone who was willing to listen to him for a moment.

The table had been set on a large cool verandah. There were drinks first, with various kinds of hors-d'oeuvre, followed by fish, fowl, and the season's fruits. Adriani had had no desire to be present at a party of this kind, but the Mayor's daughters had insisted. It was a mixed and incongruous gathering, such as might have been found round a ship's table. Plump Madam Evtychia, looking freshly dolled up under the bright light, exuberant as a ripe well-preserved tomato, so that it seemed that if you were to scratch her taut skin with your nail she would give out pulp rather than blood—Madam Evtychia waited on all with exhausting persistence, hoping for opportunities to release her tender tears. She didn't in fact have to wait long. The Mayor, half seriously, half jokingly, proposed a toast to the teachers. He thanked them on behalf of the community for their labours during the past year and for the progress the children had made. He wished a safe return to the Director and to one of the other masters who came from elsewhere and were to leave the next day to spend their holidays in their villages. The Director replied to the toast, speaking emotionally, partly because of his natural modesty and partly because of the local red wine he'd drunk. And Madam Evtychia's chick-pea tears began to well up.

Xynellis bit his nails in irritation: he'd have given anything to have been able to make a speech. He turned this way and that on his chair as though nails were sticking up through it from beneath. But when he saw Leon's mocking eyes fixed on him from the other side of the table he smiled, disarmed, and sat still in his place.

Leon was amusing himself in his own way. He watched everyone, trying to discern the characteristic lines both of their physical and of their psychological portraits, and seeing how he could reconcile what he observed as a painter with what he discovered as a psychologist. That trio, for instance, connected with the Austrian ship, was a particular study.

Sismanoglou was a pure Smyrna type, voluble, sensual, superficial, open-hearted, pleasure-loving, and a speculator. He laughed enormously, with all his mouth, all his teeth, his whole face, like all those who are comfortably off, untroubled, sure of themselves, and dressed in a suit that fits them excellently. Xynellis for example, was completely the opposite: a civil servant from head to foot, tall, thin, badly nourished, full of joints, all elbows and knees. There was nothing at ease about him. Every few moments he would set his glasses straight, for their slightest movement shifted the optical ray from the centre of the lenses and forced him to look out through their rims. This annoyed him considerably. He grimaced, raised his eyebrows up to his hair, and twisted his mouth to the right. Then his clothes betrayed all the sad and enervating story of their continual wear, beginning to die on him remorselessly, without hope of succession. And he was still a young man. Above all, the collars and the sleeves proclaimed aloud how many times up to now they'd been scoured with petrol. The sleeves were in addition extremely short, so that the cuffs of his shirt protruded several inches out beyond them. The cuffs were, it is true, clean. But Leon noticed that they were of that detachable kind which you could reverse when you wanted and wear inside out if they got dirty. And they were turned inside out now.

Mr. Scaliotis clearly revolved submissively within the orbit of his partner, economically first of all, but also morally. That was quite evident. To begin with he lacked that ease of manner both in his clothing and in his general behaviour which revealed Sismanoglou's superiority. This meant that they couldn't have equal shares in the company. Then he agreed with absolutely everything that the Smyrna merchant said, so that you saw that he kept in reserve a whole battery of assurances for any idea he might have. He laughed demonstratively at his smallest joke. He was a kind of attendant, shortish, squat-necked, round-bellied. One of those excessively servile types who'd immediately become harsh and presumptuous to his subordinates were the situation to be reversed and he to become one of the riders instead of one of the ridden. Such, at least, was the conclusion that Leon came to.

As for Mrs. Scaliotis, she might have been considered to be a stylish kind of woman, small and neat, with fish-like movements and pleasure-loving almond eyes. She also had a pair of extremely expressive, even provocative, legs, which she always kept moving. She ate with appetite, chatted a great deal with her eyes and legs, but spoke rarely, and always when it wasn't necessary. And she was always licking her thick lips.

Leon tried to discover why, from the moment that he was introduced to the woman, he had the impression that one day she would leave her husband. Then he remembered that she was called Nora, and smiled. Names had their own fatality, it seemed.

The doctor was always the type of the 'new arrival', one whose eyes had seen so much and so much and yet who accepted with sympathetic condescension these new provincial surroundings. He was continually making sure that his tie was in place, giving such importance to the movement that you might have thought it was a question of setting the earth's axle straight: if it but deviated a little whole lands and villages would sink. His suit was of the latest Parisian cut with a large carnation in its buttonhole. Also it was spotlessly clean, its pure white collar freshly ironed and starched. The flower was so impressively placed in the buttonhole that Leon thought that if the carnation was able to imagine anything it would doubtless have regarded the doctor as a most extraordinary flowerpot, specially designed by God for its use on this one particular evening.

The doctor was making eyes both at Aspasia and at Loulou.

Loulou was day-dreaming. When she wasn't day-dreaming her eyes were passing critically from Drivas to the doctor and from the doctor to Sismanoglou, rather like those a cattle-dealer sizing up the cattle at a market. Aspasia was glancing kittenishly at Leon and giving general notice to all of her dimples and her splendid white teeth. As for Xynellis, he was receiving every feminine look with gratitude, no matter where it came from; but when he spoke with the schoolmistress he was genuinely stirred. Mr. Yanni was still finding everything 'very odd', even the fact that Madam Evtychia's mayonnaise was a success. He pursed his lips together, and a whole host of tiny wrinkles mingled on his face and formed the most improbable combinations, each indicative of some particular feeling. The one ousted the other, or two of them joined together at the corners, and then a third intervened and inserted its tail between their fork, and so on.

Mrs. Scaliotis caught Sismanoglou once or twice looking pathetically absent-minded with his eyes fixed on Adriani. She tried to rouse him by giving him insistent glances. But the Smyrna merchant was far away, and wasn't to be brought back by these optical cries. In the end Nora, seeing it was useless, lowered her eyes irritably to her plate, where they sadly lighted on the provocative leg of a basted turkey. Desperately but with resignation she took her knife and began to clean the meat from it.

But the one that Leon kept continually under his observation, even at the moments when he was looking at the others, was Sappho. It was an endless interrogation, almost an act of spying.

The schoolmistress was wearings a dress of dull silk with a white collar. It was a discreet dress, and yet at the same time coquettish, spilling over her body like water and revealing her splendid figure in an incredible way. There were times when she gave him the impression of a large vigorous snake that writhed and turned only to indulge the sense of its own litheness, tasting its own delight privately, Her hair, abundant and wavy, was full of warm shadows and bronze reflections. When she bent her head forward to hear what the Mayor was saying you could see then behind the ear and over the neck two small shining curls like silken ear-rings emphasizing the robust health and freshness of her skin. The doctor had also caught sight of those two ear-rings, so that at one moment the girl, as though those male glances had become tactile and were tickling her, unconsciously raised her hand to her ear and lightly passed the tips of her fingers over the rose-coloured lobe.

Adriani brought her chair up next to that of the schoolmistress and began talking to her. They spoke quietly, almost withdrawn from the rest of the company. Once or twice Leon knew they were speaking of him, for they raised their eyes and glanced at him. The strong light shining straight down on her head made the schoolmistress's thick eyelashes play like the wings of a butterfly, while her lower lip formed a small shadowy nest on her rounded chin. At one moment she raised her head towards the powerful bulb, and for the first time Leon was able to make out their strange colour. They were of an open chestnut, and in the light they became golden, completely golden, as though they were those of the statue of some divinity. They reminded him of the eyes of some fine animal, the eyes of a wildcat for instance suddenly caught one night in some deserted spot of Anatolia in the headlights of a car. She was a woman with golden eyes. And those eyes, whenever they happened to meet his own, looked at him quietly, with a sad and thoughtful look. Then he lost his egotistical objectivity as an observer, and felt slightly agitated. He drank a glass of wine and smiled stupidly. At the moment the girl removed her glance, he felt relieved.

The doctor was doing his best to act an interesting part. He related his impressions of the war, which he'd seen from the inside of a hospital in Paris where he'd been serving 'internally' (he tried to communicate to those around him how important this being an internal doctor was.) It was during the time that the Germans were shelling with Big Bertha. A shell fell close to the hospital. It was like a meteorite, huge and mysterious. Totally unexpected, it had burst upon them through the ashen clouds without the sound of the cannon being heard. The wounded were panic-stricken, and one young English lad, both his legs smashed from the knees down, began to shout: 'Give me my shoes so I can get away. Give me my shoes so I can get away!'

The story impressed everyone. Madam Evtychia wiped her damp cheek. Leon turned and looked at his sister and Sappho: silent, they had their eyes fixed on the doctor. The doctor himself reaped his success with studied naturalness and was now explaining some details privately to Aspasia. Drivas thought how it was simply a matter of his wanting to and he could really upset the schoolmistress. He knew of another incident, which concerned a leg and some boots. But it would be disgusting to start going into competition with that idiot simply to catch attention. He then would never tell his story. Never. And he felt as if he were performing some important heroic act as he took the decision.

Then Sismanoglou told of how he'd found himself during the Asia Minor retreat in a railway carriage that was transporting the sick and wounded of a Greek hospital out of the depths of Anatolia. Sismanoglou had been a purveyor to the army and only just escaped being left behind. Well, the train was crammed full of the wounded and those sick with typhus. They all stank, their wounds, for days unattended, went bad and were full of dust and pus. They excreted where they were lying, howled like jackals, cried out for water—and there wasn't a single drop of water. The train whistled and hurtled on as fast as it could, as though it too were caught up in the panic of defeat. It shrieked with its whistle and with its wounded, and dragged behind it like a tail the sound of its roar echoing in the gorges and in the empty fields. It was like a horse that has broken free of the bridle and gallops blindly, breathless with terror. The sun scorched and the wounds stank. Clouds of flies swarmed and buzzed and glued themselves on to one's skin. Many, wounded or with typhus, died in their own filth, bent double. Then the others, those who were alive and were next to them, stirred, dragged them still warm as they were to the door of the carriage and pitched them out. In this way those who were left were relieved of their smell and gained a little extra space. The dead bodies fell alongside the burning track or on to the lines, so that the wheels cut them or jostled them abruptly, as if giving them one further powerful kick. Then, if there happened to be an embankment, the dead would begin to roll down the slope, rolling towards the bottom, their faces in the prickly scrub, their legs apart, their bellies naked.

And the train dashed on, dashed and whistled, hurtled and howled. Finally it reached the terminus, the last railway station. From there on it was by car or on foot. The wounded began to get out, fighting among themselves to be the first. They'd seen a line of big army trucks loading on soldiers and women and children, and they were desperate to get a place, a place in life. Those who'd been wounded in the legs begged the others to take them, to carry them or to kill them. Finally they would struggle forwards with their hands, dragging their wounded bodies behind them like a serpent. In this way many went head-first out of the carriage door. A sergeant of the Engineers, with a new jacket and stripes, managed to take out his bayonet and, closing his eyes, to press it slowly, inch by inch, into his breast, clenching his teeth. He was lying on his back on a stretcher, his stomach riddled with shrapnel. All the carriages emptied and the place was full of commotion. Cicadas were thrumming everywhere, the wounded were crying, voices seemed to be coming out of the earth itself.

Then a most fantastic thing happened.

A gang of Engineers who'd been in the train, riding in front on the engine, got down and turned the railway lines towards the brink of a precipice which made you dizzy even to glance over. Then one member of the gang got up into the engine alone, a young warrant officer of the Engineers, black and skinny. He put the engine into gear and the train started forward at once towards the abyss. The warrant officer coolly stayed in the cab until it was near the edge and then at the last moment leapt clear like a cat. At the same moment the carriages, the whole lot of them, linked one behind the other, hurled themselves head-first into chaos and smashed themselves with a deafening roar on the rocks below, making the surrounding mountains echo with the sound.

The engine continued hissing for a bit, and then its sound slowly died away until it too was silent, spent, and a deathly hush settled over the whole place.

When Sismanoglou had finished his terrible story all round the table also fell silent. And this silence too, round the table still loaded with fruit and food and bottles, was like a reflection of the silence that had filled the gorge after the tragedy of the train.

Madam Evtychia wept happily, lavishly, with all the anticipatory pleasure of a possible contraction. And Mr. Spanos, turning and seeing her so carried away, didn't remember to give her his usual warning: 'Your heart, Evtychia.' Through the eyes of all passed the great shades of the carriages screaming as they hurtled towards the abyss. Suddenly Mr. Yanni sighed deeply through the general silence and said in his squeaky feminine voice:

'Very odd!'

Then Leon, slowly emptying another full glass of wine, suddenly broke out into uncontrollable laughter. He tried to stop his nervous explosion, but it was no use: he only laughed more, laughed and laughed, holding his sides, till his chest ached. . . . Adriani looked at him anxiously.

'But it's terrible,' said Xynellis, thoroughly alarmed, settling the thick tortoise-shell frame of his glasses behind his ears.

'What's terrible? asked Leon vivaciously.

'Well . . . that.'

'That? What is that?'

'War,' said the schoolmaster with surprise. He opened his hands and said the word quietly: 'War . . . '

Drivas felt the wine throbbing in his temples. He spoke mulishly, and heard his voice sounding strangely isolated:

'Ah war! War! Say it then! Call it by its own name, so we can get used to the sound of it. So it's a "terrible" thing? But it's not war that's at fault. What can war do? It's its nature to be terrible, to be disgusting. But what about us? We who make a profession of it, or a business, or an advertisement? Who write poems about it and set God up as its patron? We who justify it as one of the factors of life? Who make a good story out of its beastliness and talk of a new war before we've yet had time even to forget the last? That's what I would like you to tell me: what are we?'

He spoke with genuine vehemence. But in spite of that all the time he was speaking he was thinking to himself: 'What cheap rhetoric!'

He looked at Xynellis, who was by now totally confused, he looked at the doctor, at Sismanoglou. Then he looked at the shoolmistress for a while, with a look which was intended to be offensive He refilled his glass, raised it on high, laughing and slightly drunk.

'I'm joking. All that is over and done with and forgotten. Why do we have to say it all again?—ruining our digestion when there's nothing to be gained by it. Let's drink a glass instead to the health of the excellent and hospitable family of our host. Viva!'

'Viva!' repeated everyone, sighing with relief.

He felt the drink inflame him, and at the same time an extraordinary feeling of maliciousness came over him. He spoke gaily:

'Let us now ask Mr. Xynellis to recite us one of his poems. I am going to introduce him to you. He is a poet who is a credit to Megalohori, and who will become, I'm certain, a credit to Greece.'

'Yes, yes, a poem!' they all chorused, looking with delighted surprise at the schoolmaster.

'Please, please . . .' said this latter, blushing to the whites of his eyes. 'Mr Drivas is joking as usual. I'm afraid I don't write verses. . . .'

'Nonsense,' said Sappho quietly. 'I know you write. So come on, then, don't be so modest. I even remember a few lines. . . .'

It was now Xynellis's turn to go pale. He looked at her in alarm, his eyes behind the lenses starting with astonishment.

'You know them?'

'Yes, of course I know them,' repeated the schoolmistress calmly, looking straight at him. 'Some of them have been published in the *Family Anthology.* And they're not at all bad:

> *Sorrow, the more you lodge with me*
> *The deeper shall I hide you. . . .*

The other schoolmasters made an exclamation of approval and clapped at the disclosure.

'Would you believe it? Under a bushel. . .'

'He hides his verses,' completed the doctor.

Xynellis was by this time at his wit's end, completely overcome with emotion. Drivas was only too pleased to see him like this, red as a cooked lobster, his hidden eyes darting this way and that way, as if he were seeking dimly for some way of escape, somewhere where he could conceal himself.

'Please,' he murmured, by now almost speechless.

He threw rapid sidelong glances at Sappho, rolling a ball of crumbs between his fingers.

'I assure you, I don't remember anything. . . . I . . . '

'It's no good making excuses, you've got to recite something,' said Aspasia, who liked the romantic poets.

The master turned his glasses towards Drivas. Behind their thick lenses two hidden eyes, almost myopic, sought mercy from him. Drivas pretended that he didn't understand their request.

'It doesn't matter,' he said to him. 'We don't want to offend your modesty. Let it be somebody else's poems. Two beautiful girls are making you a personal request. . . . It's not right. . . . Recite us, for instance, something from Gryparis. The "Matins of the Souls", say— it has about it a certain . . . topical flavour.'

Xynellis recovered slightly. He would recite with pleasure, since the company insisted so strongly. And he began the poem. He didn't say it badly. He modulated his voice well, and his tone was expressive without being rhetorical. Leon watched the schoolmistress carefully, surrendering himself pleasurably to the vulgar mood which had overcome him. The poem spoke of a battleground. Dawn comes and finds the place littered with dead bodies. A wounded trumpeter leaps up delirious, puts the trumpet to his lips, and blows the reveille. The blasts sound torn, savage, and discordant. The call to rise!

'But not a single dead man wakens at the call . . . '

She looked at him with astonishment, almost with fear, her eyes wide open, growing larger and larger, until they seemed like two large golden pools that filled her face, that filled the wall behind her, that filled the room: a whole golden world, pure gold, an impossible world whose sphere was circling and circling through a yellow mist.

'I must be completely drunk,' he thought to himself, turning his eyes back to the schoolmaster, to praise him and to applaud him. He felt ashamed and yet also obstinate. He got up and went and sat down next to the schoolmaster.

Xynellis was genuinely happy with the painter's excessive congratulations. He took his hand, shook it with joy, and didn't seem to want to let it go.

'Thank you,' he said, and he spoke from the heart. 'It's the greatest honour I could have. . . . Thank you . . . . If you only knew how I admire you. . . . '

He stopped, glanced sideways at Drivas, and concluded confidentially:

'I assure you, you give me a great happiness. . . . At first I thought you were mocking me, that you were wanting to make a show of me. . . Yes, indeed.'

'My God, how could you.' complained Leon in the same exaggerated tone of voice.

'Yes, that's how it seemed to me. That you wanted to shame me before her very eyes.'

Leon laughed, patting the master's narrow back affectionately. At the same time he was thinking of Xynellis's last words: 'Before her very eyes.' He may simply have said it accidentally, or he may have used the phrase on purpose. Had Xynellis in fact also noticed the golden eyes?

He again looked at the schoolmaster enquiringly, rather as an entomologist might look at an insect. He looked at his ugly eyes. the curved glasses with their thick tortoise-shell frame. They were like the eyes of an enormous ink-fish. He looked at his bent ears, pale and soft as though made out of kneaded pastry, and he thought that God must have given them to him only so that he could hang the frame of his glasses on them. He felt a vicious desire to reach out his hand and to catch hold of them and pull, pull strongly, to see how soft they were, how far they would stretch. He smiled and again he patted his back affectionately, repeating very softly in his ear:

'But not a single dead man wakens at the call.'

'Not a single dead man. . . . '

'You see?' said the master. 'It's as if the whole poem had been made for that one line. . . . '

'Yes, that's exactly how it is,' Drivas agreed, winking at him surreptitiously, as if he'd understood some great secret. Then he leant forward and spoke to him in confidence:

'Did you notice? Your own fine verses hadn't gone unremarked.'

'Yes, I noticed,' said Xynellis thoughtfully.

He raised his eyes, looked at him enquiringly, and continued:

'Yes. . . . She remembered one of my couplets.'

'Aren't you pleased about that?'

The master shrugged his shoulders, as much as to say he didn't know. Until now he'd thought that he'd have been very happy if she'd noticed them, but now he almost regretted that he'd sent them to be published: he was frightened she might be laughing at him.

Then Leon bent over close to his ear, almost embracing him, and asked:

116

'Do you love her?'

He looked closely through the lenses into the schoolmaster's troubled eyes, trying to make out the answer. Xynellis, alarmed, hesitated a moment, and then asked him timidly:

'And do you?'

The question took Drivas entirely by surprise. He burst into laughter, a ringing laughter, loud and unconstrained.

'There's manners for you. You tell each other jokes in private and you laugh at them by yourselves!' protested Aspasia. 'I don't call that at all nice.'

'But . . . Mr. Xynellis here . . . ' said Leon, and again started laughing. 'He!'

And he pointed to the schoolmaster, who paled and felt his heart sink into his boots. Drivas callously rejoiced at his embarrassment, and went on laughing.

'Well, then, what did he say after all?' asked Aspasis.

'He said. . . Oh, my God, he said . . . something about one of Mr. Yanni's theories!'

The schoolmaster swallowed dryly, and began to breathe again, like a diver that's come up to the surface. He smiled awkwardly.

'Tee-hee. . . '

Mr Yanni stretched his neck with acute interest, the wrinkles of his face forming quickly into an expression which seemed to say: 'I'm waiting for your questions.'

'I was telling him about his theory of chemical reproduction,' the master explained with relief, and again he tittered: 'Tee-hee.'

'That's it.... Just imagine....His theory of chemical reproduction.' repeated Drivas, again bursting into laughter.

'Excuse me. Does my theory seem so absurd to you?' interrupted Mr. Yanni. 'Does it seem absurd to you? Very odd!'

And he started to expound his views about the future reproduction of the human race, which was to take place in biological laboratories without either love or marriage taking any part in it at all.

'My good man, can't you stop talking such nonsense,' said Madam Evtychia, blushing furiously and thinking of her daughters who were listening to this disgusting talk.

But Mr. Yanni wasn't going to let the opportunity slip from him so easily. He moved his chair up to the doctor's, with the idea that only he, a fellow scientist, would be able to understand him, and he began speaking to him in a low voice. The whole thing was very simple. They would take spermatozoa from a man and ovaries from a woman, and in a specially prepared watery element and in a specially prepared incubator, the incubation would take place and the babies would hatch out, without pain, without bother, without labour. Love would be packed into sterilized ampoules and would be sent by post. In this way any man would be able to have a child by a woman of no matter what country or race, even if he had never once set eyes on her. He would write, for instance, to America to ask them to send him some famous film star's ovaries. . . .

'Excellent!' said the doctor, laughing discreetly. 'It's a very modern scheme, and very practical, and very respectable. It solves the problem of fertility. . . . '

'No, but truly it does, doesn't it?' said Mr. Yanni out loud, looking round triumphantly with the secret hope that he might initiate a general discussion. But no one paid any attention to him, especially as his theory was already well known. Everyone was listening to the Mayor, who was speaking about the operation with the Austrian ship.

'Yes, certainly, it's a good venture. Theoretically the profit is assured and considerable. The only thing is that no one quite knows what state the material's in after rotting for so long in the sea—— '

'Ah, ba!' interjected Mr. Scaliotis. 'The whole thing was thoroughly inverstigated before they took it on. You don't imagine they've simply gone at it blindly, do you? They sent a specialist diver down to look the ship over. There's not a doubt about it—it's an absolute cinch: five hundred per cent profit. No joking. And they got it for a mere bagatelle from the insurance company.'

He gestured violently while he was speaking, and a vein rose on his thick neck just where his collar pressed it.

The Smyrna merchant added that it would be an opportunity for them to give work to a few boatmen and some fifteen local workers—this apart from the diver who was coming specially for the job.

'That's very good news,' said Madam Evtychia with a sudden burst of philanthropy. 'It'll mean that some of the poor will have a bite of bread for a while.'

It was after midnight when the gathering broke up. Adriani offered to keep the schoolmistress company back to her house, but she declined the offer: the other teachers would see her to her door, since their road lay that way. She spoke warmly with Adriani for a while before they parted, promising finally to come and see her at the Tower.

Brother and sister walked back together towards their house, going for some way in silence. Suddenly Adriani spoke.

'You know you behaved very badly this evening with Sappho? You don't know how upset I was. . . . '

'I know,' he replied. 'I was almost vulgar to her—not even "almost". I think I was also a little tipsy.'

'It was practically as if you had some hatred for her.'

He hesitated before answering.

'Perhaps I do have some hatred for her,' he said thoughtfully. 'There's a whole pack of confused thoughts in my mind about her.'

'I'm very fond of her,' said Adriani, and her voice betrayed the sincerity of her feeling. 'I liked her from the first evening we met. it seems to me she's an exception among everyone here. Straight-forward and genuine.'

Leon didn't reply.

13

ONE afternoon the schoolmistress went to visit Adriani at the Tower, as she had promised. Leon was out, and it was not long before the two girls were deeply engaged in conversation. Their meeting was for both of them a happy discovery, and they opened their hearts to each other as if they'd been friends for years. They were still talking in this way when Leon came back, climbing lazily up the stairs, which creaked as always beneath him. He was holding his straw-hat, full of figs, in his hands, and his wet bathing-costume hung over his shoulder.

Adriani hurried gaily over to him when she saw him, to relieve him of his burden. He uttered an exclamation of surprise when he saw Sappho, and greeted her warmly.

'I'm very glad that I've got to know your sister,' she said, speaking with animation. 'It'll be really lovely for me to be able to have her company while she's here.'

'For me also,' said Adriani simply. 'I knew from that night at the party that we'd get on together.'

'Bravo!' said the painter. 'Then I congratulate both of you. In the meantime . . . am I disturbing you?'

'On the contrary,' said Adriani, tipping the dark figs out together into a red earthenware bowl. 'The proof is that we were just speaking about you.'

'About me?' he asked, making a mock bow.

'Yes. We were talking about that incident at the memorial service. Sappho told me that your words raised a whole host of questions in her mind.'

'Oh!' he said, with the same semi-ironic air. 'Would it be possible for me to hear what some of them are?'

The schoolmistress quietly explained to him that that memorial service had left her in a very confused state of mind. While Xynellis had been speaking, she'd felt that what he said was logical and right. Then when Leon had spoken afterwards she'd found with surprise that really what he was saying was the correct way of seeing things. It was a discovery which she'd accepted gladly. It was as if it were some long-lost member of the family that you were waiting for to come back from abroad. You didn't know him, you'd never seen him, but you were waiting for him. And when suddenly he came you were full of gladness. . . .

Drivas listened to the expressive way she put things with curiosity. There was in her words a fresh spontaneous note, as though water were gushing forth.

'I thank you,' he said, 'that you allowed me to change your ideas so rapidly. All that I was aware of was that in some matters you were of one mind with Mr. Xynellis.'

'How did you know it?'

'But it was quite simple. Those children of yours at school, that you taught how to make the military salute. . . . Then in your house, that medal in a frame . . . the official citation from the Division. . . . After that in the church: the inscription on the offering. . . . '

He had begun to slip into a slightly mocking tone of voice, but when he saw that she'd become as red as if she'd been slapped across the face he was ashamed of his lack of manners. . . .

'Listen,' he said to her solemnly. 'You must excuse me if I think out loud. It's a habit I got in the army. But at the same time you must let me be frank with you. It's necessary. . . . Then there are times in one's life when one discovers certain things of importance, and it's then that the attempt to hide the truth with conventional phrases and not to speak candidly results in behaviour which isn't very pretty. . . . '

'Please,' said the schoolmistress impetuosuly. 'Your candour will be for me an indication of your esteem. It is also something which I have a need of as well. . . . And it is as valuable to me as that of Adriani.'

'Very well, then. I have to confess that all those things that I saw about you filled me with horror.'

She raised her head, shaken by the strong word he'd used.

He tried to explain to her how war degrades a man, how incredibly it degrades him, and how only the systematically misguided education of several centuries still results in its being regarded as a means to human happiness. He spoke with passion, with violence almost. The schoolmistress listened to him, watching him carefully. The light in the window fell straight on her face, and again her eyes showed golden, like two large drops of pure olive oil.

'You're right,' she said, after a short silence. 'I have never been able to think those things out for myself. I am ashamed.'

The painter looked at her attentively, as he might have done at someone whom he was beginning to respect.

'There is no need for you to be ashamed,' he said. 'I myself went off and enlisted as a volunteer in order to fight. I believed in war and its ethic. And because I believed its ethic I believed also in its "justice": the shooting of soldiers who were cowardly, the burning of villages. . . I was able to justify the lot. Because fundamentally I was without love. Yes, that was the reason why I didn't see what war was. It's that which is wanted if man's eyes are to be opened. . . . '

'Love . . ' repeated the schoolmistress quietly. 'What love?'

'Love. For a human being, or for man in general. The thing that leaves our hearts as soon as we submit ourselves to any system. The thing which, for instance, that Spartan woman didn't have who said to her son: "Die or be victorious"; which the Russian worker didn't have when he slaughtered his child in front of Lenin's tomb.'

He looked her straight in the eyes, almost harshly, and went on:

'The thing that you don't have either. You didn't love your husband. That's why you put that inscription round the offering and tied the national colour to your candle. . . . That is why you are unable to see what war is.'

'No, I didn't love him,' the schoolmistress bravely confessed, a deep flush spreading over her face to the tips of her ears.

It was an abrupt, almost forced, confession, suddenly breaking out violently as if it had been suppressed for a long time.

Brother and sister exchanged glances, a movement which she followed, quite still. Then she lowered her eyes and looked down at her hands, which she was holding, palms together, between her knees. She stayed sitting in that unassuming pose and spoke now slowly and quietly.

'I think,' she said, 'that I'm able to speak to you in this way. I realize now at last that I have to speak to you. I have to because it's more than necessary for me not to have you despising me, you two. . . . Yes, in four months' time I shall finish my twenty-second year, and this is the first time I've opened my heart to anyone in all those twenty-two years. Do you know what twenty-two years of such isolation means? I must explain things to you from the beginning. It will be a relief for me. When I lost my mother I was twelve years old, and I went to live with an old aunt, who was also my godmother. She was the only person I had in the world, a good woman, may God forgive her. She'd once been a schoolmistress. It was she who sent me into the town so I could finish my schooling. When I came back to her she didn't live for long. She was already ill and failing—one foot in the grave. And her one desire was to get me married before she died. It was at that time that the schoolmaster Vranas was wanting to marry me. I said "Yes", as if marriage were a kind of game. I didn't know any better. I was seventeen when he took me, and he was twenty-six. He was in love with me. Truly. It was a kind of ponderous love, almost barbaric. He broke me like a rock. But it had got hold of him as a disease gets hold of you. I too tried to love him. With all my heart I struggled to. It was then he began to get jealous. He behaved harshly with me. One day he raised his hand against me.'

Drivas listened with astonishment.

'He did that?'

She nodded.

'Yes. He thrashed me, he beat me.... Afterwards he would repent. He used to cry like a child—he who would have rather died than be humiliated. He used to search for the marks he'd made on me, to kiss them. He would clasp me round the legs, caress me.... And then after a while the same thing would happen again. I stopped going out, because he was jealous and suspicious of everyone. I closed the windows, shut myself in the house, and there I stayed. This, I said, is where you have to be. You've got to keep a watch. I tried to guess what might possibly make him angry, so I could forestall it. But it was no use. It was all the same. He only suffered more when he couldn't find anything to accuse me of. He couldn't even tolerate my sadness. "Playing the rôle of a victim." he used to say. It was a terrible life. I got to the point of thinking of suicide: gas, the sea—it was on such things as this that my mind dwelt. Then I got pregnant and I began to breathe again. A child. At once my bad thoughts left me. I would live for the child. I began to feel something like gratitude towards my husband who'd given it to me. "God willing," I said to myself, "this feeling may develop into love later." . . . The child came, which I wish I'd never had. An idiot child. . . . I've never loved it as I should, let God punish me even for saying it. Later I learnt, altogether by chance, that my father-in-law had had an ugly disease when he was young. Since then I've regarded that unfortunate thing as an evil which has fallen upon me. A strange infection that has struck me down. . . . I say: "Is it its fault?" And then: "Is it my fault?" I am sorry for it. . . . I alone know how my heart is torn each time that I hear it. . . .But I don't love it. I am sorry for it as I was sorry for its father. I never loved him, either. . . . There you are, that's all I have to say. . . . Perhaps even I shouldn't . . . it wasn't . . . '

She began to weep quietly, without sobs, the tears only running down of their own accord.

Adriani wept with her, holding her hands in her own.

'Ah, forgive us,' she said.

'I'm very sorry,' said Leon, now thoroughly ashamed of himself. 'Please excuse me. I'm a brute.'

He felt his heart swollen with sorrow, and thought how fatuous his outbreaks were in the face of this incredible distress.

'No,' said the schoolmistress. 'On the contrary. . . . Thank you, both of you. You don't know what a relief this has been for me. Think: I've never opened my mouth to say anything to anyone. And it's so many years. No one knows anything. . . . This is the first time. . . . And it's such a relief. Only for this I'll be grateful to you for the rest of my life. Here they all look at me so strangely. Ah, how I've learnt to read what their eyes are saying. They flirt with me vilely, or look at me with hatred. Either one of the two. These are insulting looks, which I feel like unclean touches on me. . . . I'd like at once to rub myself with eau-de-Cologne. And there are others again that tell me that I'm responsible for my husband's death, that it's my fault that the child's been born with the marks of his family's disease upon it. . . . '

She wiped her eyes, twisting her small handkerchief in her fingers.

'That many times has exasperated me, has filled me with despair. At night I hear the child screaming. I shut the doors, the windows. Nothing. It goes on screaming as if it's pursuing me for some crime I've committed and know nothing about. . . . Sometimes when I lie down to sleep I make up my mind to leave everything—the house, the child. . Let come what will, I say, I'll go away, go away to where the villagers' hatred doesn't reach me, or the child's cries. The villagers, that I never trouble. . . . The child, that I'm not to blame for. But again when dawn comes I cross myself and go off to work. Yet, with the exception of the Mayor, I despise and loathe the villagers. They're endlessly abusing me with their looks, with the stones they sling at me with their mumbled talk. And I do all I can to show them that I despise them.'

'The Contessa!' Drivas involuntarily interjected.

She raised her head.

'You know of it as well?'

'Yes, I know of it,' he said. 'And I like it.'

'One day I heard Xynellis condemning women who wore lipstick. From them on I began to wear it myself. Scandal! In the school, in their houses, at their club. . . . I painted my lips even redder.'

'They're not painted now,' remarked Leon.

'They were until that morning. Till the memorial service. And when you came to the house with the wallet I put an extra lot on, waiting for you. For I saw you in exactly the same way. "Another judge," I said to myself, "this one as well. . . . The wrist-watch, the bit of shrapnel, the photograph. . . . What am I going to do with all those things, here in my unhappiness? Anyhow, we'll see," I said "We'll see whether he turns out to be a Romeo or a prosecutor." In the beginning, at the school, I thought it would be the first. Afterwards, at the house, the second. You had something of a judge about you when you were handing me those things one by one. The watch, the time he was wounded at, the shrapnel. . . . It seemed to me I could also hear you saying: "Murderess, it was you who killed him." And I wondered what I could say to vent my anger. Because it's in the same way that my villagers torment me. The honours they do in front of me in Vranas's memory are all meant to provoke me. So I hang up the medal for them. "Behold," I say to them, "I am the wife of your glorious hero. Whether you like it or not, I'm Mrs Vranas." Such things...Later, after that memorial service, I realized I was wrong about you. I thought about it a lot. And at the Mayor's party—

'At the Mayor's party I behaved like an ass with you,' said Drivas. 'I must ask you to forgive me for all my loutishness.... Quite apart from the fact that I was almost drunk....'

14

IT WAS a splendid morning. The sun still needed some time before it was fully up, and Drivas was awakened by the chatter of a flock of birds on the almond tree. They chirruped and chirped, carrying on a great conversation, and their gossip came through the open window and woke him. He leapt up, feeling in high spirits, and leant on the window-sill. The birds had fled, taking their chatter away with them off to a pomegranate tree growing at the edge of the vineyard. But he saw a squirrel on the tree, taking its breakfast of fresh almonds. It was the great spoiler of the almond crop every year. Treading quietly, he fetched his pistol and took aim. The pretty little animal caught sight of him, stopped chewing, raised its front legs up in front of its face as though it were wiping them, and looked at him without moving, ready though to dart off.

'You haven't an idea about the sanctity of private property,' smiled Drivas, lowering his pistol.

The animal made as though to continue breaking its fast, but again stopped, looking full of suspicion towards the window. It seemed as if it were thinking something similar about Leon:

'Where and the hell has this peasant sprung from, coming to disturb people on their tree at this time of the morning!'

Drivas again raised the pistol, aimed at one of the high almond-laden boughs, and fired. The bough was shattered, one or two others were damaged, and the squirrel leapt away like smoke in its fright—he just caught a glimpse of its enormous tail as it vanished. He enjoyed that playful shot. It was like Easter. He'd like to greet each of his days with a pistol-shot, as a fresh delight. Adriani was still sound asleep: she'd heard nothing.

When he went downstairs the maid and her little boy were already up and about. The child was drawing water from the well, Kyra Christina was cleaning fish—bright red scorpion fish which Letsas the fisherman had just brought in still wriggling. He stretched his hand out towards them.

'Don't touch them!' shouted the woman, alarmed. 'They wound badly, and their spikes are poisonous.'

'And I wanted to paint them,' said Drivas, drawing his hand away.

Kyra Christina shook her head sadly.

'I know,' she said. 'Like the other day with those red mullet, which I still can't get over. You'll take them away all fresh like this and bring them back good for nothing but to throw away.'

Leon assumed a serious expression.

'You know what, Kyra Christina? When we sell their picture with the money we'll get we'll be able to buy a whole boat-load of fish....'

The maid looked at him foolishly. Then she smiled.

'They'll buy a kilo of painted fish and give us back a boat-load of real fish? You're teasing me, Mr. Leon. You like a joke, I say.... Better just leave them for me to clean them as they are. And at lunch-time I'll have a fish-soup ready for you that you'll wonder at.'

Leon laughed warmly, feeling himself happy.

'I don't believe anyone can deceive you, Kyra Christina!'

The little woman shook her head contentedly and went on with the cleaning. Then she stopped for a moment, hesitated, and asked conciliatively:

'Mr. Leon?'

'Yes?'

'Wouldn't it do to paint them when they're cooked? I'm only going to take the juice from them. It's the same thing, isn't it?'

'Not exactly, Kyra Christina,' said Drivas, that child-like laughter taking hold of him again.

He took the stick he had for walking and told the boy to be down at the Portara in an hour's time with a basket. In the meanwhile he'd have a bathe and afterwards they'd go and get fruit from the other property at Anerragi, some way off. They must tell Adriani as soon as she wakes up, so she'll know. They'll be back by lunch-time for the fish-soup.

By the time he reached the beach the day had opened, a lily. The sea was silent and dead calm, the water just breathing, there where it met the sand. And the sun was rising over the horizon like a huge fresh rose.

Leon quickly undressed and stood facing the sun, more and more of which was now becoming visible. He stood quite naked before the sea, before the sky and the sun, his feet rooted in the cool sand. Birds were chattering madly in the wild bushes that surrounded the vineyard, pecking at the thick black berries. A thousand sweet voices rose from the fields, and the small town opposite woke drowsily in the early mist.

An ox lowed slowly and complainingly. Its voice had such a solemn passion and sounded so like some religious instrument that it moved him like a prayer.

The sun rose and rose, spreading its warmth everywhere, and the sea filled with pomegranate flowers. It was with compunction that

Leon heard the multiple murmur of adoration that ascended from everywhere towards the enormous god. He felt within his youthful body the frenzied dance which primitive men danced each dawn to celebrate the return of the terrible Sun when he rose up bearing his red shield. He himself now would have liked to have had an echoing drum, an Anatolian war-drum made of the skin of an ass, and to have beaten it as at a festival. He would have liked to have had a companion like himself, clothed only in his nakedness, so they could have knocked their heavy shields together in battle, making the rocks and the waters resound, filling the place with their cries of praise.

So he stood, full of ecstasy and delight before the new-born star, until his eyes couldn't bear its radiance any longer. Then he plunged into the cool water, shouting with the strong sense of life that lashed his young flesh.

He swam outwards with powerful strokes, swam full of youth towards the east. It was as if he were setting off to meet the sun!

Leon and the boy had about half an hour's walk before reaching the property at Anerragi. A stream ran there, and the deep stream-bed divided the place lengthways into two, continuing down to water the olive-groves and vegetable gardens of the village. Anerragi was an excellent property spreading out on the sides of a shady ravine and full of olive trees and various kinds of fruit trees and vegetables. All along the side of the stream-bed Leon's father had planted poplars— that is to say he'd planted some five hundred green poplar shoots, which need only to be plugged into the watered earth and they throw off roots and grow into complete trees. So it was that Anerragi had today some five hundred poplars, tall as the masts of the biggest ships, straight as enormous silver candles, their tender foliage shaking like silk in the slightest breeze. There isn't a more sprightly and playful tree. But let a butterfly pass and its leaves flutter. All day it is as if powdered with a shining silver dust, and the sum spills in drops upon it like rain falling from leaf to leaf. The stream couldn't be seen, hidden as it was by oleanders and blackberry bushes. Only the water could be heard chattering through the dark shade with invisible birds. In winter, in the old days, Leon's father used to set traps there made from the hair of horses and catch fat blackbirds.

Leon and the child lay down exhausted in the shade of the big walnut tree which served as the reception room at Anerragi on the occasion of such visits. There with their bread they ate figs still cool from the dews of night. The gardener came down from his cottage. He'd been appointed there years ago by the godfather to look after the property and guard it from the ravages of bird and animal. In summer it was the fruit, in winter the olives. He now brought them cucumbers and some large peaches, swollen with juice.

Leon went up to see the cottage, which he remembered from his childhood. It had some sort of mud roof and inside a big hearth where the gatherers and the beaters used to cook during the olive harvest. Figs used to be spread out on the roof during the summer, covered by a layer of wild marjoram, the piquant smell of which they always kept.

Leon revisited all the old spots. He saw again the ceiling, black with old smoke, tested the large wooden beam that fastened the door. He had the same curious sensation he'd had when he first came back to the Tower—that Tower which in his imagination had been as huge as a castle with its gate, the Portara, as wide as Hadrian's Arch. He'd found there everything so shrunk. The verandah had been as large as a threshing-floor, as it must have been, since he'd played ball there and had pursued Adriana up and down its length. Now when he measured it he needed but just over three paces to cross it. It was the same with this cottage at Anerragi. He climbed up on to the roof and found a space about as big as an open hand. And he'd thought it as large as the main square in Athens. He remembered they'd climbed up there one Easter and eaten the Easter lamb. The camomile had grown and was now half a man's height, giving some idea of what the hanging gardens of Babylon may have been like.

The gardener filled the basket, weaving over its mouth slender osier shoots with blue flowers. The boy shouldered it, and they set off down again.

They went down towards the sea, Leon leaping the 'steps' like a goat—'steps' being the name given by the villagers to those low terrace-like belts which they build in dry-stone round the olive trees and fruit trees in order to hold in the soil, which otherwise would be washed away down the slopes by the rain. Descending in this way, they came out above the beach to the left of the village. The Portara was to the right. On this side there wasn't an inch of sand or any plain, but a circular hill, the Sentinel rose straight up cliff-like from the shore. The shore itself was like a surrounding defence-works of savage rocks: the Sentinel's teeth, as they were called. They stood on the brink of the precipice. Drivas remembered from his childhood the path that led down from up there to the sea—a steep narrow goat-track among the wave-eaten rocks at the sea's edge. In winter, with the northern gales, the waves leapt up there and their salt had eaten into the 'teeth', making deep holes in them, so that while the storms were on, spouts of water gushed from these great mouths, as if they were spitting angrily at the sea beneath. Leon was pleased to be able to find that secret path again decorated with silver tufts of sea-pink and the green capers which his mother used to gather and pickle. He felt a strange tenderness, treading again over the tracks of his childhood. He saw the holes of uprooted stones and he remembered the game that he used to play, the Cyclops. As in the old days he leant his back against the rock, braced himself, and with his foot uprooted a large stone. He gave it a kick, to send it over the edge. It went rolling down, gathering speed as it went, until it came to an abrupt drop, where it gave a horrifying bound and leapt across to another rock. There it hesitated a moment in a piece of scrub, and then continued its mad course thumping and banging until it reached the sea's edge, when it made another fine bound and plunged into the water, like those rocks which the Cyclops had hurled behind Odysseus's ship. The water foamed, raced upwards, and swallowed it, while the Sentinel echoed deeply the sound it made as it had struck the sea.

At that moment they heard from below a terrified cry. The cry of a woman:

'Ach!'

Leon's heart froze, and the boy stared with fright, trembling from head to foot.

'There are people down there,' he whispered, getting ready to bolt.

Drivas stopped him with a gesture, as again the voice sounded from below:

'Look out what you're doing!'

Drivas breathed again and the child crossed himself.

They began to go down slowly and carefully, trying not to dislodge small stones with their feet. Now and again they saw the sea beneath them, transparent down to its bed covered with blue sea-weedy stones and other green plants. Then it would be hidden for a while. But the shore was still invisible, and they saw it only when they reached the bottom and stepped out on to its clean pebbles.

There Leon received a further shock.

Before him stood Mrs. Vranas, the schoolmistress. She was still considerably frightened, although her smile tried to conceal the fact. Leon told the boy to go on to the Tower, and went towards her.

'My God, I must nearly have killed you,' he said, horrified.

He would have given her his hand, but both hers were holding her sunshade.

'I'm terribly sorry,' he went on. 'I've almost committed a ghastly crime.'

She smiled, as if with her golden eyes alone.

'It doesn't matter,' she said. 'There's no danger. I often come here and I'm used to it. Quite a number of such surprises come down, you know, from up there. Not only from the children, who, like you, enjoy setting the stones loose, but from the goats as well that go after the capers. So I take my precautions. When I'm not swimming I lie up out of danger in there.'

She pointed out to him a large hollow in a reddish-coloured rock, pitted with holes like a sponge. Leon knew that hiding-place well.

'In the "Gudgeon's mouth",' he said, reassured. 'That's a marvellous refuge. There's nothing to fear there.'

'I didn't know they called it the Gudgeon's mouth,' said the school-mistress.

'No, that's only what we called it. I and Adriani and the Spanos's girls. When we were young. But imagine if there'd been an accident because of my stupidity. . . . '

The schoolmisters smiled again.

'There's no reason why I should imagine it,' she said. 'And then . . . what happens, happens. You know something curious which took place last year? A barber, the one that has his shop outside the club, had a son in the war. A true hero. He fought in a whole number of battles and in the end was hit by a hand-grenade. Forty wounds, if you please. When he came out of the hospital they gave him leave. In order to give his parents a nice surprise he came at night, without warning. As luck would have it, they were putting up a building in his neigh-bourhood—Mr. Daphnis's power-station. They'd opened a pit for lime at the side of the road. He came walking up there and fell into it, and in the morning when they found him they could hardly make out who he was from what was left. That's what was in store for him. What do you say about it?'

'That you're a fatalist. . . . '

She didn't reply at once. She sat down on a rock, stirring the pebbles with her shade. Then she shrugged her shoulders and said solemnly:

'My whole life's been a series of fatal events. They've all happened without my willing them and without my wanting them. . . . I'm ready to accept anything without question. . . . And without objection. . . . '

She breathed deeply, so you couldn't tell whether it was a pleasur-able draught of the salt sea-air or a sigh.

Drivas didn't know what to say. He dug the metal tip of his stick into the beach, too full of thought to be able to say anything.

'Shall we go?' asked the schoolmistress, rising. 'It must be midday.'

She opened her sunshade and led the way. At the foot of the Sentinel the strip of beach was extremely narrow—a path of large rounded pebbles, which knocked and scrunched together as you walked over them. And walking was difficult. In winter, indeed, the passage was covered by the sea.

Drivas followed on behind her, full of admiration for the fine harmony of every movement of her body. He wondered how this girl, who was still almost a child, could think like a mature person with many years' experience of life. He trod almost in her footsteps. The sun beat down from above and the rocks burnt like hot metal. The capers, broken by Leon's stick, gave out their piquant smell strongly. In the flat shallows by the shore the light endlessly wove and unwove a net of gold air-like straw. It was the shadow of the water.

At one moment the schoolmistress stood on a small isolated rock which at once became the pedestal of a statue.

'Look,' she said, pointing with her hand.

There was a shoal of tiny fish, hundreds of them, all bunched together in the shallows at the sea's edge. It was as if you'd emptied into the sea a box of brand-new steel nails, like those that shoemakers use, and they'd come to life on the instant and now were all swimming with their blue heads pointing in the same direction. A signal from their leaders and at once the whole pack would turn about or make a half-turn to the left. It was as if they all acted according to some common understanding.

They set off again. The sun fell like scalding rain on her sunshade and spilled over on to her shapely shoulders, and from there down to the hips whose movement bemused like the movement of the sea. Her thighs were long and well knit, and as she walked it was as if they were dancing a secret dance, a sacred dance. It was a splendid sight, one that surpassed a merely sensual enjoyment and stirred the pure sources of artistic vision. He would greatly have liked to have been able to set down that moving harmony in a picture—in a picture which he suddenly conceived as the great work of his life.

It would be *The Undancing Salome*. A Salome standing naked before a heavy, waveless sea, a sea of quicksilver. She would be dressed only in the noonday sun, which would set fire to everything about her, making it glow with a sulphuric light. She would have to be a motionless Salome, but one whose limbs were all tensed ready to plunge into an orgiastic dance, crying out down to the marrow-bone, down to the most hidden nerve, that they were the limbs and the joints of a frenzied dancer. So also would be the sea that spread out before her, heavy as a bitch about to give birth: beneath the thick skin of the water would be biding its hour the fierce spirit of the tempest and the waves' turbulence.

'Do you like the Sentinel's teeth?' he asked her, to change the course of his thoughts.

'Yes,' answered the schoolmistress without turning round. 'I come here regularly. I bring a book and sit for whole hours.'

'And in the heat?'

'Of course. I like the strong sun. Above all . . . when I'm in the shade,' she added, and laughed. 'There in that hollow I nestle up like a crab. It's cool and always shady. Sometimes I take with me something to knit, or a book. But I don't do anything. I simply sit in there and look at the waves and think about things. Sometimes even I don't think about anything. I just look, listen, breathe. . . . '

'Do you swim?'

'Very much!' she said vivaciously. 'The sea . . . what a wonder it is! Don't you agree?'

In her voice he heard and recognized the tones of a fanatical swimmer.

'As soon as I find some girl to come with me,' she continued. 'I come out here and in I go. There're some rocks back there where we shelter for changing.'

'So that's how it is,' thought Leon to himself. 'She's got my disease. The sea-lust.' He liked the term he'd found to describe it.

The defence-works with the Sentinel's teeth which till now had sheltered them ended at this point, and they came out on to the beach which fanned open ahead of them to below the houses of the village.

Drivas stopped.

'Would it be better,' he said, 'if I stayed behind and you went on alone?'

'Why?' she asked turning to look to him.

He pointed with his stick at the village.

'Because of the people,' he said. 'I've heard that they discuss and keep watch on all your movements, all your relationships; that they were even waiting for me behind their grilles when I came up to your house. . . . '

She shrugged her shoulders.

'I imagine it's as you've heard,' she said. 'From the time I became a widow till now they've been longing to discover some man in my life. I feel it continually all round me: an endless spying which they're never tired of. But it seems they've never gathered enough evidence against anyone to accuse him of playing the part. I stick to my work and am formal with all of them. I expect it's that that infuriates them. They miss him enormously, this lover of Vranas's wife.'

She laughed and went on:

'Perhaps finally I should, out of kindness, throw them . . . some victim.'

'That would be a terrible part,' said Leon, also laughing. 'I don't suppose anyone would find it particularly enjoyable being between the teeth of your villagers.'

'I can assure you from experience they wouldn't,' said the school-mistress. 'But, still, it would seem to me cowardly for us to separate now. In any case if we did it would be a confession of guilt for them, wouldn't it?'

'Without a doubt,' said Drivas, relieved. 'I only suggested it because I don't want to be the cause of a single further worry for you.'

She moved on again. After a moment she said:

'I don't believe they'd dare where you're concerned. They've got a pretty good respect for you. As for me, I can assure you that a new insult wouldn't add very much to things. I scorn them and I despise them. . . . Would you believe it? There are times when I don't even love their children they send me at school. I'm ashamed to confess it. They wound me deeply, fill me with bitterness—me, who was ready to love the whole world. . . . '

They were walking side by side now, at the sea's edge.

'I don't think it's right,' he said 'for you to exasperate them in this way.'

'But when one feels oneself innocent and misjudged?'

'Then perhaps. But it's dangerous to provoke the brutality of the social herd against oneself. It's terribly powerful. It can crush you beneath it like an ant. . . . '

He spoke in this way, but in himself he was certain that in similar circumstances he would act with the same and with even greater reck-lessness.

They walked on, and he continued talking, but all the time there came into his mind that phrase of hers which she'd spoken at their house: 'Will he turn out to be a Romeo or will he be a prosecutor.' When they reached the point where the path forked and they were to separate, he said to her suddenly:

'Listen, Sappho. There's something I want you to get quite clear. Please. Always, always bear this in mind where I'm concerned: that I shall never for one minute cease being for you the brotherly companion of a very unhappy man, who was your husband. And that I shall never see in you anything other than the widow of Lieutenant Vranas: a woman whom I respect and honour as I do my own syster.'

He felt that it was a very sacred moment, as if he were giving an oath, as if the tormented dead man stood by as witness. She listened to him in silence, her eyes far away. Then she raised her glance from the water and looked directly at him.

She reached out her hand.

'Thank you,' she said, blushing. 'Thank you. . . . It is very nice of you.'

When he reached the Tower the table was laid. A moment later

Kyra Christina appeared bearing triumphantly the old soup-tureen with the blue handles. She held it up on high in both her hands and came forward slowly, ritually, as if she were bearing the Holy of Holies.

'The scorpion-soup!' he cried delightedly, clapping his hands like a child.

15

THE days passed blissfully; his senses reacted to everything around him with a new intensity; and he was immensely gratified to find he could throw himself wholeheartedly into his work. In this green luminous landscape under the azure sky his shattered emotions made a swift recovery. His impressions were stamped with a new freshness; his eyes were like those of a new-born baby opening for the first time to behold a world full of beauty, strangeness, and sorrow, just emerging from the hands of its creator.

In his work he veered between extremes of enthusiasm and self-disparagement. The self-criticism to which he subjected himself was so severe, so exaggerated, as to be almost pointless at times. But he was fond of this inner taskmaster of his, who would bring him down to earth so brutally whenever his fancy began to soar too high. His judgement thus became sharpened and harsher; and when he selected five of his latest paintings and sent them to Athens he was satisfied that they were works of sincerity and self-assurance. He sent them to a journalist friend, asking him to have them hung in an exhibition of *Free Painters* which was being organized at the Zappeion Hall by a group of young artists who, like himself, had just returned from the war and were still influenced by a spirit of revolt against the academic principles of their pre-war teachers at the Polytechnic.

In Athens the exhibition was awaited with impatience as an artistic event that would set the seal of peace on Athenian intellectual life after nearly ten consecutive years of war. It was given excellent publicity and the Press was already full of notices and snippets of information referring to the provocative technique of the painters, to the maturity of their talent, and so on.

He heard of all this in a gossipy letter from his journalist friend, who was full of exaggerated enthusiasm for his works and enclosed all the Press cuttings. The bulging envelope was brought to him by a group of students who had arrived from the capital to spend the summer at their native village of Megalohori.

Among the students was Menos, the only son of Daphnis, the factory-owner. Menos had been reading law for six years, but instead of a degree he had so far succeded only in acquiring a fiancée. She was also a law student: a rather attractive girl with ostentatiously modern manners. They were accompanied by a medical student, a cousin of

Menos, and a chemistry student. They formed a noisy little group which soon began to scandalize the inhabitants of Megalohori, filling them with dismay at the startling news they brought from the capital. It seemed as though these young people were bent on turning the world upside down; they believed the established order to be dying, if not dead, and regarded such institutions as the family, religion, marriage, property, to say nothing of the capitalist system and the ideal of nationhood, to be ready for consignment to the scrap-heap.

A row started up immediately between Menos and his parents about the girl, whom they refused to have foisted on them. They tried to save appearances by making arrangements for her to sleep in the house of some relatives, thus hoping to silence gossiping tongues. But Menos would have none of it; he announced categorically that if she was not allowed to stay in the parental home he would leave at once. And that, he added, would be the last his parents would ever see of him.

Mr. Daphnis nearly had a stroke. That his only son should speak to him in such a fashion—what was the world coming to! But since his wife had accepted the situation there was little he could do but resign himself to the inevitable and let the girl—she was called Mina— settle down comfortably in his house as his son's official girl friend. So their protests had to be toned down, and Menos's mother, effecting a quick turn about, lost no time in expatiating on the qualities of the new generation. How fortunate it was, she declared, that it bore so little resemblance to her own generation, which she likened to an over-ripe plum about to drop from the sagging branch. There was a great deal of talk about outdated ideas being swept away in the whirl- wind of war and of an imminent change in the basic laws governing society. Poor Mrs. Daphnis repeated these catch words until she gradually came to accept them, just as she had come to accept the girl's presence in her house. The same eventually happened where Mr. Daphnis was concerned. He had no alternative; and in order not to seem to have been forced into capitulation he soon followed in his wife's footsteps and would be heard discoursing at length, during card-playing sessions at the club, on the progressive qualities of the new generation.

'Ah, youth, my friend! Youth! It has its rights too, after all. Eh? That's how it is, isn't it? The wheels go round. And who can stop them?'

He even went so far as to accept a cigarette from the packet that Menos had the audacity to open in his presence—and not only to open the packet but actually to smoke one, under his very nose. The nose of the established order itself.

The little group certainly did its best to shock the villagers. They began with mixed bathing, the students swimming with Mina off the jetty on which the café was situated, with the whole village gaping. The girl's two-piece bathing-dress was a sensation. They would form a circle in the sea and Mina would scramble like a cat on to their shoulders. Carrying her aloft triumphantly, the cortège would then stagger along until the pyramid of bodies suddenly collapsed and Mina would dive head first into the water, to the accompaniment of loud cheers.

At first the village was beside itself with the shamelessness of such behaviour, and the inhabitants would watch their antics with raised eyebrows. Hooligans made loud comments on various aspects of Mina's anatomy. Old women made the sign of the cross.

'It's these people, these high and mighty people from the capital, with all their learning and education, who'll bring the world to an end!' cried a refugee woman, shaking her fist at the young people frolicking in the sea. 'That's why the Almighty turned the Turks into a whip, to beat us the rest of our days.'

After a while the excitement died down. Admittedly there was no hostile manifestation in front of Mr. Daphnis, who was, after all, a pretty important personage in the village. The situation was gradually accepted, and the audiences gathered to watch the aquatic exhibitions dwindled considerably. The details of Mina's anatomy, including the mole on her left thigh, had become all too familiar.

Then there was a new accession to the group. Aspasia, Mr. Spanos's daughter, joined it. She didn't actually scramble on to the students' shoulders, but she certainly went swimming with them. Loulou objected to this. In her natural modesty she took exception to the sight of Aspasia's generous breasts flopping about in her bathing-dress. Madam Evtychia grumbled: not as much as she would have liked, because of her heart. Nevertheless she grumbled. But Aspasia grumbled even more; and in the end, of course, she won. Mr. Spanos, it is true, didn't approve; but he disapproved far more strongly of grumbling. Above all, he wanted peace; and he had never yet brought himself, not even in the full ripeness of years, to get worked up over a matter of principle. So he left the women to settle matters between themselves.

His wife tried to argue on a practical basis.

'The girl's reputation will be ruined if she's involved in such shameless activities.'

Aspasia cut in with penetrating logic:

'I've got my dowry, haven't I? I can afford to turn up my nose at anyone who disapproves of me.'

Mr. and Mrs. Spanos exchanged glances. They might have been watching Columbus stand his egg on end. The elementary logic of the girl's reasoning set their consciences at rest. So they referred the matter to the doctor who was treating Mrs. Spanos at the time.

The doctor refused to take sides. Having decided that it would be a good thing for him to marry one of the two daughters of the Mayor—no matter which—he coldn't risk offending either. Had not his professional dignity been a stake he would not have minded joining the little group himself. But then what inhabitant of Megalohori would have had any faith in the diagnosis of a man who wandered naked amid the seaweed in front of the whole village? Leon Drivas was another. Such indecencies did not carry the same implication where artists were concerned.

'After all,' he said, fingering the knot of his tie, 'there's not very much difference between a painter and a music-hall artist or a strolling musician, is there?'

One day, as Leon was bathing off Portara, he saw the group of students swimming towards him. He was genuinely pleased to see them. They all lay down in a circle, basking in the sun, and the maid's boy brought them three large water-melons. They had no knife, so they broke the fruit open with their hands, eating it greedily, their faces buried in the rind.

Leon watched them delightedly. They were charming young people; they passed with ease and assurance from one subject to another, whether art, politics, religion, or sociology. They possessed, of course, the usual complacency of youth: the kind of complacency that's inspired by immature ideological fanaticism. They informed him confidentially that they were members of a Communist student organization. Menos, in fact, contributed the editorial to the *Red Student,* which circulated once a week in the university. He wrote under the pen-name of *The Flint.*

After he'd finished eating his slice of water-melon he glanced at each of his companions in turn and leant over towards Leon.'We've been wanting to talk to you privately,' he said.

'Privately?' Leon smiled.

'Yes,' he replied with a serious air, nodding his head significantly and casting his eyes furtively round the beach. 'There're traitors everywhere, you know, informers. . . . '

'Swine!' said Mina gloomily, lowering her eyes, as though to confirm Menos's words. She was lying face down on the sand, her chin cupped in her hands. Turning towards her as she spoke, Leon's gaze

unwittingly rested on the two firm young breasts, only partly concealed by her bathing-dress, pressed against the sand. Mina was without
false modesty; and she didn't in the least mind his grey eyes hovering
over her. Seeing what was happening, Menos's bourgeois instincts
immediately got the better of his advanced Communist views. He
raised one knee discreetly, and the gap between the girl's bathing-
dress and her breasts was concealed. Not unaware of the little
comedy, Leon smiled again.

'Come on, then!' he cried. 'We're alone. Only us. Just us, the sea,
and the fish. And fish don't talk.'

'The party in Athens,' Menos informed him, 'has heard of the way
you spoke about the reserve officers killed in the war, and how your
words annoyed the bourgeoisie—in other words, my father and
people like that.'

He went on to say that he and his companions had been authorized
to approach Mr. Drivas and find out whether he would like to take
part in the common struggle, provided he did so in all seriousness. His
job would be to work in the Union of Reserve Officers and form within it an Executive Commitee consisting of Communists. He would
then proceed to establish a local organization analogous to that of the
Communist Reserve Officers functioning in Athens..

'Fine,' Leon interrupted him, 'that would be fine, if I were a
Communist. But unfortunately I'm not. Dictatorship, whatever its
form, is something I detest.'

'But why?' Mina cried sorrowfully, and they all gazed at him with a
pitying air. 'You don't mean to say you support the existing order?'

Leon could not restrain his laughter at their forlorn expression. He
tried, as best he could, to explain that he was in sympathy with their
condemnation of the capitalist system and its injustices. 'But I find
myself bound,' he continued, 'to disapprove of the way Communism
is practised in Russia today. I object to the way the Communists treat
the masses, to the falsehood and demagogy which seem to constitute
one of the basic elements of their policy. I object to their vindictive
attitude towards the class system, to their philosophy, aiming at the
suppression of the individual, to their administrative methods which
are little more than the most savage form of military repression. I can,
of course, understand your enthusiasm. At your age you naturally
look at the more attractice side of the picture—its human idealism. If I
were twenty years old . . . But how can I shut my eyes to the thousand
and one questions that remain unanswered, to the thousand and one
so-called "political necessities", terrible and inhuman "necessities",
which, if put into practice, would mean nothing less than return to the
methods of the Middle Ages. There's only one way of arriving at the

truth: by acting as one does when earning one's living. By oneself. And by taking upon oneself all the responsibilities resulting from each successive truth. It is only through personal experience that one can hope to attain true knowledge, and at the same time enrich the mind and retain a clear conscience—that is to say, step by step, with the aid of each new experience. Trial and error, accompanied by pain, sorrow, and disappointment, are the only means by which we're ever likely to achieve the goal. No system of organized thought, no philosophical conclusion, is of the slightest value to a thinking man unless he can experience—and by experience I mean actually experience—all that the creator of the system or philosophy in question has himself already experienced at first hand. Take war for an example. Now that's a reality I've indeed had to confront. I had to face it—yes, face to face, and get wounded into the bargain—before I could emerge from it sufficiently well equipped to prove how utterly false the whole thing was: false in every one of its hideous aspects. In connection with war the Communist slogan is "War against war". This simply means war all over again. And the most horrible, the most cruel and the most senseless of all wars. War between men and their fellow men. What follows? The war spreads from the frontiers to the heart of the country, to every town, village, and household. And the moment a non-Communist country is engaged in hostilities with a Communist one the war once more assumes a national character. For how long is this to go on? Who knows. The prospect is certainly gloomy. But I no longer believe in the creative force of hatred, in the imposition of ideas by force.'

'You previously mentioned an example in terms of your profession, as a painter,' said the medical student, 'when you said that we only saw the attractive side of the picture. May I now cite an example in terms of my profession? D'you believe that a child can be brought into the world without a drop of the mother's blood being spilt?'

Leon smiled. 'Assuming that mother and child are to survive— presumably that's the object of the entire process of birth, isn't it?— it's surely preferable then to let nature do the work, without resorting to the aid of a midwife's forceps. Communism, you see, is the mid-wife's forceps applied to a society.'

Mina raised her eyebrows and smiled mockingly. 'Mr. Drivas believes,' she said, 'that the oligarchy—the oligarchy of wealth, I mean; the governing class, in fact—will of its own accord hand over its main defences, its privileges, and its riches, and declare: "There you are, by all means try out your system!" '

They all laughed approvingly. Leon also laughed.

'I must say, I don't see it quite that way,' he declared. 'I do, however, believe that the oligarchy you mention will surrender its defences when it finds the fortress abandoned by the garrison. The solution in my opinion does not rest with any one of the oligarchies—that is to say, with either of the two extremes. Nor can I visualize a regime protected by an iron curtain, incapable, if it's to have any hope of survival, of laying down its arms. Why not instil the spirit of justice into the conscience of the people, instead of letting the Communists impose it on them by means of democratic slogans for which they have at heart the deepest contempt? Justice cannot become the handmaiden of class warfare.'

'Each class has its own system of justice,' declared Mina sententiously. 'Why should Communism be denied its rights?'

'I'm afraid you misrepresent the issue. It seems to me that what you want is revenge, not justice. Beware of revenge—it employs a murderer's weapons.'

'Oh, come on, let's change the conversation.' Menos cut in sulkily.

They saw the schoolmistress approaching the Tower, her dark slender silhouette advancing across the sand.

'Now there's a beautiful woman for you,' declared the chemistry student enthusiastically.

Mina cast an enquiring look at Menos.

'M'mm,' he murmured, 'she's not all that famous.'

'I don't agree,' said the other medical student. 'She's the kind of woman who'd make any Athenian turn round in the street to look at her.'

The schoolmistress passed them on a level with the fence. She called across to Leon and asked if Adriani was at the Tower.

'Yes, she's in the vineyard.' He jumped up with a cat-like spring and began to walk towards her, wiping the sand off his legs. As soon as he had reached her he was overwhelmed by the scent of jasmine which seemed always to cling to her: the pure fragrant scent of jasmine opening its petals to the sun.

'There's a group of students over there,' he told her. 'Perhaps you'd like to meet them.'

'Not now, thank you.' She smiled faintly and walked on. 'Another time, perhaps.'

Leon returned to the students and offered them cigarettes. Mina was the first to take one. She tapped it several times on her thumbnail, like the most hardened smoker. 'She's a woman of great distinction,' she said generously. ''There's no denying it.'

'You know they've christened her "La Contessa" here,' said Leon. There was a note of pride in his voice. He sensed it and immediately regretted it.

'Quite rightly!' cried the boys in unison.

'Listen now,' he cried, smiling gaily, 'let's forget all about ideologies. Let's remain friends. D'you agree? To each his own faith, to each his art. I'll always be pleased to see you. You'll always be welcome at the Tower.'

'I understand. You want to go now,' said the medical student, raising an eyebrow in the direction of the Portara, through which the schoolmistress had just disappeared.

Leon fixed an eye on him for a moment and then said: 'No. My sister is there. She'll receive Mrs. Vranas. Why don't we go for a swim? Let's see if we can swim with our cigarettes alight. . . . '

'And the one whose cigarette goes out first . . . ?' asked Mina, as she got up, rubbing the sand and water-melon seed off her arms and legs. Leon noticed two cup-shaped little hollows imprinted on the sand where she had been lying.

' . . . will stand the rest a round of drinks,' Menos finished the sentence off for her.

16

ONE day Leon set up his easel in one of the village streets and began painting. It was close on midday. The sunlight flowed like molten lava down the steep winding lane; it lip up the red-brick tiles of the roofs, turning them to the colour of flame. The white-washed walls of the little houses threw off a dazzling glare, and the whole neighbourhood seemed to be alive with the incessant throb of the cicadas. The street was empty, and the vine-leaves hung motionless from the trellises. Black and yellow striped hornets burrowed greedily into the hollow half-eaten grapes. The August sun beat down on the marble slabs with the violence of a hammer striking the anvil, so that one could almost imagine the smell of stone-chippings scattering in showers across the pavement under the shock of the blow.

But this solitude, so necessary to him for his work, did not last long. Spotted by a little boy, the alarm was quickly sounded; and he was soon surrounded by children and old women scuttling out of courtyards and passageways. From past experience he knew that in these circumstances there was no other solution but ignoble retreat. So he folded his easel and handed it, along with his paints and brushes, to a little boy, instructing him to take them back to the house. He then went down to the café on the sea-front. Seated by the wooden doorway, under the large awning, he found Xynellis playing backgammon with Menos. The schoolmaster, who was anxious to bring the game to an end, kept rattling the dice on the board in order to draw the waiter's attention. It was time to offer his opponent a drink—a confession of defeat.

'I haven't seen you for days,' he lamented to Leon. 'Where have you been?' And he made a sweeping gesture of the arm, embracing the sea and mountains.

'I work a lot, I read very little, I go swimming and rowing, and then, you know, I climb trees. What about you?'

The schoolmaster smiled with an air of modesty. 'I give private lessons to students who failed in the June examinations. As for the rest of the time? I read the papers and periodicals and play backgammon.'

Leon noticed the edge of a red paper-back peeping out of his pocket. He stretched out his hand. 'May I?'

'Of course.'

It was a Communist brochure. Leon cast one glance at it and gave it back to him.

'Are you a Communist?'

The schoolmaster looked round nervously. 'Well. . . one likes to keep up with things, doesn't one? Now Mr. Menos over there... But a civil servant, as you know, can never be anything else but a civil servant.'

'I don't agree,' said Leon. 'First and foremost one must be a physical entity. That gives one a sense of equilibrium and protects one from all kinds of psychological aberrations. . . . '

The doctor was seen approaching the jetty. In spite of the heat he was dressed up as though he were going to a reception: in a suit, with collar and tie.

'You'd better change the conversation,' said Menos. 'He's a reactionary. You know the type, ready for anything. . . . I think I'll be off now.' He got up and slouched away, his hands in his pockets.

The schoolmaster managed to slip the book quickly into his pocket.

The doctor greeted them and sat down.

'Tell me, Mr. Xynellis,' said Leon, as though resuming an interrupted conversation, 'do you like poetry?'

'Do I like poetry?' One had the impression that he was slavering. 'The poet . . . but the poet is the darling of the gods. A privileged being. Isn't that so? And you, do you also like poetry?'

'I like poetry, but I detest poems. In my opinion it's time people stopped writing poems in order to give poetry a chance.'

Xynellis's little eyes opened wide behind his spectacles. Was he being made fun of ? he wondered.

The doctor pecked at a slice of tomato from the plate of little titbits served with the ouzo. 'Exactly,' he said. 'Like the English-woman in Rhoidis, who liked garlic sauce without garlic.'

'Exactly,' repeated Leon, jumping up suddenly. He began to wave his arms and call out to a fisherman who was approaching the shore in his boat. It was Letsas, a fisherman from Moskonisi, who often lent Leon his boat and fishing-tackle. When he had reached them Leon offered him a *raki* and then went off in the boat. It was called the *Swallow*: a small light craft, painted red and yellow, and very swift.

He took the oars, the anchor, and the hook for spearing sea-urchins from the fisherman. 'I'm going to look for sea-urchins,' he called out. 'Would you like to join me, Mr. Xynellis? We can also swim off the boat. I don't suggest the doctor's coming. He's too smartly dressed. . . . '

The schoolmaster thanked him profusely, but refused. In this heat! He'd be certain to get a headache and be sick. The only water he ever entered was that of a Turkish bath. And, anyway, he didn't know how to swim.

Leon laughed loudly. He took off his skirt and rowed out into the open. He laughed at the idea of a 'poet' preferring a Turkish bath to the sea. No doubt the schoolmaster was capable of extolling them both very adequately in verse. He wondered what Xynellis would look like without his clothes on: the knobbly elbows, the hairy white-skinned shanks, and the pustular face with the flapping ears, all dazzled by the sun, beside the shimmering sea.

He rowed naked to the waist, bending back and forth, to the steady rhythm of the dipping oars. Occasionally he glanced over his shoulder at the little courtyard which could be seen disappearing in the distance, beyond the long tapering line of the boat's wash. When he got farther out he took off the rest of his clothes, remaining only in his bathing-dress. The light breeze set up by movement of the boat blew around him. The sea was dead calm, aquamarine in colour, reflecting huge patches of sunlight. The water dripped off the oars, drenched in light, glistening like silver. Tiny miniature whirlpools kept forming where the blades dipped, and spread across the surface in ever widening spirals, like blue streamers speckling the sea. This was indeed the 'measureless laughter of the sea.' It reminded him of the smile of a girl. Aspasia smiled like that. He wanted to sing—gaily, exultantly. He remembered a song he had heard from some fishermen from Cesme. They sang it as they bent over their oars. He tried to sing it too, and he felt happier.

> *'This poor cockleshell of ours*
> *Here today, tomorrow there.'*

The boat sped on, the oars beating time. He was approaching the shallow waters of the Sentinel; the sea was dotted with rocks covered in seaweed and thick with sea-urchins—so many that one tired of catching them. The water was getting shallower as the boat skimmed over the sandy sea-bed. Drifting past a dark patch of seaweed, he reached the pebbly shore of the Sentinel. Thousands of years ago great rocks had crashed down from the cliffs above; most of them lay submerged; others rose above water, in a long line, like an array of formidable medieval bastions. The bases of others had been whittled away, eroded by the ceaseless lapping of the waves, with the water gurgling and swishing in the crevices, nibbling away mercilessly at the foundations.

As he rowed he sang:

'The sea eats the mountains, mountains eat the lions,
And the pretty girls devour all the lads.'

For the first time he realized the uncanny significance of the words.

The crannies of the rocks were black with sea-urchins: some huddled together, like balls of wool; others scattered about singly, their little round teeth nibbling at the green slime. Below the surface of the water they looked very black, but the reflections of sunlight cast a faint bluish tint on their spines which kept revolving like the spokes on a wheel as they moved about the rock.

Laying down the oars, he spread out the nest and began to prise the sea-urchins out of their hiding-places with the aid of a prong, pausing every few minutes to lift them out of the sea. But it was even more difficult to extricate them from the meshes of the net than to detach them from the rock. He caught masses—the boat was filled with them; but still he went on, singing all the time.

'And the pretty girls devour all the lads.'

He was thinking of Stratis Vranas's dark sallow face when he suddenly heard the plop of a stone. It landed just in front of him. Straightening his back, he swore angrily, blaspheming as though he were back in the barrack-room. He shaded his eyes with his hand and gazed up towards the heights of the Sentinel. There was no sign of the villain who had the audacity to throw the stone at him. Just as he was about to stoop down to catch another sea-urchin, he heard a tinkle of mocking laughter coming from the Gudgeon's mouth. Swivelling round, he saw two heads, one fair, the other dark, peeping over the top of a rock. Adriani was laughing delightedly, and Sappho's eyes were smiling.

'You certainly fooled me!' he cried, wagging a finger at them. 'I thought it was some beastly little ruffian. . . . '

"We were here all the time,' said Adriani, 'and we now want to protest against the words of your song. Girls don't "devour" young men. Imagine having an "appetite" for such things. Sea-urchins, on the other hand . . . '

'You needn't get on your high horse. The song refers to "pretty" girls.'

'What compliments! From an officer too!' retorted Adriani, emerging from their hiding-place. Her black bathing-dress and cap set off the almost rose-petal quality of her skin.

'Coming for a swim?' she called out.

'Provided the mermaids of the Sentinel grant me permission.'

She leant over and whispered something in Sappho's ear. Sappho shrugged her shoulders.

'The mermaids of the Sentinel,' declared Adriani, 'have decided to grant permission to the impudent Triton to swim off their beach.'

He cast anchor and seized a large conch full of holes which was lying in the stern. It was the shell which Letsas always blew on when he returned from a fishing expedition in order to warn the fishmongers and loafers in the harbour that he was bringing back a large catch.

Taking up a theatrical pose, Leon announced in stentorian tones: 'A Triton, indeed I am. And a very well-brought-up one too. My conch is a most ancient one, and after I've blown three times on it I shall plunge into the brine. Of course, if the mermaids of the Sentinel are afraid . . . '

He raised the conch to his mouth with a great flourish and blew three times on it.

'Boo! Boo! Boo! '

At the sound of the third blast there were squeals of mock terror and consternation, followed by a splash as the girls flopped into the water.

Sappho swam straight for the open sea with wide ample strokes, her head rising and dipping rhythmically; each time she raised it the water seemed to caress her cheek. She also was wearing a black bathing-dress, and her neck and back looked as if they were chiselled out of marble. One of her arms emerged regularly out of the water, as she swam with steady rhythmic strokes.

Adriani followed part of the way; then she gave up. 'I think I'll go back and look after the sea-urchins,' she cried, painting for breath. 'You two are capable of swimming to Turkey.'

Leon laughed and continued swimming outwards. The sea was marvellous. He swam in a line parallel to Sappho, a distance of about ten yards separating them.

'Further?' he called out enquiringly.

Her movements were relaxed, effortless, showing no sign of weariness. 'Yes, further,' and she nodded, looking in his direction.

He noticed her smile; her eyes were half shut, her cheek resting on her water. But he knew she wasn't smiling at him. It was the exhilarating effect of the sea that made her smile in this way.

'Won't you get tired? he cried. 'We're pretty far out, you know!'

'I can swim like this for hours.'

There wasn't the faintest suspicion of breathlessness in her voice. But he was afraid lest she should tax her strength in an attempt to prove to him, and to herself, that she could indeed go on indefinitely.

'Let's go back, please!' he cried. 'Adriani will be getting anxious.'

'All right.' She turned back with a grateful sinuous wriggle, which reminded him of a fish. He followed suit, making for the boat, while she swam towards the Gudgeon's mouth, where Adriani was vaguely looking for crabs. She had thrown off her cap and her hair glistened in the sun as though it were spangled with gold.

Sappho was now floating on her back. Her wet bathing-dress clung to her flesh. Only her hands moved: like two oars in unison. Tiny wavelets rippled over the tips of her fingers, spreading to the dark patch under her armpits, playing round her breasts, which just showed above water.

There was an anxious look in his eyes as he raised them towards the bosky heights above the beach. He didn't want anyone to see her: not as he had seen her. And he had a feeling that she was being watched, that a pair of eyes were gazing down furtively at her from above. It seemed to him that he had detected some kind of movement, as though the branches of a shrub had been hurriedly parted and something white, probably a face, had appeared between them.

'Why don't you dry off in the sun where you undressed? I'll go to the boat. And when I've dressed there'll be a roll-call.'

'You're a very well-brought-up Triton, aren't you?' declared Adriani. 'A real gentleman Triton.'

Leon got into the boat, put on his shoes, and set out to climb the hill. He tried to make as little noise as possible. It was not long before he came upon the figure of a little man lying on his back in the shade of a fig tree. His hands, with fingers interlocked, were placed behind his head as a rest, and from under his hat, which covered his face, came the sound of snoring.

Standing above the recumbent figure, Leon suddenly stooped down and snatched the hat off the man's face, which was now revealed to be that of Mr. Yanni. The snoring, after continuing for a few seconds, was followed by all the signs of a slow painful awakening caused by the sudden removal of the hat. First one little colourless eye was opened, then another: as though the process of waking up was to be carried out in instalments. The face was seared with wrinkles. These were indeed so numerous that it was impossible to tell whether their tortous creasings and uncreasings were intended to express any particular set of emotions. Finally he yawned and made the sign of the cross over his lips three times in order to prevent the devil from entering his body through the mouth.

'Ai-ai-ai! What's this? Mr. Drivas! Where've you come from? What a start you gave me.'

Flinging the hat across at him, Leon said: 'Yes, it's me. Is there anything strange about that?'

Mr Yanni caught the hat in mid-air and sat up, trying rather feebly to laugh. He was making an attempt to pass the matter off with an air of indifference. 'I found a shady spot up here,' he said, 'and I dropped off.'

'Just fancy that. And I imagined you were chasing butterflies.'

Mr. Yanni hardly knew where to put his face. In a futile attempt to behave naturally he took out an old cigarette tin filled with smuggled tobacco. All the wrinkles of his face were taken up in the effort to give an impression of a man absorbed in rolling a cigarette. But the acute anxiety which his features depicted destroyed the effect. He looked far more like a man who knew he was 'in for it'. Leon noticed this, and his anger suddenly vanished. It was all he could do not to laugh.

As he was about to leave, he said: 'Look here, the shade of this fig tree is very oppressive. It can't be good for you. Particularly at your age. You hadn't thought of that? You'd better listen to me. I shouldn't come up here for a snooze again if I were you. I'm telling you this for your own good. You'd better think of your health.'

He clambered down to the beach, threw off his shoes, and lay flat on his stomach in the stern of the boat. His mind began to wander. The successive images suddenly resolved themselves into one. His lips were roaming feverishly over the naked flesh of her back and arms. He imagined his fingers playing with her wet hair. Then he stirred. He felt a buzzing in his ears. Perhaps some water had got in while he was swimming. He remembered what they used to do when they were children. He took a dry pebble and placed it against his ear—how deliciuosly warm it felt! He then tapped it lightly with another stone. Having completed this little operation, he lay down again, cupping his chin in his hands. But again he felt his senses quickening. It was that vision of Sappho—Sappho floating towards the shore, while he watched and bided his time, waiting to feast his eyes on her naked body as she came out of the sea. Sappho standing erect, her firm slender limbs bathed in sunlight, dripping with sea-water, glistening like one of those smooth wet pebbles; then she bounded off, leaping with small agile steps from rock to rock.

He could hear the scratching sound of the sea-urchins trying to disentangle their spines. One of his legs dangled over the side of the boat, and the water lapped round his heel. He could see the coloured bands painted round the boat reflected in the shallow water, wriggling sinuously like water-snakes trying vainly to embrace one another. He was aware that his feeling of acute distress was the direct result of having given way, having surrendered to the unlawful desire to gaze on Sappho's body in a state of semi-nudity. Perhaps the words 'given way' and 'surrendered' were not the most apt, because he had in fact been waiting, deliberately, for the moment when she would come out of the sea. Did the same apply to his ascent of the cliff in order to catch Mr. Yanni? At which of the two girls, he wondered, had the dirty old man's lascivious stare been directed? All the most unsavoury aspects of harem life were probably contained in that poor wretch's soul: the soul of the eunuch of the Anatolian harem whose job it was to see that not a single particle of female flesh was ever exposed to the eyes of any man other than their owner. Wasn't it the brother's obligation to avenge the wrong done to his sister, to fulfil all those other old-fashioned notions of honour? But then what was Sappho to him? Wasn't she like a sister? She was the wife of Vranas, his dead friend. But she was also an extremely pretty young woman of twenty-two. And he not only knew this, he felt it with the whole of his being. So there it was. He had now seen her in the full apotheosis of her beauty, against a background of sea and sunshine.

The light playing on the water kept changing the pale colours of the reflected bands painted round the boat, as though gentle brush-strokes were moving across the surface of the sea in a tireless uninterrupted rhythm.

Certainly she had a very unusal, utterly individual way of holding herself, of swaying as she walked. Indeed, even when she was seated, there was the same wavy quality about the outline. He tried to analyse the reason—anatomically; and decided that it was probably due to some special formation of the spine: somewhere in the vertebrae of the waistline, above the hip-bone. It was like the drooping branch of a tree: an apple tree, perhaps. Obviously she would never surrender her body easily. Perhaps the whole aura of desirability in which she was enveloped was the natural consequence of the unusual formation of a couple of spinal vertebrae. Nonsense. These were details of no importance. The important thing was that a luminous aura, like that of an exploding star, did definitely cling to her.

He shifted his position slightly and noticed a small crab crawling over the pebbles by the water's edge. Its progress was cautious, faintly comical; it looked like someone walking on high heels. Reaching the flat summit of a stone covered with slime, it dug its claws into the soft green coating. Suddenly the keel of the boat bumped noisily on the pebble of the sea-bed. The crab instantly took fright and disappeared into the water.

It was astounding, wasn't it, that a deformed cripple, like Vranas's child, with its howling slavering mouth, its distended belly, and atrophied limbs, for ever grovelling in its own excrement, should be

151

the offspring of such a paragon? How was it possible? How? It suddenly struck him that he could almost smell the fetid breath of innumerable sighs: the sighs of every man and boy in the village gazing on the tragic mother with hungry eyes. He could see them, sweating, panting, dribbling, in pursuit of their vain unsatisfied longings. What unjust god had planted the seed of his own terrible frustration in their cursed souls? Why didn't they get married and produce families? Then it would be lawful for them to taste of the forbidden fruit. Unless, of course, they chose to cut it open with the assassin's knife. An image rose up before him of all these ravening males forming a circle round her, their eyes inflamed, like Xynellis's, their hands damp and sweaty, their tongues hanging out of their dreams; all of them cursing their terrible desire, reducing it at last to a little piece of frothing saliva which they would have liked to spit in her face. He realized then what an unbounded hatred she must feel for these miserable creatures. And he couldn't blame her for taking her revenge on them by parading her beauty, her youth, her unconquerable feminity, under their very noses, while their lascivious longings distorted their features and the ugly defamatory epithets formed on their contorted lips. And so she passed on, a vision of sea and sunlight, with the fragrance of flowers, of flowers in full bloom, clinging to her.

Fine. This was all very well. But what of himself? What was his rôle in all this tragi-comedy of 'Penelope without a loom'? Was he no better than the rest? Just one among the throng of village suitors? A frustrated maniac, a victim of bucolic lust and provincial sex starvation? 'Each of us finds his erotic release in his own way,' he had once told Xynellis. The schoolmaster's 'way' probably led to the sublimation of desire in slander and verse; Mr. Yanni's in furtive spying; his own . . . ? Perhaps it was not so very different to Mr. Yanni's 'way', after all. For all his moral and ethical pretensions, was he no more than just another Mr. Yanni, a repressed satyr, a Peeping Tom, with swollen eyes starting out of their sockets like a snail's? Only a few minutes ago had not their furtive gaze been directed at the nipples of her breasts, erect, pointing to the sky, as she floated towards the shore. In heaven's name, what difference was there between him and that dirty old man? He was filled with self-disgust; the pain of it seemed to eat into his flesh. So that was it. He and Mr. Yanni. Identical twins. Remarkably unclean twins. One spirit in two bodies. Suddenly Papadiamandis's story, *Dream at Sea,* began to unfold before his imagination. The shame, the disgusting shame of it. *Dream at Sea!* And then his memory performed one of those unpredictable somersaults, concentrating on the most irrelevant details. He remembered. It was the last time he'd read a story of Papadiamandis's to Vranas before his mind began to wander.

'Papadiamandis?' the stricken man had said blinking his eyes restlessly. 'As though I don't know him. He was here only a short time ago.... "How are you?" he asked. "What am I to do?" I replied. "It's Fate ... " But the workings of Fate are so slow sometimes.'

It was from that moment that Vranas had gone into a delirium. Then one day his eyes stopped blinking, his lips no longer quivered and the vein in his neck ceased to throb. He was dead. From the end of his bed they removed the chart with the crazy zig-zag squiggles, indicating the course of his temperature which would never be taken again. On the commode beside his bed stood a glass with a drop of water which he'd not had time to drink before he died. Later on the sun shone through the window and the light was reflected in the glass. An insignificant detail, which only now seemed to assume any importance in his imagination, but it had made a powerful impression on him at the time. The grief caused by the death of his friend, the consequent emptiness of the room had suddenly seemed to be intensified, spotlighted on that glass of water on the commode.

Adriani's cheerful voice roused him.

'Hi, you there on the *Swallow!* What's happened to the poor old Triton? Has he gone to sleep or have the sea-urchins eaten him up?'

Sappho laughed. It was a murmuring laugh, like the ebb and flow of rippling waves on the sea.

'I'm drunk with sun,' he said, getting up.

His head felt muzzy, as though he'd been drinking a lot of wine. He dressed quickly, raised the anchor and steered the boat towards the Gudgeon's mouth. He then blew three times on the conch.

'Splendid,' he said. 'Come on, jump in.'

He fixed the hook in a little crevice of the rock. First Adriani jumped in and sat in the stern, followed by Sappho. The boat was still rocking from the impact of Adriani's leap when Sappho, in order to avoid losing her balance, found herself leaning against Leon's back and instinctively grabbing hold of his shirt to steady herself. For a moment he felt her nails dig into the flesh of his back. 'Now it'll always bear the print of her fingertips,' he thought. In his crouching position her skirt brushed against his face and he felt the coolness of the silk hem on his burning cheek. The calf of her leg touched his hair, just above the ear. He inhaled the scent of her fresh young body with its faint hint of jasmine: a burning aromatic fragrance which vanished as quickly as it had come.

He rowed slowly, truly intoxicated, immersed in his thoughts.

'Why don't you sing?' asked his sister, raising her head. She'd been leaning over the side of the boat, trailing her hand in the water. 'What a face! You look . . . as though you'd just swallowed a sea-urchin!'

'I'm drunk with the sun,' he justified himself. 'I sat too long without a hat. Well, madam, what kind of song would you like?'

'Anything. A folksong. D'you know,' she turned to Sappho, 'he's got an immense repertory of island songs.'

'It's true,' he agreed. 'An immense repertory. I mean it. All with their scores too. Music and words—like body and soul, they're inseparable. I don't understand why Politis didn't devote more attention to them.'

'Sing one to me, Leon,' begged his sister.

He smiled at her, stopped to think a moment, and then began to sing in his deep bass:

> *'Rosy cheeks and violet-coloured eyes,*
> *To you the nightingales in the thickets sing,*
> *To your fair hair and blue eyes,*
> *With two sword-blades for eyebrows.'*

'Lovely! Now sing one for Sappho.'

'For Madam Sappho. . . ? I wonder what song would suit her? I doubt if I've got one dedicated to a pair of golden eyes. But I'll try.'

He began to sing. Like all island songs it was a melancholy rather sensual tune.

> *'With your lowered glance you wound me,*
> *Don't look at me sweetly, you'll drive me mad.*
> *Your eyelashes close,*
>   *And I cannot go my way.'*

'Thank you,' she said, smiling with her magical golden eyes. Terrified, he refused to meet their glance.

The three of them spent the whole afternoon together and when Sappho left, Leon felt a sense of terrible emptiness. It was like the indefinable melancholy which follows the moment of awakening from a vivid dream, while one's still trying vainly to recapture the happiness of the fleeting vision. She left as it was getting dark and her black dress merged into the shadows of the vineyard. She might have been a symbol of daylight itself, for daylight had now departed from the house and the seashore below. With her departure also his spirits dropped, and that strange feeling of the ecstasy of living, which he had experienced in her company, now eluded him.

So he withdrew into himself, anxious to reason with his inner being, posing himself a mass of disturbing questions in his usual merciless way: 'Am I perhaps in love with her?' He then tempered it with a less categoric form: 'Am I perhaps *beginning* to fall in love with her?' Again, as though in reply to his question, he heard the suppressed cackle of cruel laughter coming from his friend the Fool. It was a very bitter laugh.

Had not Xynellis asked him the same question at the Mayor's house that day? On that occasion he had replied with the same chuckle. It was remarkable that the schoolmaster should have actually asked him a question that he hadn't even dared to formulate, let alone put to himself. It was indeed a laughing matter—Xynellis assuming the rôle of his conscience. Or more likely his conscience assuming Xynellis's features in order to lecture him all the more effectively. A schoolmaster's conscience with thick-lensed spectacles and heavy-lidded eyes. Yes, a schoolmaster's conscience, with a long thin neck growing longer every minute, like a fireman's hose, bringing the face ever nearer to his, until the eyes were on a level with his own and able to peer into his soul through that pair of thick-lensed glasses.

'Do you love her?'

'And do you?'

This train of thought finally began to unnerve him. What was he driving at? To fascinate—even if only in a platonic sense—the woman who'd been Vranas's wife? The idea filled him with horror and disgust. He would never dare look at his face in the mirror again. For he was profoundly vain where his sense of self-respect was concerned; it was his main prop in life.

He rubbed one hand across his forehead.

He must try to keep calm. Looking back, there was no cause for panic. After all, he'd made his position crystal-clear to her down there on the beath at the Sentinel. 'I shall never be more to you than the friend of your dead husband.' The words had been simple, direct, full of sincerity. And she had looked at him straight in the eyes, pleased, trusting, and obviously moved, as she said: 'Thank you.' A little earlier he had spoken to her in terms of scorn and loathing of the village Romeos. So far so good. Fear of being laughed at was the most efficient watchdog one could have for the protection of one's self-respect. There was therefore nothing to worry about. His behaviour had been perfectly normal. It was natural for a man to air his graces in the presence of an attractive woman. Sometimes he magnified his faults in order to be all the more prepared for the pitfalls they were likely to present. The same thing applied to women in the presence of men: it was something quite natural and spontaneous, without any special significance.

He sat down beside the window in his room high up in the house, his hands on the wooden rail, and gazed out at the expanse of burnished sea, which still mirrored the splendours of the recent sunset. Two fishing-boats poked their way slowly out of the harbour, their oars dipping lazily in the water which had now turned to the colour of molten gold.

It was as though the colour of her eyes was reflected in those still waters, he thought.

'Leon,' he heard his sister's voice, as she crept quietly into the room and leant against him. He felt the refreshing coolness of her arm against the back of his neck.

'Listen,' she said, 'dinner's ready. What d'you say to eating nice and early tonight?'

'Not a bad idea,' he replied. 'We can go out in the boat afterwards. The stars will be mirrored in the sea. The perfect poet would be able to cast his net and draw in a huge catch of stars.'

'If you intended going out in the boat why didn't you say so before?' Adriani scolded. 'We could have arranged to take Sappho with us.'

'Sappho!' he exclaimed almost angrily, 'We could, I should have thought, have gone out for a row without her for once, couldn't we?'

He tried to read the expression on her face in the dim light, as she said: 'Go on with you! One would think you had something against her. After all, it's not her fault we had war with the Turks and your friend got killed.'

Her face was resting on his shoulder, and he stroked her cheek. 'I've got nothing against her,' he said quietly.

'And why should you?' she said with a great show of feeling. 'She's a most remarkable woman, I assure you. And terribly unhappy. Imagine. Her whole life wrecked—at her age!'

'I wouldn't take it quite so tragically,' he cut in. 'She could very well get married again.'

'And the child? D'you forget the existence of that living cross she's got to bear, and always will have to bear? Who'd want to—'

'Don't say that,' he interrupted with a touch of irony. 'She's very pretty and men are generally capable of being very stupid where such women are concerned.'

'She's really lovely, isn't she?' Adriani cried enthusiastically. 'Everything about her is perfect. You saw her in her bathing-dress, didn't you?'

'I did indeed,' he replied; 'a veritable Venus Anadiomene. You know, it made me think of a biblical composition one could paint....'

He told her about the picture of Salome and her famous dance, which she'd performed with every nerve and fibre and muscle of her body. He went on: 'I'd have her standing erect, ready to pounce, like a hungry serpent at high noon, with gold hypnotic eyes. In front of her there'd be a silent motionless sea, but below its surface violent storms would be lying in wait, ready to be released in all their fury. The air would be yellowish, sulphurous....'

Later, when he went to bed, he again asked himself: 'Ought I to stop seeing her?'

No. Categorically no. It would not only be an act of cowardice but an admission that he was in love with her and therefore in danger. Actually he was not. He had sufficient confidence in his sense of self-respect, which had always stood him in good stead in the delicate business of adjusting a standard of moral behaviour to the ups and downs of everyday life. The lover of Vranas's wife? No. That was impossible. He was not cut out for such a contemptible rôle.

He slept badly that night. Towards dawn he had a dream; but he couldn't be certain whether it really was a dream, or a vision— if a vision, it had been so alive, so intensely perceived, as to possess all the elements of reality. His mind was still obsessed by it when he got up in the morning.

The setting of the vision was the shallow pebbly shore beneath the Sentinel. Sappho was swimming oblivious, unaware of being secretly watched. She was completely naked (he wondered how he could have acquired such an intimate knowledge of every little detail of that marvellous body). She was playing by the water's edge, throwing pebbles in the sea, leaping gracefully—she gave the impression of skimming—from rock to rock. Huddled behind one of these rocks, he sat and watched; there was such concentrated intensity in his stare that he might almost have been possessing her visually. His entire body seemed to consist of a huge staring eye, a hungry lascivious eye. He was aware of a sense of terrible shame, of a hopeless frustration. She was standing still now, and the vision became fixed, static. It was a painting, a completed composition. And she was at the centre of it, at the heart, with her terrible eyes, glorious in her nakedness, erect, menacing, like a snake rearing its head. Then she was also Salome, no longer dancing, standing on the edge of the sluggish sea: the calm before the storm. A hot wind blew across the bilious-coloured sky, and the air was malodorous with sulphur fumes. It was indeed Salome, carrying the Baptist's head on a salver. He felt the whole of his attention riveted on that head. The face was somehow familiar. He had seen it somewhere, and he knew those features. . . . Suddenly he uttered a terrible scream, and he felt an icy wind freezing every particle of his body. The Baptist's face was pale, his skin transparent and yellow like parchment. Beneath the skin the bone-structure of the thin nose was visible. The eyebrows were thick, like a heavy brush-stroke drawn across the whole length of the forehead with printer's ink. One of the Baptist's eyes opened slowly. The other remained shut. He knew that this was being done in order that he might focus his attention on the black pupil of the open eye, which looked like a bead of jet. So that he should recognize it. When the eye was fully open it stayed staring at him fixedly. Then, while the rest of the features remained motionless, a little nerve began to quiver round the mouth: to tremble ever faster under the transparent skin, like the needle of a stopwatch.

17

THE decision to blow up the wreck of the sunken ship had been taken. Sismanoglou went ahead with all the arrangements and, as he wanted to make a little ceremony of the occasion, he invited all those who'd been at the Mayor's dinner party, together with a few other officials and notables, including the Customs officer, the gendarmerie lieutenant, and Mr. Daphnis, the factory-owner. It was to be quite an informal affair. The boats would be ready early in the morning and they would go in them to the cove where the wreck lay submerged. The waters would be blessed by the priest as a propitiatory measure, and then the fuse would be set. It was to be quite an event.

The sun hadn't yet risen when most of the party gathered on the jetty to drink coffee. There was quite a hum of activity. Four large boats, freshly spruced for the occasion, were moored by the wooden jetty, rocking jauntily on the water. Sismanoglou had ordered the boatmen to decorate the boats with sky-blue bunting. He was always moved at the sight of the national colours. It reminded him of the good old days: especially of the day the Greek warships anchored off the quay in the Gulf of Smyrna and the Greek soldiers and evzones poured out in the face of a hail of Turkish salvoes. Of course, all that was past history. Sometimes, however, it seemed as if it were only yesterday. Thinking of it all now, after the shame and catastrophe of 1922, was pretty painful. But how could one forget? He was haunted by the memory of all those soldiers disembarking, four by four, down the companion ladders. The disembarkation went on for days. Men, beasts, ammunition. It was on the very first day that he'd seen his chance, for he had a good eye for profit whenever the occasion offered. He would supply the army. There were thousands and thousands of troops. How he used to cheer them, weeping for joy. It was the fulfilment of a centuries-old dream. And while he cheered and wept he also counted the heads. Heavens, how many there were to care for! They might be soldiers, but they were also mouths to feed. So he got down to it. In no time he'd penetrated the inner sanctum of G.H.Q. and was talking to divisional commanders and corps commanders; he met all the leading personalities; he gave parties; he made promises all round; he drank gallons of beer and ate mountains of those spicy Smyrniot titbits which they served with the drinks. He was all things to all men, dining in the houses of gourmets, drinking in the company of tipsters, and flirting with pretty girls at parties. Not ungenerous by nature, he often gave the pretty girls little presents. He was in the swim. One job led to another. He dealt with army corps, army formations: with all the various army services, in fact. And then he also dealt with all the important wholesale merchants in the city. In a twinkling he'd mastered the rules and regulations, the anomalies and perversities of Greek currency, so admirably designed by a bunch of clever Athenian lawyers to enable any poor wretch to wriggle out of a difficulty of almost any description.

His master stroke, however, was the affair of the rotten cod-fish. How he fixed the commissariat, got the fish delivered, and cashed the proceeds was a lesson in astute business dealing. The result of it all was an enormous warehouse stinking of rotten fish for a radius of more than a hundred yards. Had the army eaten the fish there'd have been little left for the Turks to do but to throw down their arms to go home. The Greek army would have ceased to exist. A special committee—a 'Hygiene Committee', they called it—was formed to investigate the case. It passed a resolution that the fish was in fact rotten. Then another committee was formed to witness the actual destruction of the fish and issue a warrant attesting to the 'said destruction'. The entire contents of the warehouse had to be removed, loaded on barges, and thrown into the sea at a specified distance from the quay. The job of jettisoning the fish was then put out on tender: a pure mockery of a tender, however, for the contractor who got it turned out to be none other than Sismanoglou himself. He was therefore paid all over again to cast a mountain of putrefying cod-fish into the Gulf of Smyrna. Unbelievable as it may seem, the members of the committee 'for the destruction of the said material' bothered to witness only the completion of half the operation and then repaired to Clonarides Café where they spent the rest of the morning, drinking coffee and gossiping. Only half the fish thus found its way to the bottom of the sea; the other half was re-sold to the committee.

So the money simply poured in. Millions of it. The sacks of new bank-notes arriving from Athens seemed to have a way of making straight for his coffers. Then the lean years followed. Venizelos fell from power; the Royalists came in, and ruined Greece. The curtain was run down on all his little 'enterprises'. He'd also had to abandon a mass of supplies at Kutaja and Eski-Sechir which fell straight into the hands of the Turks. It was extraordinary bad luck. In the confusion resulting from the Turkish offensive he'd not had the time to obtain a receipt. Consequently he had nothing, not the merest chit of paper, to prove that he'd ever delivered the stuff. So there it was. If it was the will of God . . . well, there was nothing one could do against that. That's life. The world goes on. One's up one day, down the next. It's the same with men and nations. The main thing is not to lose one's head or to let oneself get downcast. But then Smyrniots aren't easily downcast. It's the way they're made—friendly, talkative, open-hearted, pleasure-loving creatures.

Scaliotis and Madam Nora took it upon themselves to act as hosts until everybody arrived at the café—until, that is, they could see how many were going to come. They kept offering rounds of Turkish coffee, passing from one guest to another, shaking hands, smiling, and making themselves as agreeable as possible. The expression in Nora's mischievous eyes was sweetness itself. Her pretty legs didn't keep still for a second. Their constant self-conscious restlessness was like a conversation piece carried on in mime with every male present. A language of the blind; or rather of the deaf. A language that Mr. Philippas, who was rather touchy about his hardness of hearing, understood very well.

He had come dressed up to the nines. He might have been going to a wedding; and he was deeply distressed when he saw the doctor in a light flannel suit, without a waistcoat, a sports shirt, leather belt, and a little camera slung over one shoulder. The Customs officer realized that the days when men could talk of being smartly dressed were long since past. What had happened to Athenian chic? Supplanted by new-fangled Parisian modes, no doubt. So he approached the doctor, smiling with the gentle air common to deaf people, and said: 'That's a neat little outfit, Doctor. Well, well, the wind of change from abroad, I suppose. . . . ' His meaning couldn't have been clearer. The doctor accepted the compliment in the most natural manner, accompanied by an accommodating smile, as though he were accepting nothing more than his due. France, indeed!

By seven o'clock, the appointed hour of departure, they were all there, the only absentees being the Daphnis couple, Adriani. who had sent word to say she wasn't feeling very well, and Madam Evtychia, who was afraid of exposing her heart to the risk of one of its famous 'contractions'. On the other hand, Menos was there with his girl friend and the two university students who had come in place of Mr. and Mrs. Daphnis. The Mayor was wearing a large straw-hat. Loulou, her bosom bouncing, kept coming and going along the jetty with that peculiar waddling walk of hers. Aspasia looked as fresh as a spring rose. The doctor kept asking both girls innumerable questions about the state of their mother's health, emphasizing the importance of carrying out all his instructions. He obviously considered Madam Evtychia's heart his special responsibility, thought Leon. He frequently went to the Mayor's house; and it was evident from the familiar tone he adopted when addressing the two girls, to whom he was full of ostentatious little attentions, that he already considered himself thoroughly at home in the family circle.

At last the boats set off. Leon, Sappho, Xynellis, young Daphnis, and Mina were in one. There had been a bit of a fuss; a perfectly friendly, though slightly embarrassing, fuss, as to which boat Paisios, the old priest, should go in. Nobody wanted him, because there was a superstition that members of the clergy, for all their aura of sanctity, often brought bad luck. The priest himself didn't seem to be in the least upset by the discussion, and kept smiling with an air of benign modesty at everyone in turn. Finally Sismanoglou, adopting a protective manner, took him in his boat and declared he wouldn't have dreamt of letting him travel in any other. At the same time he gently reprimanded the rest of the company for their lack of respect towards the Church. 'I'm joking, of course, but at the same time, you know, it's not quite . . . quite . . . '

With them were the Mayor, the Customs officer, and the gendarmerie lieutenant. The official hierarchy. Mr. Philippas was seated next to Nora, with Mr. Yanni crouching at the feet of a stocky servant girl whom Madam Evtychia had insisted on sending to attend on the girls. Sappho looked so upset when she heard of Adriani's indisposition that Leon was obliged to whisper in her ear that there was nothing in the least wrong with her; she just didn't care for large noisy parties and she seemed to have taken a dislike to the trio from the Austrian boat.

The boats proceeded in a line, one behind the other, Sismanoglou's leading.

'Look at the absurd rôle religion has to play in this affair,' Menos was saying. 'Fancy getting God involved in the demolition of an Austrian boat!'

'There are still stranger rôles,' replied Leon with an air of ingenuousness. 'Look at the one reserved for Lenin's body, for instance. It's got to be regularly injected with antiseptics in order to avoid putrefaction, so that people can kneel down and worship it. . . . '

'Religion is the opiate of the masses,' declared Xynellis sententiously; and he smiled, confident of having made an important contribution to the conversation. But after a while he began to wonder why his statement hadn't created more of an impression, and he wiped his glasses nervously.

'Do tell me,' said Menos, turning towards Leon, '—but candidly now—what are you really? A pantheist?'

Leon shrugged his shoulders. 'Candidly?' he repeated. 'All right. I'll tell you what I am—candidly. One day I'm a revolutionary, the next a nationalist. Sometimes I cease to be a pantheistic nature lover and get lost in a haze of improbable mysticism. I respect the material world as much as anyone, and I take off my hat to the creators of those practical laws which govern our lives in certain circumstances. I recognize the rôle played by the individual in society, as well as the influence of society as a whole on the individual. And there are moments when I feel that this mean and miserable little "I" is the very heart of the universe, since that universe will cease to exist empirically the moment I'm no longer there. That's what I am. And that's what I believe all of us are. Only with different degrees in honesty, resolution and personal characteristics....'

'I agree,' said Sappho quietly. 'It's clearly impossible to feel exactly the same at all times, on all occasions.'

'In other words.' explained Xynellis with a laugh, 'we grow older from one minute to another.'

'On the contrary,' Leon corrected him, without making it absolutely clear whether he was teasing or in earnest, 'we get younger. The past's already old. It's only the future that's young, fresh, in a sense unattainable. So--'

'You seem to like making a mockery of my ideas.' cut in the school master, 'without offering an alternative....'

'Ah, my friend, but then it's not my job to do so!'

The larger boats were moving slowly through the calm water for the early-morning breeze was too feeble to fill even a single sail. The boatmen rowed leisurely and the sun, which had now risen, shone straight into their eyes. The women had opened their parasols. The shore extended deserted, limitless. The depths below were of infinite variety and fascination, and they passed some beaches where the water was so translucent that the sandy sea-bed gave the impression of being only a few feet below the keel of the boat. The sand had the smoothness of a sculptured marble, azure in colour and of an extraordinary density; and so fine in quality that each grain might have been passed through a sieve.

'I wonder how those indulating little banks of sand are formed.' said Mina, leaning over the side of the boat.

'It's true the currents,' explained Menos.

The movement of small waves on the surface imprinted on the sand,' elaborated Xynellis.

'You're all wrong,' Leon smiled. 'I'll tell you what it is. On the night of the full moon the nereids tie the moon's rays into bundles; they use these as silver brooms and sweep the sea-bed. The undulating lines of banked-up sand you see are simply the dump-heaps left from their sweepings.'

'Charming!' aprröved Xynellis.

Small fish swimming close inshore had erected little mounds of sand, like ant-hills, on the sea-bed, and every now and then a starfish would be seen extending its arms across the sand, bright orange like a corporal's stripes. Shoals of little fish passed under the keel of the boat. But the gylos was something apart: twisting, wriggling, showing off its multi-coloured stripes.

As they rounded a headland, cries of 'Here we are! We've arrived' were heard coming from the leading boat. Hardly had they entered the bay when the three masts were seen emerging out of the water. The middle one was slender and intact; the other two were lower in the water and somewhat damaged. It was a large ship and its shape could be dimly discerned under the water. The boats circled the wreck. The diver and workmen were in two little green boats moored to the middle mast. The diver had already placed the explosives in the hold of the ship. A long fuse was tied with wire to the mast-head. Sismanoglou was explaining everything in great detail and all the other boats crowded round him in order that everyone should hear what he had to say. The priest then donned his cassock and said the appropriate prayers over a white bowl of holy water, in complete silence. He held up a sprig of basil, together with a silver cross, and proceeded to bless the waters, the boats, the excursionists, and the workmen. Afterwards he shook hands with Sismanoglou and Scaliotis and Madam Nora. Taking advantage of the priest's handshake, Sismanoglou pressed a bank-note into his hand. With an air of great humility, the priest slipped the note into his pocket without looking at it, while everyone smiled discreetly.

Sismanoglou clapped his hands. 'All the boats must now move toward the shore. We're going to set the fuse.'

The boatmen immediately began to pull at the oars, and there was a great deal of noise and commotion. Only Sismanoglou and one of the workmen remained in the little green boat in order to light the fuse. Sismanoglou continued to make facetious jokes, calling out to them to hurry if they wanted to reach the shore before the explosion went off. The women giggled and screetched, casting terrified glances in the direction of the fuse.

'Don't worry,' he shouted, laughing heartily at his little joke, 'there's plenty of time. You'll have anoter seven minutes after I've set the fuse. There's nothing to be afraid of. Look at me! Would I be sitting here on top of all that dynamite if it was just about to go off?'

The shore was rocky and treeless. The boats bumped against the flat stones in the shallow water and everyone started jumping out in the highest of spirits. The doctor offered a hand to Aspasia who was standing on a ledge of rock, shrieking her head off with laughter for no apparent reason. He then suggested helping Loulou, who kept losing her balance as she staggered about in the bows, crying: 'Which foot shall I put first?'

'Put both feet first,' called out Leon, whereupon Aspasia went into another paroxysm of laughter.

Mina took off her shoes and stockings, lifted her skirt well above the knee, and, with the sun glistening on her thighs, waded knee-deep to the shore.

Xynellis was trying to look after Sappho; but after nodding a curt 'Thank you' at him she leapt unaided onto the shore with her usual agility. Mr. Philippas opened his arms for Madam Nora to fall into— to 'pass her through the Customs', as he so wittily put it. She, however, preferred to hesitate; she was being excessively arch and kept lifting her skirt just sufficiently to attract all the men's glances.

'Today you're no longer the Customs officer, Mr. Philippas,' teased Leon, wagging a finger at him.

'What am I, then?' cried Mr. Philippas naively.

'What are you?' And he shouted in his ear: 'An old Pharisee!'

Mr Philippas laughed, blushing to the roots of his hair.

Mr. Yanni was completely absorded in the Mayor's housemaid. Heaven knew what he was talking about, but she certainly appeared to be listening, her eyes wide open, cackling with laughter.

By this time they were all ashore, their eyes riveted on Sismanoglou who was standing up in the little rowing-boat beside the mast.

'You don't think there's any danger here, do you?' the gendarmerie lieutenant asked Scaliotis in serious, almost official tones.

Scaliotis smiled reassuringly. He had an almost heroic air. 'Heavens, no! No danger whatsoever. Look at the distance. . . . Then there's the resistance of the water. You mustn't forget that. It weighs tons. There's nothing to be afraid of.'

'I'm not afraid,' replied the gendarmerie lieutenant rather testily, raising an eyebrow. 'But we've got women here, after all. . . . I have a certain responsibility. . . . You understand my position. . . . '

'And I'm in a position to guarantee your safety,' rejoined Scaliotis firmly, speaking as a member of the shipping company. 'It'll be a jolly fine show. That's all. Just a jolly fine show.'

They were all silent now. Sismanoglou seized the oars and shouted: 'Look out!' The workman beside him in the boat ignited the fuse with a lighted cigarette.

'Push off!' yelled the other workman from the stern of the boat.

Sismanoglou pulled hard at the oars, making for the open sea.

The atmosphere couldn't have been more tense. Most of the women, their eyes blinking furiously, had blocked their ears with their fingers. So had Mr. Philippas, in spite of his deafness. Aspasia and Loulou were peeping over a ledge of rock. The entire fuse, specially designed for underwater explosions, was now alight. Leon was standing on a patch of level ground close to the water's edge, with Sappho immediately in front of him. Her eyes were fixed on the mast to which the fuse was attached. He watched her delicate nostrils dilating and contracting nervously, her bosom rising and falling. She looked slightly pale as indeed they all did. Then it happened. It was a matter of seconds. A loud rumbling sound came from the bottom of the sea, like some immense sea-monster writhing in its death agony. The water made a great gurgling sound and spouted into the air in a fantastic white jet with showers of snowy-white spray. The women, digging their nails into their hands, screamed hysterically. The mast rose out of the water as though wrenched from its socket, leant over sideways, and then collapsed with a great clatter. At the moment of the explosion the air was rent by a shrill blast.

Leon, with a soldier's automatic reaction, flung himself to the ground, carrying Sappho with him. The blast passed directly over their heads and a piece of metal struck the ground close to them with a shattering impact.

He got up and helped her to her feet. His heart was pounding. He smiled, trying to give her courage.

'Come on . . . it's nothing . . . . '

She stood up dazed. Her face had turned very pale: a sort of lemon-yellow pallor. Her knees felt weak, and as she leant against a rock for support she burst into tears.

Everyone gathered round them, talking at the same time, all offering different and equally expert advice. The doctor, even more agitated than Sappho herself, kept asking her the silliest possible questions in a very professional tone of voice. Madam Nora alone showed any acumen. She went off to the boat and returned with a bottle of champagne which she proceeded to open with an obviously practised hand. At the sound of the 'pop', Mr. Yanni shot into the air. When the students started to tease him he pretended he had done it on purpose in order to amuse them. Sappho took a sip of champagne, her eyes expressing her gratitude.

Leaping ashore from the little boat, Sismanoglou ran anxiously towards them.

'No harm's done, happily . . . ' Mr. Scaliotis called out reassuringly before Sismanoglou had time to reach them. 'Nothing to worry about. Madam Sappho just had a bit of a shock. That's all. . . . '

''I was afraid of something of the kind happening,' the gendarmerie lieutenant informed Scaliotis with ill-concealed self-satisfaction. 'The main thing is to possess foresight. That's why I told you . . . '

'But nothing serious has happened. . . . '

'Nothing very serious because Madam Sappho's guardian angel fortunately happened to be standing beside her. Had not Mr. Drivas flung her to the ground we should now be returning home with a corpse. . . . '

A slight shudder ran through the assembled company.

The gendarmerie lieutenant then congratulated Leon in his most officious manner and the Mayor embraced him with real affection. Everybody thought they had better do the same and proceeded to file past him, congratulating him warmly. He was scarlet with embarrassment. The affair seemed to be assuming the proportions of a ceremony, and now that the initial sense of exhilaration had worn off he saw the humour of the situation.

'Thank you very much,' he addressed the company, 'but I'm afraid I shall now have to shatter your illusions. I assure you that I flung Madam Sappho to the ground without actually meaning to. I just somehow carried her down with me as I fell,' and he bowed slightly, mockingly, in Sappho's direction. 'Madam, I beg you to forgive me for having been the inadvertent cause of dirtying your dress with all that sand.'

Sappho tried to smile at him.

Everybody laughed and Mr. Yanni clapped his hands. Knitting her brows, Madam Nora murmured just loud enough for Leon to hear: 'I must say, I think that young man's charming.'

Father Paisios glanced significantly at Sismanoglou. 'The hand of God . . . it was the hand of God.'

'Shows how a mere coincidence can save one, doesn't it?' was the doctor's comment. 'Had Mr. Drivas not been frightened and dragged Madam Sappho down with him accidentally as he sought cover—'

He broke off abruptly in the middle of the sentence, somewhat flustered. Sappho was looking at him in a way that made it impossible for him to go on.

Mr. Yanni was examining the piece of metal. 'Very odd . . . '

Mr. Philippas touched it gingerly with one finger and said to Mr. Yanni, in his usual distinctive note of voice: 'How it whistled as it passed overhead, eh? Did you hear it . . . ?'

They were interrupted by Madam Nora who came up, accompanied by the Mayor and the servant girl, laden with champagne bottles and glasses. Giggling and chattering, she uncorked the bottles and poured out the champagne.

They drank to the health of Sismanoglou, and Madam Nora replied without thinking on his behalf: 'Thank you, thank you!'

This little woman with the pretty roving eyes, Leon was thinking, probably constituted one of the shipping company's principal 'capital assets.' Scaliotis's share anyhow. Probably his sole 'asset'.

By this time they were having a second round of drinks. Madam Nora refilled Leon's glass. 'To your very good health, young hero,' she said, clinking glasses with him.

She spoke slowly, gazing at him through the glass, one eye half shut, for the bubbles tickled her nostrils and they went up her nose.

'To your good health, Marine Goddess,' he replied, smiling gaily, but with a faint touch of irony in his voice.

He drank up the contents of the glass which reflected the rays of the sun as he tilted it back. He thanked her, laughing happily like a child.

Sappho, who now appeared to have completely recovered, was

surrounded by the students, the Mayor's daughters, and the doctor. But whenever the doctor addressed her she replied with an absent-minded 'Yes, of course,' as though she were not listening to him. Her glance kept turning towards Leon and Nora, who were smiling and looking into each other's eyes, their lips still glistening from the moisture left by the wine.

He felt extraordinarily, unaccountably happy. He knew this was partly due to a sudden intoxicating awareness of his own youthful vigour; to the sun and the sea; and to the woman's admiring glances; but he deliberately did not add: 'and to what happened when the piece of metal stuck the ground'. The champagne was singing in his ears.

There was no shade on the beach and the sun beat down mercilessly. They climbed into the boats, shouting and laughing, and the boatmen began to pull at the oars. Sismanoglou, Scaliotis, and the workmen remained behind to complete the work of demolition. As the little flotilla rounded the headland there was much waving of handkerchiefs and parasols.

Leon, the Mayor and his daughters, Sappho, Nora, Menos and his girl friend were all in the same boat. Leon started to sing a folksong and the others soon joined it.

> *When I die from over-drinking, bury me in the tavern,*
> *So the barmaid and her daughter may tread on me for ever.'*

Nora was seated next to him and there was a strange expression in her eyes as they wandered over his chest, then up to his face and hair. Sappho, the only one who hadn't joined in the singing, was gazing thoughtfully at the expanse of shimmering sea with the mountains of Anatolia beyond. Her slender torso swayed with the motion of the boat. The clean lines of her profile were outlined against the black silk of her parasol.

Leon sat opposite her. Leaning over the side of the boat, he gazed through the blue transparent water at the strange underwater vegetation carpeting the sea-bed. It reminded him of a kitchen garden, full of frilly lettuces and fresh spring onions. Shoals of tiny multi-coloured fish wound in and out of the marine forest. Rolling up his shirt-sleeves, he dipped one arm into the water.

'My God, it's warm!' he told Nora. 'This isn't sea, it's . . . soup.'

Nora laughed. She leant over the side too and dipped one of her bare arms into the water.

The boat moved with a steady rhythm, the water washing over their hands. Suddenly he felt Nora's plump little hand, which had been carried back by the force of the wash, touching his. This unexpected physical contact, concealed by the white foam, caused him an unusual sensation of pleasure. He nevertheless made an attempt to remove his hand; changed his mind; left it there, and waited. He didn't have long to wait. The plump little hand was soon brushing against his. Again it was withdrawn, only to return, with a kind of homing instinct, to rest cosily in the hollow of his palm. Her fingers were playing with his; he caught hold of them and pressed them. The moment he released the pressure, the hand slipped away again, like a frightened fish.

During all this time her head was turned towards the passengers sitting opposite her. She chatted briskly, in the most natural manner possible, telling the Mayor all about the labourers employed on the work of demolition. These demolitions, she said, were carried out with nitrates and other explosives. The company had rented a abandoned hut from the municipality and used it as a workshop and storehouse. The rent demanded by the municipality was very high, she claimed. 'You agree with me that the company's been over-charged, don't you,' she insisted, 'for a derelict shack like that?'

'No, I don't really think the rent's too high,' declared Mr. Spanos. 'Admittedly the decision was taken by the municipal council, but that's beside the point.... Furthermore, the proceeds of the rent go into the refugee fund.'

The plump little fingers continued to play gently in Leon's broad strong hand. 'The refugee fund, did you say? Ah, I didn't know about that.... Well, of course, that does make a difference.'

Before landing Leon suggested they should all come to the Tower first. Only Sappho objected. She said she had to go home immediately. She'd hurt her knee slightly. Only then did they notice that she was limping and that one of her stockings was torn.

'But, my dear, your knee's bleeding,' said Mr. Spanos anxiously.

She was distressed to find herself the centre of attraction again and regretted having mentioned the matter at all. 'It only needs a little iodine,' she said. The doctor intervened and suggested they had better go to the pharmacy first.

Xynellis also butted in. 'Of course, of course, it might easily turn septic. Tetanus, you know, streptococci...'

Sappho laughed. Thanking them all for their solicitude, she assured Xynellis that it was no more than a scratch and there was no occasion whatsoever for anxiety. 'Poetic feet are far harder to deal with,' she added.

The students applauded her pun enthusiastically, while Xynellis blushed and Aspasia laughed without knowing why. The doctor, who was looking the Mayor's daughter in the eyes, laughed reflectively.

Before they all separated, Sappho shook Leon's hand. Slowly, quietly, but without meeting his glance, she said: 'Thank you.'

He went straight home and described the day's events to Adriani. She confessed she'd had a feeling of foreboding. 'When I saw the boats setting out all gaily decorated I felt a curious sensation of constriction. It was agony waiting for you to come back. I didn't say anything in the morning because you'd have made fun of me.'

'I wouldn't have made fun of you,' he said.

'But you don't believe in premonitions and things like that.'

Taking her hand, he said thoughtfully: 'I believe in everything, Adriani—above all, in the unbelievable. There're times when we look for the truth like people searching for their spectacles. And then you know, of course, what happens. They find they've been wearing them all the time.'

Adriani wasted no time in going to see Sappho.

Her knee was really no more than grazed, but she was still suffering from shock. Her movements were jerky, her talk inconsequential. Everything pointed to a state of repressed agitation.

As the two girls were talking, the deaf-aind-dumb woman entered the room and made a sign to Sappho. From the open door they could hear the long-drawn-out wailing of the crippled child. It was like a distant howling, muffled by a succession of closed doors. The refugee woman, dressed in unrelieved black, stood waiting by the door. Adriani felt an inexplicable sensation of fear at the sight of this tall spectre-like figure, with the dark mysterious eyes, and the head hooded in a black kerchief. Sappho got up, her face flushing, her hands trembling.

'Please forgive me,' she said. 'I'll just go and see what's wrong with the child. I'll only be a moment. . . . '

'But look how you're limping!' cried Adriani. 'Let me come and help you.'

Sappho's eyes opened wide with terror. 'No!' and she held out a hand as though to prevent her from advancing any further. 'Stay here. . . . I won't be long. . . . '

The deaf-mute woman disappeared with her. Left alone, Adriani wondered whether her offer to accompany Sappho could have been interpreted as a manifestation of vulgar curiosity. The idea distressed her, and she felt thoroughly ill-at-ease as she sat on the sofa and mechanically opened a round work-basket in which she'd seen Sappho place her knitting as she entered the room. She also re-membered seeing Sappho carefully closing the lid of the basket. Opening it now, she found it contained a ball of grey wool and a piece of knitting obviously nearing completion. She took it out of the work-basket and looked at it absent-mindedly. Then suddenly she experienced a sensation of utter horror. The piece of knitting was completely round, like a basket. She understood. It was an enormous knitted cap, large enough to fit a pumpkin, designed as a child's cap. She suppressed a shudder, put it back quickly, and closed the lid of the work-basket.

She got up and paced restlessly across the room, trying to shut out the image of that monstrous head for which the outsize cap had been designed. She stopped in front of the walnut table placed against the wall. It was apparently used as a writing-desk. On it were placed a bronze inkstand, two large piles of books, the titles of which indicated a discerning literary taste, some periodicals, and a large glass containing a few yellow reeds. Their scent was so sweet that she thought she could almost taste them. Behind the glass there was a photograph of a short man in the uniform of an officer, with thick eyebrows that met above the bridge of the nose and a black clipped moustache. He was leaning on his sword; the white stripes on his arm indicated his years of active service. The photograph was a cheap one, touched up in the worse possible taste; but the face was that of a man with great willpower and dogged obstinacy. The words. *I'm always with you, I think of you day and night, T.T. 906*, were written in a clear upright hand at the bottom of the photograph.

Sappho appeared in the doorway. Her eyes were red, and her attempt at a smile was a complete failure.

Adriani approached her. She longed for an explanation, to get her to open her heart.

'Sappho, please . . . '

Sappho's eyes suddenly filled with tears; she bit her quivering underlip and fell sobbing into Adriani's arms.

Adriani could feel the flutter of her long eyelashes on her neck. She made her sit down on the sofa beside the open window.

'Forgive me, Adriani,' she cried, between sobs, 'but you've no idea how miserable I am! Sometimes lately I've felt it's more than . . . I keep asking myself why, why, and I can't find the answer. . . . If only I could I believe it would be easier. . . . '

As she spoke, her body bent forward, as though hoping to find some kind of support. Her words came out jerkily, sometimes in sudden little spurts: words that had been too long suppressed, locked away in her heart; words that had tried desperately to find some means of release; and now that they'd at last found it they came tumbling out in utter confusion.

Adriani caressed her hair. Her own eyes were brimming with tears. 'You mustn't take it like that', she said. 'You mustn't. You're so young still. With time, things are bound to get better. . . . You'll see, you'll see. . . . '

Her young girlish voice had assumed a tone of maturity, almost a maternal quality. Seizing her hand, Sappho covered it with kisses. She longed for words to express the gratitude she felt for Adriani's affection. The girl's kindness and understanding was like a vision of a rose suddenly blossoming before her dull tired gaze. And all she could do in return was to weep salt-tears and utter disjointed words.

Adriani said no more until the little crisis was over. She pushed aside a strand of hair which had fallen across Sappho's forehead, concealing the broad firm line of her eyebrow, and kissed her. 'Sappho, I can't tell you how miserable I'd feel,' she said, 'if I thought you suspected me of anything but true affection when I suggested coming with you to see the child. . . . '

Sappho gazed affectionately into her blue eyes. 'If you only knew, Adriani, what honesty shines in those eyes of yours. They remind me of the sea. . . this morning. One can see right down to the depths. You need never be afraid of being misunderstood.'

She looked out of the window. The light was playing on the sea.

'It's you who must forgive me,' she said. 'Forgive me for not letting you come with me. But, you see, it fills me with such grief, such shame. . . . That's why. The child . . . it's the most hideous punishment that anyone could have invented. Why did it happen? Sometimes I weep all night, out of sheer love for it. . . . I lock myself up with it, spend hours with it. . . . That's when I say to myself: "This is my place, where I ought to be. After all, I'm its mother." I go to caress it . . . to kiss it . . . to sing to it. . . . But there're also moments when I see it as it really is—a dumb soulless monster whose only object in life is to torment me. It's really horrible, Adriani. You've no idea. You can't have. It's shapeless, formless. Why should I be punished like that? Neither of us were to blame . . . . Is this divine justice?

She fell silent for a moment, running her fingers through her hair. She wiped her eyes and a golden beam flashed across them. Then she began to speak again, and there was an angry obstinate tone in her voice.

'Sometimes I fell it's all a sheer mockery. Believe me, Adriani, don't ever make the mistake of marrying a man you're not in love with. At least there must be physical passion . . . if nothing else. I didn't understand this then. Afterwards, when the truth dawned on me, I was appalled. I used to surrender my body to him without a scrap of feeling, without a spark of desire. It was like throwing off some piece of underclothing. Just like that. Nothing else. And inside me I'd be weeping all the time—out of sheer disgust. He knew it, and he couldn't forgive me . . . because he loved me. . . . But can I be blamed for feeling

like that? I don't mean that he was to blame either. I realize that now...
One day he pushed me away from him and my head struck the edge of
the table—there. It made me feel faint, and there was a little blood just
behind my ear. But I didn't say a thing. I couldn't. I was afraid lest the
neighbourhood should suspect.... He then came to me; he knelt down
in front of me and started kissing my hands. . . . '

Her glance strayed to the photograph: the photograph of her
husband, her only lover, the father of her child; a man innocent of all
blame, yet responsible for all her suffering.

'And you can bring yourself to put flowers there . . . ' Adriani said
hesitatingly, 'in front of his photograph?'

Sappho turned her eyes away from the flowers. She seemed to be
going through some kind of inward struggle.

'Yes,' she said thoughtfully at last, 'I'm sorry for him. My heart bled
for him, even when he used to strike me. He loved me very much; I was
the only woman in his life. Then . . . but how strangely things work out.
As long as we were together we lived in separate worlds. We'd call out
to each other, and neither of us would hear. But now that he's dead he
seems to be closer to me in a way. Last night I dreamt of him. He was
coming towards me—but from a great distance. And I could see him
smiling and waving to me with a red handkerchief. . . . '

After a brief pause she added: 'I thought of the dream this morning,
during the excursion. . . . '

Adriani felt strangely moved as she left the house. She was
determined to do everything in her power to cherish and cultivate
Sappho's friendship.

At dinner that night Leon questioned her closely, gazing absent-
mindedly at her as she answered his questions. A multitude of
conflicting thoughts raced through his head as he grasped hungrily at
each detail of Adriani's narrative.

'Hasn't she got the medal and divisional citation framed on the wall
any longer?'

'No,' replied Adriani. 'Only his photograph. She's placed a glass
with some flowers beside it.'

He experienced a strange sensation of satisfaction at these words.
Clearly his influence was beginning to tell.

In bed that night he couldn't keep his mind off the subject.
Suddenly an idea came to him. She used not to place flowers in front of
his photograph before. Why now? Was it possible that her conscience,
like his, was no longer clear? Could her action have been prompted by
remorse? Was the bunch of flowers an attempt to atone? To atone for
what? He was simply arguing, he assured himself, for argument's
sake. But why should she feel any remorse? Was it possible that. . .?

18

HE COULD no longer deny the fact that the schoolmistress's company had become indispensable to him. He often tried to escape from it, tormenting himself by deliberately seeking opportunities to avoid her presence. But the moment they were together again he would experience such a sense of intoxication that the atmosphere would become charged and inflammable and he would be afraid lest the merest spark should set it alight. Alternating between the extremes of rapture and dejection, he was in a state of constant emotional stress. At times he felt he was deprived of all manly fortitude and would succumb to this cowardly sense of abandonment with an almost feminine voluptuousness: the voluptuousness of surrender. Then, at the other extreme, he would strut about with a great show of bravado, obstinately pretending to himself that he was immune to all the shafts aimed at him from her armoury of charms. This petty victory was necessary to his vanity. She was the wife of Vranas, he would insist, the mother of a deformed child. Nothing more. But in order to gain this cheap victory he was often compelled to resort to the most craven means, such as repeatedly describing Vranas's death to her down to the last gruesome detail. He marvelled that he could do do—he who had always considered it 'bad form' to refer to anything remotely connected with the war. But he experienced a curious satisfaction in witnessing the look of horror that passed like a dark cloud across her eyes. With morbid patience he would spin the web of his story—the story of her husband's great love for her—like a black net to enmesh her. A love, he claimed, that had been at once strong and exclusive, forged out of steel, jealously and obstinately concealed in the dark places of his silent soul. He applied himself to this task with an unusual meticulousness, trying to represent the bond that tied her to the dead man as something indissoluble, something that time could not touch. Whereas in his own soul he had to make every effort to keep alight the flickering candle which they had placed at the head of his friend's bier so that its sanctified glow should illumine and expose the hideous erotic fantasies that dwelt like venomous serpents in the inner recesses of his subconscious mind.

This continuous absorption with his war-time experiences was like a flail, torturing him through the long hours of the night. He would wake up with a pounding heart, drenched in sweat, almost incapable of shaking off the hideous dreams of murderous battles and slow death in the trenches.

A variety of wild iris with a delicious intoxicating scent grew on the beach at the Portara. From childhood he had loved this iris which he used to pick in great bunches and place in earthenware vases in the dining-room.

One day he presented Sappho with a bunch he'd just picked. 'Please put them in front of his photograph,' he told her.

The incident was repeated. He would either present them himself or ask Adriani to take them to her. Thus the dead man drew closer to them; he acquired a semi-reality and seemed to come to life in their midst.

'You know, Sappho, Vranas loved you terribly,' he would tell her again and again, with such persistence that she would look wonderingly at him. 'He loved you in his own way, of course. We all love in our own ways. These ways can, of course, be as different as one face from another, or one voice from another. In love, Vranas was both a fanatic and an ascetic. That was his way. . . . '

'But that doesn't prevent people from preferring other ways, just as they may prefer one face to another, or one voice to another,' she said. 'Personally, I can't agree that love is a feeling wholly dominated by egoism. Love surely springs from a spontaneous desire to make the loved one happy: if necessary, at one's own expense; if necessary, with humility and self-sacrifice. Love is something one offers; one can't impose it.'

'No, I don't suppose one can really define the different categories of love,' continued Leon. 'There's a violent aggressive love, rapacious, possessive. Then you have the kind of love which is all giving and tenderness. Vranas's belonged to the first category. Harsh, almost barbaric. . . . He was capable of killing for love. He told me so once, you know. . . . '

Another day he told her the same thing all over again. They were on the beach, in front of the Portara. 'Vranas was capable of killing for the sake of his love . . . capable even of killing you.'

'D'you know,' said Sappho thoughtfully, 'every time you say that I'm almost on the point of telling you something—about a curious feeling I had that day. And yet, I don't know why, I can't bring myself to. . . . '

'What day?'

'The day you saved my life. The day of the excursion.'

'Oh! The day . . . I saved your life!'

'Of course, I should have been killed,' she said with a very serious air, 'or at least badly hurt, if you hadn't been beside me.'

He laughed. 'But then if you hadn't been beside me,' he said ironically, 'you wouldn't have been on the spot where the piece of metal fell. Consequently——'

'Consequently,' interrupted Adriani, 'why don't you let her finish what she's saying?'

'All right. I'll tell you. You'll probably laugh. But, you see, I had a feeling that the danger I'd just escaped was a kind of revenge. . . . '

'Revenge . . . ! On whose part?' asked Leon, horrified at the thought of her probable answer.

She looked at him in a strange way. She saw her answer agonizingly reflected in his eyes. She hesitated, but said: 'Yes.'

'D'you mean to say you believe in premonitions and all that childish nonsense?' broke in Adriani.

'Yes,' Sappho insisted. 'The feeling came over me suddenly, the moment I sensed the danger. Afterwards, when I saw the piece of metal lying on the ground, I thought of a dream I'd had the night before. He was coming to me from afar, waving a red handkerchief. And the same feeling came over me again, the feeling that he'd actually thrown the piece of metal at me . . . '

'But why should he?' asked Adriani naively.

Sappho shrugged her shoulders. She might have been trying to raise an invisible weight pressing down on her. 'I don't know," she said, 'but that's how it was.'

'Imagination,' scoffed Leon. 'The imagination of a highly strung woman.'

Adriani, always anxious to distract her friend from unhappy memories, carried her off to show her some new roses in the vineyard.

Leon remained alone. Sappho's words had already begun to acquire the proportions of a major event in his imagination, with the piece of metal representing a murderous weapon in the hands of the dead man. So even in the grave his fierce unquenchable love was still on the prowl, seeking her out furtively, ready to strike her down at a moment's notice. The time, the place, the circumstances, joined to the dark passion brooding in his silent soul, had all come to his aid in the attempted crime. He tried to draw another reference from the events of that day. He remembered his spontaneous reaction to the danger they were suddenly confronted with. It had been a muscular reflex, an instinctive reflex to protect Sappho as well as himself. What instinct had prompted him to act so swiftly and decisively, bringing them together in a sudden violent embrace the moment they were threatened by the flying piece of metal? He realized now that henceforth something would always be driving them apart and, paradoxically enough, drawing them closer together. It was evident that she was aware of it too; and he appreciated her attempt to be so frank, so open and correct with him. But the imprint of his embrace would remain stamped on her body. Perhaps that 'feeling,' as she called it, about the dead man's revenge sprung from this fact, without her knowing it.

There was another point to consider. The moment he had seized her with the instinctive intention of throwing her to the ground he hadn't been consious of any physical contact. But later, when the danger had passed, the physical reality of the embrace had struck him with overwhelming force. His skin still tingled at the thought of her body's proximity to his. He remembered the feel of the firm breasts under his right arm, the intoxicating warmth and softness of her flesh below the thin petticoat pressing against his. The memory haunted him and he would relive the moment, in all its terror and enchantment, with a persistency that became positively nerve-racking.

When she was preparing to go he began to pick some irises for her. 'In memory of Vranas,' he said, offering them to her. 'But don't hold them too low down. The sap that runs out of the stalks is very sticky.' He said this without *arrière pensée,* but he could have kicked himself immediately afterwards as he heard a little voice inside him echoing his words in tones of mocking ridicule.

They accompanied her part of the way back; and then stood and watched her figure gradually disappear along the flat waste of the beach. The breeze had freshened up and long rolling waves were breaking on the shore. He could still just see her black dress billowing around her slender figure, and for a moment he thought he heard music in the wind.

'How well she carries herself, doesn't she?' murmured Adriani admiringly.

He nodded his head in agreement; then muttered mockingly: 'The Contessa, of course!'

He laughed and jabbed the iron spike of his walking-stick fiercely into the sand. He might have been planting a flag on the spot.

19

THERE was good news from Athens one day. The exhibition of *Free Painters* had opened and the notices in the newspapers were almost entirely devoted to praise of Leon's pictures. The reviews created quite a stir, and the fashionable world of Athens flocked to see the pictures. Leon's attacted the most flattering comment. This unstinted and unanimous praise was all the more remarkable in that it came from rival coteries and from artists and art critics who normally held widely divergent opinions. It was a wholly personal success: something quite new and strange to the public, considering that Leon's name was unknown in the art world of the capital.

In some of the more discerning reviews his pictures were given titles. The one called *The Refugees* depicted a row of female masks with features drawn with suffering.Then came *A Boy by the Sea:* a synthesis of colour, full of simplicity and a deep feeling for nature. The limitless expanse of blue sea and sky was separated only by the horizon; a naked boy stood on the rose-tinted beach gazing at the magnificent spectacle. It could well have been called *The Prayer.* Another bore the title *The Sunlit Alley.* The dazzling August sunshine beat down relentlessly on a little village street; so fierce was the impact that the canvas itself seemed to be on fire, with the paint itself sizzing in the furnace of light. This was followed by *The Castle with the Poppies:* a view of the castle of Megalohori, seen from the side of a hill carpeted with poppies. The sharply defined colour-scheme was three-fold: the blue of the sky, the grey of the ruined castle walls, and the scarlet of the poppies. So simple was the composition that it had the air of an allegorical representation depicting the indomitable force of nature exploding out of a chrysalis in a shower of scarlet fireworks; the eternal reawakening: spring itself, ever virginal and invincible, emerging out of the tomb of winter; and high above, the blue sky, the blue eye of God himself, an unmoved passionless God, riding above the storm of life, tranquil, almost unfeeling. The fifth was called *The Departed One.* It was an evocation of his mother, a tall woman with a pale face, in the long silk dress she always wore on Sundays: a composition steeped in nostalgic memories, a vision from a distant improbable world, almost transparent, like a wraith. One had the impression that if anyone blew on the canvas the colours would start waving like streamers. Visitors to the exhibition paused repsectfully in front of it and, to quote one of the critics, 'lowered their voices'.

With the large bundle of newspapers came a chatty letter from his friend the journalist. The most important part of it was the postscript.

P.S. All five have been sold. At the price you mentioned. In all 50,000 drachmas. Take away sundry expenses—the bills will follow—*and you have 45,000 clear. That's to say fifty gold pounds. You'll receive a postal order in a few days. Unprecedented for a début!*

Leon was thrilled. His heart beat as though he'd been running. He was drunk with success: it was like breathing incense—the incense of triumph; and its fumes were intoxicating. More important, it was a triumph over himself. Fundamentally he had never doubted his ability to create a genuine work of art, but he had been afraid of the danger of over-enthusiasm; that inner taskmaster, the spirit of doubt and cynicism, had so often sapped his self-confidence. The first decisive battle, the battle he had so often dreamt of in the trenches, had now been fought and won. It was a victory over the demon of negation. And the most remarkable aspect of it all was that for the first time in his life he was earning money from his own work. This, he felt, must be a proof of the work's intrinsic value; it was a triumph of immense moral significance.

He ran in search of Adriani and found her in the courtyard of the Tower. He flung the large bundle of papers at her; then he raised her in his arms and carried her round the courtyard as though she were a trophy.

'Hurrah!'

Life was indeed sweet. He was bursting with happiness.

Leon's sudden success created quite a stir at the club. Of course his triumph was viewed with that narrow yet touching parochial vanity common to all provincial communities when one of their members achieves fame or notoriety. But like good provincials they had no intention of being fooled or of recognizing success until it had received official benediction. In Leon's case there was the irrefutable proof of the newspapers; and hardly had the members of the Arion Club glanced at them before every one of them proceeded to point out that they had always known that 'that young man would go far.'

'It's extraordinary,' said the barber, 'when you come to think of the times I've cut his hair.'

'It's incredible,' echoed the grocer, gazing at Leon's name in his delivery book.

Others recalled the numberous occasions they'd drunk coffee with him at the café. 'And then you wake up one morning and find he's famous, winging his way to the stars, far above the common herd, with the whole country talking about him. You must admit it's most peculiar.'

No, whichever way one looked at it, it was a triumph for the village. Suddenly the grocer's delivery book, in which Leon's name figured, the scissors with which his hair had been trimmed, the cups from which he'd drunk coffee, all acquired the aura of venerable objects.

'And think of it, he's almost a native of the place. What's more, he's immortalized the village in these pictures.'

'Almost a native? Come now, what d'you mean by "almost"?' exploded Mr. Spanos, bursting with pride and emotion. 'Why don't you ask me—me, who brought him up? Or ask Evtychia, who nursed him, if he's native or not. You've only got to look up the church register to see that his father was a Megalohorian, that he's actually related to me through his grandmother. Almost! Twaddle! Leon's as genuine a Megalohorian as any of us. I now propose the club sends him an official letter of congratulation and makes him an honorary member.'

'We'll commision him to paint the church at Platitera,' said Mr. Adamellis, the commissioner for Kato Panaghia, whereupon Mr. Daphnis, the president of the club, pulled him by the coat-tails and pointed out that Leon painted pictures, not içons.

'Of course,' said Mr. Daphnis, who was regarded as the financial wizard of the village. 'Forty-five thousand drachmas, eh?' His mouth literally watered. He had acquired a profound respect for Leon's business acumen. 'Hard-headed business men and factory owners, accustomed to dealing in millions of drachmas don't earn as much. And then this boy goes and does it. Why is that? Now let's see. How many working hours do those five pictures represent. Five, eh? Well, let's say ten. You realize what that means? I'll tell you what it means. It means he's paid at the rate of four thousand five hundred drachmas the hour.'

'True enough,' said the police officer. 'Four thousand five hundred!' And he raised his upper lip so that his moustache touched the tip of his nose where a few sparse hairs curled out of his nostrils.

This was a new aspect of the matter, and the most fantastic. They looked at one another with bulging eyes.

'Well, well, well!'

'That's fine,' Mr Daphnis silenced them. 'Hardly a day's work! A little paint and five metres of canvas. D'you understand?'

The same day the students made a mass descent on the Tower to offer their congratulations. Menos also brought a copy of a leftist journal *The Vanguard,* in which every 'conscientious' little shop-assistant poured out his views on art (with a capital A), without making the slightest reference to the paintings under review. Leon's work was praised in general terms, but he was warned—after all, he was an elightened progressive man—of the pitfalls confronting him if he continued merely to paint for the delectation of the bourgeoisie. Henceforth his art should be used as an instrument to arouse the masses and make them throw off the yoke of their oppressors.

In order to illustrate the point *The Vanguard* carried a photograph of a piece of sculpture described as a masterpiece. It represented a workman with brawny arms holding two enormous stones in either hand. The caption ran: 'The sole weapon of the proletariat—the stones in the street.'

Madam Evtychia came to the Tower with her daughters to con-gratulate him. She kissed him on both cheeks, her round little eyes brimming with tears.

'My boy! My dear boy! If only your poor dear parents were here to share your happiness!'

The good woman wept, within the limits permitted by her ailing heart. Not since the Olympic Games, when Louis beat the French, she declared, had she felt such a surge of national pride.

Leon and Adriani didn't omit to enquire after her health. They knew how to play up to their godmother's weakness. This was her cue to embark on the subject of the doctor's admirable qualities. What a dear man! He came two or three times a week to relieve her suffering, first with one medicine, then another.

Leon smiled at her naive enthusiasm. His smile was not lost on Aspasia, who said provocatively: 'It's true enough. The poor man comes regularly. He's the only person who takes any interest in Mamma's health. And he's prescribed a new treament with all the latest medicines. He brought them from Paris for her—specially for her. Yes, he's such a civil man. One can tell at a glance that he's lived abroad.'

Leon didn't flinch. He kept nodding his head and saying: 'Yes, yes.' But he continued to smile with one eyebrow raised; and this only irritated Aspasia still further.

'The doctor's undoubtedly a man in a thousand,' she continued. 'The girl he decides to marry will be a lucky one.'

Leon glanced stealthily at the two girls. Aspasia was biting her lips to stop herself from laughing. Loulou was blushing and trying to stare at her feet, but finding her field of vision obstructed by the large intractable mass of her bosom, her glance veered to the right and remained fixed on the fringe of a Persian carpet.

'Ah, then it's the eldest one the doctor's picked on.' he thought. 'The eldest—that's very correct and proper.'

Madam Nora congratulated him one evening when they met strolling on the beach. She was attended by two of her beaux, and she gave Leon the impression of wearing nothing under her dress. She had soon manoeuvred her companions into walking ahead, while she dawdled behind with Leon, constantly increasing the distance between them by stopping down to pick up little shiny pieces of broken tiles which she sent skimming over the water.

'I can't tell you how pleased, how very very pleased, I was to hear of your great success,' she said. 'I should be terribly happy to have my portrait painted by you. . . . '

He bowed slightly, half jokingly, almost mockingly. 'Madam!' was all he said.

She looked into his eyes in the way men generally look at women whom they desire. Her look seemed to contain a reminder, an agreeable little reminder of two hands touching in the sea.

'Yes, indeed, I'd willingly sit for you, if you want me to! *Décolleté*, I suppose, very *décolleté*, in the interest of Art. . . . '

He slapped his thigh as though he'd just thought of something. 'That's precisely what I've been looking for. D'you know, I've been thinking a great deal lately about a composition I'd like to do, and the only thing I hadn't got was the right model.'

'What is it about?' Nora asked wiltingly.

'Salome.'

'Salome with the seven veils!' gasped the good woman.

'With no veils, my dear, no veils at all.' Leon burst out laughing at the thought of this plump attractive little Salome, as round as a cream bun.

'When we go back to town,' she suggested to him. 'Wouldn't that be better? It's such a small place here, and you know what peasants are like. Art shocks them!'

She bent down, picked up another piece of broken tile and sent it skimming over the water. As she did so, he could see the whole of her body wriggling like an eel under her dress.

'Shall we move on, if you like?' he said. 'We've lagged a long way behind.'

She walked so slowly, so close to him that one of her breasts brushed against his arm. Suddenly she sighed and said: 'Ah, I wish you'd recite something to me. . . . At this hour of the evening I love to listen to poetry.'

He looked at her, mildly yet quite agreeably astonished.

'I remember some...ancient Greek lines. Would you like me to...?'

'Of course, of course.'

And he began to declaim rather pompously, as though he were back in the classroom:

> *'Thracian foal, why with a sideways glance*
> *do you pitiless flee me? Do you think there's nothing I know?*
> *Learn that only too well could I bridle you*
> *and taking the reins ride to the end of the course.*
> *Now though through meadows you graze, lightly gambol and frisk,*
> *not having a rider of skill to put your strength to the test.'*

'D'you like them?' he enquired.

'Marvellous!' she cried enthusiastically. 'But . . . what do they mean? French, you see, is the only foreign language I know . . . .'

'Ah, well, it would take too long to go into now,' he laughed. 'I'll explain it to you when . . . we meet in town again. We'd better be getting on now if we're to catch up with the others. Mr. Sismanoglou keeps looking back at us as though he were rather annoyed. . . .'

'And what business is it of Mr. Sismanoglou's?' she asked wonderingly, as though she hadn't understood what he really meant. 'What right has he to . . .'

But the words froze on her ruby lips as he half turned round and looked at her. It was impossible for her to mistake the meaning of his glance.

20

THERE was quite a commotion that day. It was the fifteenth of August, the feast of the Virgin. It had been decided to evict a group of ex-soldiers from Kouphovouno, a large estate formerly owned by the Turks. The soldiers had established themselves on the property without official sanction. It was a magnificent estate, extending across the entire side of a mountain, thick with olive groves and orchards of fig, pear, quince, and pomegranate. There were also some cottages, and water installations, including two water-mills.

A certain Silellis from Aivalik, one of the most able leaders of the refugees, had got wind of the existence of the property. He was one of those Anatolian chiefs of a village who'd managed to lay hands on the best properties abandoned by the Turks through the system of the so-called 'groups'. These 'groups' were simply bands of refugees from Asia Minor, to each of which the government allocated a certain acreage of land. They were the creation of the Organization for the Relief of Refugees. Each group consisted of a number of families in proportion to the amount of land allocated, led by a shrewd and generally rapacious village leader.

The leader selected these families from among pedlars, boatmen, fishermen, and other gullible people, including a number of old women, widows, and under-age orphans, who would be likely to keep their mouths shut. They were then allotted a piece of land as far away as possible from the village where they were temporarily 'squatting'. Lacking the means to travel across the island, the refugees remained in ignorance of what was virtually theirs, had they chosen or known how to claim it.

That was what had happened in the case of Kouphovouno. So Silellis spread out his tentacles from Chora and began to work up his 'group' of refugees about the property, which, he said, was 'theirs for the asking'. But in the meantime a number of ex-soldiers, consisting of natives of the island as well as refugees from Megalohori, who had returned destitute from the war, had settled with their families on the property. Those who couldn't find room in the cottages erected shelters roofed with branches of plane and laurel trees. Three tents were soon pitched near the water-mills and the place took on the air of an encampment.

Silellis had made all the necessary arrangements for the eviction. He brought with him from the town the district Agricultural Officer and a clerk of the Ministry of Agriculture who'd just been appointed and didn't know the first thing about his job. To every suggestion made by Silellis and the Agricultural Officer he simply answered: 'Yes.' He seemed to be far more interested in making eyes at the daughter of the Agricultural Officer whose guest he was.

As soon as the service was over they went to the estate with five gendarmes from the police station, led by a sergeant. It was about midday. The property was near the Sentinel, not far from Megalohori, and quite a number of people, hearing of the proposed eviction of the soldiers and their families, were strolling in that direction. One of the gendarmes jumped over the fence and opened the gate from the inside. It was an old-fashioned country gate in the shape of a cross, made of poplar wood, and intended for the passage of men and beasts alike. A number of small children were perched on the fence, watching the proceedings.

The soldiers had foregathered in front of two adjacent cottages and were busy attending to various odd jobs, as though unaware of what was impending. Among them was a stocky swarthy man, the obvious leader, named George. Like the rest of the ex-soldiers, he was wearing an old army kilt, with a black handkerchief tied round his head, and he was making a show of pruning a branch, stopping every now and then to measure the height of a climbing grape wine which apparently needed supports.

The officials and the gendarmes approached him. Some of the children, brats with running noses and filthy drawers, got in among their legs.

'Take the children away,' cried the swarthy man severely.

A young woman with a prematurely aged face left the fire, on which was a kettle on which she was blowing, and rubbed her fists across her eyes which were red and inflamed from the smoke. She began to shoo the children away, and as she walked the flip-flop of her bare heels on the wooden sandals could be heard.

The rest of the soldiers—they were about ten in all—began to converge from the outer ring. Their movements were deliberately leisured, almost casual.

'It's you we've come to see, George,' the police sergeant told the leader of the group.

'You're welcome,' replied George, casting a frigid glance at him and continuing to prune the vine.

The police sergeant came a bit nearer and placed a hand on his shoulder in a friendly manner.' Come on, let's stop all this nonsense and get down to business. It's you I'm addressing, d'you understand?

You've got a good head on your shoulders, George. And you're a family man, and an honest one at that.'

With a shrug of the shoulder George was relieved of the friendly hand resting on it. 'Aren't the rest of the bunch honest family men too?' he said.

'I just wanted to have a word with you,' said the police sergeant, 'like a colleague.'

'Colleague?' George stopped pruning for a moment and cast a look of extreme derision at him.

'Weren't you a corporal in the army?'

'Yeah.'

'Well, corporal and police sergeant . . . they're much the same thing, aren't they?'

'And if they are, what then?' said George, and his companions laughed rudely.

Silellis was standing a little farther back, holding his straw hat in one hand, wiping his bald pink head with a white handkerchief. The more he wiped it, the more the perspiration seemed to pour from it.

'What I want to tell you,' the police sergeant was saying patiently, 'is that you know as well as I do what orders mean. You know the meaning of duty, of responsibility. Can't you understand then that we're simply here—I mean we and the officials from the Ministry—to carry out orders? And our orders are to see that you get out of Kouphovouno.'

Sillelis looked as though he wanted to speak. He extended a hand towards George: a soft plump white hand; and in it he held the handkerchief drenched in perspiration from his head.

'Please . . . ' the police sergeant stopped him.

George turned away for a moment to measure the supports for the vine. As he did so he shut one eye. The other seemed to be fixed on Silelli's plump hand which was being slowly withdrawn.

'You're right, I suppose,' he said finally to the police sergeant. 'Government orders, eh? Must be respected, eh?'

'So! . . . ' cried the Agricultural Officer delightedly.

'We've got a paper,' said George, 'a government paper. Right here. That's why we're here. Hi, you Procopius,' he turned to one of the soldiers, 'go in and get the paper. It's on the shelf over there. . . . '

One of the soldiers, who had a complexion the colour of sulphur, went in and returned with the document, which he handed to the Agricultural Officer.

The Agricultural Officer put on his glasses and unfolded the paper. Silellis and the official from the Ministry glanced over his shoulder. As they read they each smiled in turn.

'Is it possible?' said the police sergeant, holding out his hand in order to emphasize his incredulity.

'Charming!' said the Agricultural Officer as he put his glasses in their case.

'You chaps think it funny, eh?' said George. 'All the same, you know, it's a page from what they call the *Government Gazette*. D'you see those signatures and seals? There, at the bottom. Venizelos. And all his ministers. It's not what you'd call bullshit, eh?'

'It's the signature of the revolutionary government in Salonica,' said the police sergeant.

'That's it,' affirmed George, 'the Prime Minister and all that. It was the government that told us to go to the war. It says so. You can read, can't you? It says the chaps who go to the war'll be given "lands" when they come back. So, you see, we're all right. Sitting pretty here. We went to the war. We've come back. We sold all we had, our animals, our ploughs, so as to buy bread for our wives and children. And then we took these lands.'

'Come on,' said the clerk from the Ministry of Agriculture, who was getting tired of standing about. He'd been whistling the latest tunes from the Athenian revues. 'Let's stop palavering and get on with the job.' He took out his watch from his waistcoat pocket.

Silellis nodded his shining head nervously. 'Get on with the job. Yes, get on with the job.'

The police sergeant looked at the ex-soldiers with a stern air. 'Come on, boys. Collect your things and get going. No fuss, please. Otherwise . . . '

The women, who were huddled together in a little group, were talking in whispers. They looked frightened and angry. The soldiers were looking fixedly at George, looking to him for a lead.

'Leave us alone, will you?' he said curtly. 'We're staying here.'

'Careful, George,' said the police sergeant sharply. 'That's obstruction of the law, you know. I don't want to have to handcuff you. . . . I'm sorry for your wife and children, my good man.'

'If you're sorry for' em why d'you come here and try to throw 'em out in the street, you son of a bitch?' burst out George. He flung the piece of wood he'd been trimming on to the ground. It might have been a savage curse he had hurled at the sergeant.

'Will you go?' said the latter, scarlet in the face. 'Yes, or no?'

'No,' shouted George. 'I'm not going. I'm staying put. See? and let any son of a bitch who wants to try to throw me out.'

'Come on, then, take him to the station,' the police sergeant ordered two of the gendarmes. 'And if he resists bind him.'

'Yes, bind him,' echoed Silellis, making a gesture with his hands to illustrate the proposed action.

There was a rustle of movement among the soldiers, who exchanged glances as their fingers closed round the various farm-tools they were holding: spades, shovels, scythes.

'George,' the police sergeant shouted, 'for the last time, I warn you, don't go too far. Think of the others. . . . '

'Look here, my boy,' said the somewhat naive Agricultural Officer. He had a sedentary nature and had spent a lifetime sitting in an office chair. 'Look here, don't let's have any fuss.'

'Go away!' shouted George, black with rage. 'Go away! If you don't, by God . . . '

'Bind him!' cried the police sergeant, now pale in the face, drawing his revolver.

Two gendarmes fell on the demented George, who clenched his teeth which showed white, a brilliant white, against his swarthy complexion. And as he clenched his teeth he swung the hoe he was carrying and brought it crashing down on the head of one of the gendarmes.

An ugly sound broke out from all sides, followed by a loud trampling of feet as most of the spectators tried to get out of the way. A piercing scream came from the wounded gendarme as he fell to the ground. Women shrieked and tore their hair. The children, crouching at their feet, were crying: and a boy of about ten years old began to throw stones. Then came the pistol-shot, followed by another. Without a word, George fell to the ground, face down, his fingers stretched wide apart. Everybody started shouting. Silellis and the officials were panic-stricken and immediately decamped, along with all the people who had come out for a stroll and who were now only too anxious to get home as fast as their legs would carry them. All the way back to the village their footsteps could be heard clattering along the road. In the field, however, the struggle went on. One of the soldiers still refused to surrender. Raising a shovel with both hands, he brought it crashing down on one of the gendarmes. The latter, in an attempt to evade the blow, bent forward, thus exposing his back to the blow. Spitting blood and firing wildly with his revolver in all directions, he crumpled up. The police sergeant took the revolver from him and struck the soldier who was wielding the shovel a heavy blow in the face with the butt-end of the weapon. The soldier staggered away dizzily, blood pouring from his nose and mouth.

Finally they were all dragged, their hands tied behind their backs, to the police station. The thud of blows delivered with the butt-end of rifles on men's backs echoed all along the route to the station. At their heels trailed the women and children, cursing and blaspheming.

The convoy soon crossed with a party hurrying in the direction of Kouphovouno. It consisted of the adjutant, the Mayor, the doctor, Leon, and the chemist, who was carrying a little black chest. They were accompanied by a gendarme armed with a rifle and bayonet.

As soon as they had reached the scene of the tragedy the police sergeant ordered the gendarme with the bayonet to guard the entrance to the property and to allow no one to enter.

George was lying spreadeagled, face down, on the ground. His wife, her hair dishevelled, was wailing over him while her two children howled and tugged at her clothes. In another corner of the field an unconscious gendarme was groaning. The blood pouring from his sleeve coagulated into a kind of blackish-red substance mixed with earth which looked like a piece of blackened raw liver.

The doctor turned George's body over and raised one of his eyelids. The half-open eye gleamed white. Lowering the eyelid again, the doctor shook his head sadly, making a gesture of finality. It was all over with George.

The woman remained perfectly still while the doctor was examinin-George's body. She held her prominent chin cupped in her hand, her eyes riveted on the doctor's face. His solicitude probably roused a last forlorn hope. But when she saw the gesture of finality she broke out in renewed screams, beating her breast all the while. It was as though George had died all over again.

The doctor left her hurriedly and went to attend to the gendarme. Taking a pair of scissors out of the little black chest, he cut off the bloodsoaked shirt sleeve at the armpit and threw it away with a pair of tweezers. A gaping wound was revealed. The shoulder-blade had been smashed and the arm dangled limply like a broken branch. It looked white and soft, almost childish, drenched in blood. He cleansed the wound with peroxide and tied it so tight with gauze that the blood seemed to ooze out redder than ever through the bandage.

Four men then carried the gendarme wrapped in a blanket to the station. The police sergeant asked the doctor if the gendarme should be driven to the hospital in town by bus along with two other gendarmes and four soldiers who had been less seriously wounded.

'Yes, it's imperative he should be taken to hospital immediately,' replied the doctor. 'He'll be lucky if he escapes tetanus, but they're not likely to save his arm,' and he began to take notes for his casebook.

George's body was then lifted by the arms and feet and carried into the cottage. His shirt had slipped out from under his trousers and a band of flesh showed round the waist. His arms dangled loosely. The woman had run ahead and placed a long blue bolster on a kind of sofa which served as a bed for the entire family. It consisted of a wide mattress, patched with yellow squares, placed on a wooden frame made of boards of unplaned poplar wood. There was no flooring in the room: just the bare soil. The woman hurriedly tried to fluff up the mattress, as though the lumps and hollows might have added to the discomfort of the dead man. As they laid him on the bed the boards creaked loudly. Having arranged his head on the bolster and straightened his hands and feet, the woman bit her lips; drawing in her breath, she then tucked his shirt under his trousers. As she kept moving about from one end of the sofa to the other the two children followed at her heels.

The doctor asked her politely to keep out of the light streaming in from the open door (there was no window in the room) and examined the wound very carefully again; for he would have to fill in a report on the man's death. The bullet had penetrated the left ear and come out through the right temple where the skin and the cranium were pierced and a reddish-coloured pellet, the size of a blackberry, was lodged.

Turning round, the doctor found Leon beside him. 'It was instantaneous,' he said, putting his notebook in his pocket and lighting a cigarette.

The woman was still crouching at the foot of the bed, close to the dead man's feet, the entire weight of her body resting on her heels. She'd placed her hands, with fingers interlocked, between her kness. Stunned by grief, she had stopped wailing; occasionally she shook her head slowly from side to side. She was a dark girl, with a worn face and large eyes, the whites of which shone gruesomely in the shadow where she crouched, gazing fixedly at the face of the dead man. She was alone now, alone with her children and her dead husband. All the other women and children had scurried off behind their husbands to the police station. She had no one to follow.

Two yellow butterflies flitted in through the door. They chased each other round the room, rested for a moment on the dead man's brow, and flew out again into the benign light of day.

The drawers of the smaller of the two boys, a stocky child with black curly hair, hung below his knees; suddenly he lifted a small brown arm and placed it round the woman's neck. He wasn't crying any longer. Rubbing his face against her cheek, he asked: 'Mother, why did they kill Father?'

The question was repeated monotonously several times. The elder boy, standing behind her back, was swallowing the tears and mucus that streamed down his face.

Outside a hen cackled. It wanted to lay an egg. It approached the doorway, picking its way nervously, and squinted inside. It was probably accustomed to laying eggs in some corner of the hut and couldn't understand what had happened to interfere with the routine. Its annoyance was evident.

The woman looked up; her eyes fell on the hen; mechanically she indicated a corner of the room with a sweep of her hand.

Faint clucking sounds came from her lips.

As they left the cottage Leon thought how even in this idyllic village one could meet death face to face. And it wasn't war this time. Nor even a battle. And yet how it resembled it. Men killing other men. The curse of Cain, bequeathed to humanity, like an incurable cancer, from one generation to another.

He returned very late from the club that night. He couldn't keep his mind off the child's words: 'Mother, why did they kill Father?' Other words began to impinge on his consciousness; they were somehow connected with the child's question, but they just managed to elude him. Suddenly he remembered. It was the story of the white man in Africa, trying to explain to a cannibal something of the horror that cannibalism inspires in civilized man.

'All right', replied the cannibal with an air of naive wonder. 'We kill our enemies in order to eat them. But since you don't eat human flesh what on earth do you kill them for?'

21

A NEW angle to the Kouphovouno incident emerged in the course of the interrogation of the ex-soldiers, It concerned the Daphnis family.

The ex-soldiers and their wives referred to repeated nocturnal visits paid by Menos Daphnis to Kouphovouno. He used to take a bottle of spirits with him, and in between rounds—'Well, let's have just one more.' and 'One last one, eh?'—the indoctrination began. The evidence, however, showed that the young man's attempts at proselytizing had had little or no bearing on the subsequent tragedy. He had declaimed on the benefits of the ideal state, in which all land would belong to the community and the peasants who worked it would own nothing—'not even an olive tree!'

In one of these discussions George, so far from being converted, had apparently said half jokingly: 'See here, Menos, that's all right, but until it happens, why don't you get your father to give me back my vineyard? I owed him some money, and he took it away from me. He even made my wife pay interest when I went to the war.'

'These accounts will be settled with the signal for revolution.' replied Menos. 'Then you'll see the heads roll!'

'What sort of a chap are you?' George had said. 'Ever heard of a son wanting his father's head to roll?'

The soldiers had obviously enjoyed pulling Meno's leg while they drank his spirits.

As soon as the police sergeant learnt that young Daphnis was involved he made a series of separate investigations confined to the political aspect of the affair. He also removed the three incriminating depositions, placed them in a separate file, and locked them up. Consequently Meno's name didn't appear in the ducuments forwarded to police headquarters in town.

But he wasted no time in taking Mr. Daphnis into his confidence. He rose early the next morning and went straight to the factory-owner's office. Mr. Daphnis was dipping biscuits in a cup of milk as he dictated letters to an elderly clerk with long drooping moustaches.

The police sergeant stood in the doorway smiling. 'Good morning,' he said.

Mr Daphnis looked up with an air of faint annoyance. He was not at his best early in the morning. He didn't like being disturbed while at work and he was not in no mood for conversation. Moreover, he had never given the police sergeant much encouragement, treating him with the polite though distant condescension he'd shown to all the gendarmerie officials stationed at Megalohori over the course of the years. Throughout this part of the island he was regarded as the official party leader supported by the Ministry of the Interior. Although a mainlander in origin, he had been repeatedly re-elected in this constituency: a feat achieved by means of an organization of his own creation consisting of all the local factory-owners. He retained their allegiance by the dispensation of political favours and occasional judicious loans. He was definitely a power in the land. Consequently the transfer or promotion of a police sergeant might well depend on his good offices.

He greeted the sergeant coldly and continued both his breakfast and his correspondence. He seemed to have some difficulty in finding his words; and he kept glancing sideways at the intruder without asking him to sit down.

The sergeant smiled again, rubbed his hands, and entered the room uninvited. Sitting down on a leather-upholstered armchair, he crossed his legs and smiled all over again.

The clerk peered in horror over the rim of his spectacles at Mr. Daphnis, who in turn gazed with astonishment at the sergeant.

'You'll excuse me,' he said peevishly, 'I'm very busy, as you see. I've really no time for--'

'It doesn't matter,' replied the sergeant, with an air of extreme goodwill, accompanied by the same maddening smile.

'I've got all these letters to write,' insisted Mr. Daphnis firmly.

The sergeant struck his boot with his whip. 'I understand,' and he continued to beat his boot with the whip. 'But couldn't you break off for a minute or two?'

'Break off?' gasped Mr. Daphnis, banging his cup on the saucer with a loud clatter. 'Well, that, for instance . . . D' you mean to say you're so anxious for a chat?'

'Yes, I am,' the sergeant nodded emphatically. 'And I'll ask you to grant me a few minutes of your time; only a few.' The glance he cast at the clerk clearly indicated that he wished their chat to be a private one.

Mr. Daphnis finally realized that the sergeant meant business, so he dismissed the clerk. 'Well, what is it?' he asked impatiently.

'Thank you,' murmured the sergeant, and said nothing more for a few moments, stroking his moustaches reflectively with the handle of his whip.

'You know how much I esteem you, Mr. Daphnis,' he said at last with deliberate slowness, 'though I may not yet have had the chance of showing it. But I've always had your interests at heart. And not only your interests, but your security, your reputation, as well. . . . '

'What on earth . . . ?' Mr. Daphnis looked at him suspiciously.

'It isn't all that serious, of course. But it could lead to unpleasantness. That affair at Kouphovouno, you know.'

Mr Daphnis shrugged his shoulders. 'My dear man,' he said wearily, 'in what way could that unfortunate business be any concern of mine?'

The sergeant leant forward. 'That's just the point,' he said, lowering his voice, 'in certain circumstances it could. It's about Menos, you see, that I'd like to have a word with you. According to the witnesses we've interrogated, he used to go up there every evening and incite the soldiers to pillage, murder, arson. Bolshevism, in fact.'

The implications were not lost on Mr. Daphnis. This was an affair for the courts; it had nothing to do with politics. He pulled his chair so close to the sergeant's that their knees touched.

'Menos? You don't mean it?'

The sergeant raised an eyebrow and nodded, protruding his thick lips as though he were about to whistle. 'It's clear enough in the depositions. Mr. Menos is described as "provoking disorder" and "inciting to revolt against the established order". "The disorders which indeed ensued," it goes on, "were not without victims, including servants of the state." It's all too clear that the moral responsibility for the bloodshed at Kouphovouno lies with . . . '

Mr Daphnis's fingers twitched nervously. He placed a hand on the sergeant's arm. 'Now tell me,' he asked anxiously—he was almost pleading—'what d'you expect will happen? The young scoundrel. . . . God knows what troubles he's laid in store for me. . . . '

The sergeant was thoroughly enjoying himself. He took out a packet of cigarettes, tapped one several times on the arm of the chair, and placed it between his lips. He then held out the packet to Mr. Daphnis, who took one mechanically and started to roll it between two fingers. The policeman slowly replaced the packet in his hip-pocket and produced a lighter.

'Allow me,' he said, offering a light to Mr. Daphnis, who could only repeat:

'What d'you expect will happen?'

The sergeant looked at him. But his glance was a kindly one, the glance of a saviour; and his smile was that of a guardian angel.

'Don't be afraid,' he said. 'Don't forget I'm here. A case of childish irresponsibility, I suppose. That's what it was. I'll save your boy. . . . '

'That's all very well, but what about the depositions? They'll go t
headquarters in town—and you can then imagine what it'll be lik
trying to get hold of them. . . . '

'They've already gone,' said the sergeant. 'They went with the
early-morning bus.'

The pallor spread over Mr. Daphnis's face as he gazed at the
sergeant, who was still smiling.

'As soon as I learnt,' he said, 'what a dangerous game Mr. Menos
had played in this ugly business I realized the difficulty, the great
difficulty, of my position. I was faced with a dilemma: the choice
between duty and friendship. Not very pleasant for me, eh? To tell
you the truth, I hesitated for a long time. Divided loyalties, you
know. There it was. Friendship on the one hand, duty on the other.'
With a show of modesty, he concluded: 'Friendship won.'

'And the depositions?' repeated Mr. Daphnis in an agonized tone
of voice.

'Set your mind at rest. They're safely locked up in my office,' and
he showed him a tiny key which he tossed in the air and then replaced
in his pocket.

Mr. Daphnis got up and shook him by the hand. All the affection
he bore his only son seemed to be expressed in his flushed face, his
trembling voice, as he said: 'And you did this for me? You good man,
you did this for me?' His eyes were brimming with tears.

The sergeant also rose. He patted Mr. Daphnis's hand
affectionately and said in a very dignified tone: 'Calm yourself. It
was nothing, a mere nothing. Nobody'll ever hear a word about it. I
only told you so as to reassure you. Now I think I'd better be going. .

'Please, I beg you, sit down,' and Mr. Daphnis caught him by the
arm. 'How can I thank you? . . . How can I express to you . . . ?'

'Now, now, there's no need, I assure you. Please. If you go on
you'll make me sorry I told you and then . . . '

'Very well, very well,' he said, his face radiant with relief and
emotion. 'When will you come and dine with us?' he added, his eyes
gazing pleadingly into the sergeant's 'When? Tonight? What about
tonight?' And he continued to gaze at him, as though the Almighty
himself were about to pronounce a blessing.

'M'mm, we'll see,' said the sergeant almost coquettishly. 'It's true,
I haven't been in your house since the Minister's last visit. . . . By the
way, how is Mr. Papadatos? Does he ever write to you?'

'Regularly,' replied Mr. Daphnis. 'Why, only yesterday I had a
letter from him. An excellent man. And capable. Devilishly capable.
One must own it, when it comes to politics, most of us here are
nonentities compared to you mainlanders.'

'Capable, is he, eh?'

'Remarkably. You'll remember my words some day when you see him Prime Minister. You can tax him with the most ticklish problem and he'll find the solution in no time. He's a real benefactor to us here.'

'That's it. But you've done a lot for him too, no doubt. He got in in the last elections on the Megalohori vote, didn't he? And weren't the voters nearly all your people?'

'Nearly? My dear man! All, all!' replied Mr. Daphnis complacently. 'Apart from my own share in his newspaper, apart from the eighty subscribers in Megalohori alone, what I do sometimes is to forget, or pretend to forget, about the little sums of money I've lent them from time to time. You understand?'

The police sergeant smiled as though he had just thought of something. 'Just imagine!' He might have been talking to himself. Then he turned and looked at Mr. Daphnis. "Would you like to do me a small favour?'

'Would I like to?' cried Mr. Daphnis, bounding with enthusiasm. 'If only I could. If only. If only it's something I *can* do. . . . Tell me, what is it?'

The police sergeant swung his whip nonchalantly.

'It isn't anything very important. Only this. When you said you'd had a letter from him yesterday it passed through my mind that when you acknowledge it you might like to mention the question of my promotion. . . . It keeps being put off. . . . I can't understand what's happened. You see, if the Minister really wanted . . . '

'If he really wanted?' cried Mr. Daphnis. 'Listen to that! If he wanted! I'll write to him at once.' He repeated with dramatic emphasis: 'At once.'

He sat down at his desk, took out some headed paper, and wrote a cordial letter to the Minister, which he then read aloud to the sergeant. He begged the Minister to do his utmost in order that the good man should obtain his long-awaited promotion. If he didn't grant him this little favour he'd have to conclude that the Minister no longer set much store to their friendship. He concluded:

. . . .With every respect towards your esteemed person,
Yours very sincerely,
Petros D. Daphnis.

In a postscript he added:

My wife, as well as that young scoundrel, Menos, send you their kindest regards. I enclose herewith all the relevant information concerning my great friend, the police sergeant. In the meantime I await your answer, which surely cannot be otherwise than favourable, with impatience.

'Fine!' cried the sergeant, taking the letter from him. He scribbled some notes—the 'relevant information' pertaining to his career in the force—on a separate sheet and said:

'Will you let me post it myself? I'll do it at once. I know you'll want a quick reply. I'll send it registered.'

Mr. Daphnis looked at him for a moment and then nodded his assent. Smiling and patting him affectionately on the back, he led him to the door.

'My friend, my good friend! And, as we said, you'll come to dinner one night. . . . As we said, eh?'

In the doorway the sergeant said playfully: 'I trust the answer won't take long. And I promise you, the day I get the good news, I'll bring you those depositions as a souvenir.'

Mr. Daphnis's face clouded over for a moment.

'Of course, of course,' he said hurriedly. 'You may rest assured. If necessary I'll write again. Whatever happens you'll get your promotion.'

As a result of these melancholy events, Megalohori remained in a state of ferment for several days. Emotions were exacerbated by the Press: both Athenian and local. The Athenian papers, of course, presented the incident according to their party lights. The Venizelist Press wrote of guerilla tactics mobilized by Royalist forces; the Refugee newspapers described it as an attempt on the part of the natives to seize ex-Turkish property allotted to the refugees by international agreements, while the Communist sheets hailed it as an uprising of the downtrodden peasants against their capitalist oppressors.

The soldiers were flung into the dungeons of the castle in town, and their houses were left empty and unguarded.

One day the wife of one of the imprisoned men, half demented with despair, made her way to Mr. Daphnis's house, accompanied by her three children.

It was early afternoon. With a shove of the shoulder she pushed open the iron gate usually reserved for horses and mules, and entered the courtyard with a firm step. There, under the dense arbour of creeping vines, were assembled the Daphnis family, reclining in deck-chairs, sipping their after-luncheon coffee. Mr. Daphnis raised his eyes slowly from the newspaper he was reading. He was not wearing a jacket and the two top buttons of his trousers were undone in the interests of comfort.

'What d'you want, my good woman?' he asked.

His voice sounded gentle and drowsy as he lay back comfortably relaxed after a good meal. Mrs. Daphnis half opened her eyes like a cat. Mina looked up, lay back again, put a cigarette between her lips, and blew out a great puff of white smoke.

Menos immediately recognized the woman's distracted face and was seized with agitation. It was one of the faces he used to see by the light of the hanging bulb in the course of those nocturnal visits to Kouphovouno when he talked to the ex-soldiers about the class war. He cast a quick glance at his father. Mr. Daphnis knew the cause of his agitation. The woman, taken aback by the peaceful scene, lost the courage that had sustained her at first. She stood erect in the middle of the corridor with the grey and white panes of glass arranged in such a way as to form the word 'Welcome' on the glass doorway. In her bewilderment she kept plucking at her apron. The three children, sucking their thumbs, clung to her.

'What do you want, my good woman?' Mr. Daphnis repeated in the same gentle tone.

Deflated, she lowered her eyes and began to babble: 'Well, you see. . . . I'm Stylianos's wife. Mr. Menos there remembers me. . . . My husband's a muleteer. They've put him in prison now, you know, because of the revolution. . . . What am I to do? Without a husband . . . with these three children. . .? How can I work when I have these . . ? What's going to become of me?'

Distress, if not fear, was expressed on all their faces as they gazed pityingly at her, waiting for a pronouncement from Mr. Daphnis.

The woman turned to Menos. 'D'you see my children now? D'you see them?'

Menos was fully aware that what she really wanted to say was: 'See? We killed people—as you, your lordship, told us to. And now you lie back snoozing comfortably while we starve to death.'

It was apparent that she'd set out determined to get even with him, but it was also apparent that she'd lost the game before it ever began.

All this was perfectly clear to Mr. Daphnis.

'Poor creature! It's certainly not your fault. You're just a victim . .' he said at last.

He summoned the maid and told her to give the woman a double portion of bread. To the woman he said: 'Come to my office tomorrow and I'll see what we can do for you. Either in the tobacco factory or somewhere else . . . There it is. We're all going through difficult times. A little Christian charity. . . . We're all His servants. We must give each other a helping hand whenever we can. . . . '

The woman, although defeated in her original purpose, departed showering blessings on him. Her eyes filled with tears of gratitude. She dragged the smallest of the children by the hand, as though it were a recalcitrant dog on a leash. Its face was turned back, gazing wide-eyed at the receding scene of peace and plenty.

A few days later Menos and his fiancée returned to Athens before the end of the summer vacation. 'They've gone back to study,' Mr. Daphnis explained to his friends, adding to himself: 'For better or worse.'

22

COMING back to the house one day at noon, Leon was struck by Adriani's strange behaviour. She kept blushing, leaving her sentences unfinished and laughing for no apparent reason.

'Come on,' he said, 'you've got something on your mind, and you can hardly wait to tell me. Come on, get it out. You know you're not going to have a moment's peace until you do.'

She leapt up with a lithe movement, sat on the arm of his chair and tweaked his ear. Then the words came out like a pistol-shot:

'D'you ever think of getting married?'

'It depends.'

'Don't evade the question. What would you say if you were asked: "What is marriage?" '

'I'd say it's the best cure for love. Cure guaranteed. The only trouble is it's a pretty long and tedious cure. It lasts a lifetime.'

She looked disappointed, but went on: 'Isn't love incurable sometimes?'

'In such cases . . . well, the cure in superfluous. Come on, for God's sake, tell me what it's all about. Stop going round in circles.'

'All right. I'll tell you. Your godmother's been throwing out hints about you.'

'My godmother?' He started, and looked at her. After a brief silence he began to shake with laughter.

'Heavens, what a romantic bridegroom you'd make!' Although her tone of voice was quite serious, there was more than just a mere suggestion of mockery in it.

'And . . . which of the two am I supposed to choose?'

'Whichever you prefer,' replied Adriani, still trying to look serious.

'Oh, it's too wonderful, really. Look for trouble and you're bound to find it. Well, what sort of hints did she make?'

'She says she's been given to understand Aspasia rather likes you.'

'And how has my godmother been "given to understand" Aspasia rather likes me? Has Aspasia said so?'

'No, but she's constantly running you down and hasn't a good word for you.'

'What an admirable exercise for a future wife. So Madam Evtychia doesn't only suffer from contractions of the heart. Garrulousness, in an advanced stage, must obviously be added to her list of ailments.'

'She also says Loulou, if you preferred her, wouldn't say no.'

'And the poor doctor?'

'I said exactly the same thing, as tactfully as I could. But she says she's certain Loulou wouldn't give the doctor another thought if you came to the point. . . . '

'Of proposing ? To Loulou? Thank you. I hadn't quite visualized myself as a kind of bust bodice for Loulou's ample bosom. Quite apart from the fact that she's my godfather's daughter, and therefore any thought of marriage between us is out of the question.'

This time Adriani tweaked both his ears quite hard. She was trying not to look too obviously relieved.

'You're the limit,' she said, 'and very ungrateful. Think what a wonderful opportunity you're missing of becoming a wealthy landowner and heir to the mayoralty of Megalohori.'

'That's to say two opportunities. Impressive, isn't it?'

Adriani suddenly dropped her bantering tone and asked: 'Tell me, seriously, have you never thought of getting married?'

'Never. The only marriage I ever give any thought to is yours. I don't think marriage is my vocation.'

'And if you really fell in love with somebody one day?'

He scrutinized her face. There wasn't the slightest hint in the expression of her clear blue eyes that she had anything particular in mind.

'If I really fell in love . . . ?' he repeated. 'Why then . . . I wouldn't get married for the very reason I've just told you—in order to preserve that love.'

'My dear,' she said, 'I predict your old age will be as full of philosophical contemplation as Mr. Yanni's.'

'How very odd. . . . '

It was not long before Mr. Yanni, inventor of the theory of the chemical reproduction of the human race, became one of the two leading protagonists in a scandal which created such a stir in Megalohori that it even brought on one of Madam Evtychia's heart attacks: a terrible attack which taxed the strength of that ailing organ of hers to the utmost.

It was a Saturday afternoon when Sultana, the Mayor's maid, appeared before Madam Evtychia squealing like a pig being led to slaughter. She wept noisily, wiping her eyes with her pink little fists.

'Madam, Madam!'

Madam Evtychia was terrified. Had there been some terrible

accident? She approached the girl, her kindly eyes bulging, her heart filled with the secret rapture with which the prospect of public lamentation always inspired her.

'What's the matter with you, my child?' she cried. 'Don't go on like that. What's happened? Is there anything wrong with your mother? Have you had bad news from the village?'

'No, no.' Sultana shook her head in between sobs which made her breast jerk up and down as though she had the hiccups. She tried to speak but succeeded only in stammering some disjointed words.

'Come, come, my child, don't go on like that,' said Madam Evtychia, almost disappointed. 'Tell me what's the matter. In this house am I not a second mother to you?'

The girl began to regain a little courage. 'It's . . . it's because I have to take communion tomorrow, madam,' and she swallowed the tears coursing down her cheeks with great gulping sounds.

'Heavens above! And what's wrong in your taking communion tomorrow? Who's preventing you from . . . '

'I can't!' cried Sultana, in a renewed paroxysm of weeping. 'I can't . . . ever, madam!'

'Well, it's not the end of the world really. . . . Have you been so greedy again that you've broken your fast?'

'No, no,' Sultana shook her head again and moaned despairingly. 'I . . . I've sinned, madam!'

Her misery and sense of humiliation were obviously acute, and Madam Evtychia immediately sensed what lay behind her words. It was like a hint about whose meaning there could be little doubt.

'Heavens, what a calamity!' cried Madam Evtychia, catching hold of the girl's cheek. 'Heavens, what a calamity you've brought down on your head, accursed child!'

Sultana's lamentations grew louder. 'What's going to happen to me, madam? . . . Oh . . . what's going to happen to me? How can I face the priest? How can I go and confess? How am I going to take communion, madam? Oh-h-h, madam!'

Madam Evtychia was driven almost out of her wits.

'D'you mean to say you never thought of the shame you'd bring on your house, let alone on mine?' she shouted, stamping her foot. 'How d'you think you'll ever dare look anyone in the face again? Where d'you think you're going to hide your shame? Ah, you didn't think of that, eh? And all you can talk about is taking communion. Communion! How d'you dare let the word pass your lips, you brazen hussy!'

Sultana stopped weeping and listened attentively for a moment;

then she burst into renewed sobbing. Madam Evtychia's words had thrown a new and terrible aspect on the matter.

The Mayor's wife was pacing up and down the room, slapping her hands against her thighs in her agitation. 'Oh dear, oh dear!' she murmured. 'And who's . . . the . . . the. . . who . . . you shameless hussy?'

'Mr. . . . Mr. Yanni, madam,' the words were almost catapulted out of the girl's mouth. 'Mr. Yanni, yes, it's him.'

Madam Evtychia nearly had a fit. For a moment she remained speechless; then she approached Sultana and removed the grubby hands in which the girl's face was buried.

The face was round with crimson cheeks bursting with health. Sooty smudges, mixed with tears, surrounded her eyes which she'd been rubbing with her dirty fingers.

'Mr. Yanni!' cried the Mayor's wife incredulously. 'You're lying, you slut. That old man . . . that bundle of bones!'

'I'm not lying madam,' Sultana assured her, making the sign of the cross and quickly kissing her crossed fingers three times. 'May I burn in everlasting hell fire if I'm not telling the truth!'

Dumbfounded, Madam Evtychia made the girl sit down on the sofa beside her; she made her tell her everything. Not that Sultana showed much reluctance. No details were spared.

So Mr. Yanni was the villain of the piece. For about a year now he'd been trailing after her, winking, ogling, cracking jokes. Occasionally there'd been a bit of slap and tickle. Sultana, simple-minded and unsuspecting, had sometimes listened to him, sometimes rebuffed him, and sometimes, the little idiot, positively encouraged him. Who'd have thought it possible? Well, to cut a long story short, she had once stroked his neck—that sparrow's neck! Why hadn't she thought of strangling him instead!—And so, what with one thing and another, the old satyr had got what he wanted. It was one day during the fig harvest. In the hut. Behind all the baskets. She hadn't even realized what had happened at first!

Madam Evtychia listened with mounting horror. Finally the climax was reached: the girl was pregnant.

'A baby! But weren't you afraid? . . . . Aren't you afraid of how God'll punish you?' cried Madam Evtychia, turning pale, her knees shaking. 'A bastard child! What's going to happen to us all? Oh, you slut!'

Sultana confessed she'd done everything she could think of to bring on a miscarriage. She had tried single-handed to lift the heavy table on which they ironed the clothes; she had carried basket after basket of laundered clothes; she had beaten the carpets fiercely with her hands; she had attemped to jump over the vines like the men do at the grape harvest. She had done everything. What had she not done?

Madam Evtychia sent for her husband. She told him everything in detail. The honour of the house was at stake. The Mayor's house. Mr. Spanos immediately sent for Mr. Yanni. He was to be brought to the house by hook or by crook.

Madam Evtychia's nerves were in such a state that she very nearly had a contraction. Left alone with her daughters in the little sitting-room, she said she felt it coming on. But, thinking it over, she decided it was wiser not to have one. If the doctor were sent for all the neighbourhood would be alerted; in the circumstances it was better to hush the whole shocking episode up until her husband had decided what they had best do. So she remained in the little sitting-room, weeping in the arms of her daughters.

When Mr. Yanni arrived, Mr. Spanos, his hands behind his back, was pacing up and down the large drawing-room, his highly polished shoes squeaking officiously. He was ready to burst with indignation when he saw Mr. Yanni enter the room with his docile, apathetic air. Noisily shutting the door of frosted glass, he stood in front of the wretched man with clenched fists.

'There, that's for you, sir!' and he spat in Mr. Yanni's face.

Mr. Yanni took a small handkerchief out of his pocket, wiped his face, folded it with great care and put it back again.

'What's the matter?' he asked feebly.

He looked feeble—so small and feeble—standing there like a prematurely aged child. The wrinkles gathered round his eyes, screwed up as though to ward off a dazzling light.

The Mayor's shoes still squeaked officiously as he paced across to the other end of the room. He returned and stood in front of Mr. Yanni. Complete silence reigned. There was not even the sound of the squeaking shoes. It was like the silence in an auditorium just before the curtain goes up. It was clear that Mr. Spanos was trying to be angry, very angry, as indeed the occasion demanded.

'I spit on you, wretch!' he cried out at last. 'May the bread with which I feed you turn to gall and wormwood in your rotten intestines. Scoundrel! Blackguard!'

'But why?' piped Mr. Yanni almost unconcernedly.

'Wretch! Couldn't you have respected my house? Weren't you ashamed of your white hair when you did it? Didn't you think of the poor innocent girl's reputation? Scoundrel!'

'Is it about Sultana?'

'Yes, it's about Sultana,' thundered Mr. Spanos. 'It's about Sultana I'm talking to you.'

'How extraordinary!'

'Ha, you find it extraordinary?' and he imitated Mr. Yanni's piping voice. 'You'll find it even more extraordinary when they chuck you into prison for your misdeeds. What are you going to do about the child now, the bastard child?'

Mr Yanni nearly jumped out of his skin. A shaft of light passed across his faded little eyes and seemed to illumine the countless wrinkles round them.

'She's going to have a baby?' His voice trembled.

'Listen to the man's impudence!' exclaimed Mr. Spanos in amazement, '"She's going to have a baby?" you ask? Just like that? As though it weren't any concern of yours? To what depths have you sunk, you wretch?'

He continued to growl, pacing up and down and around the room, his squeaking shoes most effectively expressing the petulance of his mood.

Mr. Yanni finally stirred himself—that little scarecrow of a man standing in the middle of the Mayor's drawing-room like a wooden puppet, the Mayor's cast-off clothes hanging limply on his skinny limbs.

Running his tongue across his lips, he said: 'Listen here, your honour. What's done, can't be undone.' His squeaky little voice suddenly acquired an almost official tone. 'I fell into temptation. I don't deny it. I'm to blame. I was a victim of human frailty—the flesh, you know. But,' and he struck his chest with his hand, 'I'm a man of honour.' The emphasis he placed on the word 'man' seemed to give him confidence. 'And I don't intend to bring dishonour either on your house or the girl or the brat--'

'D'you imagine an affair of this kind,' interrupted the Mayor, 'can be patched up so easily, like darning a hole in a stocking? Come, come, man!'

Mr. Yanni raised a hand, as though about to take an oath, and said with a very tragic air: 'I shall do my duty, your honour. My duty. I shall marry Sultana!'

'What?' said the Mayor distractedly.

'It's my duty as a man of honour,' the old man squeaked theatrically.

The Mayor scratched his cheek; he fixed Mr. Yanni with a penetrating all-embracing glance.

The little man was standing, as though at attention, below a picture entitled Oedipus and Antigone.

'Fine figure of a bridegroom you'll make,' said the Mayor, hunching his shoulders. 'But there's no other way out. Unless you put your neck in a noose, tie a stone to it, and throw yourself into the sea.'

'No, no . . . I prefer the first alternative!' said the old man. Suddenly all the wrinkles of his face seemed to quiver and concentrate around his mouth. It might have been an attempt at a sly little smile.

From the top of the staircase the Mayor shouted for Sultana. She climbed the stairs and shuffled in with bowed head. Her vacant cow-like eyes were red from weeping. She proceeded with the shrinking gait of a dog that knows it's going to be soundly whipped.

Seeing Mr. Yanni standing below the picture in his Napoleonic stance, she raised her head and said to him: 'There, see what you've done now!'

Mr. Yanni didn't reply. But he smiled in an affectionate, even protective, way. Placing one knee forward, he began to shake his leg in his baggy trousers.

'Listen, Sultana,' said the Mayor, 'Mr. Yanni's going to do the right thing by you. He's going to marry you. He's going to make you his wife. As for me . . . what can I do? I'll help you as much as I can.'

Sultana raised her eyes; gazing at her future bridgeroom, she said very simply: 'How d'you feel about it?'

The Mayor then began to shout and scold her. He expatiated on the extent of her iniquity. 'What'll you feel like when you can't hide your condition from the world any longer? How do you like the idea of being the mother of a bastard child, eh?' He added: 'Unless, of course, you intend to do away with it. But that can't happen in my house. Understand? That no. I'd have to report it to the police. If you think I'm going to be another Herod you're mistaken.'

He was shouting so loud that the window-panes rattled as in a thunderstorm. The squeaking of his shoes added to the general tumult. Never in his life had Mr. Spanos succeeded in getting so angry. He realized this; and he was full of secret admiration at his achievements as he paced up and down the room like a caged animal. His wife should have been there to see him.

Sultana, terror-stricken at the spectacle presented by her master, glanced at Mr. Yanni again. Her childish mind was trying to solve a little problem: how would this bony little man fit in her narrow bed—night after night—and in winter, with his feet like blocks of ice. She thought of him in his calico drawers. Her train of thought was distracted by her master's furious thunderings. Well, he ruled here, after all, didn't he? That's how it was. That's how it had to be. Do this, do that. And she did it. For Sultana, like a good servant, was an obedient girl.

She raised her shoulders, glanced curiously at Mr. Yanni again, and turned her pink face towards Mr. Spanos.

'As you say, your honour,' she said, 'I'll do whatever you say.'

There was a short silence and then she asked timidly: 'And now . . . can I take communion?'

23

THE effect of the scandal was like the plop of a stone in a sluggish bog, ruffing the smooth surface of provincial life. The underwater convulsion had barely subsided before all the little frogs, long concealed under the mantle of slime, leapt to the surface. Naked, slippery, with distended green bellies, they began to croak hoarsely. In every café, at every street corner, the sole topic of conversation was the strange idyll of Mr. Yanni and Sultana. Imaginations boggled at the thought of the old man and the girl, a mere child, tumbling about in secluded corners of shady vineyards. Every aspect of the amorous episode was conjured up by the villagers. They got a lot of fun out of it too, identifying themselves with the two protagonists, experiencing the distress, agitated by their lust. It became, in fact, a screen on which the entire village could project its own frustrated desires.

The summer sun beat down mercilessly on the little town and on the walls of its ruined castle, casting a dazzling sheen over the expanse of tepid sea and wooded mountain slopes. The red-brick tiles of the roofs were baked red-hot, the fig trees grew heavy with the burden of their fruit, and the parched soil contracted and cracked into numerous small fissures. The earth itself seemed to gasp with the heat. Every breath of the air was like an exhalation from a furnace.

At first the Mayor was beside himself with despair, and the hints and innuendoes of the villagers very nearly made him lock himself up in his house and refuse to see anyone. Finally he decided to treat the whole thing as a joke. 'Think of it. Just think of it! Mr. Yanni of all people! Makes one think, doesn't it? One feels one can hardly trust one's own grandfather!'

The least concerned by all the commotion was the chief protagonist, Mr. Yanni. He even put on airs as he formally accepted the mocking congratulations of his acquaintances. His whole face seemed to break out into laughter, pride and self-satisfaction exuding from its countless wrinkles. He strutted about like a bedraggled old cock, suddenly reminded of the fact that it still has a masculine rôle to play in the roost. He wore his hat as though it were a cock's comb, red as a Turk's tarboosh, and devoted himself to the task of overcoming the disabilities of his age so that he might crow as loudly as the proudest rooster. But in his own way Mr. Yanni knew how to crow. He straightened his narrow shoulders, shaved frequently, and at night he laid out his trousers neatly under his mattress. He also began to acquire a peculiar way of walking, as though he were tripping. One could imagine a pair of little wings sprouting under his green jacket, ready to open the moment the jacket was removed and waft him gently in the air to the top of the belfry, like one of those winged dragonflies. It was with difficulty that he kept his feet to the ground.

One day Leon went for a walk and suddenly came upon him in a field of vegetable marrows. He was carrying a basket and appeared to be delighted to see Leon. 'They've sent me here to pick vegetables,' he said.

Although Leon had no intention of offering him an opening, Mr. Yanni was obviously itching to bring the conversation round to the burning topic.

'Sultana was to have come with me,' he said. 'This is a woman's job really ... but, I think you'll agree with me, it's better she shouldn't be seen too much out with me ... There's no stopping people talking... When we're married—in a month's time, if all goes well, it'll be a different matter.'

'True enough,' said Leon. 'You must forgive me for having forgotten to congratulate you. You've certainly gone and done it, as they say, haven't you?'

The wrinkles in the old man's face creased with pleasure. He placed the basket on the ground and took up a stand (he was wearing an old pair of trousers of the Mayor's), his legs wide apart, like a wrestler full of confidence in his prowess.

'Well, I suppose I was lucky, eh?'

'But how did you manage it, man?'

'Desire ... the desire to reproduce oneself ...' squeaked the old man. 'Let the village gossips have their say. Who cares? Let them ask themselves the why and the where and the how... "Father, forgive them; for they know not what they do." ....'

Leon laughed. 'And what about the theory of chemistry?'

A more serious expression stole into Mr. Yanni's face. He raised an eyebrow.

'That, excuse me,' he said, 'is a different matter. Science is science, and the business of living is something else. At least, that's how I see it.'

He stooped down and, selecting a small tender cucumber from the basket, presented it to Leon.

They parted and he soon came upon a boy engaged in putting up the supports for the branches of some quince trees which were giving way under the weight of their fruit. Taking an axe, he descended into the valley and chopped up a bundle of sticks in order to give the boy a hand. They were very young trees with slender branches and coarse matt-coloured leaves; the ponderous fat quinces hanging from the branches were like the udders of a cow just after it had given birth to a calf.

The job lasted until midday. He was happy. He had something comforting to think about: he had just begun a new picture, it would be there when he got back, ready to welcome him as its creator! He felt an intoxicating sense of pleasure, well disposed towards everybody and everything. He bounded as he walked, carefree as a truant schoolboy. Youth, liberty! How sweet they were, after all. He felt he'd never really been allowed to enjoy them before. It reminded him of that time during the war when he had first learnt to prize life for its own sake.

He reached a steep rough-hewn stairway. In order to shorten the distance between the zig-zag bends, he scrambled down the slope, clinging to the branches of shrubs for support. He sat down to rest on a boulder near a water conduit and picked up a moss-covered stone, stroking its furry surface as though it were the head of a child. The velvety moss was cool to the touch. Suddenly a snake slid from under a loose dry stone. In spite of a sensation of revulsion, he raised his stick and struck it just before it had time to slither away under the stones. The blow cut off the tail, which was left quivering and squirming on the ground, while the head with the rest of the body succeeded in wriggling away and vanished from sight. It was a grass snake. He remembered them from childhood days. They weren't venomous. There was an old wives' tale that if provoked they would pick up pebbles with their tail and sling them at one, as though from a catapult. There was also a story that they were suckled by cows and goats. What nonsense, he thought, gazing at the tail lying motionless on the ground; as he was doing so, it was suddenly shaken by a last violent convulsion. Long columns of ants began to converge. They surrounded the lifeless tail. They seemed to parley between themselves before making up their minds. But it wasn't long before they were nibbling greedily at the unexpected morsel.

He continued towards the beach at the Sentinel. On the way he saw a cluster of small blue flowers; they had tall slender stems like metal hairs. He picked them and looked for more, delighted when he came across another cluster. By the time he reached the Sentinel he had picked quite a large bunch. He went straight down to the shore, knowing he'd find Adriani and Sappho there. He had told Adriani in the morning that he would fetch them. He descended slowly in order to surprise them, knowing only too well how wrong of him it was to do so.

They were lying in their bathing-dresses sunbathing on a flat rock, their heads shaded by a dark red umbrella. The surface of the rock was burning hot.

He covered his mouth with his hands and shouted: 'Booh to you! The Triton's come for you!'

They jumped up in alarm; but when they saw who it was they began to laugh. Adriani lay back lazily on the rock. She was saying something to him; he could hear the words distinctly, but their meaning made no impact. Sappho was standing erect on the rock. She had jumped up the moment she heard his voice with that peculiar elasticity that characterized all her movements. It reminded him of the reflex action of two branches after they've been parted by someone groping in a dense thicket.

She disappeared into a hiding-place between two rocks, where he imagined her getting dressed. He suddenly experienced a sensation of desire so intense that it stung like a whip-lash; it hurt, physically and mentally; it reminded him of his reaction to the sight of the snake gliding out from the stones.

Adriani was still talking to him, and he kept smiling stupidly, without taking in a word she said; he was listening to the sound of a low soft whistling in his ears, like the plaintive long-drawn-out wail of a clarinet.

'Come on, hurry up and dress. We must be going,' he called out, trying to make his voice sound as natural as possible. 'I'm dying of hunger.'

He leant back, letting the weight of his body rest against a rock, for he suddenly felt very tired. The metallic shrilling of the cicadas, with its unending vibrations filling the air, like a personification of monotony itself, came from the olive-clad hill above. The sound beat against his temples, drumming in his brain as in an empty vessel. He tried to resolve the vision of Sappho, leaping gracefully from rock to rock, her bathing-dress clinging to her glistening body, into some aesthetic parallel.

He wondered. Didn't her movements conjure up an image of a sword blade drawn back as far as it would go, then suddenly released-snap! Perhaps that was it. A naked sword erect in the sunlight.

The parallel pleased him; it comforted him, as though the effort to arrive at it had been the cause of his anguish. The tip of a straw tickled the back of his neck. The sense of touch. Nothing else. Nevertheless it gave him a slight, a very slight, sensual thrill. The vision of the parallel between Sappho and the sword rose up before him again: an unsheathed sword bending in the sunlight. Then he thought the whole thing too silly and smiled ironically.

'How much literature,' he thought, 'we have to apply to life in order to grasp the meaning of it!'

He heard the padding of the girls' sandalled feet across the pebbly shore as they came towards him. They were dressed. He shook hands with Sappho.

'It's ages since I've seen you,' he said as casually as possible. But he could think of nothing else to add.

'Yes,' she replied, looking down at the ground. She too had nothing further to say.

Of course, he had no one but himself to blame for his embarrassment. He knew that. His sideways glance fell on the tip of her ear reddened by the sun, as he thought of the intrinsic falseness of his remark: 'It's ages since I've seen you!' True enough. For he'd been positively looking for ways of tormenting himself lately, trying to find excuses to leave the house the moment she came to see his sister. Yet he'd been acutely conscious of her presence in the house: conscious of her talking to Adriani, in the courtyard, in the pergola with the wistaria, or out on the beach at the Portara. He'd go there, of course, after she'd gone and search for the imprint of their recumbent bodies on the sand, trying to guess which had been left by hers. Then he would go back to the Tower and listen to her words echoing in the drawing-room. He would think of her words in terms of physical entities floating round the room until they came to rest like birds on a piece of furniture: a chair, a table, a cupboard. The atmosphere of the room was impregnated with the fragrance of her body: the fragrance of an enormous cluster of jasmine.

Walking beside her now, he was aware of the same scent of jasmine.

'You've been picking flowers?' she said at last—obviously in order to say something. 'They're quite lovely, aren't they? You may not believe it, but I've never seen them before.'

He glanced down at the bunch in his hand. He had completely forgotten them.

'Of course I believe it,' he replied; 'it's also the first time I've seen them. May I give them to you?'

He wanted to say: 'They're for the vase in front of Vranas's photograph,' but he didn't. He offered them to her awkwardly, half jokingly. He felt he wanted to laugh, knowing only too well that he had picked every one of them for her, subconsciously repeating her name as he broke the slender stalks.

'Thank you.' She took them and he noticed the quick surreptitious glance she cast at him.

'A golden glance,' he thought, 'from a pair of golden eyes, as brief and transitory as the yellow flash from a distant gun.'

'Thank you,' she repeated. 'I've also got to thank you for all the other flowers you've sent me lately. I know it's for him—in memory of him—and sometimes it makes me cry . . . .'

'We must never forget him,' he said very deliberately. 'After all, he had no one else . . . but us two.'

What he really meant was that Vranas's ghost would never be laid until they'd banished his memory from their minds; and that would be like killing him all over again. He did nothing to clarify his words. But he sensed that she understood. It was evident from her silence.

A curious sensation came over him: a kind of double-edged sensation. One moment he was burning hot, the next freezing cold. A giant conflagration consumed him; then the ice froze the marrow of his bones. Suddenly, with a mixture of misery and relief, he realized what it was all about. The ghost of Vranas had come between them again. They were no longer alone, just the three of them, below the cliffs at the Sentinel. There was another presence among them.

Adriani had lagged behind, and he could hear the crunch of the shingle under her sandals. But it wasn't Adriani's sandals. It was the crunch of the dead man's polished army boots. He knew he had only to turn round and see him: slight, dark, his eyes bright like two lighted coals, his eyebrows drawn in a thick straight line across his forehead. And as he crunched along behind them he would be thinking what a cad the man in front of him was—a contemptible little twirp, fancying himself as a local Don Juan, a superficial, dishonourable, treacherous creature, trying to seduce his wife with bunches of flowers offered in his name and using his own death as a means to further his adulterous intentions. How could the beloved war-time friend be this traitor who had made his coffin a Trojan horse in order to penetrate his wife's bedroom? How could he be called a man in the real sense of the word, a man who had once been an officer in the Greek army and had led other men into battle?

As though in a dream he heard Adriani say: 'What extraordinary flowers,' as she took the bunch from Sappho's hands, 'they're like miniature flowers.'

He repeated her words mechanically to himself, and they seemed to merge into the chorus of shrilling cicadas. 'Mi-nia-ture flow'rs, mi-nia-ture flow'rs!'

'Oh, do look, Leon,' Adriani was now addressing him, 'they're the colour of the sky, aren't they? Real sky-blue.'

He said something in reply—he was in too much of a fluster to realize exactly what he was saying—and then suddenly he heard his voice assuming a flat official tone as he began a discourse, in the most professional manner, on the gradation of colours.

Adriani began to look for coloured pebbles. She was mad about her collection and once she had started looking for them it was difficult to tear her away. She had quite a collection at the Tower. The only trouble with them was that the moment their surface dried, the colour faded and one had to wet them in order to bring it out again.

'I had the same mania at one time,' said Sappho. 'I kept them in a shallow glass bowl and poured water over them every morning.'

She stooped down and picked up a little cherry-coloured stone, like a Byzantine seal, which she handed to Adriani. 'They're like flowers really. They fade unless you water them.'

Her words were without significance, but the way in which she spoke them moved him inexplicably.

He was walking behind her, unable to take his eyes off her swaying gait; it might have been some kind of visual music, he thought, whose harmonies were constantly woven into a series of glorious themes, elaborating into new variations which, while they soothed and lulled him, brought his love for her into ever sharper focus. At the same time he recognized the essential hypocrisy upon which his metaphor was based, and he was forced to face the situation squarely. He loved her. Certainly. It was better to admit the fact: without shame, without mincing matters. He had loved her, while hating her of course, from the moment he first saw her in the schoolroom. Worse still, he was literally tormented by desire. Ever since the day he had seen her lying half naked on the beach he mentally undressed her every time they met. 'Ah, Tartuffe,' he thought, 'Whoever looks on a woman with lust has committed adultery already with her in his heart.' How like the typical straitlaced Megalohorian villager, preaching morality, with that lust in his heart! He thought of Salome—a Salome no longer dancing. What a masquerade! Pure escapism! So he would force himself to listen to the voice of truth rising, like the voice of the Baptist, from the depths of his subconscious. But he was frightened at what he heard. The real Salome stood before him, in all her abomination. What held him back then? He would perform his little dance on the rotting corpse of Vranas. Cold cynical words raced through his mind, like the flutter of a bat's wings. He tried to keep them back, raising his hand to his mouth. But wasn't it time they were uttered? There, they were out now: 'Lieutenant Vranas's death was no doubt a very timely one for you, Mr. Drivas!'

He stuck his walking stick on the ground.

Under his breath he muttered: 'Shut up!' But the words were muttered loud enough, it seemed to him, to go on ringing in his ears. No, he could never let himself sink so low. He was sure of that. If it came to the worst he'd leave the island.

That was it. Go away. Seek salvation elsewhere. Go to Athens. Go straight to Paris: the journey he'd so often dreamed of. After all, he wasn't an entirely worthless person. By no means.

A bustle of activity suddenly broke out on two fishing-boats, painted red and yellow respectively, which had been lying motionless on the calm water. The two girls, who had been walking in front of Leon, stopped to watch. The fishermen were shouting across to each other. There had apparently been a big catch, and they were now busy casting the nets. The rim of corks attached to the edges of the nets bobbed up and down on the oily water. There was a terrific din, as the fishermen at the oars shouted to those casting the nets, while the two at the helm shouted to the rest. It seemed odd that order could emerge out of such chaos. Hardly had the circle of nets been formed than they started dragging them in. It was such a large haul that the men had to lean right over the holds.

'What a catch!' exclaimed Sappho. Adriani was practically dancing with childish delight at the sight of the quivering mass of silver-coloured fish, leaping and slithering in the nets. 'They look like silver,' continued Sappho, 'but the colour's really more like that of tin.'

'Tin?'

'Yes, you should see them when they unload the baskets at the harbour. I assure you, they're the colour of tin, with a rusty-green lime across the back.'

'That's because they live in the water,' said Leon, who had now caught up with them.

They had reached the crossroads where they had to separate.

'Listen,' Adriani told Sappho, 'why don't you come and have lunch with us? I don't know what there is to eat in the house, but there's plenty of fruit.'

Leon said nothing. Before replying, Sappho cast a hurried glance in his direction. Then she refused. 'Thank you very much, but I really must get back home. I've got so much work to do this afternoon.'

The moment he was alone he began to wonder. What could Sappho have read in the expression of his eyes to make her refuse Adriani's invitation. There had certainly been a momentary gleam of fear in her own eyes; and it was not the first time he had noticed it. It was generally on occasions when they happened to be alone. Yes, he was sure of it. But what had she to be afraid of? he asked himself. Did his face, when they were alone, conjure up some dreadful image in her mind? Unless .. she was afraid of herself.

'So that's what you're up to,' mocked that inner cynical self of his, with a lewd knowing wink; 'it would certainly suit your purpose if she were in love with you, wouldn't it? Then you could shift all the responsibility for the abominable act you're contemplating on to her, couldn't you, you wretch?'

He was often wearied by these endless acrimonious dialogues which he carried on with his conscience. They generally took place at night, before he dropped off to sleep. Frequently, in a state of strange exhilaration, he would finally decide to brush aside all moral scruples and demand the fulfilment of his rights.

It was the first time he had fallen in love. It was his right to love, after all. With whom then was he engaged in this agonizing controversy? With the dead man or with his conscience? He tried to bring reason to bear. If it was the dead man then he was engaged in a controversy with a shadow, a mirage. A dead person no longer exists. That which had once been Vranas had long since disintegrated into all its component parts, and nature had probably already transformed them by means of a whole series of chemical processes into new amalgams. The different ingredients which had once made up the synthesis called Vranas had now been transmuted into moss, lime, fruit, flowers, insects, gases. None of these elements could lay any claim to Sappho. So there only remained his conscience. A moral court of enquiry based on custom, tradition, and supersition. But they were old customs, old traditions, old superstitions. All old—like the wares of the ragman. He could almost hear his cry· 'Old clothes! Old clothes! Old clothes!' It was the conscience of the nineteenth century which not only had the effrontery to continue to dwell in the soul of a young man of the twentieth century but to raise its voice in an imperious veto. A young man of the post-war generation, vital and positive to his fingertips. It was time to have done with all these hag-ridden shibboleths. Sappho belonged to him because he loved her. What more valid claim could be made than that of love?

What claim had the dead man, who had no being other than in his own thoughts, on this love which was a living thing? It was no figment of the imagination. On the contrary it was strong and healthy, like a ripe fruit offered to him by Fate itself. By Fate, why not? Who knows whether some benevolent Fate, awesome as it was mysterious in its workings, had not deliberately contrived to put an end to that ill-assorted union. It might be that same Fate again, acting with premeditation, which had removed Vranas from the scene so that by a long chain of coincidence he should finally replace the dead man as Sappho's predestined mate.

With thoughts like these going round in his head he would gradually appease his conscience until sleep finally came: a sleep full of dreams, frightening and fantastic.

He was in a war-time dug-out. An acetylene lamp lit up the anxious faces of his companions which showed white and chalky. Their shining eyes, with dilated pupils, had a strange expression, as though they didn't dare look at him. They were strangers to him, and they behaved as though he wasn't there, or as though they couldn't see him. Was he dead? he asked himself. Why did their glance pass over him as though he didn't exist? Yet, in spite of his terror, he was aware of a tiny ray of hope and smiled to himself. Perhaps it was all part of a dream and not really happening. A dream, that was it. Then suddenly he heard a thud, the prolonged thud of falling sand. Turning round, he saw the entrance to the shelter blocked by hundreds of tons of sand. He was a prisoner inside. There was no hope of escape. In the white light of the acetylene lamp he tried to distinguish the faces of his companions. He wanted to tell them: 'Now, what are we going to do?' But which ever way he looked they ignored him. Then he understood. His companions were all dead soldiers; soldiers who had been killed a long time ago; and it was their spirits which haunted the old abandoned war-time shelters at night; their tormented spirits flitting like moths round the white glow of the acetylene lamp. He wanted to cry out, to shriek from terror, but no sound came from his lips. He wanted to escape, but he couldn't move. Every minute the supply of oxygen in the shelter was diminishing, every minute his breathing was becoming more difficult, more rapid. . . .

24

ONE afternoon he was lying back in a deck-chair under the vine trellis in the courtyard. He saw Sappho approaching and put down the book he was reading. He had deliberately avoided seeing her for three days. As she came nearer, his heart began to beat faster. He got up quickly, running his hands through his hair.

They shook hands. She quickly withdrew hers. He felt he was blushing like a schoolgirl. She asked if Adriani was in, and when he told her she had gone to the Spanos's she said: 'What a pity I missed her.' She stood still, wondering whether to go or stay. He opened another deck-chair and asked her to sit down, doing his best all the time to seem as natural as possible. He then made an attempt to sit down himself, realized how low the chair was, laughed, got up, and raised it two rungs.

'I've interrupted your reading,' she said, casting a glance at the open book on the whitewashed ledge behind his chair.

'I read when I have nothing better to do,' and he smiled.

She smiled too, and turned her head slightly. It was a familiar gesture and he was able to see the shadow of her long eyelashes on her cheek.

There was a hint of irony in the tone of her voice as she said pleasantly: 'If that's how you feel about it you ought to continue reading. Otherwise I'll imagine you're paying me a compliment, and there's surely no need for people to pay each other compliments when they're friends.'

'I'm not paying you a compliment,' he said, with obvious sincerity. 'I always find your company delightful. . . . '

'Which means you must have been avoiding "delightful" company lately, like your godmother's for instance.'

For a moment he thought he was going to break down and come out with everything. 'Careful!' warned a malicious little voice inside him. 'In a minute you'll be pouring out a confession of love. Remember, that's Vranas's wife!'

So he lit a cigarette. It was easier to put on an air of indifference with a cigarette in one's hand.

'I've avoided seeing people because I've been working,' he said. 'I've been painting without interruption—except when I'm swimming or climbing trees. It's wonderful to work with real enthusiasm, isn't it?'

'Yes,' she replied, 'work's such a refuge. It calms one emotionally. It saved me once. . . . '

'You're absolutely right,' he said in a tone of relief. 'Our salvation lies in work which we do with genuine enthusiasm.'

He talked of everything he could think of: anything to keep off dangerous ground. His defences were well guarded. But the struggle was a pitiable affair. Because inside him, within the perimeter of those carefully manned defences, treacherous thoughts, with little stomach for the fight, were struggling to break out, like an unarmed rabble, and surrender to the all-powerful enemy, waiting calmly outside—there in the green shade reflected on her face by the vine trellis. But he? No. There he stood. At his post. An obstinate commander. Severe, but honourable. It was a hard-won victory over himself, and the fruits were bitter to the taste.

'What were you reading when I interrupted you?' she asked.

'Papadiamandis,' he replied, casting a look back at the open book on the ledge. 'An old love of mine. I've read those stories so often, and every now and then I return to them as to a fresh, clear fountain-head.'

'Yes, I love Papadiamandis too,' she said. 'There's an extra-ordinary poetic feeling about his stories. That's what makes them so appealing, I think, don't you?'

'Precisely. A kind of Helleno-Christian form of poetry. An amorous pagan singing of his love to the measure of a Byzantine hymn. . . .'

He stared at her, courageously; then lowered his eyes and fixed them on his cigarette. 'I was reading *The Royal Oak*. It was the last of Papadiamandis's stories, I think, that I read to Vranas before he died.'

Her eyelids fluttered suddenly. She looked as though she were going to speak, but no words came. There was a moment of difficult silence. Then he spoke slowly.

'I was thinking of it only yesterday, to tell you the truth. The memory of it is so vivid. I'd gone for a walk beyond the Sentinel, and I came to a field with some olive and wild pear trees sloping steeply down to the sea. The field faces north, so that it gets the north wind slap in the face in winter. Consequently all the trees are bent practically double, the tips of their branches almost touching the ground. The ones facing the sea are quite bare, without a single leaf. One has the impression that the trees are trying to scramble up the hill, like panic-stricken people out of breath. But what I'm really driving at is that when I read that story to Vranas he made a remark that left a deep impression on me. He spoke of the trees' fate—rooted to the ground, incapable of moving. Like him, you see. A forest catches fire, he went on to say, and all the animals, the birds, the insects, even the worms which haven't got legs, but have the power of motion, can get away. Not so the trees. Their legs are rooted to the soil. They're like chained prisoners in a building which catches fire. They simply have to stay there and be burnt alive. Horrible, isn't it?

She made an affirmative gesture. But his head was turned the other way.

He continued, determined to reach the end of his story. 'You see, I sensed the trees' plight immediately. It was exactly as Vranas had imagined it—there they were, tossing about helplessly in the north wind which comes howling across from the sea, struggling to escape, to uproot themselves. But no. They have to remain there. Chained. What a predicament! The whole of their hideous struggle against the winds seems to be expressed in the terrifying contortions of the branches. An image of panic and headlong flight is conjured up. One feels one can actually see the struggle they've gone through to loosen their hold, to break the chains that bind them to the earth so that they might go . . . go . . .'

There was a short silence, embarrassed and oppressive. Suddenly the vine-leaves on the trellis above them rustled. It was as though an unseen hand had passed by and touched them.

When he raised his head again to look at her there was a faraway expression in her half-shut eyes. She held her head high. Something in her face had changed. She might have been some divinity the way he was gazing at her—adoringly. A deified Contessa in Athene's helmet! She turned her head round slowly, her eyelids lowered. 'It's days since you sent me flowers for the vase,' she said quietly, each word sounding like a drop of rain falling on a calm sea.

She didn't say 'for his vase,' as on other occasions.

He was longing to say: 'But I mustn't send you flowers any longer, my love. Don't you understand? I mustn't. I oughtn't even to see you. . . .' But, of course, he said nothing of the kind.

'Yes,' was the only word he could rather stupidly bring out. It was with a sense of relief that he saw Adriani coming across the vineyard.

'I've been to my godmother's,' she said when she reached them, 'but the girls have gone for a walk to the Sentinel. Shall we go and meet them?' She added, smiling: 'We needn't, of course, if we don't want to,' as she stood beside Sappho, stroking her hair. She knew Sappho didn't like the Mayor's daughters.

They went out as dusk began to fall. A cool breeze blew in from the sea. It swept lightly over them carrying the tang of salt, sweeping back the girls' dresses so that the shape of their breasts, even the nipples, could be discerned. It caressed their bare arms, ruffling the faint down into long winding little furrows. Fishing-boats in line crept leisurely out of the narrow harbour.

One of the boats was painted red and blue. On the prow stood a little boy of about five or six years old, his hands on his hips, his legs wide apart, gazing towards the east. His father was rowing; the boy's figure, bathed in the glow of sunset, was motionless, in spite of the rocking of the boat.

The man's name was Perdikis. He was from Aivalik, across the channel on the Asia Minor coast. His boat was called *The Unforgettable Maria.* He was a splendid type, short, ash-blond. Whatever money he earned was spent on wine which he drank at the tavern at night. But he never got drunk. When it was nearly midnight his wife would send the little boy to tell him to come home to eat. Whatever happened he insisted on the family sitting down to eat together.

'Mum says it's time you came home,' the boy would call out from the door of the tavern.

Then he would get up, shout 'bastard!' at the boy, curse the woman, and sit down again. Accustomed to this manoeuvre, the boy would cower against the side of the outer wall. As soon as his father sat down he would emerge out of the darkness again, approach the door of the tavern, poke his head in, and repeat:

'Mum says it's time you came home.'

This would go on until Perdikis jumped up and ran after the boy; he would seize a handy broomstick and hurl it after the child. On Sundays—he wore shoes on Sundays—he would throw one of his shoes instead. It was the child's job to go on repeating the message until the man finally got up, paid for his wine, and stamped home. When he reached the house he would beat his wife before they all sat down to eat together. It was a routine process, repeated with unfailing monotony whenever he'd earned enough money to pay for the wine.

'Bitch,' he would bawl at his wife, 'why did you go and let that baby of mine die?'

This was a reference to Maria, after whom his boat *The Unforgettable* Maria was named, a baby daughter who had died three years ago. He believed it was his wife's fault they had lost the child. They'd had no more children after that.

The other fishermen knew him, and when they saw his boat returning with a large catch of fish they'd nudge one another and say: 'He's done pretty well again. His wife'll have to pay for it.'

Leon had heard another story about Perdikis which amused him. He told it to the girls. One night Perdikis had returned home blind drunk; instead of beating his wife as usual, he began to curse her. His blasphemies apparently went on for such a long time that his wife, losing patience, finally cried out: 'Come on, beat me, will you, and have done with it. Then the child can have something to eat and go to sleep!'

Adriani, unable to contain her indignation, cried without thinking: 'How can these women accept to be treated like that? Have they no pride? . . .'

She was immediately conscious of the tactlessness of her remark and blushed. She looked at her brother and noticed how flustered he looked too. The remark struck Sappho like a blow. But she realized the girl's pitiful embarrassment and seized hold of her hand, trying to smile.

Adriani returned the pressure of her hand with a violent squeeze. A few minutes elapsed before she could bring herself to speak.

'My dearest, how could I say anything so terrible,' she murmured at last, her lips still trembling.

'Don't worry, you mustn't, please!' Sappho smiled again. 'I know you didn't mean it personally. After all, what you said is quite logical. Only, you know, strangely enough, it's not always quite like that. . .'

'How?. . .' Adriani sounded bewildered.

'You see, I, too, felt exactly like you. The first time he struck me it seemed to me something impossible had happened. I stood there gaping at him. I couldn't understand. I didn't even cry. I used to look at him and felt frightened . . . bewildered. . . . But later . . . I swallowed it and said nothing. Can you understand it?'

'Yes,' said Adriani, caressing Sappho's hand nervously, her blue eyes full of tears. 'Forgive me, Sappho.'

There was an air of melancholy about Sappho's smile as she raised Adriani's interlocked hands and kissed them. Leon adroitly changed the conversation to more agreeable subjects. They were approaching the beach at the Sentinel.

The sun, blood-red, was setting, way out at sea, beyond the Holy Mountain. In a few minutes nothing could be seen on the horizon but the enormous disc, with its rim on fire like flaming copper, sinking into the rose-coloured sea. The sky too was the colour of pink roses. They were nearing the cliffs at the Sentinel. There they found the doctor and the Mayor's daughters. The girls were sitting on the rocks, and the doctor, who was standing beside them, was lecturing them in his usual autocratic way, gesticulating like a politician in Parliament.

The moment he saw Leon and the two girls he stopped gesticulating. Some hurried words were whispered—evidently about Sappho. But as soon as Leon and the two girls had reached them the doctor and the Mayor's daughters greeted them with every show of enthusiasm and Leon was taken to task for having failed to call at the house for so many days.

'I've been working very hard lately,' he said. 'That's why.'

The doctor was very formal and pompous: his usual unsympathetic self.

It was getting dark by the time they turned for home. They hadn't gone very far before they recognized the figure of the Mayor advancing towards them. He turned and walked back with them: very slowly and with innumerable halts. He was inclined to pause and buttonhole the person nearest to him every time he spoke. Nor would he let go of his friend's lapel until his speech was over. The subject of his discourse this evening was the political situation. Politics bored Leon—politics, and the political parties, and the fractious generals who started revolutions.

The newspapers which had arrived with the evening bus were apparently full of startling news about the latest activities of one of these generals. General Digenis this time. General Digenis, whose photograph hung on the walls of Mr. Spano's office, was regarded as something of a national hero. The Mayor worshipped General Digenis because he had vindicated the honour of Greek arms during the retreat in Asia Minor when most of the brass hats had taken to their heels along with the infantry.

According to the papers this demi-god, the *Black Horseman,* as he was called, had been hunted down by a corporal and five soldiers, agents of a rival general. The legendary General, according to the papers, had been compelled to take refuge in an attic from the windows of which he had climbed on to the roof with incredible agility. The *Black Cat,* they now called him. Although his faith was somewhat shaken, Mr. Spanos couldn't accept the story at face value. He tried by every conceivable means to convince both himself and his audience that it was nothing but a malicious—nay, laughable—rumour, invented by the General's political opponents in order to discredit him. Imagination boggled at the idea of the *Black Horseman* cowering in attics and scaling roof-tops like any common thief hunted by the police. The very idea was preposterous. He thought of the photograph in his office: the proud, fully armed warrior, mounted on his fiery black steed, with all the dignity of a St. George. No. It was out of the question. It was slander. And jolly clumsy slander at that. Even supposing there'd been an element of truth in the story, the most scurrilous opposition Press ought to be forbidden to print such stuff. The General stood for the Glory of Greece. He alone had vindicated the honour of Greece at a time of great national humiliation. The General ought never to be made fun of. The man had become a symbol, almost like Coundouriotis. And when people started reviling their national symbols it meant there was something pretty wrong in the general state of affairs.

Leon, desperately bored, said nothing.

The doctor, however, did not remain silent. He agreed to every word the Mayor said.

'Quite right, absolutely right,' he kept on interjecting. 'You have a way of putting things—of hitting the nail on the head. Dead right. It's national heroes. . . . . .'

Leon felt disgusted.

'Now, am I not right?' Mr. Spanos turned to him.

'I . . . that's to say. . . . As you know, I've little love for army officers as a whole. . . .'

The Mayor said nothing. He was sorry to hear such words coming from one whom he regarded as his son, whose wound—a trophy of the Asia Minor campaign—he had almost come to regard as his own.

At this point the doctor intervened with considerable gusto.

'You exaggerate. In my opinion you exaggerate,' he declared in his most pontifical manner. 'There's one thing I'd like to ask you. But you must answer me frankly.'

'I always answer people frankly,' said Leon quietly.

'Good. Answer me this, then. Suppose a foreign power were to invade Greece tomorrow. Would these generals be called upon to save the country? Would they, or wouldn't they?'

The Mayor stretched out his hands. 'There, you see!' he nodded approvingly.

'Of course they would,' Leon answered without the least hesitation.

Under the impression that he'd scored a point, the doctor turned round to see if the girls had appreciated his little victory.

'And would you not be grateful to them for doing so, sir?' he insisted.

'Very,' replied Leon quietly, with an air of mock seriousness. 'In exactly the same way as I'm grateful to an executioner for cutting off the head of a criminal who's a public danger. But that doesn't make me like the executioner's profession particularly.'

Adriani bit her lip in order not to laugh at the doctor's discomfiture. In the dim light a delighted smile could be seen spreading across Sappho's face.

'Ah, he's got you there, Doctor!' said Aspasia archly, and she laughed.

'That's not the point,' retorted the doctor angrily. 'The point is that Mr. Drivas's morale was broken in the Asia Minor campaign. It's the spirit of defeat. It can be explained scientifically. It often happens with defeated peoples. Their vitality is sapped, their reactions become enfeebled, and the patriotic ardour, both of the individual and the group, is reduced to a minimum. The ideal of heroism . . . the spirit of sacrifice . . . they go by the board.'

Leon let him have his say and then declared with maddening calmness:

'It's perfectly true to say I never did anything in the least brave. I wasn't brave. Emotional, yes. Sentimental, perhaps. I sometimes feel it wasn't patriotism at all that prompted me to join the army. It was a nagging desire to give something of myself. A desire for self-indulgence that can be stretched to the very limits of the "will to live" —stretched to the point of wishing for death. But I was never without fear. As for the stories of heroic deeds performed in battle, you'll permit me to say I no longer believe in fairy-tales. In nine cases out of ten men become heroes without having had the slightest intention of doing so. Necessity prompts them to act heroically. As the proverb says: "Even a devil can become an angel, if need be." I don't deny that some people are probably seized by a kind of neurotic apathy the moment they're confronted with danger. It's a kind of retardment of the nervous reflexes. They are the people in whom the instinct for self-preservation is less developed. You'll admit it's the instinct for self-preservation that protects us from danger and not the will or the intellect. They've got nothing to do with it. The result is that you get people in whom this instinct to preserve themselves is less developed than in others. That's all it is. They're incapable of reacting with the same energy as others to the most obvious dangers. Take the case of the small child who jumps from a height for the first time in its life. Why does the little hero topple over the side of a sofa and hurt himself badly? Why? Quite simply because he didn't know he was going to hurt himself.'

25

A LOUD din was coming from the other end of the village. It was followed by shouting. Angry shouting, accompanied by more noise. Then pistol-shots rang out: shots aimed in the air. Church bells began to ring ominously, frenziedly. The ringing sounded hurried, impatient; it came first from a church some way off, near the castle, followed by the deep note of the bell of the Lower Church of the Virgin. Then both together.

A reddish flame suddenly belched forth, the reflection of its numerous tongues licking at the walls and roofs of neighbouring houses. A moment later a second flame leapt out of a window. It was like some fantastic beast, all tongue; it disappeared, drawn into some kind of dark invisible vortex, only to re-emerge, wriggling and waving like a flag on the castle ramparts. It fluttered and hung still; then proudly unfurled itself again.

'Fire!'

'I must go,' said the Mayor, quickening his pace. In a moment he was almost running, and his shoes squeaked loudly, officially. All the solemnity of his office was contained in the tone of those squeaking shoes. The rest of them followed on his heels.

Villagers were scurrying from all directions to the scene of the fire and the little streets were black with people. The shrill cries of mothers calling to their children mingled with the clatter of their footsteps on the cobbled stones. The appearance of the fire-engine provoked a renewed outburst of shouting from the crowd of urchins. It was like a carnival setting in a Macedonian village. The helmeted firemen in baggy peasant trousers, with unshaven faces and dead-pan expressions, mounted on the bright red pump, looked as though they had been got up for a fancy-dress party.

The Mayor, joined by his assistant, was now on the spot.

'Oh, isn't it fun watching a fire?' cried Aspasia, wriggling with excitement.

Leon looked in astonishment at this young girl with the predilections of a Nero. The glow of the fire was reflected in her eyes: like a microscopic ballerina in a red *tutu*.

Outside the burning house the police were vainly trying to hold back the crowd from approaching too near the flames; but like all crowds they seemed to take a hysterical pleasure in the anticipation of disaster. The reflection of the porphyry-coloured flames danced in the dilated pupils of a thousand staring eyes.

The building was an old Turkish house belonging to the steamship company. Machinery, cables, fuses, and cartidges were stored on the ground floor; on the top floor the workmen, in particular two refugees from Asia Minor, mixed the various materials for the explosives. They had been forbidden to work at night with the aid of a lamp; and smoking was not allowed during working hours. In order to earn an extra drachma they had been working overtime with that absence of precaution that often goes with constant contact with danger. The explosives had caught fire and the flames had soon enveloped the whole house.

The firemen were doing what they could with their little fire-engine. A crowd of men and women from neighbouring houses carried petrol-tins filled with water which they poured from the windows and roofs of adjacent houses. But within the burning building the flames had now reached the top floor and were belching out of the windows. No one dared get too near. They all knew explosives were stored inside, and they all continued to shout in an aimless bewildered way as though their cries could arrest the flames. They might have been taking part in a wild-boar hunt.

The flicker of the flames cast a constantly shifting striped effect on the ghost-like faces of the crowd. Every now and then loud cries would be heard asking whether the workmen had succeeded in getting out. But no one knew the answer. The thought that they might still be there, trapped in the flames, sent a thrill of horror down their spines. Craning their necks to see better, the expression in their eyes was that of an audience awaiting the denouement of a spectacle which they knew was fated to end in disaster.

A shudder seemed to pass through the crowd as someone shouted: 'The workmen!'

The wooden outer door of the house had opened form the inside and two men, lurching like drunkards, staggered out. One of them kept slapping his trouser leg which was smoking, but he was not seriously burned. The other, a great giant of a man, stark naked, bore hardly any resemblance to a human being. His skin was scorched and charred, full of large oozing patches of flesh, on which little tufts of clothing sizzled and simmered until they fell off, peeling layers of skin off as they did so, as though he were being flayed.

There was a collective gasp of horror and the women's voices rose in the air like the howling of dogs.

The man lurched forward, muttering disjointed words, his knees sagging, his arms hanging limply to his sides. His gait resembled that of an Anatolian wrestler who performs a few hesitant little steps backwards and forwards before coming to grips with his opponent. His head was a huge charred wound, covered in burns and sprinkled with the ashes of what had once been his hair. His moustache, his eyebrows, and the rest of the hair on his body were also reduced to ashes. His eyes, however, were open, shining very bright within two flaming wheels, the whites gleaming against the blackened flesh: two eyes without eyelashes, filled with terror and madness. He continued to mutter to himself as he staggered up the steep little street leading to his house. The dumbfounded crowd fell back, making a wide lane for him to pass.

Suddenly a piercing shriek was heard.

'Ni-i-i-co!'

A woman was racing down the incline like a demented creature, tossing her hair about widly, tearing her face with her nails.

She grabbed the man by the hand. The flayed skin came off on the palm of her hand, and she dropped it quickly, still shrieking. He continued alone, the whites of his eyes rolling, his swollen lips babbling incomprehensible words. The woman followed, a few paces behind; she was still tearing her hair. They soon turned a corner and were lost to sight.

A minute later she came running back, more demented than ever. 'Save her, save her!' she screamed. 'Have mercy on her, save her!'

She was rushing in the direction of the house, the top floor of which was now burning more fiercely than ever. Two firemen seized her by the arms and forcibly held her back.

'Who? Save whom? Who is it? Stavria, who is it? Tell us.'

'My child!' she screamed, making another desperate attempt to shake off the firemen and reach the flaming building.

'Fanoula's inside! My little Fanoula! I sent her to fetch him! I...I..'

Sismanoglou arrived panting on the scene. He was without a hat and his clothes looked dishevelled. He wrung his hands like a madman, as he shouted in the voice of a street-crier:

'Be careful! There're two cases of dynamite and other explosives on the lower floor!'

The commotion increased. Shrieking and trampling over one another, the panic-stricken spectators retreated.

'Torpedoes!' they shouted. 'They're torpedoes inside!'

'Come, quickly,' said the doctor, seizing the Mayor's daughters by the arm. He was shaking with fear.

The Mayor joined them, urging them to get away as fast as they could. Leon grabbed him by the arm and whispered hurriedly in his ear:

'Look after the women, will you?'

He indicated Adriani and Sappho, and then dashed forward. In a few bounds he was inside the burning house.

He couldn't see anything. Black smoke swirled down the well of the burning staircase from the upper floor.

'Fanoula!' he shouted. 'Fanoula!' The smoke choked him.

He stopped and listened. He could hear nothing but the sound of rafters creaking and falling on the floor above him, and the crackling sound of the fire as it consumed the wooden boards. 'Fanoula!' He entered a dark windowless room. 'Fanoula!' he shouted again, and paused to listen. No answer. He searched, groping with his hands, with his feet. He got entangled in ropes, knocked against cases, tools. He tried another room. There was nothing there either. There were no more rooms on the ground floor. 'She must have been burnt alive!' he concluded. A flaming plank came crackling down the well of the staircase and landed in front of him. The stairs were filled with red-hot coals. He drew back quickly, catching hold of a jar-like receptacle built into the floor. Unintentionally he put his arm inside; his hand touched a round little head with two hands clasped tight over it for protection.

His heart was pounding. With savage delight he dragged the little body out. The child resisted, biting the rim of the jar with her teeth in order to keep a hold on it. He then seized her violently, pinned her firmly under his arm and dashed out. The crowd had withdrawn to a considerable distance: as far as the beach. As he emerged he heard a renewed shouting: the cries of people shouting in unison. He ran towards them. A woman, weeping distractedly, tugged at his clothes, caught hold of his legs and tried to kiss his feet. He handed the child to her, with difficulty extricated himself from the clawing hands and went in search of the girls. He couldn't see them anywhere.

'Adriani!' he shouted. 'Adriani!'

Sappho was running towards him.

'Here, this way!' she called out, still running, waving her hand so that he might see her. 'She's on the beach. She fainted. But it isn't anything. She's all right now.'

He ran beside her, his temples beating so violently that he thought his head would burst. Adriani was in the arms of the other girls. The doctor was patting her hand, talking to her as though she were a child.

'That's it! Nothing wrong with you. Don't worry. . . . And there's your brother coming back. . . . '

Sismanoglou was placing a handkerchief dipped in sea-water on her forehead. The Mayor was there too. He hardly knew what he was saying or doing any longer.

Leon took her in his arms and kissed her on the cheek. 'Adriani, what's the matter?' he asked in a frightened voice.

She opened her eyes, and began to weep, sobbing on his neck.

'It's nothing,' said the doctor. He bent over her, smiling protectively in his most professional air. 'It was a little fainting fit! It's passed now. . . . '

Leon looked up at him.

'You might now attend to the workman, I think,' he said. 'It's not just a little fainting fit in his case.'

The Mayor was beside himself with emotion.

'Leon, my son,' his voice was trembling. 'Come, let me embrace you. You're a man, if ever there was one. And a good man . . . just like your father.'

He kissed him on both cheeks; his eyes filled with tears which glistened in the flickering light. He tried to conceal them and beamed all round. The flames had now enveloped the whole house. The firemen had given up trying to control them and all they could do was to turn their hoses on the little neighbouring houses in which barrels of olive oil were stored. Every now and then pieces of coal and red-hot nails would be catapulted out of the furnace. The flames—they looked like red banners waving in the breeze—belched forth from every corner of the roof and from the doors and windows of the ground floor. A luminous cloud rose above the blazing shell and wafted towards the starlit sky.

The dark silhouette of a cat appeared on the roof, mewing pitifully. Half crazed with fear, it kept turning in all directions for help, hopping on the red-hot tiles as they cracked in the heat. It peered over the edge of the roof, its fur standing on end, as though trying to make up its mind to jump, but it hadn't the courage. A large flame scorched its face. It turned; it twisted; it ran; it paused, choking in the smoke. The tiles burnt its paws; there was a desperate anguished tone in its mewing. Suddenly it straightened itself and raising its front paws to its mouth it bit them dementedly.

A piercing long-drawn-out whine was heard from the animal as it disappeared from view. The roof had caved in with an appalling clatter.

A column of fire leapt into the sky and dissolved in a shower of flying sparks. The sky seemed to be filled with shooting stars.

26

IT TOOK Adriani several days to recover from the nervous shock she experienced on the night of the fire. She wept frequently and had terrible coughing fits at night. At first the Mayor's daughters came regularly to visit her; then they stopped coming. They obviously didn't like meeting Sappho at the Tower. Leon tried to arrange his life in such a way that he would either be out when she came or at least never alone with her. This constant strain, forcing him to behave in a way so contrary to all his natural instincts, made him nervous and abrupt in his manner. Nor did it have any effect on his love for her, which grew daily until he thought he would no longer be able to restrain it.

One night it seemed as though he couldn't stand it any longer. He locked himself up in his room and wept. He wept for a long time, marvelling that he still could. It brought him some relief. Even a kind of satisfaction. It was years since he had wept. He thought the war had blocked up the source of all tears. Once more he was a little boy, the sensitive boy of his childhood. As he wept he felt he was weeping for countless sorrows. For his friends his brother officers, killed in the war; for Vranas. But the most heartfelt tears were reserved for his mother: tears long owed to her, which had refused to come when he first heard of her death.

As a result of the part he'd played in the fire he tried to avoid seeing people. He was afraid lest they should want to congratulate him, using all the commonplace meaningless expressions like 'a true hero', 'an act of heroism', 'what spirit of self-sacrifice' and so on.

He went neither to the club nor the café.

His gratitude to Sappho, who never mentioned the affair, was unbounded. Her large eyes reflected her wisdom and understanding.

As he tried to sort out the various impressions of that nightmare evening he realized to his astonishment that the one most clearly stamped on his mind was the expression of appeal in Sappho's eyes when he asked the Mayor to look after two girls. It was the moment he had decided to enter the burning house. She had held out a hand as though to hold him back. Then he had turned and dashed into the house. Her hand must have dropped limply, slowly, to her side. He tried to imagine exactly what she would have said had she been allowed to—allowed to by him and the ghost of her dead husband. Then he recalled her air of distraction when he emerged from the burning house. All her feeling for him, so long repressed, drawn taut like an arrow to the bow-string, seemed to overflow in the expression of her eyes and trembling lips.

As he continued to go over the events of that night he suddenly found himself asking an awkward question. It seemed to stand in his way, confronting him provocatively, like an erect snake.

Had the rescue of the child been nothing more than an act of bravado intended to impress Sappho? Worse still. Had this act of heroism been a reaction to all the nonsense talked by the doctor about shattered morale, sapped vitality, and so on? Would he really have plunged into a burning house full of dynamite in order to save a human life had not Sappho and that pathetic creature of a doctor, who deserved to be humiliated once and for all in the eyes of the world, been there to witness the act of gallantry?

In that case everything became clearer. With the instinct of a woman in love she had realized—certainly before him—that the show had been put on for her benefit. That was the meaning of her appealing glance. Perfectly natural. It was her automatic response to his mute but nevertheless very real confession, which fundamentally continued to be nothing more than just cheap literature and show-off.

So his passion was at last unmasked, and his declaration of war against it openly made. They stood ready in the lists, glaring at each other. In the bitter struggle that lay ahead he had only one person to champion his cause—the dead man.

One day he picked a large bunch of poppies with the intention of sending them to Sappho. As he picked them he held up the bunch to the sun; it looked like a flaming torch. He might paint a picture of a hill covered with poppies. From afar it would give the impression of having caught fire.

But as he went on picking the flowers he knew he wouldn't send them to her. He picked them with care, one by one; as he snapped off the stalks he thought of her. His thoughts also went to his friend, the dead soldier, for whose tomb the flowers should be destined—the desecrated tomb of a vindictive corpse.

Ascending the slope, he reached the top of a high rock above the beach at the Sentinel. Down below in the aquamarine depths the underwater vegetation had the luxuriance of a marine spring-time. He flung the bunch of poppies in the air, which immediately seemed to be filled with a host of scarlet butterflies; then the waters below were spattered with their petals, floating gently in the current. Drops of fresh blood rained down on the blue waters.

It was here that he had seen her half-naked for the first time: standing on her toes, on the edge of the red rock, with all the provocative immobility of a Salome who had stopped dancing. Naked, beautiful, but dangerous, like the blade of an unsheathed sword.

He would have to leave. There was no alternative. The only salvation lay in flight. He could feel his willpower disintegrating, like anchors breaking one by one from their chains. There were times when his imagination, untrammelled by caution any longer, would play strange tricks on him. He would shut his eyes and experience moments of fantastic ecstasy and anguish. These day-dreams became so real and vivid that his heart would thump and his temples throb violently.

He would then make a strange resolution. Sappho belonged to him. She stood for life itself; and no one had the right to spew his laothsome spittle over their love. Least of all public opinion. Megalohorian public opinion. The opinion of Mr. Yanni, the doctor, and the Mayor, with his shoes squeaking piously outside Sultana's kitchen. cooking up the legal abomination of her infamous union with Mr. Yanni. The opinion of the allegedly saintly Aspasia and plump buxom Loulou, of the cosmopolitan Daphnis family and the members of the highly respected shipping company. For they, with a few more added perhaps, consituted public opinion. Well, then, they had about as much right to interfere in his love for Sappho as that bag of bones mouldering in an Anatolian tomb. What was he waiting for then? Why didn't he stretch out his hand and pluck the rare fruit that was being offered to him, that might not be offered to him again? There it hung, directly in front of him, waiting to be plucked. Like that poppy which he had found in the derelict Serbian trench one terrible night during the war and which he had believed to be a manifestation of the Divine Presence. So that was love, then. That famous flower which he had thought would never take root in his heart. He now understood the significance of the cry of the poetess, who, on his very beach, had sung:

> *Love shook our minds*
> *like wind falling on a mountain thick with oaks!*

Yes. Love was like a storm that agitated the sea to its depths, so that the waters were forced to adjust themselves to new levels. Like a lone straw one was tossed in the whirlwind, exulting in the tempestuous buffeting of the winds. Then again, it was like a fresh rose that has taken root in the hidden places of the heart. Or like a fire which burns the entrails and consumes the soul.

This strugle—this war which he'd declared against himself— couldn't go on indefinitely. Some calm must descend after the storm, some order must emerge out of the chaos that surrounded him. He would simply have to go and tell her everything.

Everything. He would write first. 'My love. I belong to you. No one can come between us—not any more. Let's renounce the past and start a new life. From the very beginning. It will be our life. I'll come to your house tonight. Leave the door open.' And below it his signature, in a firm, manly, unashamed hand: 'Leon Drivas'.

As soon as midnight came he would get up, ready and resolved, a bird beating its wings in his breast. 'Where are you going?' Adriani asked from her bed. 'I'm going for a stroll on the beach. I love walking alone by the sea.' What emphasis he placed on the word 'alone'! Each step of the old staircase creaked loudly as he descended. Shutting the outer gate carefully, he went towards the beach, then turned inland. From the beach he could see her window dimly illumined by a night-light. 'I'm going to Sappho,' he kept saying to himself. 'Sappho, I'm coming, my love. To you, at last. I ask nothing else from life. Only to be with you.' When he reached the little street where she lived he trod cautiously on his toes, like a thief in the night, so that his steps shouldn't be heard by the old crones who lived in the neighbourhood. The outer door was ajar. Unlatched! He could hear his heart thumping. So she was expecting him. 'Oh, my beloved!' He opened the iron door slowly, very carefully, so that it shouldn't grate or squeak. Then he shut it behind him. Sappho was there, in the courtyard; waiting for him in the dark. How slim she looked in her black dress, flanked by two rows of pots filled with pungent-smelling plants. The jasmine glistened white in the dark. The air was balmy, the great vault of the sky speckled with stars. He put his arm round her waist and clasped her very tight. How slight and fragile she seemed in his embrace, like some fantastically delicate flower on a long stalk. She wept in his arms; but she didn't speak. She wept quietly—from joy. He felt the coolness of her arms round his neck, the delicious pressure of her head resting on his shoulder. He inhaled the bitter-sweet fragrance from her hair, which brushed his cheek. The scent of jasmine clung to her. 'I've been waiting for you,' she said very quietly. 'If you only knew . . . '

He led her gently inside and made her sit down on the sofa beside him, by the open window overlooking the sea. He then took her in his arms. She was his at last. He felt a glorious warmth pervading his body. He placed his lips on her neck, below her ear, which glowed as though it were on fire. He felt the little curls at the back of her neck touching his face, and her breath enveloping him like exhalations of incense. His whole being responded to the intimacy of her body in a hundred different ways; ways that could never be expressed in words, but that he understood intuitively. She kept repeating quietly: 'Take me, Leon. Take me. . . . '

His glance fell by chance on the night-light burning beside some books on the table. It consisted of a wick surrounded by a little wax floating in oil in a tumbler of water. A vase, rather like a large glass, stood near it. There was a gold design round the rim, and it contained some withered wild irises from the beach. The faded blooms drooped limply. They were lovely flowers. He remembered warning her about the sticky sap that oozed from the severed stalks. Unintentionally his gaze wandered on, resting on a frame containing the photograph with the familiar face, which could be just distinguished in the dim light. How well he knew it. A slight shudder shook his frame. It was as though a breath of frozen air had blown through him. He clenched his teeth, shut his eyes so that he shouldn't hear anything, shouldn't see anything; so that he might be able to hold out and conquer. But the breath of frozen air continued to blow icily in his heart. Gradually it quenched the flame of desire that had burned so brightly, so deliriously a few moments ago. The night-light flickered on a tomb-stone; and the frozen air came from within the tomb, playing around him endlessly, so that he began to shake with cold.

He recoiled brusquely from her. He unwound her arms from his neck and placed her gently at the other end of the sofa. His eyes filled with tears. Tears of anger and frustration.

Her own eyes, dark and wondering, rested on him. She saw that he was staring at the photograph, and she understood. Neither of them spoke. The shadows cast on the wall by the night-light resembled a bird's wing opening and closing.

Suddenly footsteps were heard padding along the passage. They both tried to look as natural as possible, sitting at either end of the sofa. Their hands were no longer touching.

There was no knock on the door. The door-handle turned slowly and the door opened. The dark figure of the deaf-mute woman, dressed in black, stood motionless in the aperture. Her shadowy eyes were fixed on Sappho. Their message was clear:

'He's started crying again. You'd better come for a moment.'

The shadowy form didn't move until Sappho got up from the sofa and followed her into the passage with bowed head.

Through the open door, as though from behind innumerable closed doors, a long-drawn-out scream was heard. It was like a muffled howling. The draught made by the open door and the window caused the flame of the night-light to cast a succession of rapidly shifting shadows on the walls and ceiling. The frame showed up black, and the shadows passed across the books, occasionally lighting up the gilt lettering of their bindings. In the corner of the room there was a drawer; and in the drawer a wallet. Suddenly a cold uncontrollable fear seized him. He was afraid of the night-light blowing out and being left alone in the vast room filled with the freezing air that came from an empty tomb.

He rushed out like a hunted creature, shuddering—away from the dead man's house. But the impression of an invisible hand reaching out behind him, ready to seize him by the scruff of the neck, remained with him.

He spent hours going over these imaginary situations.

There was only one thing to do—leave. He would take Adriani and leave Megalohori.

There was no other alternative.

27

HE WAS in such an obviously overwrought state that Adriani decided
to speak to him.

They were in the courtyard at the Tower. It was after lunch. He had
as usual just played with his food; and he was lying back in a deck-
chair, smoking, his hands behind his head, his eyes half shut.

Adriani made several fruitless attempts at conversation. His replies
were monosyllabic; he clearly resented being disturbed. Finally she
got up and stroked his head.

'Leon, aren't you well?'

Half-opening his eyes, he replied in a deliberaterly ironical tone:

'Of course I'm not well! I'm badly afflicted with . . . laziness. There's
little hope for the patient.'

She shook her head thoughtfully, leant over towards him, and
placed her cheek against his.

'I wish you'd stop pretending. There's something wrong. You've
got something on your mind, and you're hiding it from me. For days
now you've been behaving as though you were putting on an act. As
though you were on guard.'

'As though I were on guard?'

'Yes, stop making faces and trying to fool me. Tell me, Leon, I
understand, dear. . . . That's what I'm here for, to understand. . . . '

'Ah so!' he said angrily, 'and what do you understand?'

She didn't reply immediately. She looked at him with hurt surprise,
her eyes filling with tears. 'The way you speak to me! . . . '

He instantly felt ashamed for his boorishness.

'I'm a beast. All right. I know it.'

She smiled through her tears.

'Tell me then, what's the matter with you. I've been watching you
for days, wondering and waiting for you to say something. But you
don't say a thing. You've lost your appetite. You're bad-tempered.
You've given up swimming. D'you think I don't see it all? At night I
hear you tossing and turning in your bed, walking up and down in
your room, going to the window. One night you were even talking in
your sleep. . . . '

'Really?' he started up. 'And what was I saying?'

'Oh I couldn't make out very much. Something about a lieutenant.'

He smiled with relief.

'So you've become quite a little spy, eh?'

He had thought of the word suddenly, as she leant over and gazed into his eyes, trying to read what was going on in his mind. He looked at her again, guardedly, through half-shut eyes. He thought of the horror of a lifetime spent in such intimacy: the intimacy of a married couple. He imagined himself in the place of the husband, with the wife prying into secret places of his soul, just as she went through his pockets. Never alone, never able to lock himself up, alone and naked, in his own room. She would always be there, beside him, waiting expectantly for him to open his eyes in order to stare into the windows of his soul and ferret out what was going on inside. And it would be her right to do so. A right sanctioned by such institutions as the Law and the Church.

He tried to explain all this to Adriani, but she was at a loss and could only reply: 'But I'd be delighted to have someone who minded how I felt, who'd stare into my eyes and try to read my thoughts. It wouldn't be in the name of the Law or the Church. It would that I'd never feel I was alone in the world.'

He looked at her cautiously; after a while he said: 'I believe you, Adriani. You will never have anything to hide. You. . . . You're different. I don't think I could ever share my sorrows with anyone else. After what I saw in the war . . . I believe everybody dwells alone in his own private sphere or planet, and that a great abyss separates us from one another.'

'D'you mean to say that when two people are in love they continue to live in separate spheres or planets?' she asked.

'That's when the abyss between them becomes ever greater. Love is like a duel between two molecular cells. Which is going to defeat or assimilate the other? You can't have agreement between victor and vanquished. Only submission on the part of one. What we call agreement has a relative meaning. It's a combination of retreat, cowardice, and temporary accommodation. The most we can hope to accomplish, I believe, is to try to keep a course parallel with that taken by other people and to avoid a collision. But we mustn't deviate from our course. Oh, no. On the contrary, we must defend it fiercely, keeping our eyes wide open all the time, our fingers on the trigger.'

Adriani listened to him thoughtfully. An expression of sorrow passed across her eyes, like a transient shadow cast on the sea by a passing cloud.

'I don't want to believe what you say,' she said. 'If it were true it would poison our lives. I believe in love. I only believe in God as a reflection of love.'

'And so you should,' said Leon earnestly. 'So you should.'

'Then . . . will you give me permission to feel slightly worried about your present state of mind?'

'There we go again!' he laughed. 'All right, I'll tell you what's wrong with me, so that you'll stop filling your head with all sorts of ridiculous ideas. It's simply this. I'm fed up with life here. In other words, I'm bored. I—am—bored. I want to leave.'

'And all this time you didn't tell me? . . . '

'Well, I knew you liked being here,' he said with a rather martyred air. 'I didn't dare. But as things have turned out I'd perhaps better come out with it all. I'm bored to death, Adriani. All the monotonous green lushness gets on my nerves. There's so much of it. It's positively oppressive. Look at the sea—and there's hardly ever a boat on it. Look at all the familiar landmarks—like cardboard stage-sets in an empty theatre that's been shut for the night. And the people . . . my God, the people! Always the same secretive narrow-minded people, saying the same things, wearing the same clothes. Our godfather with his squeaking shoes, like the ones I wore as a child on Sundays. And to think there's been a world war that claimed twenty million victims between then and now. And yet the same squeaking shoes! Our god-mother, with her contractions of the heart, which she's been talking about ever since the year of the Olympic Games. Aspasia with her beastly dimples. Loulou, Mr. Yanni, the police sergeant, Mr. Philippas, Silellis, the doctor with his buttonhole . . . Oh God! Day after day, the same thing. . . . '

'How horrid you are.'

'I know. But that doesn't alter the situation. I want to go, Adriani. I want to leave this place. I pine for the bustle of a large town, for more stimulating work. I long to travel, to hear a little good music. In other words . . . new faces, new voices.'

'We'd better leave, then.'

'Let's go Adriani, do let's go.'

'Of course. The way you put it you make me see things differently. They bore me too.'

'Dearest Adriani, you're lying, I'm afraid.'

'I assure you I'm not. In a week's time I'll be ready. I'll have everything ready, packed, washed, and ironed. You'll see if I don't.'

He took her hand and kissed it, thinking what a hypocrite he was. He then jumped up and left the house whistling.

So that was the answer. Honourable flight!

The moment Adriani began to prepare for their return to town he saw their departure in the light of a fatal necessity and faced up to it accordingly. The heroic flight of his dreams was no longer a half-formulated project; it had at last become a reality. The furniture was actually being moved. The empty spaces in the rooms were concrete evidence of this change in the order of things. Then there was all the business of packing and dismantling. The house would be locked and left empty, inhabited only by memories.

So the flight had begun. He felt lacerated. He was miserable when he watched Adriani packing all the cherished little objects they'd collected from the beach and countryside: the petrified purple sea-weed which she had fished up from the sea-bed, now placed in a card-board box, carefully wrapped up in cotton wool so that the brittle weeds wouldn't break; the multi-coloured pebbles, the tiny shells gathered on the shingle; the enormous deep-water conches which she laid between their clothes to prevent them from being smashed when the bus jolted along the pot-holed road. All these objects were like tentacles trying to hold him back, to keep him at Megalohori, where Sappho was. But the grip of the tentacles grew flaccid; one by one, they began to loosen their hold.

He remembered being greatly moved by Adriani one day when they were children. They were on the beach, searching for coloured pebbles. She had picked up a large green one. It was as wide as the palm of a man's hand, the colour of rusty copper. Its surface had been eaten away by the tiny insects that burrow in the sand and it looked like a sieve. She had asked him whether he liked it and whether she might keep it for her collection. He had replied something about it not being a rare specimen, and that there were masses of them lying about on the beach. She had then proceeded to place it with the utmost care on the spot where she'd found it— where it had been originally placed by nature herself—instead of simply throwing it carelessly over her shoulder. It was as though she hadn't wanted to disturb the harmory of nature.

He was seized with a longing to do the same thing: to take all those spoils of the summer months, which were being neatly packed before their removal to the house in town, and place them where they belonged: the conches on the sea-bed, the pebbles on the beach, the rose-coloured shells on the sand by the water's edge.

When Sappho heard the news of their departure from Adriani she merely laughed. She thought Adriani was joking.

'I'm not joking,' said Adriani. 'We're leaving on Sunday or Monday.'

Adriani's voice was trembling slightly and Sappho realized that she was in earnest. She turned pale.

'Oh . . . really,' she said dumbly.

She was seized by an uncontrollable longing to run away, to shut herself up in her house—alone, by herself. The sensation gradually gained complete control of her; it was like one of those fevers that strike suddenly, spreading to every part of the body, turning the knees to water. The feeling of weariness was unbearable. She felt she simply must sit down; so collapsed on the sofa. Her body was like a dead weight. There was a feeling of hollowness inside her which increased every minute. How she longed to be in some deserted place, far away from everybody, far from the danger of ridicule, where no human being could spy on her, no human ear hear her. Then she would be able to scream, as loud as she liked, so that the sound of her scream might fill that terrible empty hollow which seemed to be engulfing her, threatening to suck her down into its limitless vortex. She clenched her teeth to prevent herself from uttering the cry; her lips trembled, her eyes filled with tears which she tried to fight back.

Adriani, her own eyes brimming with tears, sat down on the sofa beside her.

Closing her eyes, Sappho began to weep quietly. She felt a sharp stab of pain as though the prong of a long fork had pierced her heart. There was a horrid bitter taste in her mouth. Abandoned. She was being abandoned. The thought of it hung like a heavy cloud low in the sky, immediately above her head. For once a window had been opened to let the light into the darkness of her miserable useless existence: a magnificent window from which she'd been able to see the light. Thrilled and bewildered by the unaccustomed prospect, she had nevertheless been very cautious: cautious from wonder and astonishment. For the first time she had realized what life had to offer. To her amazement everything had assumed an enormous and incalculable significance. Objects, ideas, people, had adopted new forms, unbelievable forms. She wondered how she had not perceived all this before. It was only then that she had realized the significance of the act of creation, how everything flowed from it: multi-coloured, spring-like, full of sparkling beams and sunny visions. She had been intoxicated by this astounding revelation, and she had shaded her eyes, dazzled by its radiance. She had wanted to kneel down in prayer and supplication before this new effulgence. But she hadn't dared, just as one hesistates to risk interrupting a pleasant dream by thinking: 'Ah, it's a dream!' She hadn't dared to analyse the significance of the revelation, to give it a name, to examine it rationally. She had shut her eyes, almost pretending to be unaware of its existence, so that it mightn't vanish away. She had felt like a vessel, until now empty, suddenly filled to the brim with the most intoxicating potion. The wasteland of her interior life had been carpeted with flowers. She had no idea so many roses could have existed. How was it possible that a chance remark could have such meaning? A glance, an insignificant gesture of the hand, a flower, a mere nothing. From where did it come? What was it? Happiness? Love? A violent surge of youthful vigour? A breath of air from God himself? She didn't know. But it was strange, enchanting, and incalculable, like a spring gushing and sparkling inside her, like a bird warbling and beating its wings. And all around her nothing but roses and an azure sky.

Then suddenly—just now, a few minutes ago—the window opening out on to that great vista of light had been shut. Shut in such a way that she would never be able to open it again. The sound of the fountain playing subsided, the wings stopped beating, and the bird lay dead on the ground. The dream was over. And the multi-coloured lights had been turned out.

And so she would remain alone again; alone with her dead hero, and the pride of the village, who'd given his life for his country; destined to spend the rest of her life under the weight of that heroic corpse, while at her feet the dead man's monstrous child howled through the night with the insatiable wrath of its father. The hatred of the villagers, with all their erotic frustrations, would close in on her again, the freshness of her youth merely serving to stimulate their filthy appetites. And her sole revenge would lie in the pleasure she would take in repulsing their advances with her obstinate unswerving chastity. That was the melancholy prospect she had to look forward to. God! To look forward to! . . .

28

LEON and Adriani began their farewell calls, and everyone heard of their imminent departure with genuine sorrow.

Madam Evtychia kissed them and wept inconsolably.

'My child,' she told Adriani, stroking her fair hair, 'we shall look forward to the return of summer, if only because it'll bring you back to us.'

She invited them to a farewell dinner, the idea of which bored Leon to distraction. These little formalities were getting more and more on his nerves. This 'last supper' appealed to him even less when Aspasia said very knowingly:

'There won't be anyone else. Just a family affair. Ourselves and no one else.'

In other words she meant Sappho wouldn't be there. They had no intention of inviting her.

'They're all jealous of her in that house,' said Adriani. 'The girls obviously don't approve of our friendship with her.'

'Perhaps you've shown them too early how much you prefer her company to theirs,' he said, smoking his cigarette with an air of indifference.

She shrugged her shoulders and looked at him thoughtfully.

'We're not really social types, you and I,' she said, 'We show what we're thinking too much. You must admit Sappho's the only genuinely interesting person here. I'm terribly fond of her. So is she of me. You can't imagine how we both wept when I told her we were leaving. She was quite inconsolable.'

He suddenly felt his heart beating violently. He didn't reply immediately. Watching her closely, he finally said with studied objectivity:

'It's true, she's got a certain aura about her. The fact that she doesn't talk very much and lets her looks speak for themselves adds to her charm. I've noticed the same thing in other women. In most cases it's instinctive and it can be very appealing. An occasional prolonged glance seems to give a point to their silence and provides the imagination with the opportunity of filling in the blanks. Like a cinema screen on which a film is projected. Then . . . the lights are turned on, and we find the screen empty. A smooth blank surface with nothing behind it.'

'How wicked you are!' she laughed. 'You make it all sound so tortuous. It may be so with certain women. But, as to Sappho, I was simply trying to tell you what I think and feel about her.'

'Perhaps . . . I won't insist,' he said with the same objective air. 'Sappho's looks are very distinctive. And a woman's looks are, of course, her most powerful asset.'

'That's a lot of fine talk,' continued Adriani; 'personally, I believe Sappho's looks are her greatest liability. I'm sorry she won't be at our godfather's dinner party. But to make up for it let's go for a picnic to Anerragi the day before we leave. We can spend the whole day there. Just "ourselves and no one else", as Aspasia would say.'

'Fancy having the energy to organize a picnic!' Leon said, yawning with affected weariness.

But at the same time he felt a secret thrill at the thought of spending the last day with her. A whole day!

It would be the last round and he was confident of winning it. Everything was so clear in his mind now and he looked forward to the bitter triumph that would crown his long struggle. To Sappho he would behave with friendliness—a guarded friendliness. After all, he felt nothing but gratitude to this strange 'Contessa', who had initiated him in the mysteries of love and delivered him from his nightmare preoccupation with the past. The gaze of her beautiful eyes had lent wings to his fantasy, given him back the power of shedding tears which he thought the war had dried up for ever; above all, she had fired him with the joy of artistic creation. Some time in the future the flames would die down, the bright fire would be extinguished. He might even learn to love another woman. But in his heart the image of Sappho, the chaste and unapproachable wife of his dead friend, would for ever remain undimmed, bright in its holy penumbra of gratitude and friendship. Friendship. Friendship? Why not? Certainly.

The Mayor's last supper was, as foreseen by Leon, very boring. Mrs. Spanos conversation alternated between the condition of her heart and the departure of Leon and Adriani. Mr. Spanos reminisced endlessly about their parents. This led him on to the old days under the Turks, before the world had gone to pot, when life was all ease and leisure, and Turkish agas and beys could be fixed with a few *medjids*.

It was obvious that the two girls were frankly sorry Leon and Adriani were going. Taken in all the dinner party could not have been a more melancholy affair. But there was a surprise in store for them. At about ten o'clock Mr. Yanni appeared, uninvited, and not unaccompanied. His ill-considered action, however, came almost as a relief.

His companion was a hypnotist. A certain Mr. Maloukos from Athens, who edited a periodical on spiritualism and was making a tour of the provinces in order to enrol subscribers. In the course of his travels he held meetings in theatres and private houses, where he demonstrated his powers as a hypnotist. He called these meetings 'sessions'. The newspapers in town were full of articles about his experiments which had naturally stirred the imagination of the local inhabitants. Maloukos, it seems, not only hypnotized people but actually transported them back to Asia Minor, to the fire of Smyrna and the martyrdom of imprisonment.

The whole fearful drama would be relived down to the last detail, leaving the spectators shuddering with horror. The medium, no matter where he came from, would recount the fate of the spectator's relations: step by step, right up to the climax of their grisly end, with all the tortures inflicted on them by the *Cétes*, the fierce Turkish guerillas of the Anatolian hinterland, thrown in for good measure. The spectators would gather round the groaning medium, sobbing and wailing as they stumbled over one another.

It was an extraordinary spectacle.

Thanks to Maloukos, the frontiers, so jealously guarded by the Turks, seemed to disappear. How near it was in fact, that frontier: a mere two and a half hours, given a following wind; and yet so far, as far as the other end of the world.

In the daytime, when the sun shone on the opposite coast, one could see the little Greek villages of Anatolia: whitewashed, empty, abandoned. One could even distinguish the camel caravans moving leisurely along the saddle of the long line of hills. And in the evening, when the wind blew across the channel, it would carry with it the echo of the beating of drums. When night fell the triumphant illuminations would be seen glimmering in the distance; even the flicker of the *masaladhés*, the torches set on poles to celebrate the feast of Bairam, could be discerned. One felt that it was all being done to refill the cup of bitterness already drained by the routed humiliated Giaours, gazing nostalgically across the channel from their island refuge.

Maloukos's skill removed all frontiers and natural obstacles; he was able to transplant people in the most bewildering fashion and let them wander at will in the shattered villages of Anatolia.

Physically he was a short, dark little man with thick hair and a low forehead. His movements were awkward and cramped, his speech a form of popular vernacular; he sounded barely literate and floundered helplessly when he tried to explain his experiments in scientific terms.

Mr. Yanni introduced him to the assembly with an air of great triumph. Maloukos, he said, had just given a series of 'sessions' to a number of refugees and locals who were anxious to learn the fate of their relatives in Asia Minor. All free of charge. In the cause of patriotism. He had very much wanted to meet the Mayor, and he begged to be excused for the intrusion.

Having heard so much about him already, they were all naturally very anxious to meet him. Aspasia, biting her nails with excitement, was dying to see him perform one of his marvels, and went so far as to ask him to carry out an experiment on the spot.

'Of course, of course!' Maloukos cried modestly. 'I should be most happy to serve the Mayor and his esteemed family.'

Leon wondered what lay behind the man's words and his bowings and scrapings. There must be something he wanted from the Mayor.

'So', said Maloukos, 'we've only got to find the medium among us. Let's try.'

He began his exhortations. 'Now, please, will you close your fingers tight, clenching your hands together. That's the way. Good, good. Will you all now please look straight into my eyes, keeping your hands tightly clenched all the time. That's it. Good, good. There's nothing to be afraid of. Nothing at all. Now . . . now . . . just a little bit more . . . fingers tighter, please. That's it . . .'

They did what they were told, smiling bravely. Aspasia even cracked jokes. Maloukos, however, looked very serious. He gazed into their eyes, each in turn, very earnestly and intently, and gradually their smiles vanished, and there was no more joking.

'Good, good,' he kept repeating. 'That's it. A little tighter still. As tight as you can. You mustn't loosen your grip . . . not even for a second. I'm now going to count up to three and when I reach "three" you'll try to unfasten your hands. You'll find you won't be able to . . . it'll be quite impossible. Your hands will just refuse to come apart. It'll be impossible to separate your fingers. No, tighter . . . that's it. That's the way . . . Ready? One . . . two . . . three!'

They all exclaimed 'Ah!' and unfastened their fingers with a deep sigh. All except Mr. Yanni. The harder he tried, the more obviously impossible it became. His hands remained tightly clenched. The vice-like grip of the fingers seemed to get tighter every minute. His ratty little eyes darted from side to side in a frightened way, and the wrinkles of his face creased and uncreased in his agitation. In his high squeaky voice, he kept repeating:

'Most peculiar! Most peculiar to be sure!'

It certainly was.

Maloukos's gaze travelled triumphantly round the assembled group. He raised his eyebrows into his hair and patted the bewildered old man's clenched hands.

'This is nothing . . . nothing at all,' he said with affected modesty. 'I shall now count up to three, and at the word "three" his fingers will come unfastened.'

He was as good as his word. At the word 'three' Mr. Yanni's numbed fingers came apart and he began to wriggle them like the claws of a crab. From then onwards Mr. Yanni was the centre of all attraction, a plaything in the hands of the hypnotist.

Maloukos would tell him his coffee was unsweetened and hand him the salt-cellar instead of the sugar-basin, whereupon Mr. Yanni would put spoonful after spoonful of salt into his coffee and drink it up with as much relish as if it had been the sweetest most syrupy cup of coffee he'd ever tasted.

The women cried from laughing, and Mr. Yanni kept saying wonderingly: 'The company seems to be very happy tonight . . . very happy indeed. . . . '

Maloukos then said he would put the old man into a trance and that when he woke up he would find Madam Evtychia had a moustache.

Commotion.

Waking up from his trance, Mr. Yanni opened his eyes slowly. He remembered nothing. He seemed slightly embarrassed, probably feeling rather ashamed of himself for having dropped off in his chair. The others were talking about other things and weren't paying much attention to him. Occasionally, however, they cast a glance in his direction. They soon noticed that he was staring at Madam Evtychia with round eyes. He made as though to open his mouth and stretch out his hand, but stopped. He then lowered his eyes, raising them furtively every now and then to take another peep at Madam Evtychia. All of a sudden he seemed to remember something. He smiled with a more reassured air and said guardedly:

'It has been scientifically observed that when certain glands cease to function properly in the female of the species, male characteristics may appear. The woman's voice may deepen . . . hair may grow on the face. . . .'

At the same time he glanced slyly at the Mayor's wife, as though trying to read the expression in her face.

She was shaking her hand sadly, as though saying: 'It's me you're telling!' sighing and stroking her imaginary beard.

They were all choking back their laughter when Mr. Yanni, convinced at last of the reality of this biological phenomenon, rose cautiously from his seat and approached Madam Evtychia in order to examine the phenomenon at close quarters.

'Well, Evtychia,' he said, 'can you believe it? I've only just noticed what's happened to you.'

'What am I to do?' said Madam Evtychia resignedly, twirling her imaginary moustaches which must have reached to her ears. They were all screaming and laughing hysterically. As for Aspasia, she was beside herself, shaking with spasm after spasm of uncontrollable laughter.

'For God's sake! It's enough! I can't! . . . Enough!'

Maloukos looked at Mr. Yanni in the eyes and told him sharply: 'Go and sit down on the sofa at once. Over there!'

Mr. Yanni trotted obediently to the sofa.

'Excellent. Now go to sleep. A deep sleep . . . . You're sleeping heavily. You're not conscious of anything round you. You can't feel, you can't hear, you can't see anything . . . anything . . . anything . . . . .'

The old man lay on the sofa, and went off into a complete trance. Then Maloukos produced a large safety-pin—the kind with which bandages are fastened—from under the lapel of his coat. Holding it up to the light so that it shone, he suggested jabbing it into the sleeping man's flesh, without his feeling any pain and without shedding a drop of blood.

'No, no, not that!' they all cried horrified.

Maloukos made a gesture with his head as though to say: 'As you wish,' and fastened the safety-pin under the lapel of his coat again.

'He's a very good medium,' he said. 'Would you like us to try a little experiment now? We could converse with the spirit of some dead friend of yours. . . . '

'Somebody killed in the war?' suggested Loulou.

'Why not Vranas?' Aspasia jumped up and looked round enquiringly. They all nodded their heads. 'Yes, yes.'

Leon had just been thinking what a charlatan the man, what a hoax the whole seance was. But his heart began to beat faster, his breathing to become more difficult, as he heard Maloukos invoking the spirit of his dead friend. It was laughable. But . . . Mr. Yanni had now rolled himself up into a little ball on the sofa and was groaning. Madam Evtychia looked very anxious and they were all afraid lest her heart should break up the proceedings. Fortunately her curiosity was very lively and no contraction intervened to prevent the continuation of the seance. Furthermore, Maloukos assured her there was nothing at all to be afraid of. He kept patting her shoulder and making all sorts of reassuring grimaces and gestures.

Mr. Yanni was twisting and turning restlessly on the sofa; his moaning sounded like a child crying in its sleep.

'Are you a good spirit?' asked the hypnotist in a cold, detached voice.

'Yes,' whispered the medium.

'The spirit of Lieutenant Stratis Vranas?'

'Yes.'

'Do you swear it in the name of the Father, the Son, and the Holy Ghost?'

'Yes.'

They were all breathing deeply. The women's bosoms could be seen rising and falling. They were all trying to recapture the tones of a voice that came from the grave in Mr. Yanni's distorted speech. And they

247

somehow all succeeded in tracing a striking, a frightening resemblance. Leon himself could recall the deep manly tones of a voice long since silenced; a voice that had once extracted from him an oath concerning a woman as yet unknown to him.

'Lieutenant Vranas,' said Maloukos in very solemn respectful tones, 'is there anything you wish to tell us?'

'Yes . . . my child . . . my little boy . . . my wife . . .'

The sound of quiet sobbing came from between Mr. Yanni's clenched teeth. He seemed to be suffering horribly from the pressure exerted by this strange other being, this other willpower that had taken possession of him.

'Speak then, O spirit of peace!'

The medium groaned; he seemed to be trying to put up some kind of resistance. The women wept. Leon was furious because he felt his heart swelling, his eyes ready to fill with tears. He was in an agony to know what was coming next, what would be said next. The medium mumbled something again. The words were broken off, incoherent. But Leon was greatly agitated.

'Sappho . . . I love you, Sappho . . . Our child . . . our child . . . Drivas, thank you, my friend . . . my friend . . .'

The medium groaned again; his chest rose and fell with an increasingly rapid rhythm.

Suddenly they all looked round. The sound of sobbing came from the glass door by the staircase. They saw Sultana fleeing, with her head bowed.

'In heaven's name wake him up!' cried Madam Evtychia. She was terrified now. Her hands trembled.

Maloukos said a few words and rubbed the old man's forehead. He went off into a peaceful sleep. The hypnotist left him lying there quietly for a few minutes, and then brought him round. Before doing so he commanded him to forget everything he had experienced.

On their way home a full moon rose above the olive orchards of the Sentinel, shining through a tracery of feathery branches. Land and sea lay silent and motionless under the silver light which seemed to cast its hypnotic spell over the whole world. The little village nestled among the olive trees above the seashore, its inhabitants sleeping the heavy dreamless sleep of exhaustion. A row of gnarled trees was silhouetted against the horizon, their erect branches pointing skywards like the fingers of a hand.

Adriani had slipped her arm through his. After a long silence she said:

'Do you believe in all this? If it's true that we can communicate with the spirits of the dead . . . . I think it's horrible!'

Leon tried to treat the matter lightly.

'Horrible? Why? It would be very strange, not horrible. Think of Mr. Yanni serving as a kind of telephone exchange between the living and the dead!'

'Stop joking,' and she asked again: 'Do you believe in it?'

After a while he said: 'Perhaps I do. It depends on the circumstances. We're such weak creatures . . . capable of any imbecility.'

They were passing Sappho's house. It loomed dark and silent in the night. Above the tiled roof rose the tops of the two poplar trees in the courtyard. In there the Contessa lay closeted. The schoolmistress with the golden eyes. Like the Sleeping Princess, jealously guarded by two ogres: a dead lover, with one leg amputated from the thigh-bone, and a little child-monster, all head and stomach, which could do nothing but eat and howl. And a third guard: a woman dressed in black from head to toe, with eyes like burning coals, the deaf-mute servant.

On reaching his room he went to the open window, put his hand out, and snipped off a twig from the almond tree. He crushed the leaves in his fingers. They felt cool to the touch, for his hands were burning hot; and the fresh bitter-sweet scent of the leaves filled the room. The full moon cast its silver beams on the calm sea. It looked like some luminus heraldic seal imprinted on the inky-blue vault of sky: an enormous golden seal stamped by the Creator himself on his own creation.

Then he thought he heard a voice coming from the empty expanses of sea, from the arch of the sky above; the faint faraway voice of his dead friend, the voice of an embittered dead man:

'Thank you, my friend, my friend . . .'

It was as though Vranas himself had looked into his heart and understood the nature of the tragic struggle he had waged, culminating in a victory of Pyrrhic proportions.That was why the dead man's voice was so tender, so full of gratitude.

A king of melancholy contentment filled his heart. It was like a quiet nostalgic song. He could hear it in every part of his consciousness; but he slept quietly.

29

THEY set off early in the morning. It was to be an all-day excursion. Leon was conscious of a nagging sense of melancholy at the thought of the next day's separation. It preoccupied them all, but they didn't talk about it. At the same time he felt as though a weight had been lifted off his chest. The way ahead lay clear now: his conscience had triumphed.

The sun was just rising, burning hot, rose-coloured. The air was full of the murmuring sounds of morning: an occasional shout, a shrill whistle, the braying of a donkey, the rustling of birds in the trees.

They travelled light, having decided to eat whatever they found when they reached their destination. On the heights above the Sentinel they stopped to admire the view of the sea below. Her eyes glistening, Adriani gazed at the landscape which she loved so much and would now be leaving so soon. In the east the sun was already beginning to shimmer on the sea.

'If only you'd let me bring our bathing things,' she told Leon, 'we'd have had a heavenly swim.'

It was just that contingency that he had foreseen and wished to avoid.

'It would have taken up too much time,' he said casually. 'The sea's so lovely that we'd have dawdled for hours. And then we'd have had to climb up in the heat. . . .'

Sappho didn't say anything. But she was glad she wouldn't have to appear before him undressed. Adriani's suggestion had a curious effect on her: she felt as though she'd been through a kind of test.

The most bucolic imagination couldn't have dreamt of a more attractive stretch of country than the one through which the track led up to Anerragi. The rough stairway soon gave way to a path with large flat stones placed at intervals so as to serve as   steps and reduce the effort demanded of the climber. It wound through olive orchards and echoing gorges, shady with plane trees and agnus castus. Everywhere there was a smell of crushed sweet-smelling herbs which they trod underfoot and the air was full of the swishing sound made by Leon's walking-stick as he slashed a way through the giant nettles.

Adriani was so moved that she stopped for a moment.

'Isn't it beautiful?' she said slowly. 'I wonder if there's a landscape to equal it anywhere else in the world.'

Leon felt like saying that this soil had exhaled an atmosphere of eroticism ever since the days of Sappho; that for centuries the island's

poets had sung of nothing but love and desire. But he didn't. Sappho
might have read some other meaning into his words. He slowly
approached the stout trunk of an olive tree and cupped a cicada,
which was shrilling dementedly, in the hollow of his hand. For a
moment he thought of placing it on the back of Adriani's neck. He
might, with equal innocence, have slipped it into Sappho's bosom.
Exactly as in *Daphnis and Chloe.* He thought of reminding Adriani
that this was the scene of Longius's idyll—the most erotic countryside
in the world. But all he said was:

'The peasants here have a curious superstition, you know. They say
it brings good luck to bite the first cicada of the year. Quite gently, of
course. Then you let it hop away. Funny, isn't it?'

They saw a pear tree. Almost all its fruit had been plucked, but as
Leon gazed at it his eye fell on a pear, a single pear, the colour of gold,
hanging from one of the topmost branches. He began to climb up. The
rustling leaves felt cool and fresh. With the crook of his walking-stick
he caught the branch on which the fruit hung and pulled it gently
down towards him.

He was reciting the old Lesbian lines in a loud voice which echoed
across the valley:

'As the sweet apple is found at the top of the branch,
at the top-most tip, overlooked by the reapers!'

Down below Sappho replied in her deep vibrating voice, which
seemed to have acquired a strangely boyish tone, with the line:

'No, not overlooked: they were not able to reach it!'

They all laughed. Adriani could hardly wait to dig her teeth into the
pear. Looking down through the leaves, he saw their noses upturned
towards him, waiting for him to descend. Sappho was smiling; her lips
looked very full and her teeth shone, white and healthy, in the
sunlight.

He dropped his stick and leapt down, falling among a pile of dead
leaves. It was a marvellous pale-coloured pear, fresh and juicy. He
gave Sappho and Adriani a bite; then took one himself; a deep bite—
there was something almost sensual about it—just where Sappho's
teeth had left their mark.

They wandered about in the copse for some time until they found
the entrance to the Anerragi property. The gardener was delighted to

see them. He had spotted them from afar and stood on the ledge of the pond which supplied the whole farm with water, shouting words of welcome. His cries mingled with the echoing hum of insects and the sound of water running in little channels down the slope.

'Aou-aah! Ou-iih!' were the only sounds they could distinguish. They could see his blue shirt and his large straw hat which he waved above the tops of the peach trees.

They replied in unison, with the same inarticulate cries:

'Aou-aah! Ou-iih!'

How they laughed.

Leon joined the gardener and cut a mass of fresh ferns and tall grass with a scythe. They carried it in armfuls and dumped it in the shade of a large walnut tree. The gardener brought a bright-coloured rug, as wide as it was long, and placed it on the mattress of grass. They flopped down with the abandonment of well-earned fatigue. There was a pungent smell of freshly cut grass and crushed walnut leaves as they lay in the shade.

'It's really marvellous here,' said Leon, taking a deep breath.

'Well, well,' mocked Adriani. ' "All this monotonous green lushness ... all the familiar landmarks like cardboard stage-sets ..." ' She was quoting to Sappho the words he used the day they had decided to leave Megalohori. 'Leon, you see, is bored stiff in the country ...'

'And this is your revenge, I suppose,' he smiled wryly.

Adriani continued her parody.

'Not at all,' she said with affected pomposity. ' "I pine for the bustle of a town ..." For dust, I suppose, asphalt pavements, petrol fumes, newspapers, state lotteries ...'

Sappho was gazing up at the branches of the walnut tree.

'It's strange, isn't it,' she said hesitantly, 'how the country soon palls ... for people who normally live in towns, I mean. I myself never stop thinking with nostalgia of my days at the high school in town. Even the most miserable hours seem happy in retrospect. I can understand how much more monotonous this existence must seem to people accustomed to the rhythm of life in a large city ...'

Leon opened his mouth; he appeared to be about to say something. But he changed his mind. In order to do something, he began to whistle with an air of affected indifference.

The gardener returned with a basket of magnificent fruit, plucked ripe from the trees. Peaches, pears, pomegranates, and grapes from a climbing vine which wound its green tendrils round the trunk of a poplar tree, its tender shoots roaming freely along the branches like small firm hands groping their way. He also brought them a jug of foaming milk straight from the cow's udders. They drank in turn out of a wide glass bowl, like babies. Adriani was greedily licking the cream off her lips. Leon was watching Sappho. She drank thirstily, her head bent forward, her long thin fingers closed round the bowl, her lower lip submerged in the white foam. Her eyelids opened and shut rhythmically as she swallowed. She suddenly became aware that he was watching her; her eyes opened wide and remained fixed for a moment so that he had a fleeting impression of two large pools expanding across the surface of a wide plane, like the gold sky in a Byzantine icon.

She lowered her glance quickly. Whenever their eyes met she experienced the same sensation of fear: like a fit of vertigo on the edge of a precipice. But deep down inside her she longed to leap over the precipice, spiralling down to lie there at the bottom, her eyes shut, waiting.

They picked fresh vine-leaves and vegetables, cleaned them sitting round in a circle, and began to cook them.

The gardener brought them oil, salt, and pepper in a little box made of cartridge caps, a saucepan, a pruning-hook in place of a knife, a fork, a spoon, the glass bowl from which they had drunk the milk, and a large deep earthenware dish.

'It's all I've got, I'm afraid,' he said, looking worried. 'If I'd known you were going to honour us with a visit I'd have gone to the village and collected all the necessary things.'

They assured him that everything was perfect. They would eat out of the same plate, with the same fork and spoon. Like the Gorgons.

While Adriani was preparing to cook the vegetables on the primitive fire, Sappho told them the story of the Pipina sisters, three old spinsters, notorious for their stinginess. They lived in a very old house. The eldest was called Pipina, and the other two thought it would be simpler if they also adopted the same name. They thus came to be known as the Pipina sisters. They were identically alike, with hooked noses and pointed chins that practically met. They had one decent dress between them. It was of ancient silk, and the back was so frayed that it shone, a greeny gold colour. They also had one pair of patent-leather shoes between them. It was even said they had only one plate, one knife, and one spoon and fork. They consequently ate in turn. They were terrible gossips and were constantly making malicious allusions to the 'shamelessness' of Sappho who 'spent all winter in a bath and all summer in the sea.' They were very god-fearing, and every Saturday evening one of them would put on their only dress and attend vespers. Another one would go to church on Sunday morning. They kept all the fasts. The one whose turn it was to go out would put on the old dress and patent-leather shoes and bring back the holy bread tied to the end of her chin-piece for the other two. Easter week was rather a problem. But they soon found a solution. The eldest would wear the family dress at the Good Friday service, the second at the midnight Resurrection service, and the third on Easter Day. The youngest, who was fifty-five, was called 'Little One' by the other two. 'Little One's gone out', 'Little One's come back', and so on.

Sappho told the story with such vivacity and power of mimicry that she soon had her friends helplessly laughing.

Adriani then put the saucepan on the fire and disappeared in the direction of the gardener's hut. She came back with a cushion and a long rope. Leon tied the rope to a strong branch of the walnut tree, making a swing. As they sat on it in turn, they sang some well-known old song. Sappho had a pleasant voice with deep contralto notes and undulations like the vibrations of brass cymbals. It was a revelation. She admitted it was the first time she'd sung since she'd got married; and as she was saying so, she knew it would be the last.

Adriani was terrified each time the swing sent her flying into the air in a great arc. Squealing and giggling as she clung to the rope, she implored Leon not to swing her so high. He finally gave in to her entreaties and caught hold of the rope with a firm hand. She tumbled off, her hair dishevelled, her dress all rumpled.

Sappho was not in the least afraid.

'Higher,' she kept crying, as she flew past them. 'Still higher!'

Her eyes were half shut, and she could feel the wind ruffling her hair as it whistled in the ropes. She sat cushioned in the loop of rope as in an enormous sling which was being drawn back very tight in order to catapult her into infinity. The rope kept grazing one of the branches of the walnut tree, bruising its leaves which fell in showers on Leon's head, filling the air with their strong scent. He kept quickening the pace so that he could hardly distinguish her face as she flashed past. It was like a vision of velocity, he thought, trying to reach the empyrean; suddenly arrested in its course, it would shoot back to earth for a second, rest in his embrace and then fly off again in another attempt to break through its earth-bound orbit. The hem of her skirt flapped on his cheek. Backwards and forwards she passed before him, with flushed cheeks. The scent of jasmine would come and go. Her blouse clung to her breasts, which rose and fell rapidly, in the excitement of the movement. Her legs were extended forward, together, very straight, so that he could see as far as the knee. She gave the impression of flying through space, treading the air on her toes, like the Nike of Paeonius. He shared her sense of intoxication. He was conscious of a thrill of happiness. The impetus which sent her flying up to the tree-tops came from him: from the muscles of his arms. Then he thought: 'After tomorrow I'll never see her again. She would pass out of his life like some astral body which has just grazed the surface of the earth on its course through space.

Adriani suddenly stopped singing and clapped her hands.

'I've an idea!'

Sappho, placing her feet on the ground, brougnt the swing to a standstill.

'Well, let's hear it.'

He leant forward, holding on to the ropes of the swing, so that his body pressed on to her back. The scent of her hair reminded him of the smell of poppies. He bent forward, his breath coming in little short gasps. He had only to bend forward a little further and he would be able to take her in his arms, like a flower with all its petals in disarray, and bury his face in her hair, and kiss her mouth, her cheeks, her neck.

He drew back quickly, breathless, angry with himself.

Adriani was suggesting they should go down to the stream of the Oryaka and catch crabs. There were masses under the stones in the little rivulets, she said. When she and Leon were children they never left the farm without taking a basketful of crabs back home.

Leon immediately began to put difficulties in the way. 'It's true, the stream is very picturesque, but the way down is terribly difficult. In some places there's such a jungle of nettles and brambles that it will be impossible for you girls to pass. It was a different matter when we were children.'

Adriani put her foot down and Sappho's enthusiasm for the project was only whetted by the obstacles he kept presenting. 'It will make the crab hunt all the more exciting,' she said.

'All right,' he smiled eventually. 'You girls always know best. Well, forward then, to the exploration of the sources of the Oryaka!'

'Like Jules Verne's Orinoco,' cried Adriani excitedly.

She glanced at the saucepan, poked the fire, and added some water. They entered the copse, and when they came out of it the stream was in front of them. There wasn't much water, and in summer its width was sometimes reduced to the length of a man's arm. It trickled over the smooth stones, filling little waterfalls, cascading over the glistening stones which had the patina of marble. The girls were delighted. The cicadas seemed to have gone mad in the midday heat, raising their strident drumming to the heavens as though in wild protest. But within the arbour of shade formed by the network of branches along the course of the stream the air was cool, almost green from the reflections of the foliage. In places the creepers were thickly interlaced, twining their sinuous shoots round the clusters of brambles whose slender spiky branches dipped over the banks of the stream. The twittering of birds could be heard in the dense foliage. Suddenly the flutter of wings would startle the girls and large lizards, as green as the grass around them, darted past, gazing at them for a moment with their beady frightened eyes before vanishing into the undergrowth.

Adriani knew all about catching crabs and she kept telling the others what to do. One had to lift the stone abruptly and quickly cup the crab in the hollow of one's hand before it succeeded in running away. But when she found some mother-crab with a fat brown belly and claws the size of nail scissors, she was afraid to place her hand over it and she screamed for Leon. This big game was a man's business.

Sappho acted as carrier. She placed the crabs in a wet handkerchief tied with two knots at the ends. She really had the most difficult job: to prevent them from escaping. And to do this she had the use of only one hand because, as they were groping their way downhill, she had to keep her other hand free to ward off the branches and brambles from scratching her face.

Sometimes a screen of blackberries and honeysuckle barred their path.

'It's like barbed wire!' they cried.

Leon thrashed a way through the green lattice-work and a strong sourish smell came from the beaten undergrowth and the stream was filled with leaves and petals swirling down in the current.

The girls kept crying out with pleasure at each new discovery. A cavity in a stone, like a miniature cave, revealed a tuft of maidenhair, marvellously invisible in the shadowy light, and the minute shining leaves trembled in the air as though they had been embroidered on it with a green silk thread. Clusters of little black shells carpeted the bed of the stream. One had the impression they might have been lying there since the beginning of time.

They also found a hidden fig tree. It was a wild fig tree, which had sprouted there in the shade, far from the light. But it had had the courage to push its branches through the tangle of spiky shrubs and had consequently acquired an unusually slender willowy shape. Five late figs had ripened at their leisure, unsuspected by any human eye. Leon caught the branch with the handle of his stick and tugged. The tree leaned over gracefully, as though offering its fruit to the accompaniment of a bow. They were just a few figs, very fine ones, bursting with ripe seed, their thick dark skin drawn tightly across, with a drop of honey on the tip. Leon picked them one by one and placed them, without bothering to peel the skins, into the girls' mouths. He then released the branch and the tree shot back to its former position, erect and graceful. As he did so, the rustling of the leaves seemed to echo a sigh of relief at their delivery from the burden of the fruit so patiently ripened through the long summer months.

The rustling reminded him of the flapping of a hen's wings just after it has received the attentions of an amorous cock.

A drop of glutinous liquid, white as milk, fell on his hand from the little stump left on the branch where he had lopped off one of the figs. It looked like the nipple formed on a tree that has just been grafted.

There was a heavy cloying aroma about the place.

They continued downhill. When they came to a stretch of jagged rocks or slippery stones, he held a hand out to help Adriani, and she did the same to Sappho. He thus avoided any physical contact with her. If by chance they happened to touch each other they both recoiled with instinctive fear, as though they had trodden on a burning coal. But they would glance furtively into each other's eyes, where they saw the reflection of their mutual fear.

The swollen winter stream had washed the earth away from under the roots of some of the trees: strong powerful roots with multiple tentacles. They resembled thick snakes burrowing into the earth, emerging again in contorted shapes, full of brutal vigour. Others were shaped like human knees trying desperately to encase the smooth blue-veined boulders of the stream in a vice-like grip. Others shot out arms with coarse rough surfaces in an agonizing struggle to push above ground.

The metallic drone of thousands of insects came from the tall grass, as though an infinite number of watches were in a wild frenzy ticking away in order to keep up with one another.

They reached a spot where the stream plunged into a dark thicket full of laurels, fresh and green from the perpetual watering they received from the stream. They were laden with dark clusters of berries, and the delicious smell made Leon and the girls pause and take a few deep breaths. There was a ceremonial, almost a hallowed atmosphere about the place, which Leon thought must be connected with memories he associated with the smell. Then he found the answer. It was the Palm Sunday feast. With the ringing of church bells, the children in the courtyards of the houses beat the laurel branches which were adorned with silk sashes of recent brides and with little golden bells.

He cut two slender twigs which he fashioned into a crown and placed on his sister's head.

'The crown of Apollo,' he said. 'Yet better known as a condiment for a number of excellent dishes; hare stew, for instance. It's odd we should associate it with hares and triumphant heroes. That's dreadfully symbolic.'

He looked at Adriani who assumed a very noble attitude. The rough leaves with the dark berries looked charming in her fair hair.

She suddenly abandoned the pose, flung the laurel crown from her head, and cried anxiously:

'Talking of stew, I've forgotten all about the food. If it isn't actually burnt to a cinder there'll be precious little water left in the saucepan by this time. I must fly. Don't be late. It's about a quarter to twelve—at

257

least, that's what my stomach says.'

'We'll all go back,' said Sappho quickly.

Adriani had already started climbing back. 'No, no,' she shouted. 'I must run all the way. There's absolutely no need you should all come panting behind me.'

She was already practically out of earshot and had soon disappeared behind the screen of foliage.

'All right,' said Leon indifferently, anxious not to appear afraid of being left alone with Sappho. 'We'll pick a few more crabs and then go back.'

An embarrassed silence followed. At all costs it had to be broken. He walked on a few steps without looking at her, bent down and raised a large stone with some difficulty. He quickly placed his hand underneath, cried: 'Got him!' and produced a large crab. Sappho, assuming an air of interest, approached him holding out the handkerchief.

He cracked the crab's claws and dropped it in among the rest.

'There he goes too!' he cried laughing.

'What a huge one!' she laughed too.

They both felt grateful to the poor crab for having come to their rescue.

He started thrashing about with his stick, breaking off the tips of nettles, brambles, and the tender shoots of little dwarf plane trees. The ominous silence was in this way broken by the swishing sound of his stick. She followed one or two paces behind. Once he halted in front of a round tufted shrub.

'Come on,' he cried laughing, '. . . a little nearer. That's right.'

She stood near the thick stumpy bush and waited. She was relieved at his natural cheerful manner. He beat the bush with his stick and a swarm of small butterflies fluttered out. They flitted round her head in a dense cloud. She uttered a little scream as she tried to wave them off. Then they both started laughing.

The butterflies were everywhere, clouds of them, fluttering round in a circle as though they had gone blind. Their wings were speckled with brown; rose-coloured on the reverse. After a few minutes they disappeared in the dense foliage.

'They've gone!' cried Sappho wonderingly. 'How suddenly!'

He explained the reason. He remembered it from childhood days. He always liked explaining things. They belonged to a variety of night butterflies which dwelt in the foliage. They liked the shade, avoiding the light as much as possible.

He started to move on again, his head bent under the tangle of branches which formed an arch overhead; then he stopped to rest against the trunk of a wild fig tree and lowered his head again so as to take a look round.

'Charming!' he cried, and his voice, ringing with enthusiasm, echoed down the stream.

A blue-coloured rock fell away in front of them, smooth and rounded by the ceaseless lapping of the water which trickled caressingly over it like a piece of diaphanous silk. As its base a round hollow had been eroded by the water which tumbled in with a burbling sound.

Clutching one of the branches of the wild fig tree, he began to descend slowly, resting the entire weight of his body on his heels. When he had got far enough he bent his knees and jumped.

It really was a charming spot. The water trickled down the miniature waterfall, sparkling and gurgling, making little channels wherever it could through the mass of sodden weeds. The sound of the running water splashing into the pool was out of all proportion to the size of the stream. At this point the bed of the stream had widened. One of the banks was completely straight, with tangled ferns waving their large fan-shaped leaves tapering into curly little shoots. The foliage created a veritable arch, shady and scented. In the pool there were magnificent flying-fish with iridescent horizontal fins.

He looked up to see how he had actually managed to climb down and caught sight of Sappho's head between the leaves of the fig tree. She was trying to gauge the height, and there was an expression of eagerness on her face, her long eyelashes quivering.

'It's marvellous here,' he called up, 'but for heaven's sake don't try to come down. The rock is almost sheer. Better stay where you are. I'm coming back.'

He started to climb up.

'What d'you mean?' she called out. 'If you could imagine it why can't I? Just because I'm a girl?'

Her words came down to him accompanied by the sound of laughter and the splashing of the cascading water. The sound seemed to fuse into one, so that the whole ravine was echoing with laughter and song.

He saw her seize the branch he had used as a prop and begin to descend. It was not made easier for her by the fact that she had the handkerchief containing the crabs in one hand.

'Stay where you are, you'll fall!' he called out anxiously and began to scale the rock. He could at least relieve her of the handkerchief and give her the walking-stick.

'Don't worry!' she cried, anxious to get down before he could give her a hand.

But just at that moment she slipped. She clung to the fig tree, her feet barely touching the rock. She tried desperately to lodge her heel somewhere, groping blindly. Her other foot still touched the rock. The leg was trembling as far up as the knee.

He plunged the point of his stick into some strong roots so that he could rest the whole weight of his body on it, swivelled round, and held out a hand to her.

'Come. Lean on me. Quickly.' His voice was one of command.

She let herself slide into his arms. She placed the hand in which she held the handkerchief containing the crabs on his neck and slowly let go oᶠ the branch to which she had been clinging.

Holding her tight against his breast with one hand, he began to climb down very cautiously. He was careful to test the surface of the rock with his foot before he placed it down. He felt his limbs were on fire, his temples about to burst. Everything was green, a kind of liquid flowing green before his gaze, a cataract of leaves waving and rustling over the edge of an abyss.

He heard the sound of running water in his brain, he felt her warm body pressing against his, her arms winding round his neck like delicate shoots of ivy. Her firm breasts rubbed against his cheek: it was as though his face was buried in an enormous flower. He could hear her heart beating under the thin blouse, and he thought it was his own heart. His bloodstream seemed to have fused into hers; the blood pounding through their arteries was the same blood; their pulses beat to the same rhythm. It was pain: terrible, violent, exhilarating pain.

A few more steps and he was treading on firm ground. But he didn't let go of her. He only reached out one arm to remove the walking-stick which he'd planted in the tangle of thick roots. With the other arm he pressed her closer to him. But he carried her gently, like a delicate child or some object of priceless worth. He lowered his head, so that it came closer to hers, closer to her golden eyes which gazed up at him, half shut, heavy-lidded, like those of a sick person in a high fever.

But his gaze had penetrated hers. From her eyes it spread through her consciousness to every particle and nerve-cell of her body. She shuddered. Another spasm shook her; and then she clung to him with all the strength she possessed.

He looked round, like an animal searching for a convenient spot to devour its prey. He saw the ferns—a carpet of them. He carried her there, placed her carefully on the green cushioned earth. The crushed plants under his knees gave out a heady scent. He didn't wait any longer. There was something of violence, almost of hostility, in the way he took her to him.

Her eyes under the long lashes shut slowly. The hand clutching the handkerchief loosened its grip. The liberated crabs, their broken claws erect, disappeared into the tall grass, anxious to find their way back to the stream.

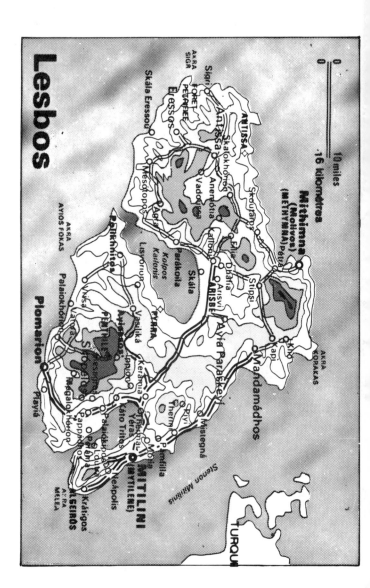

Lesbos